One Apple Tasted

One Apple Tasted

JOSA YOUNG

E&T

First published 2009 by Elliott and Thompson Limited
27 John Street, London WC1N 2BX
www.eandtbooks.com

ISBN 978-1-9040-2771-3

9 8 7 6 5 4 3 2 1

A CIP catalogue record for this book is available from
the British Library.

Printed in the UK by J F Print Ltd., Sparkford, Somerset
Typeset in Sabon

To Thoby

Prologue

GEORGIA'S VOICE FLEW UP the stairs to where Dora lay dreaming in the bath. 'Do you want an egg?' she was yelling. Dora didn't feel like breakfast but she sat up, cooling water pouring around her sides, and got out. Ultravox were feeling sorry for themselves on the radio in her bedroom as she picked her way through scattered garments, pulling on red tights, army surplus khaki shorts and a collarless shirt of her grandfather's with safety pins as cufflinks.

On went grey eye shadow and mascara and down she flew to join her flatmates. Georgia sat eating her egg and scanning *The Times*. The espresso pot bubbled on the stove. Dora poured herself a cup of coffee and sat down.

'What's going on in the world, then?' she asked.

'It's St Agnes' Eve tonight,' Georgia replied.

'Ah, bitter chill it was! The owl, for all his feathers, was a-cold,' quoted Dora.

'It says here that if we say the Lord's Prayer and stick a pin into the sleeve of our nighties, we'll dream of the man we're going to marry. And you can't have any dinner.'

'Will a safety pin do?' said Dora.

'Any kind of pin; it doesn't specify. You have to be a virgin. That rules me out.'

Dora stared into her coffee. Her virginity was a deadly secret.

'St Agnes is patron saint of virgins,' Georgia added. 'I wonder who's the patron saint of serial monogamists with the odd slip-up?'

Victoria came clattering in dressed in a navy pleated skirt and pie-frill collar, her thick fair hair held back with a velvet Alice band, for her job at a grand estate agent.

'What are you two talking about?' she said.

'It's St Agnes' Eve, when, according to Keats, "Young virgins might have visions of delight, And soft adorings from their loves receive Upon the honey'd middle of the night",' said Dora.

'Sounds a bit dodgy. Not sure about the soft bit. Do you have to be a virgin in the physical sense or in the old-fashioned sense of not being married?'

'I'm sure that'll do,' said Georgia. 'I'll break out the safety pins this evening.'

One

1982

'I FEEL SO SORRY for people like him. Cameras poking into his face wherever he goes. Particularly with that difficult-to-manage, flyaway hair and the kind of complexion that always lets you down.'

Dora knew the speaker's face but she couldn't remember his name. He shook his head. 'I would hate to be famous,' he added, shuddering.

Dora found him arch but touchingly beautiful. She assumed he was gay and therefore out of the question for anything but friendship. Not that she undervalued that. After Cambridge, her friendships still endured – unlike the relationships she'd had with straight boys.

The pretty, well-bred publicity girls known as Davoli's puffettes had fielded just one A-list celebrity for Davoli's latest splashy book launch and he'd had a grim time with the paparazzi on the way in. Dora supposed the singer felt obliged to come, as Davoli was going to publish the earnest photography he wasn't ever likely to be famous for in a big glossy book.

'If it was me I think I would never go anywhere. He'd go to the opening of a stock cube. Lovely for the puffettes to have such a tame celeb.'

There was a bitchy note in the beautiful boy's voice. Dora thought he sounded jealous. She was only half listening when she became aware of something.

She began to giggle. Laughter rose from her stomach in a bubbling stream. She tried to keep her mouth shut but the joy escaped through her nose. She snorted and clutched her middle with one hand.

'What's the matter? Are you all right?'

She was speechless. Giggles were escaping all over her face and her eyes began to stream. She wiped them with the floppy cuff of her New Romantic shirt, staggering backwards, looking for a wall to lean on but encountering only solid, disgruntled, fashionable flesh. She wheezed and ached with laughter. His anxious face only provoked fresh paroxysms.

'What have you taken?' the boy inquired, looking down at her hands to see if she had a joint. Her first glass of champagne was still half full.

Dora was held upright by the crush of the party. Davoli always gave good ones – champagne rather than warm white wine. The assembled liggers were squashed firmly together, rapidly smoking and drinking with arms clamped to their sides and hands up near their faces.

'Look behind you,' she managed to gasp, an idiotic grin wavering on her face.

The boy swivelled his head over one cramped shoulder. 'What is it?'

'It's him,' she whispered. The celeb. 'You're leaning against him.'

She was overcome again when on the boy's elfin face it dawned that the celebrity was pressed firmly against his back. There was no way that the singer hadn't heard their conversation.

She was suddenly afraid that her companion would abandon her in a sea of complete strangers. She'd been so relieved to see a face she half recognised, even if she couldn't remember his name. Excruciatingly shy, Dora had been desperately pretending to have a good time before she ran into him. She had been thinking about leaving, hoping to give off an aura of an urgent, thrilling dinner date as she went.

Due to the squeeze the boy couldn't move away, which was a temporary comfort. She thought his ears looked pinker, but it was difficult to tell in the gloom. His mouth trembled and his expression became more intense. Her heart sank. Then his face seemed to crumple.

He closed his eyes and threw back his head, not caring that he nearly nutted the famous object of his pity. He opened his mouth to the tonsils and bellowed with laughter. As far as they could, the cramped partygoers looked around to see who was so genuinely enjoying themselves.

He put his hands – a cigarette in one and an empty glass in the other – on either side of her and pressed himself against her. Bending to lean his blond head upon her shoulder, he gave way to the giggles as well. This set her off again. She put her arms around him to hold them both up.

They held on tight, glasses behind each other's backs, terrified of parting, looking for an escape route and trembling with crazy elation.

The crowd had parted crossly to let them through. They found a table and put their heads down on their arms to recover, gasping for breath, last little bubbles of laughter breaking free from their loosened mouths, faces wet with tears, feeling weak and abandoned.

Dora didn't dare look up. Then she felt him take hold of her forearm. She raised her head slightly. Only his eyes were visible. As she couldn't see his mouth, she couldn't tell what he was thinking or feeling. His eyes were enormous in his thin face. His straight blond hair was dishevelled. Dora didn't know what it was like to come back to life with a man after passionate love-making, but she thought this stillness, gasps for breath, utter relaxation, happiness and enormous warmth towards the other might be how it would – or could – be.

They turned their heads towards each other, still resting them on folded arms, their only contact his left hand on her forearm. She studied the worn gold signet ring on his little finger. She didn't want to speak.

'What's your name?' he asked. 'I've seen you before, haven't I? Aren't you a friend of Evangeline's?'

'I work with her at *Modern Woman*. My name's Dora Jerusalem.'

'God, what a romantic name. Where did you get that from?'

'My grandfather was dumped as an infant on the steps of the Jerusalem Mission in Limehouse. He believed himself to be the result of what he referred to as ships that pass in the night. I think it was his way of saying he was the offspring of a sailor and a prostitute. There's an idea that one of them might have been partly Chinese – hence the dark hair.'

'Sounds a lot more exciting than being the result of generations of country gentry humping resignedly in the marriage bed. I'm Guy Boleyn, by the way.'

'Any connection with the poor girl?'

'I don't really know,' he said carelessly.

MARIE CURIE CANCER CARE
REGISTERED CHARITY No. 207994
www.mariecurie.org.uk

04/05/2013 10:47   000312#6427
0002 CLERK2

1 x 1.00
BOOKS   £1.00
SUBTOTAL   £1.00

***TOTAL   £1.00
CASH   £1.00
CHANGE   £0.00

8 THE MALL, WINCHESTER ROAD
CHANDLERS FORD, S053 2DD
TEL: (023) 80271822

Speak to our shop manager for details.

www.mariecurie.org.uk

Do something wonderful

- Come back to see us next week.
- Bring in your

He had dropped the camp and shuffled his chair closer to hers.

'Would you like another drink?'

'Yes, please.' She handed him her glass.

'I'll get you a fresh one. This one's got a bit warm in your sticky paw.'

He stood up and left her. Insecurity immediately flooded back. There were copies of the book on the table. She flicked through the pictures of impoverished but beautiful black South Africans and weird-looking white Afrikaans families, all photographed in stark black and white.

'To make the point about apartheid,' she thought. 'Stunning but morally unspeakable.' Her mind wandered off. The book dropped. She felt vague flutterings of excitement and fear under her ribcage.

Where was he? It seemed ages since his back had disappeared through the crowd. Even sitting down she was jostled. She went around the other side of the table, taking a chair with her and picking up the book again for cover as she surreptitiously watched for his return.

He didn't come, and he didn't come.

'He's found someone more interesting,' she was thinking, just as she glimpsed him, cigarette in mouth, bringing two glasses and a bottle of Davoli's champagne.

'Sorry I took so long. I couldn't get the barman to be a sensible chap and give me a bottle. He kept saying Mr Davoli wouldn't like it. But I told him I was Mr Davoli's nephew. Anyway, here we are, this should last us for a bit. Then we can go out and get some supper. What do you do on *Modern Woman*?'

'I'm features assistant to the assistant features editor.'

'What?'

Dora repeated herself and then asked Guy what he did. She couldn't think of a more scintillating way to get into conversation with him.

'Well, I do various different things. I've just left art school under a bit of a cloud. So I do a bit of painting now and again – houses not pictures – and sell the odd picture – other people's not my own.'

'I see. What happened at art school?'

'Well, I thought it would be a complete doddle of a way to fill in time before my life started, but it turned out they wanted me to do some work. So I left.'

'Can you draw?'

'I think that was the problem. I had this romantic image of drawing fat naked men and thin naked women with interesting sticky-out bits all day long and hanging about in galleries full of plaster casts of Greek sculpture. But it's not like that these days. They want you to be as provocative and abstract as you can possibly be. I really wasn't interested. There seemed to be a lot of string involved.'

'What did your parents think?'

Dora was still at an age when this mattered.

'Well, they sent me to Dartington because of its arty reputation, but I wasted a lot of time there, so they opposed art school in the first place. In retrospect I think they knew more than me and realised I was fantasising. But I didn't listen. They're quite soft though, keen that I should be fulfilled and not too worried about the money-earning bit.'

'Oh.' Dora was confused by this. She had had no choice at all. If she wanted to come to London and have some fun, she had to earn her living and that was that.

'So what are you doing here?' she asked.

'I crashed it with one of Davoli's many bits of skirt, but

she disappeared quite quickly. I think Davoli is keen on her at the moment. She's probably in the inner sanctum on his lap.'

There was a flurry by the door and the *Modern Woman* crowd arrived in the hopes of supper. The low-fat nibbles at the American Hero shop opening in Bond Street hadn't been at all filling for girls who lived off canapés, and the understated drinks weren't up to much either. Anyway, you weren't allowed to smoke for fear of contaminating the expensive stock of faux British tweeds, velvet smoking jackets and satin column dresses.

Dora looked up and caught sight of Evangeline Flight, young gun (in her own estimation) of the *Modern Woman* fashion room. As far as Dora could see, Evangeline spent a lot of time crouched in the fashion cupboard covering the soles of shoes with masking tape to protect them during shoots.

She was a favourite of Addie Bean's though, the fashion editor notorious for her wild ideas for locations and her narrative fashion stories: all black and white, tousled hair and homoerotic overtones. James Scott, the assistant features editor and Dora's boss, had told Dora that Addie fancied Evangeline.

Addie definitely smiled indulgently when Evangeline took outrageous liberties with the clothes that had been brought in for shoots, wearing them for parties and sneaking them back, stinking of cigarette smoke, in plastic carrier bags. It all seemed so effortless for Evangeline. She had been at Cambridge with Dora but she was the year above and in a different college.

When Dora appeared at *Modern Woman* in the features department, the tall blonde beauty inexplicably began to patronise her – in the nicest possible way of course. Dora didn't mind. It meant she went to a lot more parties. She wasn't really aware that her dark curvaceous looks acted as a foil to the tall and fair Evangeline.

But she still started guiltily when the older girl said, 'Dora? What are you doing here?'

'James asked me to come. He said everyone else was going to the American Hero opening and someone must sign in for *Modern Woman*. He's gone to the opera.'

Dora could have bitten her tongue. Why did she feel the need to justify herself like this?

'Oh. I see. Well, the *Modern Woman* lot's here now. Addie Bean is thinking of doing a black-and-white story in South Africa. Miss Peebles has forbidden her in case the anti-apartheid brigade boycotts the magazine. She's not taking any notice; she's come to get a look at Davoli's new book for inspiration.'

Guy was attempting to disappear behind the pile of books when Dora felt she had to bring him to Evangeline's attention: 'You know Guy Boleyn?'

Guy swore to himself and re-materialised.

'Goodness, Guy, what are you doing back there? Of course I know Guy, Dora. I introduced him to you, didn't I?'

She turned back to Guy.

'Dora is so silly sometimes. She's quite bewildered by London. I have to tell her everything. How's Thelma? Is she here?'

'I believe she's fine,' Guy said coolly.

Evangeline drew up another chair and said, 'Guy, do be a love and get us a drink. I'm parched.'

Addie Bean came over. Ignoring Dora, whom she recognised from *Modern Woman* but felt wasn't important enough to be noticed, she picked up a copy of the book.

'That old cow won't let me go to South Africa. I've got

this wonderful black photographer. I've got a lead on a six foot four black model. If I use black, we won't be boycotted, will we? I want to put her on the cover. It would be just right for *Modern Woman* to have the first black cover girl, wouldn't it, Evangeline?'

Modern Woman was famously liberal. Founded in 1910 by a suffragette with some commercial instinct and a large fortune, it billed itself as 'The Glossy for Women Who Count'. Edited now by the terrifying Miss Peebles, it balanced its practical politics with the brilliant fashion, beauty and media coverage that brought in the advertisers.

Dora glanced sideways at Guy. He looked frozen, but when he saw her looking at him he imperceptibly cast his eyes skywards. She felt the giggles, which had been resting, bubble to the surface again.

Smiling a little, Guy said, 'I'll get you a drink, Evangeline, but I was just going to take Dora out to supper.'

'Right. OK. Fine.' Evangeline smiled back at him brightly.

He stood up, sighed and went to get Evangeline a drink.

As soon as he was out of earshot, she turned abruptly to Dora. 'Goodness, what are you doing with Guy?'

'Oh, we just started chatting.' Dora felt distinctly uncomfortable. She wasn't going to tell anyone about the giggling fit. It seemed private and significant.

'Johnnie Yeats said you were giggling like a maniac. Are you stoned?'

'No. I'm not stoned. I was just laughing at something funny.'

Addie Bean was gazing intently at each page of Davoli's South Africa book. 'Look at this, Evangeline. Don't you think it would be brilliant to have the model standing against the sink in this Soweto hut wearing one of Comme's ripped black jersey tubes? Wouldn't it make the most fabulous statement about how wearable Comme des Garçons is?'

Evangeline, her career dependent upon Addie's patronage, dropped her prey and switched, all smiles, to Addie.

Dora took the opportunity to stand up. 'Bye, Evangeline. Bye, Addie.'

Addie looked up, her subtly made-up face a mask. Dora could see her faking an expression of dawning recognition. 'Oh, it's Dora isn't it? From Features? Bye, dear.'

Having seen photography books scattered all around the Fashion Room, Dora knew that Addie was busy pillaging for visual ideas.

Dora didn't want to lose Guy in the crush, so she made her way slowly towards the bar. After she had repeated, 'Excuse me' for the fourth time without being listened to she began to push. She felt a sharp sting, looked down and saw a little smouldering hole in her full shirtsleeve. When she looked up, she couldn't see who'd done it.

Then she spotted Guy. He was standing talking to a woman in a beaded, Afghan-style dress and laced-up ankle boots. Her fair hair was long and wavy, her eyes lined with kohl and her lips painted bright shiny red. He held two glasses of champagne in his hands and handed her one. Their heads were very close together. The woman put her arm around the back of Guy's neck and drew his face down to hers. She kissed his mouth. Guy did nothing to pull away.

'Oh well,' thought Dora. 'He doesn't belong to me.'

All the same, a twist of anxiety turned in her guts as she watched the long, sweet, familiar kiss.

'He'll get covered in lipstick,' she thought. 'I hope it smudges on her.'

Guy released himself gently and said goodbye. He turned, spotted Dora and smiled at her, pushing through the crowd in her direction.

'I'll just give this to Evangeline, and then we'll go?'

'Yes, please,' said Dora, relieved. His mouth was a bit red. She handed him a tissue. 'Wipe your lips.'

He laughed and took it from her, scrubbing away furiously. Dora caught a glimpse of the fair woman's face. She seemed oblivious to everyone else in the room, staring at the back of Guy's head. Her face had drooped into longing and sadness. Guy went across to Evangeline and handed her the glass of champagne.

She saw her friend put her hand on Guy's arm, pulling him down towards her and saying something earnestly into his ear. The party was too noisy for Dora to hear what it was.

He extricated himself and came back to her, asking what she would like to eat. When she hesitated, he said, 'We'll go up to Westbourne Grove and see what we can find.'

They climbed up the stairs out of the smoky basement, collected their coats and emerged into the chilly night air. Guy hailed a taxi.

'Westbourne Grove, please.'

Dora had never been there. She had no idea that authentic curry houses lined the Bayswater street. In the taxi, she shuddered. Guy's arm came round her instantly.

'Is that better?' he whispered into her ear. It tickled and made her laugh.

'I love your laugh,' he said.

They drove on in silence. It wasn't uncomfortable. Dora

didn't feel she had to be amusing. She felt enormously happy.

They left the empty streets of Mayfair, turned into Park Lane and went past the lit-up fountains by Marble Arch.

Blade Runner was on at the Odeon.

'Have you seen it?' Guy asked.

'No, not yet. I'd love to.'

'Me too.'

'Drop us at the junction of Queensway and Westbourne Grove,' Guy told the taxi driver.

They got out; Guy paid and they began to walk.

'We won't go to Khan's. It's so noisy, and you always have to queue.'

Khan's looked vast to her, its cloud-painted ceiling supported with exotic pillars like palm trees. 'I would love to go there one day,' she said wistfully.

'I'll take you, I promise. But not tonight, OK?'

They went into the Khyber opposite, which was quiet and conventional by comparison.

She said, 'I've just got to go to the loo.'

She went into the Ladies. Her face looked flushed in the mirror, her eyes half closed. There were smudges where her mascara had run while she was giggling.

'God, you look a fright, Jerusalem. What on earth does he see in you?' She realised she was a bit drunk.

'Now, Jerusalem, you're not going to do anything silly,' she told herself as she repaired her face. She pulled out the chopsticks that held her hair up and let it fall down her back.

Guy had swivelled his chair away from the table so he was facing her as she emerged. His face was quite expressionless. She could feel her heart like a fish in a landing net do a huge flip-flop that left her breathless. It seemed to take weeks to walk towards him. She didn't even feel very welcome. Then he smiled and she was lost.

'Come and sit down. You look lovely. Goodness, what long hair you've got. I love long hair.' He was speaking fast. She wasn't really listening. She gazed at his face. He took hold of her hand and guided her to the place opposite him. He went on holding her hand over the tablecloth. He stopped talking and looked at her.

'Just like in the films,' thought Dora. The restaurant faded away. All that was left were Guy's large grey eyes fringed with thick dark eyelashes. She felt she wanted to eat the way he looked. Her gaze scanned the fine-grained skin dusted with a few distinct freckles, his soft, rather pale mouth (she didn't like red lips on a man) and his high square forehead from which the thick straight dark blond hair sprang up and back.

'Oh Lord,' he said. He put her hand carefully down, dropping his eyes to the tablecloth as she heard him sigh. He seemed to hesitate before looking back up at her face and smiling. 'Shall we look at the menu?' he said.

'Oh, yes, OK.' Dora dropped her eyes.

'What would you like?'

She was looking bewildered.

'Would you choose for me. I've never been here before.'

'All right. Do you like chicken or meat?'

'Chicken I think.'

'Right. I'm sure you will like chicken tikka masala. It's not particularly hot, but it is delicious.'

'That sounds lovely.'

Guy ordered lamb jalfrezi for himself, two naan breads, raita, a salad, and poppadums and chutney to start.

'Would you like a beer?'

'If that is the right thing, yes.'

He ordered a pint for himself and a half for her, and then sat back in his chair.

The food arrived and Dora picked at it. Her stomach was off somewhere else and not interested in eating. They tried to remember when they had first met, and talked about all the parties they had both been at without meeting. She refused coffee. She offered to pay half. He wouldn't let her. She said, 'OK, I'll pay next time.'

Then she looked at her watch. 'Goodness, it's late. I'd better take a taxi home. Shall I drop you off on the way?' She felt shivery with excitement and anticipation. In the taxi he simply curved an arm around her waist, which made her skin quiver. Then the cab stopped at his Chelsea basement. She wouldn't let him give her any money for his bit of the journey. He kissed her lips. She felt a sharp, sweet pain. He surprised her by gently removing his lips from hers after only a moment or two. There was nothing 'Not Safe in Taxis'– as her mother used to say – about him at all. Then he got out and the taxi carried her away. She turned and looked back as he disappeared down the area steps.

'You look happy,' said the taxi driver gloomily as he handed her the change. She tipped him lavishly to cheer him up. Then she let herself in. Everyone was asleep. She went to her bed hoping something significant had really happened. As she slipped into sleep, she muttered the Lord's Prayer and half remembered that her torn old nightie was held together with a safety pin.

The next day she spent the morning wading through the usual pile of dross sent in by the most surprising people claiming to be *Modern Woman* readers. Occasionally there was a diamond in the dust, and she would be overcome with relief, composing long letters of appreciation to the writers. A stark contrast to the curt notes of rejection she usually banged out on the old electric typewriter.

As she typed mechanically, shreds and patches of the dream she had been having when her alarm went off that morning came back to her.

There'd been no man in it, just an unknown barren landscape, a thin wind sighing past her ears and a sense of overwhelming longing mixed with fear and sorrow. What did it mean? It didn't have anything to do with the steamy, smoky, stuffy party where she had found Guy.

Two

THEY DIDN'T BECOME A COUPLE EXACTLY. Dora was disappointed for a while but then stopped minding as the months went by. She dreaded what being a couple meant – the awful struggle to keep things under control. She remembered the angry men she'd fancied but refused to sleep with, who then wouldn't speak to her. She'd lost so many promising friendships and had such nasty things said about and to her.

She didn't like the idea of being anyone's girlfriend, so it suited her to be sort of special but only sometimes, and it avoided the difficulty of her virginity very neatly. Having gone to boarding school at seven, squashing down her own emotional requirements and waiting months for the people she loved to take any notice of her was second nature anyway.

There was nothing to stop her thinking about him as much as she wanted – but it was always a little-girl fantasy about getting married. She'd been having these dreams for ever and felt slightly ashamed of them, but the man standing top right of the aisle had never had a face before. Now he did. Guy's. She would tell herself that she had every right to want to get married, but inside she squirmed.

She loved the heart-lifting moments when she spotted him across yet another party. They often spent evenings together, talking and laughing and sometimes kissing like teenagers. They chattered on the phone. He wouldn't ring her for a bit. She would sometimes ring him, but if he wasn't in the mood for her he would be quite short. Then he would feel sorry and ring her back and talk to her for hours. Ridiculous banter.

Guy loved her pealing laugh so freely given where her body wasn't. He went out of his way to think up jokes, the more ridiculous the better, because she appreciated them so much. He almost preferred her on the telephone: it wasn't so frustrating.

He would fill the spaces with Thelma – although she was becoming so clingy that this was risky. Then there were girls he picked up at parties and private views, and Lesley Stavely. Oh yes, Lesley – a serious symptom that something was wrong in Guy's love life.

One Friday morning in February he woke with Lesley in his bed, lying on her back snoring, her mouth slightly open. She smelt of pure alcohol and stale sweat. As he reached for his lighter and a half-smoked joint on the bedside table he wondered if he could set fire to her breath like James Bond with the aerosol.

Lesley had failed as usual to wash her face before falling into bed. Her long, unnaturally red hair extensions looked dull and ratty as they lay spread on the pillow.

He rolled out of his side of the bed, pulled on some jeans and went into the bathroom. 'Better shave today,' he said to himself. 'Wouldn't do to go and see Christopher Crane unshaven.'

He had a little Pre-Raphaelite drawing that Dorian Peak, a dealer friend who wasn't as pretty as Guy, had asked him to show to specialist dealers. Crane specialised in Victorian pictures in general and Pre-Raphaelites if he could get his well-manicured hands on them. He had an amazing client list and was opening up the Victorian market.

'Guy?'

He felt irritation.

'Guy?'

'Yes?'

'Guy, get us a coffee. I feel awful. Have you got any Alka-Seltzer?'

Guy looked at the ceiling. It was peeling with damp from the shower. Demands, demands. She was voracious in bed and he couldn't even get out without more demands.

To begin with it had been so exciting. In the months that followed it became mechanical. She wanted him to go on and on. The night before she had been so damped down with drink that nothing had lit her fire. In the end he'd given up and gone to sleep. Just couldn't be bothered. He felt squalid. He pulled off his jeans and got into the shower, turning it on full blast to wash the smell of her off his face and body. Turning his head up, he opened his mouth and let the water flow down the sides of his face.

Faintly through the rush of the water he could hear her calling, 'Can't you hear me?'

He stood until the water went cold. The thermostat was unreliable. Then he stepped out and wrapped himself in a damp grey towel. 'Sleazy, sleazy,' he thought.

He could hear Lesley moaning next door. It was a pointed criticism of his performance of the night before. She was telling him that she could give herself a better time than he ever could.

He felt sick and grasped the loo seat, bitter saliva dribbling out of his mouth. Unable to face Lesley again, he went straight into the sitting room, where his clothes from the night before lay in a heap on the floor.

The shirt was crumpled and stained. He'd better buy a new one on the way and change before he got to his meeting. He didn't want to go back into the fetid bedroom. He sprayed himself liberally with L'Heure Bleu. He hoped the creases would drop out of the chocolate brown velvet before he got down to the West End, and that he could have a coffee on the way.

When he was dressed, he picked up the small sanguine Conté crayon drawing of two children in vaguely Tudor dress embracing each other. Almost certainly by John William Waterhouse, it was called 'The Princes in the Tower'. Their faces were particularly well drawn – frightened but trusting. He wrapped it in a piece of old blanket and put it in a carrier bag. Then he called out, 'Lesley, I've got to go straight out. I'll be late. Sorry. Get yourself some coffee and let yourself out, won't you?'

He couldn't help the questioning tone; he could have slapped himself. He really didn't want to find her there when he got back. She was an actress, currently resting and therefore inclined to slob about all day in his flat, recovering from her hangover and waiting for him to come home.

She didn't answer. He imagined she had gone back to sleep or else she was sulking. He was beginning to hate her.

Guy had first seen Lesley in a production of *The Threepenny Opera* at the Almeida Theatre in Islington three months before he met Dora. She had been a wonderful low-life Jenny the prostitute. Her raucous singing voice had suited the part. Her dark eyes blazed. Her long magenta hair had seemed to crackle with energy. Guy had been drawn to her – she seemed so reckless and extreme. She'd played the part in a bodice that exposed her breasts. Her nipples were rouged bright red, her skin powdered greenish white. She looked just like a George Grosz drawing from 1930s Berlin. Guy had made the mistake of confusing part with person. He had a trace of nostalgie de la boue, and it had seemed to him a better idea to have sex with an actress playing a prostitute, than with a real prostitute. He didn't consciously realise that Lesley was a good actress, well directed.

He'd gone round to the stage door to see her when she came out. He had taken her for a drink and they had gone to bed that night. They hadn't talked much – it had been pure lust. She'd smelt of greasepaint, which reminded him of productions he'd been in at school and the curious ambiguities of dressing up as a girl. It had been wonderfully grubby to begin with, but he tired of it quickly. The crackling electricity of her performance did not extend into her life. She was a blank, rather lazy woman whose moodiness was worsened by drink and drugs. He was finding it difficult to get rid of Lesley now. The night before he had been too drunk to resist.

Stupid nights like that made him want to be with Dora all the more. Sometimes it was all too much and he became depressed, hiding in the flat unwashed and unshaved, unable to go out.

He didn't really know what to do with his life. Selling the odd picture, being turned down by Christie's, painting people's walls, waiting for his trust fund – it didn't add up to much. He lay on his bed, an insignificant speck, feeling the enormousness of time stretching out into infinite space. The idea of filling it made him panic. He knew it was self-pity, but there was nothing he could do to shift it – not drink, drugs or sex; they just made it worse because they filled minutes only and left him hungover, bad-tempered and filled with self-disgust.

When he got back from showing the drawing to Crane – who'd said it was a fake, been rude and dismissive, put his hand on his leg and then offered him a fiver for it – Lesley was still in his bed. He lost his temper and yelled at her to get out. She sulkily dressed and left.

He sensed that Lesley was as terrified of life as he was and was trying to hitch a ride on him. There just wasn't enough of him to try and pull her up when he was so down. The two of them dragged at each other. He had noticed that Lesley was particularly persistent when she wasn't in work. When she was, he hardly saw her. How she afforded the cocaine he didn't like to ask; and it was all very hilarious getting high. But the next day black depression descended on both of them, and they vied with each other as to who could be the most sullen and difficult. The contrast between Lesley and Dora bore down upon him like a blow, and he felt like crying with hungover self-pity.

He felt no better the next day, which was a Saturday. Unable to stop himself, he rang Dora. He wanted to warm himself on her hopefulness, her capacity for joy. She seemed to him to be staring open-eyed into her own future. He wanted to join himself to her and let her pull him forward, no matter how annoying he found her in the flesh. But he didn't know how.

She realised from the flat note in his voice that all was not well.

'Would you like me to come round?' she asked.

'If you like, but I'm not really worth seeing.'

Dora had to ring the bell twice before he let her in. She was dismayed by the stale whiff and the waves of misery that came from him. She hid her reaction. Depression had pulled his face downwards and his pink mouth drooped.

She had the sense not to whisk about tidying up, which she thought might irritate him. So she said, 'Why don't you get dressed and we'll go out and have a late lunch?'

He felt quite blank. The easiest course was to go along with what she suggested. He went into the bathroom and Dora could hear the shower. When he came out, clean, dressed and shaven ten minutes later, Dora had opened a window to let in some fresh air. He went over to the telephone.

'Mrs Jarvis? Look, I know it's Saturday but do you think you would come round and clean up this afternoon? I'll pay you a bit more... I know. I haven't been very well. Right, I'll leave the door unbolted so you can let yourself in. Thanks.'

He put down the telephone and turned to Dora. He was beginning to feel pleased to see her; the black dog slinking away.

'Sorry about all this.'

'Don't worry. It can happen to all of us.'

'It's a disgusting mess. I am sorry you saw it like this.'

'Well, it's better if we know the worst of each other, isn't it?'

He thought, 'She doesn't know anything like the worst of me yet.'

They went to a café and had cheese and pickle sandwiches, a carafe of red wine and coffee. Dora's happiness at being with him came across the little, marble-topped table and cheered him. He thought to himself, 'I can't be that bad if this lovely girl is happy to be with me, can I?'

By the time they had finished he felt better and took her to see *Blade Runner* at the Chelsea Classic. Then they had supper and went their separate ways.

When he got back to his basement Mrs Jarvis had been and put all to rights. She was wonderful; she cleaned for his mother and never told tales of torn Rizla packets, funny-looking cigarettes, mirrors and razor blades and stained sheets. The place was as immaculate as it could be with its battered and faded old servants' furniture from his father's country house.

It smelt of Pledge and Mrs Jarvis had obviously had the windows open. His bedroom was innocent of the rumpled grey sheets that would have brought the sour taste of Lesley back into his mouth. He put on some old pyjamas, got himself a beer out of the fridge, rolled a joint, put The Stranglers on the record player and thought about Dora. At that moment, he didn't want to be seedy any more – he wanted to try and do things on purpose, not just impulsively.

Dora wouldn't let him pay for things, or if she did she was strict about paying for the next thing – even though he knew that *Modern Woman* paid a pittance. It expected its well-educated young employees to have an allowance, but he knew she didn't.

There was never any pressure. She left him alone if he seemed to want that. She didn't come across as needy. He was used to an exasperated feeling when some girl he'd screwed fell in love with him. 'It's not my fault that I didn't fall in love with her,' he would excuse himself with when he found some poor hopeful creature on his doorstep with a bottle of expensive wine she couldn't afford.

Dora didn't know that he had other girls but she must

have assumed it. He did wonder sometimes why she was so dead set against full-on sex. She was much too young to be thinking about marriage, certainly to him with his unformed life and uncertain future. He was a good two years younger than her for starters, and wasn't going to get his trust fund until he was 25. Sometimes he felt this was paralysing him.

He was becoming hugely affectionate towards Dora, as well as exasperated. She seemed to him to be associated with the happy rush he got when he sold a picture well or had some other success. He would like to capture that pleasure and make it more permanent. It was so utterly unlike feelings evoked by Lesley and Thelma, inextricably linked with all that he felt was wrong in his life.

Three

GUY STOPPED FROM TIME TO TIME, wrapped his arms around a blissful Dora and kissed her. She tasted the bitter espresso on his lips and felt she was drowning with love. Her skin shuddered with desire like a horse shaking off flies. She also felt quite drunk. A group of Guy's friends, including Evangeline, had all been having Sunday lunch in an Italian restaurant in Chelsea. The table had been covered with bottles by the end.

In the months since the book launch, Dora had harboured secret longings that she had the self-control not to reveal. They kissed a lot, but that was all. Mostly they just enjoyed themselves hugely. Dora felt her London life was lit up because Guy was around somewhere – not necessarily at exactly the same party just then, but bound to appear across a smoky room any point soon.

She thought about him constantly but knew better than to be clingy or demanding. This lunch had been different though. He'd hardly spoken to anyone else, and now they were reeling home through the quiet Sunday streets.

Joined at the hip like Siamese twins they dropped behind the others. Their friends were waiting by the railings outside Guy's basement, shuffling their feet and looking embarrassed when Guy and Dora reappeared.

Evangeline said loudly, 'I don't think we're wanted here. Guy's got a bit of an agenda, haven't you, Guy?'

Guy looked straight into Evangeline's face. 'I just go with the flow, just go with the flow.'

Dora was happy to flow along with Guy. She was so hungry for his love. Then she looked at Evangeline. Her fair skin was flushed; her eyes glittered. They were all quite lit up, but Dora suspected her friend was very drunk indeed. She'd noticed that the older girl had ordered Armagnac after lunch, when everyone else had stuck to the wine.

'Remember what I told you, Dora dear. Be a sensible girl, won't you? You've drunk an awful lot and I wouldn't like you to do something you might regret.'

'What a hypocrite,' Dora thought. What did she mean anyway? Did she think Dora was a drunken little pushover? Was that what Guy was up to? Dora knew more about his philandering ways now and didn't entirely trust him. It certainly didn't put her off him, as he never seemed to have anyone who lasted more than a night or two. Also, she was a veteran in the campaign of saying no and meaning it.

She drew slightly away from his insistent arm. The others had all turned to go, muttering tactfully about being green and hairy. The spring day that had seemed like summer was chilling into dusk.

'Bye, Guy. Bye, Dora.' Kisses all round, then they were gone, leaving her outside Guy's flat. Only Evangeline remained.

'Don't you need a chaperone, Dora?' she said, propping

herself up on the railings. 'Guy's got a terrible reputation, you know.'

'I can look after myself, thank you,' said Dora, all dignity, in spite of the spiteful glow that was lighting up her entrails. She wished Evangeline would leave too, and then asked herself why she wanted to be alone with Guy. What was her body planning?

Evangeline had turned to Guy. 'What about whiling away the rest of this dull and depressing Sunday with both of us, Guy?' she slurred.

Dora realised what she meant and felt her face grow hot. Guy had turned to go down the basement steps, trying to draw Dora with him. His averted head didn't convey anything in particular. She pulled herself away from him. He looked around, startled.

'I'm going now, OK, Guy. I've got to go home. I've a piece I've got to finish for Monday,' Dora explained.

'You didn't say anything about it before. Do come at least and have a cup of tea. Please. You can do it later, can't you, when you've sobered up?'

'I write rather well when I'm a bit pissed.' Dora was determined now. She found the idea of losing her virginity in the company of another woman utterly squalid. If she was going to take the plunge, she wanted to be the only female witness.

'Do come down, please.'

Guy was ignoring Evangeline, who still stood there with a slightly mad smile on her face. He turned and came back up. Dora had her back to the railings, and he grasped the cold iron on either side of her, his right shoulder shutting out her friend. He bent down deliberately and kissed Dora's mouth. Then he said, 'Dora, I'm so madly in love with you that if you leave me now, I'll get into the bath with the Carmen rollers.'

'In your hair or out of it?' Dora inquired solicitously.

'Oh, in it I think, don't you?' He puffed up the back of his thick straight hair.

'Then I won't worry about you a bit, because they can't present a threat to your health if they're not plugged into the mains.'

'Oh, you cruel woman. You will break my heart. I make a very good pot of tea. Everyone says so. You must be very dehydrated by now. Please come in.'

Evangeline stood silent and astounded. Guy didn't usually say so much. The tender note in his voice disturbed her. The Guy she knew was far harder and more predatory.

'OK, but just tea, please. I wasn't fibbing when I said I had a piece to finish.'

'Bye, then,' said Evangeline, defeated. 'Shall I come back later when she's gone?' she asked Guy.

'I won't require your services tonight, Miss Flight. Would you like to make an appointment with my secretary for later in the week?'

She at least had the grace to laugh and leave. Dora and Guy went down the steps. He kissed her while he was trying to put the key in the lock, which meant it took a long time. He had one hand twisted into the back of her loose hair. Her whole skin felt electric. He kissed her as he pushed the door open. He pulled off her jacket. He put his arms around her and fell with her on to the sofa. He kissed her again and undid the buttons of her tight bodice, releasing her breasts.

Although she was enjoying Guy's energetic attentions, even with alcoholic logic and slightly dulled senses, she was disturbed by Evangeline's insinuations. Her long-held virginity had taken on a hideous significance. Losing it couldn't be casual now. She wasn't too drunk to stick to her conviction about not joining the throng that trooped through his bed, and began half-heartedly to push his hands away.

He let go of her abruptly and slipped to the floor at her feet, where he knelt down on the bare boards.

Dora blinked. Without his warmth, the chill of the unheated room struck on her bare chest, raising goose pimples.

He said: 'Shall we get married then?'

She was silent for a minute, and then she said, 'OK'.

'Right, my darling, let's go to bed.'

He stood up, holding out his hand to help her to her feet.

'Hold on, Guy.'

She didn't accept his hand. She leaned back on the sofa. The world was beginning to tip. She felt slightly queasy. She tried to think.

'Shouldn't we wait until after the wedding?' she asked carefully.

He was still laughing.

'I don't think I can wait another minute. And this is the 1980s, not the 1880s.'

'We hardly know each other.'

'I know everything I want to know. That you are beautiful and good and kind, and I don't know – that I'm desperate to fuck you right now. Here if you like.'

He sat down beside her on the sofa again, hoping that he might overcome her scruples physically. He scooped her on to his knee and began to kiss her again. Her arms went around his neck. In spite of all the booze he was feeling very aroused. He bent his head, released a nipple from her bra with his tongue and sucked quite hard. It had an electric effect – the sensation shot through to her groin and she clung all the closer and kissed him enthusiastically back.

'Here we go,' he thought to himself, smiling inwardly. He'd really meant it when he'd said he loved her. She was special and different, but not too special and different to fuck.

Then she pulled back, her eyes glittering, her cheeks red. 'When do you want to get married?'

He felt shocked. Marriage wasn't the sort of persuasion technique he usually used. These days every girl he met was on the Pill and it wasn't necessary. He might be a chancer but he didn't employ cheap tricks like declaring undying love. He was confident enough of his own attractions to get anyone he wanted into bed. He wasn't quite sure why he had used marriage now, but it had seemed right. He had felt overwhelmed by Dora herself, not just by lust.

She rested her head on his shoulder, hiding her face from him, her hands still linked around the back of his neck. He felt very frustrated and had the urge to pull up her flounced skirt and just get on with it. He put his hand on the damp warmth of her cotton knickers. She murmured a protest and clamped her legs together, wriggling to dislodge him. He resisted a parallel desire to push her sharply off his lap on to the floor.

Dora was aching with desire, and trying to deal with this peculiar proposal, rampant lust and her usual reluctance to let anyone go too far. She wished he would just put his hand in her pants and make her come that way; but this had always led to requests she couldn't fulfil.

Guy gave up and let go of her, glaring at her hot face and naked breasts in frustrated fury. She wanted to cry and he wanted to scream.

Lost for words, he shoved her away from him, stood up and left the room. It felt like some stupid 1950s heavy petting session.

'For God's sake,' he said to himself over and over again. 'Why don't you just leave her alone. She's obviously frigid as hell, or religious or something. Maybe she doesn't fancy you. Not your type at all.'

He shut his bedroom door and leaned against it, his erection gradually subsiding. He could hear her gathering herself together in the next room, and the sound of the front door opening and closing. He sighed. What was wrong with Dora?

'I wouldn't marry me,' he thought.

For the first time in his life, he wondered what was going on inside a girl's head. Hitherto, he had worried a great deal more about what was going on in their knickers.

Four

DORA HOISTED HER TOWEL HIGHER over her breasts and sat down on the chair by the telephone to answer it. 'Who's that?' she said, although she knew damn well.

'It's me, Evangeline. Can I come and see you?'

Dora felt uneasy. Evangeline did telephone sometimes, but only to invite her out somewhere. She never seemed interested in visiting Dora at home.

Dora's heart started thumping in her chest and she didn't dare say, 'Why?'

'Yes, I suppose so. I'm in this evening. Do you want to come now?'

'Yes, all right. Are you alone?'

'Er, I think so. Why?'

'I want to talk to you in private.'

Dora felt as if she couldn't breathe properly. She knew what Evangeline was going to tell her, and she didn't want to hear it.

She wanted to tell Evangeline to go to hell. She also wanted to hear what she had to say. It was like licking an ulcer.

She went upstairs, rubbing her hair with her towel, and hastened back into her clothes. She had intended to put on her cotton pyjamas and dressing gown, but if she had to face Evangeline, she wanted to be armoured in stiff fabric. She chose midnight blue corduroy jodhpurs and a matching beaded cardigan. Then she went to make a pot of tea, damned if she was going to pour wine down Evangeline.

She turned on the television and caught the news. Mrs Thatcher was doing something or other. She felt rather bemused and considered having a stiff drink herself first. There was some cooking brandy left over from the Christmas cake she had made. She went into the kitchen, took the bottle down, unscrewed the lid and took a swig. It burned down her gullet, making her choke, but when it settled in her stomach it glowed more gently. She took another couple of nips, wiped her mouth on the back of her hand and put the bottle back for next Christmas, or crisis, whichever came first.

The doorbell rang and Dora jumped guiltily. She went and let her in. Evangeline was immaculate. Her floating blonde hair was crimped into perfect little curls. Her face was artfully made up to look unmade up, and she was wearing a soft suede wrap-around skirt and an extravagant natural cashmere throw. When Dora looked at her objectively, she thought the whole effect was much too old. Evangeline was only 25, for goodness' sake. That look suited the senior fashion editors, but not a young woman.

'Hello, darling,' she said to Dora. Unhappiness always made Dora clumsy and the two of them got stuck in the narrow end part of the passage. Evangeline's smile became rather fixed.

'Come on, Dora, let's sit down.'

'Would you like some tea?'

'Haven't you got anything stronger?'

'Sorry, Evangeline, I haven't.'

'Oh, but what can I smell on your breath?'

Dora thought quickly. This was going to be a very tricky interview. She'd better pull herself together and start playing Evangeline's game at least as well as she did. She had come to hurt and wound Dora, her little protégée who'd ventured too far into her territory. It was time to punish her transgression – but Dora didn't consent to be punished.

'I was just finishing up a bit of Christmas cake with my tea,' said Dora, opening her eyes as wide as she could.

This disconcerted Evangeline, as it was April. She came back with, 'A little bit of this and a little bit of that? I must get you one of those fridge magnets which says, "A minute on your lips, forever on your hips."'

'That would be lovely, thanks.' Dora smiled broadly at her. 'Now, you said you wanted to talk to me.' She stood waiting for Evangeline to begin.

'Right.'

'Do sit down.'

'OK.'

Evangeline unwound herself from her cashmere throw and sat down on the saggy old sofa. Dora remained standing, her hands linked in front of her, still smiling.

'Aren't you going to sit down?'

'Me? Oh, not for a minute.'

Dora walked over to the fireplace and leaned on the mantelpiece, picking up an old invitation and smiling what she hoped Evangeline would think was a secret smile.

'What did you want to say?' she asked.

'Well, I'm sure you must know by now how much I like

you, Dora. It's been such fun having you in London after being such friends at Cambridge. Particularly when you came to work at *Modern Woman* with me.'

Dora didn't remember being such good friends with Evangeline at Cambridge. Evangeline had belonged to a very cool collection not given to mixing with the year below. Dora had always thought that Evangeline enjoyed the company of men more than she did women, a trait that Dora found particularly disquieting, as she had made her best and closest friends at single-sex boarding school. She didn't realise that her smaller stature, roundedness and dark hair set off Evangeline's willowy fairness rather effectively. After a year in the fashion room, even picking up pins, Evangeline had come to understand how to show herself off.

'Well, Dora, I just don't want you to get hurt. The fact is—'

'The kettle must have boiled by now,' said Dora in a bored voice, and walked out of the room.

As she went down the passage to the kitchen at the back of the house, she could feel the anger rising in her belly. People only said that they didn't want you to get hurt when they had the intention of inserting the knife and giving it a leisurely twist.

She slowly laid the tray with cups, milk, tea and sugar. She had another swig of brandy. She added a packet of biscuits and carried the tray back to the sitting room.

Evangeline was in a nonchalant pose, staring straight ahead, and seemed to start when Dora came back in. 'Sorry, I was in a little dream,' she murmured.

'No need to apologise,' said Dora.

She made a great ceremony of pouring out.

'One lump or two,' she asked, knowing very well that

Evangeline took her tea black, with perhaps a slice of lemon. Evangeline was intensely aware, as all aspiring fashion editors are, of the need to keep her figure under control to fit into sample-sized garments.

'No sugar, please, Dora. Do you have a slice of lemon?'

'I'll just go and look.' Dora, the brandy coursing around her veins, got up and drifted gently back to the kitchen.

She spent a long time at the vegetable rack, brandy bottle in one hand. Eventually she found a lemon that someone had sliced and left behind the onions. One side of it was a beautiful verdigris. Dora looked at the combination of lemon yellow and bluish green with pleasure. 'I'd love some fabric like that,' she thought.

She had a little more of the brandy, sliced off most of the furry bit, and took the lemon back to the sitting room. She was aware that she was running out of delaying tactics. The brandy lent a little courage, so she decided she had better let Evangeline have her say this time. But she was very pleased that so far she had been in charge. Evangeline's first mistake had been tackling her on home territory; she wasn't as calculating as she thought – although Evangeline was older and meant to be more sophisticated, she seemed innocent and clumsy now, whatever her mission. 'If I was planning to destroy someone,' she thought, 'I would catch them on the telephone at work or invite them on to my territory.' She found Evangeline in a similar pose to last time, and snorted down her nose.

'Sorry?'

'Sorry, I've got a bit of a cold.'

She dropped the ragged piece of old lemon from a great height into Evangeline's tea, hoping that it was cold enough to be quite nasty.

She went back to leaning on the mantelpiece.

'What was it you wanted to say?' she said again.

Evangeline took a deep breath. 'Well, Dora,' she began.

'Why did they call you Evangeline?' Dora inquired. She knew she was stalling and that when it did come out it would be so much more spiteful and cruel than if she had just left her alone. The brandy was beginning to talk.

'Some old aunt, I don't know. I think my father expected a legacy. But she left the lot to the old horses from the Crimea or something – and me with this name. Why are you called Dora?'

'My father was a big fan of Augustus John. He wanted to call me Dorelia, but Mummy drew the line at that.'

'How interesting. Now, Dora. I came here to give you a little sisterly word of advice.' She drew herself up a little. 'Don't fall in love with Guy. It's fatal.'

'Oh, really?' Dora thought, waiting for Evangeline to go on. 'She's months and months too late. I fell for him within minutes of seeing him properly for the first time. When he laughed.' She remembered the look of the under-side of his chin, like a flat-topped pyramid. Then his head had come down and his eyes were screwed up, streaming with laughter. He had held her to support himself. Dora loved him then, and she loved him now. She didn't know when she was going to stop loving him, even though she knew he slept with other girls. She felt she couldn't blame him, as she was in such a state of confusion about her virginity. She knew that Evangeline was going to tell her everything she could to put her off. Guy belonged in her world, Evangeline's world. And she didn't want the people in her world to relate to each other without her permission.

Evangeline was talking again. 'He has such a dreadful reputation for pumping and dumping. He's got a whole collection of girls, you know. All ages too. He has no discrimination.' She looked up at Dora under her lashes to see how she was taking it.

Dora was looking down at the toe of her flat bronze slipper, anaesthetised by cooking brandy.

'He's terribly charming, but totally fucked up. His parents divorced when he was quite young. He used to play one off against the other. From the age of about 12 he would tell one he was with the other and vice versa, when he was with his girlfriend. Of course, she was much older than him and should have known better. You've probably seen her around; she's called Thelma. She was at least 30 even then, and lived in a caravan in the woods on his father's estate. I wouldn't be surprised if she was his father's mistress as well. In those days she was some kind of hippy, flower-child type, left over from the sixties. She introduced him to marijuana, sex, free love. I think it was there he got his taste for three in a bed.'

Dora spoke slowly, 'How do you know all this?'

'Oh, everybody knows about Guy's weird childhood. He was so out of hand that they sent him to Dartington. Everyone knows what goes on there. He came out with straight Fs. No, I'm wrong – I believe he got an E in Art O-Level. Everyone screwed everyone else there. He was exceptionally pretty as a young boy. I'm sure he got up to everything you can think of. Sex, drugs and rock and roll. He played in a band, of course. Very badly, I believe. Too stoned to learn the notes.'

'You seem to know an awful lot about Guy. Why are you so interested?'

Evangeline stood up and came over to where Dora was standing. She put her finger under her chin, and said, 'Look at me, darling Dora. I just don't want you to get hurt. You're new to London; you just don't know how bad it can be.'

'I survived Cambridge.'

'Oh, that's terribly safe in comparison. A limited number of people all pursuing the same aim – roughly. Most of the people we hung around with there are far too ambitious and bright to be as hopeless as Guy and his ilk. Don't you understand what I'm telling you? He's no good for you at all. I suggest you forget him, right now – for your own good.'

Dora found it safer to look at her shoes and the carpet. She thought for a bit and didn't say anything. Then she walked out of the room and back to the kitchen. She swallowed some more brandy. It was quite pleasant when you got used to it. Evangeline followed her, and saw her putting the bottle back in the cupboard.

'What have you got there?'

'Only cooking brandy, Evangeline.'

Evangeline glowed inwardly. She realised that she was getting to Dora; her instincts had been right. Something had happened after that Sunday lunch.

Her voice was softly solicitous when she said, 'You've got him bad, huh?'

'Yes, I've got him bad. You're much too late, I'm afraid.'

This time Dora looked directly at Evangeline. She could see a strange mixed collection of expressions on her pretty face. There was triumph, but it was mixed with disappointment and a kind of unease and incomprehension.

'Yup,' Dora went on. 'I would gladly die for Guy Boleyn. Just for one glance, one touch of his hand, I would jump off the roof of Modern House. I adore him. I love him. I want to have his babies. I want to tell the world.'

She looked at Evangeline again. It was clumsy, but it seemed to working. Another expression had joined the party. Was it relief? Did Evangeline really want to rescue Dora from Guy's clutches?

'You're teasing me?' Evangeline said uncertainly.

'Of course I am. Do you think I would let you come round here to tell me things I didn't already know if I was really in love with Guy? You must be mad. He's very attractive, I'll give you that, and kissing him is heaven. But I know how to look after myself, and falling for someone like him isn't on my list of things to do.'

But she was screaming inside, 'Get out of this house. Leave me alone!' She said instead, 'Have you slept with him? Of course, you are so much more sophisticated than me, I'm sure you wouldn't let him through your defences. Just another notch on the bedpost for you, eh?'

Evangeline looked disconcerted. 'Well, as a matter of fact, he did pester me for a bit. I made it clear that I wasn't interested.' She didn't add the truth: that she had become very interested indeed when Guy had developed a soft spot for her funny little plump friend. She didn't like the way he looked at her. His eyes would droop and he'd have a silly smile on his face. She didn't understand and she wanted it to stop. Evangeline felt very confused; she wanted to get things back to normal between her and Dora.

'Dora, there's a dance at the Polish Club on Saturday – do you want to come? Everyone will be there. I thought you could come round to my place and we could get ready together.' She was back in charge of unsophisticated little Dora from the sticks – any feelings Dora had for Guy were surely doomed anyway. It would blow over and then she could say, 'I told you so.'

Dora was feeling sick. She was glad that Evangeline wasn't going to tell her anything else she didn't want to know about Guy. If her dreams came true and he did love her, he could tell her himself in his own words.

She looked slyly at Evangeline. 'Will Guy be there?'

Evangeline tried to read her expression. 'Yes, I suppose so.'

'Oh good. How much are the tickets?'

'About five pounds, but you get lots of wine and breakfast.'

'That sounds fun. Is there a theme?'

'Masks.'

'Right. I'll think of something. If you don't mind, Evangeline, I'm rather tired. I was going to have an early night tonight.'

'Ah. OK. Head over to my flat for seven o'clock. I've got some people coming to dinner beforehand, and we can help each other dress up and cook the dinner.'

Dora knew of old what that meant. Evangeline would do lots of dressing and making up, chiefly of herself, and Dora would cook the dinner. She didn't mind. But there was one thing she did have a problem with.

'I'll bring a bottle of wine, but you really will have to provide the food this time, Evangeline. I have a lot to do on Saturday and I can't do your food shopping for you as well.'

Evangeline felt that their relationship had shifted. Perhaps it had been a mistake coming round this evening. She couldn't analyse exactly what had happened, but Dora seemed stronger rather than weaker after what she had had to say.

'Of course I'll get the food. Oh, don't worry. Just come round at seven and we'll help each other get ready.'

'Right. See you then.' Dora had no intention of going early. She would ring at seven and say she had been delayed. She hid a smile. Then Evangeline would have to cook for her own dinner party. Ha bloody ha.

Five

AT SEVEN O'CLOCK DORA WAS RINGING Evangeline's bell. She had calmed down after her friend's visit the day before and could see that in a sort of kind of way Evangeline meant well, even if Evangeline's 'concern' for her was rather over-whelming. Also, she couldn't forget the amount of fun she had had in London. Evangeline could be generous, charming and funny. Why shouldn't Dora do something for her in return for all the parties, clubs and new friends? Dora had been happy at Cambridge, but she had never penetrated the really cool lot that Evangeline ornamented. She had been working too hard. To discover that Evangeline found her interesting enough to drag along behind her in London was very flattering. Evangeline's voice came down over the intercom.

'Darling Dora, how lovely, I really need you. Come straight up.'

'Come on Jerusalem, don't be so grudging,' Dora thought. She reminded herself that when you're single in a big city, it is very nice to be needed.

She pushed open the heavy door and walked up the shallow steps to the flat on the first floor, her cocktail frock over her arm. Evangeline was standing in the doorway waiting for her, wearing a white towelling dressing gown and small Carmen rollers.

She kissed her friend enthusiastically.

'I've only just got in myself. I was having lunch with Johnnie Yeats in the Savoy Grill and couldn't tear myself away. Do you think you could fill in the gaps? I can't go out shopping dressed like this.'

Dora's heart sank. She walked into the flat and hung her outfit on the white-painted, bentwood hatstand. The whole flat was pale and light, with cream-coloured sofas and carpets. However, Evangeline's friends being what they were, if you looked more closely there were many grey red-wine stains, liberally sprinkled with salt. The kitchen was at one end of the sitting room, cut off from it by a row of units, so you could see out while you were cooking.

'Let's have a look at what you've got so far, Evangeline. Then we'll see what's needed.'

Dora opened the little fridge. It contained a half-finished bottle of Frascati, some Ski yogurts and a squalid packet of Anchor butter smeared with red jam streaks. Evangeline giggled nervously.

'Actually, I was a bit inaccurate about the food. Not even you can make much out of that lot, can you?'

Dora didn't trust herself to look round. She felt really angry but was nervous of expressing her anger. She didn't want to lose Evangeline, however uneven their relationship. At work it would be unbearable if she fell out with her only fashion-room friend. Socially, Evangeline had been responsible for most of her fun. She couldn't risk it. She kept her voice deliberately even.

'No, I can't. You'll have to get dressed and buy some food for me to cook.'

'But I've got my curlers in,' she wailed.

'Never mind. You look enchanting.' Dora tried to smile. 'Gloucester Road will be very edified by your appearance. You can go to Europa and pick up everything we need. I'll have my bath while I wait for you to come back.'

She wouldn't have dared to be so straightforward previously, but something about that interview at Dora's flat had shifted things between them.

There was a silence. Evangeline was thinking. She was used to people doing what she wanted when she was charming and helpless. She was used to Dora smoothing the practical path to successful dinner parties. Before Dora had emerged as her tame cordon bleu, she'd invited people round to supper and they'd always had to go out and share the bill because Evangeline had never managed or bothered to produce any food.

'Let's all go out instead,' she said brightly. 'That would be much more fun and save you the trouble.'

'I can't afford to go out, Evangeline. I'm quite happy to cook for your friends if you get the food. Everyone will bring bottles; it'll be much cheaper.'

She knew Evangeline was parsimonious, always adding up her share of a group bill if she had been restrained and only had a first course. Dora had noticed that when she had ordered Armagnac for herself after that Sunday lunch, she had been just as keen to divide the bill equally. Evangeline's bottom lip shot out.

'I don't see why—' she began.

'I do.'

'Oh, OK then.' She went back into her bedroom and shut the door on Dora.

'She's quite a little girl still,' Dora thought kindly. She knew Evangeline was an adored only child of elderly parents, that she had always had exactly what she wanted. She also respected Evangeline's ambition. Spoiling can wreck a girl's chances of success.

She helped herself to a glass of the Frascati, made a list of what she needed and was leaning on the worktop drinking when her friend re-emerged in jeans and a sweatshirt with a scarf over her curlers. Dora was ready for renewed combat and had herself well under control when Evangeline disarmed her by saying, 'Look, I'm really sorry. Lunch went on for such a long time that I thought I wouldn't be here to let you in if I went shopping. Then I just got into the bath and forgot about it. OK?'

'Yes, that's OK. Please don't worry. Of course I'll do a good dinner. I've made a list. I thought we would have a fish pie with peas for simplicity. You can get some cheese and apples for pudding, and a big box of Smarties.'

'What fun. You are clever.'

Dora let herself rest for a moment on the flattery. She wondered who was coming and hoped that Guy was but didn't like to ask.

'I won't be long. It all looks very straightforward. I've already got some potatoes – they're in the vegetable rack.'

'Bye, then. Got your keys?'

'Yup.' And she was gone.

Dora investigated the potatoes. They were a bit soft and some were green, but there were enough. She cut off the worst bits and put them on to boil before she went to have her bath.

Evangeline always had the most delicious things in her bathroom. Dora chose Floris Rose Geranium and put a couple of drops into the water. Then she borrowed a bath hat, smeared on some face pack that was open in the soap rack and lay back. The mask smelt of lavender and she giggled when she looked at herself in the mirror tiles. She relaxed, completely happy. Even if he wasn't coming to dinner, she would see Guy at the dance later. The prospect started the fluttering under her diaphragm and she tried to breathe deeply and calm down. She sipped her wine. The glass was misted with the steam. She rinsed off the mask, washed herself all over and got out of the bath. All the towels were damp, but she didn't mind. She borrowed a bathrobe and padded barefoot back to the kitchen to check the potatoes. The scraping of a key in the lock heralded Evangeline's return and she turned to her smiling.

'I've just bumped into Guy,' Evangeline announced, hefting the yellow plastic carrier bag on to the work top. 'He said he would see us later at the party.' She glanced discreetly up at Dora to see how she was taking this. Dora was smiling cheerfully. This irritated Evangeline.

'He was in Thelma's Rolls Royce. She's married to that old has-been Billy Kidd now, but it doesn't stop her chasing after Guy. They're going to have dinner at Le Gavroche and then come on from there. I can't imagine why Thelma's husband lets her drive Guy around like that. He must be a very unjealous man.'

'Oh.' The happiness seemed to drain out of Dora like her sweet-smelling bath water swirling down the plug. 'Perhaps there's nothing for him to be jealous about. They're very old friends, aren't they? Guy and Thelma?'

'Yes, but Billy's away touring in Japan, I believe.'

Evangeline suspected what her announcement had done to Dora. She felt a pang of pity, which quickly passed when she remembered that Dora had been warned – and by her as well. Dora would just have to take the consequences and be a bit more realistic about London.

Dora had turned back to the potatoes and prodded them viciously with a knife.

'I think the potatoes are nearly done. I'd like to put the fish on please.'

'I got everything on your list.' Dora couldn't help noticing that her friend's voice had a pleading note in it. 'Thanks,' she said.

She took the food out of the bag. The smoked haddock was dyed bright yellow, but you probably couldn't get the natural sort in Europa. A good big fillet of cod. Milk. Quail's eggs. Button mushrooms. Capers. Prawns. Evangeline had done well, but she was looking uncertain.

'You get dressed and made up, and I'll get on with this. I've had my bath, and it won't take me a moment to get ready.'

'Right.' She still stood there. 'You don't need any help?'

'No. I'm fine. The food you bought looks great.'

Evangeline smiled her little girl's smile and went back into her room.

Dora put the fish in milk in the oven and began to make a white sauce with the rest of the Frascati. She mashed the potatoes, used the milk from the cooked fish to complete the sauce and put the dish together. Then she laid the table, arranged the fruit and cheese and put the Smarties in a glass bowl. Evangeline came back just as she had finished.

'God, Dora, you are so quick.' She genuinely admired Dora's abilities.

'The fish pie's in the oven heating gently. I'll go and transform myself now.'

She looked admiringly at Evangeline, who had tied a striped ribbon across her forehead and under her hair. She was wearing yet another designer outfit from the fashion cupboard, in draped red silk velvet: Zouave pants and a low-cut waistcoat with a wide, striped sash. Dora went to dress herself, knowing that her dressing-up box tat could never compete but hoping to do her best.

The doorbell rang as she disappeared. She climbed into the 1950s black strapless cocktail frock and pulled on a pair of tights and bow-trimmed low court shoes. Then she did her face: pale, with red lips and lots of black eyeliner. She twisted her dark hair into a bun and stuck in black lacquered chopsticks to hold it up. She tied a black velvet ribbon around her neck and experimented with the strip of black lace she planned to wear as a mask. Some black lace fingerless mittens, a quick spray of Opium, and she was ready.

If she half closed her eyes and ignored the worn satin of the dress, she thought she looked quite nice. She was most of the way down a second glass of wine and feeling almost free of the twisting sickness of knowing Guy was with another woman. 'He doesn't belong to me,' she told herself firmly. 'He's got lots of girlfriends willing to sleep with him, no doubt. I've got no right to feel jealous.'

Then she remembered his jokes, his kisses, his big grey eyes looking into hers. The shivering happiness she felt when she was with him. The way he walked around London with her, his hand twisted into her hair at the nape of her neck. In particular she couldn't get out of her head the image of him turned in his chair to watch for her in the Khyber. What had happened after Sunday lunch didn't seem to matter now.

'He's only 21 and you're an old bag of 23. You take what

you're given and don't ask for more.' She was positively scolding herself now. She drained her glass, smiled brilliantly in the mirror and sallied forth to find Johnnie Yeats flirting with Evangeline in the sitting room.

'God, Dora, you look wonderful,' he said, putting her friend down and coming to kiss her. 'You smell wonderful too.'

'Mind out, you'll smudge my lipstick.' Dora evaded him with a broad smile.

'Can I have another drink, please?' she asked her friend.

'Help yourself.'

Johnnie rejoined Evangeline on the sofa and started whispering in her ear. The doorbell rang again and she made no move to get up, so Dora answered it.

'Cook is a little unnerved,' she said to herself.

The fish pie was browning nicely in the oven. She put the peas on and gave herself another drink between answering the door. Richard Tate came into the kitchen to see what was for dinner. He loved food, and Dora and he had had many happy sessions concocting inventions since she had met him with Guy.

'What are we doing now?'

'Oh, just fish pie, Richard.'

'I bet it's got a twist if I know anything about you.'

'Well, yes, it's got smoked fish, prawns, mushrooms and capers.'

'Ah, capers. Brilliant touch. Original?'

'No, I got it from the mother of a friend.'

They discussed food for a bit. The air was filling with smoke. Everyone had brought bottles of wine. Johnnie, a Lloyds broker, had come armed with three bottles of champagne.

Dora found herself serving the food as usual, and clearing away. She drew the line at washing up, but knew it would be left for the cleaning lady on Monday. Richard helped. Evangeline was so engrossed with that dull Johnnie that she didn't lift a finger. Still it was all very noisy and great fun. 'Better than sitting at home on a Saturday night anyway,' she thought.

They went down into the spring evening and all tried to get into one taxi. The driver had a sense of humour failure and would only take four of them. They could have walked – it wasn't far to Exhibition Road. They didn't. Dora tied her bit of lace around her eyes in the taxi. Richard was very impressed and said she looked like a houri. Evangeline overheard. 'Oh, no, you've got her all wrong, Richard, if you think she's a whore. Our Dora's frightfully innocent. Aren't you, Dora?'

'He said houri, not whore, Evangeline. One of those virgins in paradise. For goodness' sake, Richard's a nice boy.'

'What's the difference?' Evangeline wasn't really interested and turned back to Johnnie.

They arrived very quickly and piled out on to the street. Dora felt quite lit up, and Richard took her arm and her ticket to show to the bouncer on the door. Almost the first person she saw was Guy, and he walked over.

'Hello, Dora. Hello, Richard. Pots shifting all right?'

'I had a good day. Lots of tourists in Portobello. They love all that kitschy thirties' stuff with fairies and things. You ought to join us, you know, have your own stall.'

'I was too busy today, Richard. Dora, come with me.'

He led her away unprotesting. 'Dora, I want you to come to the country with me tonight.'

'Oh, Guy, how? We're both much too pissed to drive.'

'Well, we could go tomorrow, couldn't we? First thing. I'll come and pick you up at about eight.'

'But you won't be awake at eight o'clock. Not after this thrash anyway.'

Guy drew himself up. 'Well, it might be a bit later. But will you come?'

'I'd love to, thank you.'

'I just wanted to ask you before we get separated in the crowd. I'm sure it's going to be a beautiful day tomorrow. I want to show you my home.'

Dora glowed with relief. After their rather unsatisfactory parting in his flat the Sunday before, this looked like a return to the old friendliness. Evangeline appeared beside her.

'Guy, will you dance with me?'

'Yes, of course. You look beautiful.' He picked up Dora's black lace mitten and kissed it. 'You look beautiful too. I'll dance with you next.'

Dora watched them go downstairs to the dance floor in the basement, and then began to circulate. With the prospect of a day in the country with Guy in front of her, she didn't need to hang about waiting for him.

Midnight came, the party waxed fast and furious. Guy hadn't come back to dance with her. Masks were torn off and the pretty faces underneath kissed. The ebb and flow of people bent on fun swept Dora along with it. She danced, she flirted, she kissed people and they kissed her. She drank the cold white wine that came with the ticket.

Then she spotted Guy again. He sat, not speaking, with the fair woman whom Dora now knew was Thelma. She thought he looked a bit bored and might need rescuing. She knew perfectly well she wasn't sober.

'Hi, Guy. Would you like to dance?'

He looked up at her. She could see he was extremely drunk. The glass in front of him contained something clear that wasn't water. He didn't reply. Thelma did. She got to her feet, swaying slightly. Her make-up was awry, her red lips and mascara smudged, as if she had been crying. She glared at Dora.

'You're so stupid,' she said. Then she repeated it louder. 'Stupid, stupid, stupid, stupid. Why can't you leave him alone? You're not his type.'

Dora, reactions slowed by alcohol, reeled a little at the unexpected attack. She glanced at Guy. He was looking into his drink as if his life depended on it. She faced Thelma and prepared to weather the storm.

The older woman was in her stride now, yelling out, 'Stupid, stupid, stupid,' in a sing-song playground chant that made Dora feel ill.

She waited until Thelma had ground to a halt. Then she found the presence of mind to say quietly, 'I've got a Cambridge degree. I'm meant to be quite clever.' It wasn't brilliant, but it would have to do. She turned and walked away to find the Ladies, run cold water over her wrists and try to recover.

She sensed the destructive tentacles reaching out of Guy's past to destroy what little there was between them before it could develop. Dora was willing to give Guy plenty of time and make every kind of allowance. They were both very young. Deep in her heart, she was convinced he was the one for her: her platonic other half. She didn't want to put a foot wrong for fear of losing him.

Sometimes she wondered at her own self-control and determination. It had made her believe that her most basic instincts were guiding her towards a safe harbour at some unspecified time in the future. But now she was afraid. She had never seen Guy so drunk. He had completely ignored the scene Thelma was making. She supposed that he must have been embarrassed and hoped that by pretending it wasn't happening he might be able to evade responsibility.

She felt quite cheerful when she emerged, face repaired. After all, Guy had invited her to the country when he was almost sober. She thought she had better leave Guy alone now, given his state. She would wait until tomorrow, although she guessed he would be in no fit state to leave London. Never mind; she was sure he would invite her another time. She also found it in her heart to feel sorry for Thelma, who was obviously besotted with him.

A couple of hours later, she had had enough of the party. The bright, taut balloon of enjoyment was beginning to deflate. She didn't want to hang around with the drunken hopeful dregs. She helped herself to some fruit from the breakfast buffet, and found Evangeline to say goodbye. Johnnie Yeats was still much in evidence, one broad paw parked inside Evangeline's waistcoat. Dora couldn't see the attraction.

She walked out into the early dawn to find a taxi. Drawn up at the curb was an enormous 1960s pink Rolls Royce. Guy lay curled on his side on the bonnet. He seemed to be asleep, or at any rate unconscious, and his head was pillowed on a pink feather boa Dora recognised as Thelma's. She went closer to have a look at him. His still, young face moved her and she was bending to kiss him when she felt someone's eyes upon her. She glanced up. Thelma was in the driving seat, glaring. Dora smiled at her and kissed Guy on the cheek. He stirred. One eye opened, taking a moment to focus.

'Dora?' he muttered.

'Yes, darling, I'm here.'

'What are you doing in my bed, you naughty girl?'

'I'm not in your bed.'

'Don't be silly.'

His eyes closed again as he lapsed back into unconsciousness. Thelma mouthed at her through the windscreen. She seemed to be having trouble getting the car door open.

Dora shivered. Her mind's eye, always overactive, visualised the Rolls upside down in a ditch with Guy dead and white and bloody. She couldn't let that happen. She needed a lot more time with him. He couldn't be killed in a drunken accident. She looked down. She had a banana in one hand and an apple in the other.

She went round to the back of the car and crouched to examine the exhaust. The apple fitted best. She shoved it in and then stood to ram it home with the toe of her shoe. It was invisible from above.

'They won't be going anywhere tonight with the exhaust blocked,' she said to herself. 'And Thelma won't dare call the AA in her condition.'

The thought cheered her up. She hailed a taxi, and snorted from time to time with laughter all the way home. The birds were shouting in the trees along the street. She struggled out of her dress, but was too tired and drunk to wash her face. She tumbled into bed naked to sleep it off.

Six

THE TELEPHONE RANG. Every time she went to answer it, it dissolved into pink cotton wool balls. Dora felt herself dragged back to the surface, and awoke realising that she hadn't answered it, and there was no one else in the house. It was ten o'clock.

She jumped out of bed, and regretted it.

'Oooh,' she groaned, clutching her head. The telephone kept on ringing. She stood up carefully and went into Victoria's bedroom at the front of the house where there was an extension. Warm sun flooded through the big bay window and Dora sat naked in a panel of hot light thrown on to Victoria's duvet cover. She picked up the receiver and said, 'Hello?'

'Hello – Dora, is that you?'

'Yes, Evangeline, it is.'

'Are you OK?'

'No, I feel dreadful.'

'Oh, poor you. So you know, then.'

'What?'

Dora became alert. 'No, I've got a hangover. What's happened?'

'Well, you'd better brace yourself.'

Dora thought quickly – what was Evangeline talking about? Had Guy and Thelma managed to drive off, even with half a greengrocer's stuck up the exhaust, and crashed?

'Has there been an accident?'

'Oh, no, no, nothing like that. Only, I heard Guy asking you to go home to the country with him today. But he went off with Thelma to her husband's grand pad in Berkshire.'

'Right.' Dora didn't want to give her friend the satisfaction of a reaction.

'It was really funny though. Apparently Guy went to sleep on the bonnet of the Rolls and Thelma had to get the bouncers to put him in the back of the car. Then she tried to start it and couldn't. She was pretty pissed. Anyway, she went into the office to call the AA, and a friend of hers warned her not to, as she was so drunk they would be likely to call the police. So then she summoned Billy's London chauffeur from his bed. He came. Couldn't work out what was wrong with the car. By this time it was broad daylight.'

Dora giggled.

'Dora, are you there?'

'Yes.'

'Anyway, Guy slept through the whole thing. The AA came and found fruit stuck up the exhaust, which was why the car wouldn't start.'

'I know,' said Dora.

'What?'

'I know about the fruit. I put it there.'

'You put it there?'

'Yup. Thelma was so drunk that she couldn't even find the car door handle let alone drive safely.'

Evangeline laughed down the phone. 'But Dora, don't you mind Guy going off with her?'

'He didn't have much choice if he was asleep, did he?'

'No, that's true. Anyway, let's hope Billy Kidd doesn't come home from Japan and murder them both.'

Dora worried momentarily about this further threat to her beloved's life. Her hangover was too insistent. She had to go and find the Alka-Seltzer.

'Well, Evangeline, did you have a nice time last night?'

'Lovely. Isn't Johnnie a darling? We're going to Martinique in two weeks time.'

'How lovely, you lucky thing,' Dora said mechanically. 'Plink, plink,' prompted her sore brain, 'fizz, fizz. Oh what a relief it is.'

'What are you doing today, Dora?'

Dora thought quickly.

'I'm going to have lunch with my godmother in Kent. I forgot about it last night, but I wouldn't have been able to go to the country with Guy anyway.'

'Oh right. Well, have fun. I must go. I've got to repair my face before Johnnie comes to pick me up. We're having brunch at the Brasserie. Bye.'

'Bye.' Dora put the phone down. She went as quickly as her head would allow to the bathroom cabinet, put two large fizzing tablets into a glass of water and ran herself a bath. She was shuddering with excess alcohol. Why did she do it when she felt like this the next day? She really had no idea. She slid into the bath and, retching at the second-hand toothpaste flavour, swallowed her healing potion.

She decided she really would go and visit Tirzah, which

she had been promising for months. She imagined Tirzah would probably have a brilliant hangover cure at her fingertips, much used at Chelsea School of Art in the 1950s. Dora loved Tirzah – so clever and talented, but so warm and loving as well. She had no children of her own, and Dora sometimes felt that her godmother invested a motherly interest in her progress, quite unlike her own mother, whose best friend and foster sister Tirzah was. Funny that friends should be so different.

Dora dressed in loose, undemanding clothes. There were red marks on her body, where the bones of her strapless bodice had burst unheeded from their confining tape and ravaged her waist. She telephoned Tirzah.

'It's Dora. Are you busy? I'd really like to take the 11.15 train and come and see you.'

'Dora, darling, how lovely. I've got some food. I'd love to see you. I'll pick you up from Folkestone.'

'Look forward to seeing you there, then.'

Dora, feeling slightly better, rushed to Parsons Green tube as fast as she could and jumped on the District Line to Victoria. There she scraped on to the 11.15 without buying a ticket. She had enough cash on her to pay at the other end.

Tirzah was waiting at the barrier, and hugged her. They made for the car park.

'Well, Dora, how are you?'

'Hung over and troubled, darling Tirzah. I need your advice.'

'Why don't you go to your mother? She's very sensible.'

'I can't talk about this sort of thing with her.'

'Oh I see,' said Tirzah, unlocking the car. 'OK, hop in and let's go home. Can you stay the night?'

'Only if I catch a very early train tomorrow,' Dora replied.

'Why don't you do that?'

'It's a bore for you getting up so early.'

'I always get up early, particularly in the summer. And I'm hungry for as much of your company as I can get.'

Dora smiled; her head was thumping less, although she found it difficult to look at the sun sparkling on the sea as they drove along.

Tirzah had a studio at Littlestone, a modest seaside resort in Kent. Why she chose to be there, rather than with so many of her contemporaries in Cornwall, defeated Dora. Tirzah and her beloved Dougal had been very happy. They both had an appreciation for the peculiar shifting qualities of Romney Marsh. Dougal had drawn and etched the ancient marsh churches. He had also loved the Romney, Hythe & Dymchurch miniature steam railway and had often taken Dora for a ride on it when she was younger.

Dougal had died two years ago, and Tirzah had been staggeringly brave. Dora knew that Tirzah had gone and stayed for a long time with her mother, Hilly, in her cottage after the funeral, and that Dora's mother had been a source of comfort. She couldn't quite understand this; she found her mother singularly cool and unsympathetic.

'How is Hilda?'

Dora started guiltily. She hadn't been home for ages. There had been so much going on every weekend, either in London or just outside. She wanted to be available to Guy as much as possible. Besides, she was afraid her mother might notice that she was in love. Dora sometimes wondered if her neurotic virginity was something to do with her mother's complete disapproval of anything to do with sex and boyfriends.

'I haven't seen her for a bit. I talk to Dad on the phone and he says she's fine.'

'Your dear father. Such a nice man.'

'He took me to see your exhibition in February. We loved it.'

'Thank you. It's selling quite well. The Tate are interested in one of the Sorrow pieces, and a big American gallery has contacted me about a Baby.'

Dora was used to Tirzah's status as a successful sculptor. Her husband Dougal had been well known for his water-colours, fabric designs and etchings. He was a Scotsman from Aberdeen, but never seemed to miss the blunt, heather-covered mountains. He had drawn Tirzah down to dwell upon the marsh with him after they left London at the end of the 1960s.

When they arrived at Tirzah's house, Dora scrambled out and breathed in great draughts of sea air. The house was black-painted clapboard and had been converted from some sail lofts, with huge windows set into the north-facing roofs. The living bit of it consisted of a large kitchen, now filled with good smells, and a bedroom. There were a couple of small spare rooms over the kitchen in the roof. The rest was an enormous studio where Tirzah's work stood about: small clay maquettes under damp sacking, the odd marble piece – though Tirzah found bashing away with a hammer and chisel too exhausting now – and some of her recent bronze casts in all sizes, from a few inches high to several feet tall.

There was a Sorrow standing in the middle of the room – a slender female nude, hands up to her face, every angle and plane conveying grief. Dora felt like crying when she saw it, partly because she had a hangover, but also because she had loved Dougal and missed not finding him here as well. There was an early marble Baby, conveying strength and purpose in its rounded limbs, like a netsuke or Maori sculpture. Dora touched it and it rocked on its rounded back.

'I do love your Babies.'

'Yes, I love them too.'

Dora, filled as she was with love for Guy, felt far more grown up with Tirzah for the first time – less like a daughter and more like a friend.

'Why did you and Dougal never have any babies of your own? Was it because your art was more important?'

'Oh no, not at all. The thing was, we got married so young – we were both 20 and still at art school. We had to get married though. We adored each other on sight and felt the need to show the world how much. Of course, all our friends were living together and being terrifically bohemian. But Dougal comes – sorry, came – from a traditional Scots family, and he didn't want to upset his parents. Also, we felt so strongly it was right. And it was. It lasted until death did us part.'

'I'm sorry, Tirzah. Don't talk about it if you don't want to.'

'Oh, but I do. I want you to know how happy we were, in spite of everything. We lived in a single room at the top of a crumbling house on Cheyne Walk. It was six flights up and there was only a cold tap and a gas ring when you got there. We got married in Chelsea Registry Office about a month after we met, and then told Dougal's parents and Leora. They were worried about us, particularly about babies coming along. Leora took me to a very old man on Harley Street called Mr Lawrence, and he fitted me with a Dutch cap. So no babies came then.'

'Is it all right? The cap, I mean.'

'Oh, all you young girls are on the Pill now, aren't you?' Tirzah said casually.

'Not me, Tirzah. I've never needed it.'

'Right.' Tirzah didn't comment further, but went on, 'I was very fond of my cap, and it certainly did the business. We couldn't leave each other alone to begin with. Dougal sold the odd drawing, and I posed for life classes to make a bit of money for the gas meter and food. It was very cold in our nest in the winter, but we wore lots of clothes and cuddled each other at night. We got used to it really. I still can't stand central heating.'

She smiled at Dora. 'Would you like a drink?'

Dora shuddered. 'No thanks. I'm sure that whatever's in the Aga that's producing that lovely smell will cure my hangover instantly.'

She was already beginning to feel better with sea air and distraction.

Tirzah helped herself to a large glass of brown sherry.

'Anyway, when my work began to sell and Dougal got that gallery interested in doing limited editions of his work, we thought we might as well chuck the cap out and try for a baby. We were both 30 by this time, and things were going fine for us. Nothing happened. Month after month we tried, and month after month I bled.'

Dora sensed that the wound was still deep and Tirzah needed to talk. She kept quiet, just nodding sympathetically.

'I thought I was pregnant several times, but my period always turned up a bit late. I couldn't come near Hilly and you for a bit. You were such a dear little girl, and Hilly adored you so much. But I had angry feelings about you, and didn't trust myself not to hug you too tight and frighten you.

'The first of the Babies is modelled on a photograph I had of you naked when you were about three months old. Of course, they became more stylised after that as I tried various forms and materials. You were my first inspiration. I've left you one in my will.'

Dora didn't like thinking about wills, so she ignored this.

'By the time we were both forty, we were making plenty of money. We'd bought this place in 1969 and converted it to suit us. I had got used to being childless. I loved Dougal so much, and he did allow me to mother him a bit. And you would come to stay. Then...'

Dora reached across the table and pressed her godmother's hand. She knew what had happened next. Dougal had developed a particularly nasty form of testicular cancer, which had spread quickly. Whenever she pictured him in her mind's eye, he was standing at his easel, palette spotted with brilliant blobs of gouache in one hand, brush in the other, screwing up his eyes against the smoke of his cigarette while he contemplated the next brush stroke.

Tirzah was a very young widow at 42. Dora hoped she would find someone else, but Dougal was a hard act to follow.

'Now, I must give you some lunch. Goodness, look at the time.' Tirzah stood up and went over to the Aga. She took out a golden chicken sitting on a bed of roasted vegetables and rosemary. Dora's mouth filled with bitter water.

She laid the table, and Tirzah directed her to the fridge where a bottle of chilled Muscadet was waiting. Tirzah made regular forays across the Channel to shop, and most of the food in her store cupboard was French. The chicken was a maize-fed free-range one from Normandy, which tasted completely unlike any pallid British battery bird.

'How did you meet Dougal?' Dora asked over lunch.

'You could hardly miss him. He was well over six feet

tall, and his hair blazed like a beacon in those days.'

'It was still pretty red when I knew him.'

'He was in the year below me at Chelsea, even though we were the same age. It had taken him a little longer to get himself down from Aberdeen than it had taken me to get myself up from Surrey. With the help of Leora's family in America – and your grandfather, of course.'

'I never knew that grandfather. Was he nice?'

'He was terrific. A father to me. He never treated me differently from Hilly.'

'Did you ever find out any more about what happened to your real father?'

'Leora went back to France after Geoffrey died. She picked up a clue that Philippe had joined the Resistance, but records of who did what are not very reliable. So many of the French collaborated, I'm afraid to say.

'He was Jewish, of course, so in mortal danger once France had fallen. There is some evidence that he was near Lyon, helping Jews to escape into Switzerland. Leora sent me lots of copies of his articles, which she found in libraries. He wrote the most brilliant stuff, trying to warn the world about what was happening to the Jews in Hitler's Germany. But I'm afraid the world was quite used to Jews being ill-treated – and so desperate to avoid a war like the last one.'

'Did he end up in a concentration camp, do you think?'

'It's unlikely, darling. The Nazis kept meticulous records, and Leora looked through as much as she could. He just disappeared from Paris one night after France had fallen. She questioned her old concierge, who said that Philippe had said goodbye to her and taken a bag. She thought he must have been killed on some clandestine mission, and his body never found. He is officially dead.'

'How is Leora by the way? Have you been to see her recently?'

'She's fine. I popped over to the States to discuss this possible gallery purchase, and dropped in on her. She and Harry live in Boston. She is still just as tiny and vivid and elegant. I feel like an elephant next to her. Philippe was apparently very tall. She's terrific. She's coming over to Britain later in the summer to see Hilly and me. You must see her – she always asks about you, and was so pleased to hear about your degree and job on *Modern Woman*. Harry wanted a European tour this year. His company makes very good copies of Italian and French shoes, you know. Leora always did love shoes and found them hard to find in her small size.'

Dora looked at Tirzah's pale oval face. She wore a scarf around her head to keep the dust out of her thick dark hair, now gradually turning iron grey. Her eyes were large, with deep lids and thick lashes.

'Now, Dora, tell me your news. I've been going on.'

'No, not at all. It's very interesting,' Dora replied, filling her mouth with chicken. 'This is delicious, by the way. I feel much better.'

'I'm so glad you came.'

Dora knew that Tirzah wasn't lonely. She had dozens of friends of all ages, from the local vicar with whom she would argue, to the youngest art student who wanted help and advice. The thought of art students brought her round to the subject of Guy.

'I'm in love.'

She said this so earnestly and suddenly that Tirzah almost laughed.

'Darling, how lovely. Who is he?'

'He's called Guy, and he's quite hopeless in some ways,

quite wonderful in others. I love him madly, and I'm always so afraid I'll only have enough really serious love for one man. I'm afraid Guy's the one, and I don't know what to do. He asked me to marry him the other day.'

'Well, that sounds hopeful. I don't know what your parents will say but we both married young and stayed married.'

'That's just it. I don't think he really does want to marry me. He's always wanting me to go to bed with him but I'm afraid it won't be wonderful, and I'll just be another girl he's screwed, and I think he's getting fed up.'

Tears began to run down Dora's face. Tirzah came around the other side of the table and drew her on to the sofa, where she could cuddle her more satisfactorily.

Dora, through her sobs, told Tirzah everything that had happened since she had got the giggles with Guy at that fateful party, including the incident of the night before with the fruit.

'I know Thelma Kidd,' Tirzah remarked at one point. 'She must be nearly as old as me. And married to Billy. I don't think she can possibly be a threat, darling. You really are very lovely. Are you telling me that you're still a virgin?'

'Yes.' Dora blew her nose into a piece of kitchen towel.

'I didn't realise there were any virgins any more. Not after the sixties and seventies.'

'I know. I feel a bit silly about it and try not to tell people. I've developed quite a good line in being enigmatic.'

'Things have changed a bit since the fifties. There was a summer towards the end of the fifties when two very keen men avidly pursued your mother and me. We resisted, oh how we resisted. At least I did. I was never so sure about your mother.'

'I don't want to think about my mother's sex life if you don't mind.'

'What is it with you and your mother, Dora?'

'Oh, I don't know. She's always so critical. Of my clothes, my work, my friends. Dad is so friendly and sweet. I spend hours with him. Mum is always telling me to unload the dishwasher or something when I want to talk to her. The only time we're really happy together is when we're cooking.'

'It is odd, you know. When Hilly was young she was very like you: warm and confiding, and falling heavily in love—'

'Anyway,' Dora interrupted. 'What do you think I should do now I have told you the worst things I can think of about Guy?'

Tirzah thought she could detect how Dora felt about her young love. She was taken back to that chilly attic where she and Dougal had loved each other so warmly. Dougal hadn't been a saint either. The first time she saw him he'd been leaving the changing room used by the life models, looking pleased with himself. But he had married her almost as soon as they met and never looked at another girl again. He said it was a relief. In Scotland, Chelsea had a reputation for debauchery, and he felt he should do what he imagined everyone else was doing. She remembered with a shiver the passion of their lovemaking. She missed him, and she missed the sex as well.

'Next time he asks you, particularly if it is in a non-bedroom type situation, I suggest you accept and get him down to the Registry Office. You can sort out the details afterwards. Where does he live?'

'In Chelsea, funnily enough.'

'So you could go to Chelsea Registry Office, like we did

and all the pop stars and so forth since. Could you live in his flat with him?'

'I suppose so. It's not very big. I could make it much nicer.'

Tirzah's words had broken down a barrier in Dora's mind and thoughts and fantasies came belching forth. She sat there stunned. She could, she really could, just get on with it, not put her life on hold while he grew up but get married now and grow up together, just as Dougal and Tirzah had. She glowed and gleamed.

'Oh Tirzah. You've made me very happy. I'll try it. It can't do any harm if he never asks again, I'll just have to try and recover and get on with my life. If he does ask again, properly and not just to get into my knickers, we can maybe get married.'

Then she thought of something.

'Would Mum be hurt if I didn't have a big church wedding?'

'Oh no. She'd appreciate the romance of it. She isn't particularly religious. I'm sure she'd love to give a party for you when the dust clears.'

Dora hugged Tirzah hard. 'I think I'm ready for my pudding now.'

Seven

TIRZAH TOOK HER TO THE station early the next morning.

'Do you like him?' she asked Dora in the car.

'Who? Selwyn? Yes, I thought he was terrific. A bit evangelical for me though.'

'I find that rather attractive.'

Dora glanced sideways at her godmother, who was looking suspiciously dreamy.

Selwyn Landon was the local vicar, in his early 30s, young looking. Dora hadn't realised at first that he was a vicar when he dropped by the previous evening, as he had been wearing jeans and an open-necked shirt. She was surprised that such a nice, unattached man was hanging around in Littlestone. Tirzah had switched from warm, middle-aged maternal mode to a sparklier younger self when he came through the kitchen door. It was obviously something he felt very comfortable doing – not your average parish visit to a grieving widow.

Dora felt almost jealous, and then slapped herself mentally over the wrist. 'You've had lots of attention this afternoon. Tirzah has every right to a lover.' Lover? Goodness. Well, there certainly was something between them. He was an attractive man.

'He's got that slightly silly smile Christians always have,' she thought spitefully. But when she looked at him again, she realised that this was blind prejudice. He looked happy. She was so used to tortured souls in London, men who claimed to be sensitive but were really just touchy. Selwyn was refreshing. Tirzah was only 42, for goodness' sake. No age at all. She had got the whiskey out and the two of them got very cosy around the kitchen table. Dora, feeling green and hairy, wished she'd said she would go back to London that same day, but she didn't want to disturb Tirzah and ask her to take her to the station.

'I didn't get to bed till six this morning. Do you mind if I go to bed now?' she said at nine o'clock. Tirzah started a little guiltily.

'Of course not, darling. I've made up your usual. Do you need anything else? No? Well, sleep well. I'll bring up your Horlicks in a minute.'

Dora smiled and forgave her completely. Tirzah was a firm believer in Horlicks. Littlestone was the only place Dora ever had it.

She had climbed up into the little attic room with its dormer window overlooking the sea. Tirzah had put out one of her own antique nighties, starched and ironed, on the bed, and Dora had revelled in the clean sheets and salt air. She'd been asleep when Tirzah had come up with the steaming mug.

When Tirzah pulled up outside Folkstone station the next morning, Dora turned to her and hugged her passionately before jumping out to run for her train. From Victoria, she fled straight to Modern House. She didn't look particularly ready for work, but popped into the Ladies to add a bit of powder, lip gloss and mascara. It was extraordinary how undebauched she looked. Must be her age, she thought. She went into the features room, empty as she was early, to find her telephone ringing on her battered, red-painted desk.

'Hello, Features?'

'Hello, is that Dora?'

'No.' Why did she say that? She had no idea.

'Can you give her a message, please?'

'Hang on. I'll just get a pen.' Dora scrabbled a bit on her desk to sound authentic. 'What was it?'

'Could you tell her Guy rang?'

'OK. Bye.'

'Bye.'

She put the phone down, smiling. What little demon was prompting her?

There had been a series of articles over three months in the 1950s, which Dora had read in old copies of *Modern Woman*: 'How to Find, Get and Keep Your Man', they had been called. For such a proto-feminist rag as *Modern Woman* pretended to be, this was pretty strong stuff. Still, it had been in keeping with the zeitgeist.

In the second article there had been a paragraph subtitled, 'Keeping Him Keen'. The tip about pretending to be someone else on the telephone to keep a distance had been there – along with not ringing back, saying you had forgotten he had rung at all, cancelling dates at the last minute and other rotten tricks.

The next paragraph had issued dire if veiled warnings about 'Not Going Too Far' on the first, or any, date. Dora examined herself. Was she a mindless relic of the 1950s?

Clinging to her pointless little virginity while everyone around her was losing theirs? She was frightened of her mother and wanted to please her. She felt her brooding presence whenever she got herself into a sticky situation. It had helped her avoid many a sticky situation and, if she was honest with herself, possible good and happy relationships as well.

Was she investing too much in the idea that love and marriage were inextricably linked? She could not shake off the idea that her capacity for love was weak and could only power one episode. She thought of Tirzah, obviously attracted to Selwyn. 'Perhaps she misses the sex,' she thought. Then she giggled. 'He's a vicar and an evangelical at that. She's not going to get much joy there.'

She decided she would just exist and let Guy make all the moves. Then she stopped dreaming and put some paper in her typewriter and began to write a short review of a fringe theatre production for the Young View section, to which James graciously allowed her to contribute.

When she arrived home that evening her flatmates wanted to know where she'd been. It was a habit at Hamden Road to spend Mondays in with the girls, provided nothing more exciting and preferably male turned up.

'Will you cook supper, Dora? You're so good at it,' said Georgia.

'Flattery will get you everywhere, dear,' said Dora. 'Is there any food or shall I go and do a bit of a shop.'

'No, it's OK. Vicky and I went to Waitrose on Saturday afternoon.'

'On the King's Road? Isn't that a bit beyond our budget?'

'It is a bit, but we were very careful. Anyway, Vic heard you could meet the most fantastic men if you hung around the game counter.'

'Did she?'

Georgia laughed. 'No, but I did. In front of the patisserie of all girly places. He asked me whether I knew what a Japanese was.'

'A Japonais.'

'Ooh, you should have been there, you bossy know-it-all. Anyway, I gave him a huge smile and asked the girl behind the counter. So we found out, and we got chatting.'

'What did he want a Japonais for?'

'His pregnant wife.' Georgia went off into peals of laughter. 'Never mind. Better luck next time.'

'I've got an idea,' said Dora. 'Why don't we get some kind of wine-buff book and then we can hang around the booze department making knowledgeable comments. That's far more likely to work. Anyone buying cakes, unless they're a bit porky, is bound to be doing it for a girl.'

'That's a good idea. Victoria's going out by the way.'

'With Justin?'

'Yes.'

'Right. So it's just the two of us.'

The telephone rang. Dora was on her way to the kitchen, and could hear Georgia answering it.

'Oh hell,' she thought. 'I should have briefed her.' She stopped to listen.

'Oh, hi Guy. Yes, she's just about to cook us some supper. Please don't take her away.'

Dora came back and took the receiver from Georgia.

'Hello?'

'Hello Dora, why did you pretend to be someone else this morning and then not ring me back?'

Dora blushed but tried to remain sounding cool.

'Because I didn't want to talk to you.'

That didn't sound cool. It sounded as if she cared, as if he had got to her; although it was the truth, it was no good letting him know.

'Look, Dora, I'm sorry about the other night.'

'That must be one of the most spoken lines in the English language,' she remarked.

'I was very drunk, OK?'

'I could see that.' Dora let the silence persist.

'Dora, I did mean it. I want to take you home, possibly this weekend if you aren't doing anything.'

'Why?' She knew this was irritating, but couldn't help it.

'Because I want to show you where I grew up.'

'Oh, how touching. By the way, did you have a nice time in Billy Kidd's house? I hear it's spectacular.' She had to admit to herself she was very jealous. She felt quite sick with it as she imagined Guy and Thelma in a rock star's no doubt completely vulgar bed having passionate sex all day long. Satin sheets or something ghastly. Yuk, sweaty and slippery, the last thing she imagined you would want for athletic activity. Her mind's eye was overactive with nerves. She saw Thelma lunge at Guy and Guy slither off the shiny surface and land with a thump on the shagpile. She smiled grimly.

'As a matter of fact, I had a horrible time. I woke up not knowing where the hell I was or remembering anything about how I got there. I had a hangover to end all hangovers. Worst of all, I remembered that I had invited you to the country – and you definitely were not beside me and we definitely weren't at home.'

'So you thought home surroundings might work where London so far hasn't?' Dora knew she was handling this badly but couldn't stop.

'For goodness' sake, Dora.'

She went quiet.

'Are you still there? Can I come and see you?'

'No, the girls are here and we're having an evening in.'

'Can't I come and join in? I love girls' evenings.'

Dora couldn't help being amused by the longing in his voice.

'I bet you do,' she remarked. With a heroic burst of self-restraint, she managed to say, 'I can see you tomorrow if you like.'

'Right. What about lunch?'

'I'll look in my diary.' Dora knew perfectly well that Tuesday was a blank. 'That looks OK. Do you want to come and pick me up at Modern House at about one?'

'Do you mind if we meet somewhere else?'

'Why?'

'I just don't want to bump into someone with you, that's all.'

Dora didn't ask who. She found it difficult to cope with Evangeline in Guy's presence as well. Except that these days Evangeline seemed wholly wrapped up in Johnnie Yeats, so perhaps she would lay off.

'Where would you like to meet, then?'

'There's a wine bar in Kingly Street. You know, that alley that runs down beside Liberty. It's called something ghastly, like Shampers.'

'All right, Guy. I'll see you there.'

She managed to put the phone down. Lunch was a good sign. There could be no agenda attached to the lunch hour. There just wasn't time.

Dora went back into the kitchen and began to make supper for Georgia herself. Her whole skin felt warmed by the conversation she had just had. She remembered what

Tirzah had advised and she shivered with anticipation. Then she switched off from thinking about lunch the next day, prepared lasagne and a large green salad and settled down for an evening of television and gossip with her flatmate.

Guy was alone in his flat when he put down the telephone. One of the reasons he had started drinking the Polish vodka on Saturday night was that Thelma was making terrible demands. He felt assaulted and trapped by her. Marriage to Dora looked like freedom to him in comparison. Thelma was talking about leaving Billy and moving in with him. The more she tried to get a reaction out of him, the more he drank. He really wanted to stand up and walk away, find Dora and go home. When he tried, he couldn't trust himself not to stagger. It seemed easier just to carry on drinking and Thelma was buying the booze.

He was vaguely aware that Thelma had made a scene in front of Dora. He couldn't remember the details but some little devil in him was always amused when women fought over him. Dora's response came back to him, and he laughed down his nose.

'Thelma's got what she wants. Why does she want me as well?' he asked himself. 'A big house, a rich husband, a studio to work in, all the status symbols that her American heart craves. A long way from a trailer park in Arkansas.'

He remembered when she had married Billy two years after he'd met her. Billy was well past his sell-by date but had been cannily advised and was also still big in Japan. It was a shock when Guy had read in Dempster that he had married 'Thelma Garvey, well-known American artist'. He had tried and tried to get hold of her, but realised they were on their honeymoon. The balance of power in their relationship had been very different in those days.

She had telephoned him when she got back from the Bahamas.

'Hello, little Guy.' It always irritated him when she called him that. 'Happy for me?'

'Thelma, why didn't you tell me? I didn't even know you knew him.' 'I've known him for years, dear.' She wasn't going to tell Guy then, but she had been a groupie when she met Billy Kidd, or one particular bit of him, in 1968. He hadn't even known her name for at least two years, but she persisted.

'Now I'm on the up and he's going down, he wanted to hitch himself to my star,' she explained to Guy.

'Do you love him?'

'I adore him but I'll always love you, darling. You see I want lots of things that little boys can't give me. I'm not making enough money myself to get them. Hence Billy. He's not around much; he's always in Japan. It's perfect. You and I can carry on as before.'

'Carry on? Like *Carry On Camping*?'

'Something like that, yes.'

Guy had been revolted. He might have slept with dozens of girls since, but Thelma had been his first love. In her he had invested some of his feelings for his absent mother. He had been very jealous and wanted to hurt her.

'So you're just a little gold-digger after all? All that idealistic nonsense about birds and trees and flowers and living with nature and going with the flow was so much crap.'

'I'm not as young as I was, Guy.' Her voice had hardened.

'No, I've noticed. Getting a bit saggy, Thelma.'

'You bastard. I want things, don't you understand? I want to know I won't be alone and poor when I get old. You don't know anything about me, do you?'

'No. Obviously not. I thought you believed in freedom

and art and love. Not in fat bank accounts and fat has-beens.'

'Billy isn't fat. Look, this isn't getting us anywhere.'

'No, it isn't, but we were never going anywhere anyway. You were just using me, weren't you? A nice little toy to play with when you wanted.' He remembered how remote she could be when she was caught up in a painting. 'I don't want to see you.'

'You will, Guy, I bet you will.' She'd said this in a taunting tone. Infuriated he slammed down the receiver. Then he'd sat and the anger drained away leaving the familiar black dog in its place. He'd thought he could rely on Thelma to be a fixed permanent spot in his turning world; that he would always be able to go back to her for reassurance that he was loved and admired. Then she'd made it quite clear that she needed a rich husband far more than she needed Guy.

And now she wanted to leave Billy and move into Guy's tiny Chelsea basement with him. He shivered with disgust. Her bedroom in Billy's opulent Berkshire mansion had been pure Biba Mistress Department. All feathers and black satin and none too clean.

'Not that I can talk,' he said to himself, looking around his sitting room. For him dirt signified misery; he was utterly fastidious at other times. He thought about Thelma trying to cram in her personality and possessions. He folded his arms around his middle and curled over so his forehead rested on his knees.

'No, no, no, no, no,' he muttered. He didn't want her. She was the past. He didn't want to be dragged backwards. He wanted to move and change. He had sold 'The Princes in the Tower' to a private client and his friend Dorian Peak was pleased. He had mentioned something about sending Guy to

New York to assist in his gallery there and help open up the market for Pre-Raphaelite drawings. Guy was seriously considering it. It would simultaneously be a way out and a way in.

What about Dora? He uncurled his body, went and fetched a can of beer from the kitchen, and rolled a joint. He had better do some thinking. What was it about Dora? She had made it quite clear that she wouldn't sleep with him unless he married her.

He felt so furious about this sometimes, he didn't know whether to laugh or scream. He was in this ridiculous position in the 1980s? Guy Boleyn who had charmed the knickers off anything he fancied since he was 15? Buried deep within him was the feeling that most of his relationships hadn't lasted much beyond a few fucks. Apart from Thelma, but that was almost worse. This wasn't necessarily very good news.

He took a long pull at the cold beer. How long had he known Dora? It seemed like ages but it was probably no more than a few months. He remembered with crystal clarity meeting her and getting the giggles. He couldn't remember anything about the last time he had slept with Lesley, or the first for that matter. He remembered things about Thelma because she had been his first experience.

He wasn't remotely bored of Dora. Granted, he didn't see her very often. They talked constantly on the telephone, but when he did see her, they got into uneasy situations where they misunderstood each other. It was delicious in a way, like being a monk.

Why shouldn't he do what she wanted and marry her? They could sort out the details afterwards. He was sure she would make a good wife. Wasn't it meant to be a good idea to start out with a virgin? The royal family had gone to a great deal of trouble to find a virgin for Prince Charles. Lady Diana Spencer was meant to be one. And Dora was obviously the other last virgin left in Britain. Maybe it was the fashionable thing to do – marry a virgin. Guy was somewhat stoned and the more he thought about it the more right it seemed. He would marry her and reserve her for himself.

They didn't have to tell anyone or do anything about it until he was more successful. He would get his trust fund when he was 25 and they could buy a house together. Meanwhile he would go to New York and make a name for himself as a dealer and she could get on with her life here, secure in the knowledge that he loved her and would come back for her. Otherwise she might forget about him and marry someone else.

He had never been so sure about anything in his life. He would tell her tomorrow. He would find out how to do it with the minimum of fuss. Chelsea Registry Office was a very cool place to get married. Didn't all the rock stars do it there? Including Billy Kidd.

Thelma wasn't going to devour him this time. If he knew Dora, she would wait. In one fell swoop he would fill that terrifying future and get his revenge on Thelma. Maybe he could punish Dora too for making him wait so long, by making her wait in turn. Dora made him feel good. Why should he think about anyone but himself?

Lunch tomorrow. He would ask Dora to marry him and then just go with flow.

Eight

Tuesday morning crept by. Whenever Dora glanced at the clock, it seemed earlier than when she had last looked. Some glitch in the time-space continuum meant that eleven o'clock went on for 20 minutes. Getting cups of coffee didn't help. Neither did going to the loo to look at herself in the mirror. Finally her boss, James, noticed.

'Hot lunch date, babe?' he inquired.

She smiled at him radiantly.

'Ah,' he said. 'Will you be working this afternoon?'

'Of course.' She felt touchy. She wasn't going to become completely unprofessional.

James decided, quite maliciously Dora was sure, to ask her to return an embarrassingly large backlog of unsolicited manuscripts.

'You are naughty, Dora. You should do this within days of their arrival, not months later,' he scolded.

She began to read them, wincing at the bad grammar, the complete inappropriateness of the subject matter: 'Trainspotting for beginners', 'Some leaves from my garden'

– might that make a nice series? – an obscene one that James caught her putting in the bin.

'Write a nice letter, Dora, and I'll sign it. Otherwise he might want to strike up a correspondence with you.'

'Thanks.' She couldn't help sitting sucking the end of her pencil and dreaming. 'Isn't it odd how the lyrics of pop songs seem so relevant to one's life sometimes?'

'Indeed,' James agreed. 'Noël Coward said, "Extraordinary how potent cheap music is." James was inclined to camp – a hangover from his membership of the Piers Gaveston Society at Oxford. 'It's because they record the actions of our hormones rather than our brains. I can see your hormones are rampaging. Who is he then?'

Dora returned to her work without answering.

'Seriously, Dora, I'm interested. Who are you having lunch with?'

'If you must know, it's Guy Boleyn.'

'Oh, I know him. Art dealer, and a bit of a painter himself, isn't he?'

'Yes.'

'I've always heard he has strings of girls like polo ponies. I wouldn't mess with him if I were you. Might get that heart broken.'

'I know. I know all about him and the other girls. I've known him for ages.' Those few months had certainly felt like ages. 'I'm not in love with him anyway; he's just a friend. I'm looking forward to going out to lunch for a change instead of having a dismal sandwich at my desk while reading proofs.'

She said this to deflect any criticism should she be late back.

'You'll probably need a long lunch hour today then, won't you?'

She smiled gratefully at James. He was a kind boss sometimes. His lunches were of legendary, almost Fleet Street, length. Miss Peebles often hauled him up about them. He made her laugh and she always forgave him. Dora often wished she were a man – they seemed to get away with everything, and no one ever expected them to type a letter. But not at this precise moment because she was meeting Guy for lunch. Something big seemed imminent; stirring in the depths of her hopelessly romantic soul was hope.

She hoped that Guy, product of a fractured marriage, seducer, drug-taker, drinker, over-sexed and under-educated, was going to transform into one of the easily reformed rakes of her endless reading. That he would pull off his mask, marry her for love and they would live happily ever after, Dora playing the part of reforming angel virgin from a Victorian novel.

She'd lived long enough in London to know the world had changed, though. Even Cambridge should have taught her that life wasn't like that any more, if it ever had been in the first place. But she lived as if it was the nineteenth century – minus the consumption and corsets – and this in no way decreased her charm for Guy or anyone else.

At last it was quarter to one. She made another dash into the Ladies to look at her make-up. She was carefully dressed in a Laura Ashley cotton frock with a tight bodice and full skirt, worn with laced-up black granny boots and red tights. Her long dark hair hung loose down her back. When she came out again, she said to James, 'How do I look?'

'You look very pretty, but be back here by three at the very, very latest, do you understand?'

'Thank you.' She bent over to kiss his cheek. He looked a

little surprised but smiled, infected by what she was feeling.

She couldn't bear to wait for the lift so she fled down the stairs. She darted out into the sunlight and told herself to slow down. She didn't want to be early. She walked around the block once and was five minutes late, just as she had planned.

Guy was there already, watching the door for her arrival. Her face was shining with happiness. She looked delicious. When she bent to kiss him, he caught a glimpse of her breasts down the neck of her dress, and smelt a warm waft of lemon groves. There was an open bottle of cold white wine on the table. Dora, speeding entirely on happiness and nerves, sat down and drank her first glass in one long gulp.

'I haven't got long,' she told him. 'James is such a slave – driver. He's got me sending back unsolicited manuscripts. You wouldn't believe how daft some of the ideas are that people think are suitable for *Modern Woman*. Drivel about their cats, their gardens, attempted humour. It's depressing.'

She could feel herself wittering.

Guy took her hand. 'Dora, would you like something to eat?'

'Yes, please.'

Guy ordered another bottle at the bar and came back with two plates of various mixed salads.

He filled a fork with mushroom salad and, looking at it rather than her, said, 'Dora, I've been thinking...'

He put down the fork and took another sip of his wine. Then he tried again.

'Dora, were you quite serious when you said yes to me?'

'You mean about the food?'

'No, silly. About marrying me.'

She thought her heart would choke her. Tears sprang to her eyes. She gazed into his face as if she could absorb it.

'Of course,' she said slowly. 'I never joke when I accept proposals of marriage.'

'Oh, have you accepted many?'

'Dozens, if you must know. But they all died of the plague, alas, before I could get them to the altar. You should have seen the buboes. Purple, shiny, bursting with pus. Quite disgusting.'

'Look, Dora. You're leading me astray. Would you like to get married? It wouldn't be conventional, in that I have to go to New York for work soon, so we wouldn't be able to move in together. But we would be married. I want you to know that I love you. I have never met anyone else I wanted to marry.'

Fantasy and reality collided for Dora but she had a shred of sense left. She said, 'And you want to get inside my pants, and you can't think of another way to achieve this?'

'Oh Dora. Don't belittle it. I want to spend the rest of my life with you. In a way, I want to reserve you for later. I want you to know you are married to me, so you won't marry anyone else. Just being engaged doesn't seem enough to fix it. Then, in a year or so, we'll have a big party and tell everyone and move in together. What do you think?'

In all her romantic dreams, Dora hadn't thought of a secret marriage. Maybe a secret ceremony, quick and neat, but she wanted to tell the world as soon as possible afterwards.

'You see, Dora, I won't get my trust fund until I'm twenty-five, and I don't think my father would be any too pleased if I saddled myself with a wife before then.'

'Well, why do it?'

'Because I love you. Because I have been around for long

enough to know there aren't that many girls like you and I want you to myself.'

'What about Thelma?'

'She's married to Billy Kidd. I don't see her any more.'

'Are you sure?'

'Yes.' He looked wearily down at his drink. He didn't like the hard jealous note in her voice. He'd heard it before from so many other girls. She seemed like all the rest. Perhaps he was mistaken. He tried to remember what it was about her that was so special. Surely it wasn't just her virginity, which was merely eccentric these days. He felt embarrassed, but then he thought about the other things: the peace he felt with her, her curious classlessness. There were no clouds of ancient glory floating about her name. Her foundling bastard grandfather was one of the most attractive things about her. She seemed freshly sprung from nowhere. He liked that.

'Have another drink,' he said.

'I'm sorry,' she said in a gentler voice.

'That's all right. I don't blame you. I haven't been very good.'

Dora felt agitated. What should she say? Should she consent to this kind of half marriage he was offering? No flowers, no presents, no white dress.

Tirzah's advice came back to her: 'Next time he asks you, accept and then you can sort out the details afterwards.'

She smiled across at Guy and drained her glass. She hadn't touched the food. She felt that she should dare him to see if he was serious.

'OK,' she said. 'It's Monday today. Shall we say next Thursday?'

He surprised her. 'Yes,' he said. 'I've looked into it. We

can do it with a couple of days' notice if necessary. I'll book us in. It should be fairly simple on a weekday. Not much of a queue. You have to go to your town hall – I suppose it's Fulham – and register, so that we can get a special licence.'

She felt a sense of unreality. He was being as prosaic as if he was booking a dentist's appointment.

'Look,' she said. 'I've got to go back to the office. Will you call me with the details?'

It was only two o'clock, but she had a violent desire to get away from him and think. She was also beginning to feel rather drunk and knew if she stuck around she would just drink more, which wouldn't help.

She stood up, fishing for her purse in her bag.

'How much do I owe you for this?'

'You don't owe me anything,' he said, sounding exasperated. 'Look, do you want to go through with this or not?'

She sat down again with a bump.

'I do, I really do. It's just that I'm nervous.'

He took her hand again. 'I can understand that. I'm nervous too. Let's dare each other to go through with it. Then we can sort out the details afterwards.'

He was echoing Tirzah's words, and to Dora this was the signal that she must surrender, that it must be the right thing to do. She leaned forward, narrowly avoiding getting mayonnaise on her breasts, and kissed his warm mouth. He kissed her back. She drew away from him.

'Thursday, then?'

'Thursday.'

'Thanks for the lunch.'

'That's my pleasure.'

She slipped away a little clumsily between the tables

looking over her shoulder once to blow him a kiss. Then she headed back to the office, stopping in a café to drink a bottle of mineral water and a large, strong cup of black coffee. She felt slightly less dazed and ready to face James at exactly three o'clock.

Nine

UP TO THE LAST MINUTE Dora didn't quite believe it would happen. Guy telephoned her on Tuesday evening to say he had managed to book them in for eleven on Thursday. He hadn't wanted to talk at length. There was none of the usual banter. Dora felt edgy and nervous. He had, after all, done what he said he was going to do. What was there to worry about? He had reiterated the need for secrecy.

'Don't even tell your flatmates, OK?'

'OK.'

On Wednesday, Dorian Peak made Guy a definite offer on the gallery job in New York. He accepted. Initially it was for a three-month contract to see how he got on. Then Dorian could swing a green card for him, with Guy's 'specialist knowledge' – by which Dorian meant his good looks, urbane manner and Englishness.

Guy began to question why he was marrying Dora so quickly. He could run away from England and Thelma. He didn't need Dora to close that chapter of his life. They could just be engaged, or he could even promise to come back for her at some vague time in the future. He knew he wanted her but perhaps not right now. But the time fled away. He couldn't decide what to do. He found it easier to do nothing and the wedding was organised. He would go through with it. Dora agreed to wait until he was ready for her; meanwhile he wasn't going to lose anything by marrying her.

As the child of a marriage broken almost before it was made, he didn't have much faith in vows and promises. It was what Dora wanted. He didn't care either way. He thought he might just as well go along with her convictions in the absence of his. She wouldn't have any more excuses for pushing him away.

Deep inside he knew that he loved Dora; that he might be damaging her more by marrying her than by abandoning her. He preferred to gamble on a long-term project than risk certain immediate pain.

Dora told her flatmates on Wednesday night that she had a dentist's appointment the next day and would be going into work late. She took Thursday off. She was sure there would be no honeymoon. She wasn't sure what would happen to her on Friday or for the rest of her life. Until that night, she hadn't much cared. She had been so incredibly happy. Why was she now so miserable? It had been Guy's voice on the telephone.

Doubts seized her. She couldn't sleep. He had sounded so different. Maybe Evangeline had been right to warn Dora about Guy, instead of just jealous as Dora had supposed. Maybe he really was hard, cold and predatory, and that the soft, playful, loving Guy was just an illusion.

Didn't they say that falling in love was a kind of madness? Well, Dora felt mad. Her sensible nature, having brought her so far in her short life, just flew away. She was stranded on a shore of lunacy. She burned and ached with love for Guy and was willing to do anything, even risk total humiliation, to keep him with her. Even for a moment.

On Thursday morning she came down to breakfast in her dressing gown. Her flatmates were in too much of a flurry to notice how subdued she was. If they did, they would have put it down to the dire prospect of the dentist.

When she was sure they had all left, she went upstairs. In a rush she'd bought a dress the day before. It wasn't right. She could seldom find a dress she liked, particularly as she was curvaceous and didn't fit neatly into a size category. Bits of her were size 10, bits 12 and sometimes bits were 14, although she preferred not to think about those bits.

Already she hated the dress. She'd paid far too much for a black silk shirt-waister, with thin stripes of turquoise, pink and mustard, which *Modern Woman* had told her was a style whose time had come round again. It just made her look frumpy, shapeless and middle-aged, not insouciantly formal yet dashing, like the six-foot-tall, fifteen-year-old American model whose short silk skirt had flowed so liquidly around her slender thighs. Thank goodness she hadn't bought the matching tricorne in mustard straw with fluffy feathers dyed to match.

It was the kind of thing Princess Diana wore. It didn't suit Dora at all. She'd wanted so much to look irresistible, to give herself courage on what should be such a special day. Her hands trembled so much as she got ready that she put a huge blob of mascara on the bridge of her nose.

She took the Tube to Sloane Square, feeling awkward and conspicuous. Clumsy with nerves, clutching her silly little bag and feeling her personality trailing dismally along in the gutter beside her.

After standing for a quarter of an hour, waiting for him on the draughty steps of the registry office and so often nearly running away, she saw him approach, hands in trouser pockets, a preoccupied expression on his face. Her heart lifted with relief. It was going to happen, wasn't it?

'Hello,' she said, and forced herself to smile. She was careful not to gush or reproach about his lateness.

'Hello,' he said without returning the smile. 'Let's get this over with, OK?'

Guy was repelled by how afraid she looked. He thought to himself he would rather be at St Mary's clap clinic than Chelsea Registry Office. What the hell was he doing? He knew perfectly well that he should tell her that it was off, that it was mad, that they hardly knew each other. He started to speak. She put a hand on his forearm and looked up at him. He saw her strange eyes with their very slight suggestion of the East, and hesitated.

'OK,' she replied. If he was going to be cool, she was too. She noticed with pleasure that he had put a lawn daisy in the buttonhole of his suit.

All Guy's suits were made to his design by an old tailor in Hackney. When he married Dora, he was wearing a new one he wasn't pleased with – which added to the awkwardness of the occasion. It was sky-blue corduroy and he resembled Tom Kitten. However, he was very thin, so the buttons were in no danger of popping off.

When they emerged from the registry office after the brief exchange of vows, he glanced up and down the street and took the little posy she had gathered from her Fulham garden, chucking it in the nearest bin.

'Don't want anyone to know what we've been up to, do we?'

Dora felt dashed. She'd tried to make it feel like her wedding. The whole event was so far from her fantasies that she could hardly bear it.

'What shall we do now?' she asked tentatively.

'Oh, I don't know. What time is it?'

He hadn't even kissed her. He seemed impatient and unwilling. Why hadn't she listened to her misgivings?

He turned and put his arms around her, pressing her briefly against him, staring over the top of her head, before letting her go.

'Oh, come on, petal. Don't look so glum. Let's go and have a coffee.'

So they descended the steps and became part of the herd of King's Road shoppers, not special at all. She looked down at where her ring should have been. He'd had to borrow the female registrar's to marry her and then give it back.

'We'd better go and get you a ring,' he said. 'Sorry I didn't have time to do it before.'

They walked into Antiquarius, the covered antique market, and he stopped at the first jewellery stall inside the door, looking down at battered little antique rings under the glass counter. Dora began to feel a bit better.

'Can I look at that one?' he asked the assistant.

She saw he was pointing at an old gold Claddagh ring, with two hands holding a heart. The assistant handed it to him, and he took Dora's left hand and pushed it on to her ring finger. It was a bit loose.

'Do you like it?'

She didn't really – she would have liked a proper wedding ring, a plain gold band – but she said she did. At least it was a token of sorts. He paid and told Dora to take it off again and put it in her pocket.

They walked out through the crowd. Dora felt intensely self-conscious. Guy was slightly ahead of her now. He turned back and said, 'Do you have to go to work today?'

'No. I took the day off. I thought we might go out to lunch.'

'Sorry, Dora. I can manage a quick coffee but I've got to fly to New York this afternoon.'

'I don't remember you telling me you were going today.'

'Oh well perhaps I didn't. You don't mind, do you? We haven't even got time to go to bed really. What time did you say it was?'

She looked down again. He wasn't taking in anything she was saying at all. She felt desolate. There she was married to a stranger. Walking along the King's Road aimlessly with a chill draft around her ankles.

'Oh Goneril,' she muttered under her breath. 'You are not worth the dust that the rude wind blows in your face.'

'What did you say?'

'Nothing.'

'Look, Dora, don't be such an old misery. I married you, didn't I? That's what you wanted, wasn't it?'

He thought to himself: 'I was wrong. She's just like all the other poor droopy darlings who think they're in love with me after one drunken fumble. She's not really special at all. Only, I've gone and married her.'

He felt panicky and absurd, but hid it under a cool manner. Sometimes he thought he was always at the mercy of women, doing what they wanted rather than what he wanted to do himself. Dora was talking. The agitation in his mind blocked out her words.

'Well, if you haven't got time for lunch, perhaps I'd better go back to work after all.'

'Yup, good idea. Look, let's have a coffee here.'

He pulled her into Picasso, with its co-Picasso mural on the wall, sat her down and went up to the counter. When he came back, he had a large brandy in one hand and a coffee in the other for her.

'Cheers, darling. Don't look so glum. I can't bear depressed people. Well, here's to us.'

It was all Dora could do to stop herself from crying. She'd thought that maybe giving in to his incessant demands might change things, might make her feel more secure. But it had the opposite effect.

She'd hardly managed a sip of her hot coffee when he'd swallowed his brandy and stood up. She rose clumsily and tipped her chair over. She felt her cheeks grow crimson and hot as she heard him tut. She bent to pick up the chair and banged her head on his, which was lowered to the same task.

When she rose, she looked studiously down at the table, unable to meet his gaze. She felt his finger under her chin, pushing it up quite hard.

'Are we crying? Oh dear. Not quite the wedding you'd been brought up to expect, was it? A bit short, no white dress, no nuptial mass. Poor little Dora. Why did she say she'd marry mean old Guy, huh?'

He kissed her lightly on the lips, still holding her chin.

'Bye, darling, I'll send you a postcard. Remember not to tell a soul, won't you. It'll be our secret. One day we'll surprise them all.'

That comforted her and she gave him a watery grin. She'd remember that. Perhaps it was as exciting as she'd thought before and now she was just being a weed about it.

Then Guy was gone.

Dora sat down and stared at her cooling coffee, stretching her eyes to try to contain the tears. It was no good; they began to slide over the edge of her lower lids like a stream slipping its banks and trickle slowly and uncomfortably down her face. Her forehead furrowed and she developed that instant headache that goes with trying to control violent weeping in public. She began to sob and scrabbled miserably in her bag for a hanky. Guy came back just as she was blowing her nose and wiping the mascara from her eyes.

'I forgot my paper. Oh, come on, Dora. It's not that bad. I'll be in touch next week or something. You will keep this quiet won't you? If it got back to my parents, they'd cut off my allowance and probably my balls as well. They've got a low enough opinion of my activities as it is.'

He laughed, dropped another kiss on to the top of her head and left. She removed herself to the Ladies and had a look at her face. She wasn't surprised by his lack of enthusiasm for his new bride. Her face was swollen and blotched with make-up, her hair messy where she'd run her hands through it. Her dress was truly dreadful.

She made a decision. She wasn't going back to work. She had a day's holiday so she was going to enjoy herself without Guy. She would go up to Hatchards for a good browse, buy a book and take it out to lunch in Fortnum & Mason's Fountain Restaurant. She smiled at last. Books had always been an excellent substitute for beloved people ever since boarding school.

She used to come up by train to London at the beginning of half-terms from prep school, and her father had always taken her to the Fountain for tea. She had a ritual that involved ordering Elegant Rarebit cheese on toast with bacon, and an iced lemon tart with Citron scribbled on it in chocolate icing. To her it symbolised happiness and hope. Funny that her wedding day should include lunching in that dear old-fashioned place with her chief solace – a good novel.

When Guy came back from New York, she could move into his flat with him. She would go back to work tomorrow and pretend to herself and everyone else that things were exactly as they had been before – before she met Guy even. There was plenty of time. Tirzah had said they could sort out the details afterwards and that sounded very sensible.

She could even wait until he felt more secure and had inherited his trust fund, although she had heard that two could live more cheaply than one. She could earn a living and he could share it. She would have to see about getting a Dutch cap, although she hadn't the slightest idea how to go about it. They couldn't possibly have babies just yet. Being married meant she was a step closer to motherhood, which was a lovely but remote possibility at 23. When Guy was settled, that was soon enough to worry about telling people, finding a place to live and perhaps having a church blessing. Then she'd feel really married.

She went to the bus stop and caught a 22 to Piccadilly.

Ten

1939

THE SLIGHT, DARK WOMAN CROUCHED on the red plush sofa on the other side of the Harley Street waiting room. Dismal rain seeped slowly down the large panes of the Georgian sash windows. There was a table stacked with old copies of *Vogue*, *Tatler* and *Modern Woman*. Emma watched her across the magazines. She looked terribly young, no older than Marjorie. Was she frightened? Emma stood up and went to choose something to read, and also to take a closer look. The young woman's knees seemed jammed together and she was compulsively chewing the skin around one of her beautifully manicured nails. Then she whimpered.

Emma froze in the act of picking up a two-year-old copy of *Modern Woman* and walked briskly over to her. She was obviously in trouble, and it wasn't in Emma's motherly heart to leave well alone.

She sat down on the sofa beside the girl and said, 'Is there anything I can do to help?'

Emma noticed she seemed on the verge of tears. She put

an arm around her shoulders and said, 'I'm sure it will all be all right. I was very frightened the first time. It's fine. It hurts a bit, but you forget very quickly about the pain and then you've got a lovely baby.'

'It's not that,' she said. Her English was fluent but with an extraordinary hybrid accent. 'I don't mind about the pain.'

Emma squeezed her shoulder. The girl began to cry, taking out a small, lace-edged linen handkerchief to wipe her eyes. The mascara quickly made her look like a panda. Emma took out her own handkerchief and wiped it off as best she could. Once she had started crying, it seemed to be such a relief that Emma just held her against her plump bosom and let her get on with it. Her arms had come up around Emma's neck and she was pressing her face against her shoulder in the most confiding manner. Emma moved her mink stole out of the way.

When the sobs had subsided the girl drew back embarrassed, particularly when she noticed a small black stain on Emma's grey crêpe dress.

Emma looked down, following her eyes. 'Oh, don't worry about that. I'm sure it'll sponge off.'

'I'm so sorry. I have been trying to control myself. You were so kind. I couldn't help it.'

'Women are always weepy when they're pregnant,' Emma remarked.

'How did you know I was pregnant?' she looked surprised.

'Well, we are both in Mr Lawrence's waiting room and he is a gynaecologist and obstetrician.'

'Yes, of course.' The girl began to smile. Then a thought came to her. 'He's not an abortionist, then?'

Emma was shocked. 'Goodness no. Whatever gave you that idea?'

'Just something the woman I'm staying with said.'

'Good heavens.'

Emma took a minute to recover. Then she thought that this woman had been thrown in her way and she had a responsibility to do something about her.

'What's your name, dear?'

'Leora de Rosemann.'

'What a pretty name. Mine's Mrs Vane – Emma if you like. Where do you come from?'

'Paris. I've been in London for a couple of months, staying with friends. When Philippe – that's my husband – heard about Kristallnacht last year, he made contingency plans for me to go abroad in case the Germans invaded. I came over in August. Just in time.'

'Have you been married long?' It didn't seem likely but Emma wanted to draw her out gently and find out why she was so miserable.

'We got married about a month before I came to England. My own family were to leave Paris for America, so we brought the wedding forward. I know it sounds awful, but I didn't want to go with them. Marriage seemed the only way out and I was hoping Philippe would keep me with him, but he insisted I came to stay with these awful people.'

'What's so awful about them?'

Leora was tempted to confide, as one does when faced with an impossible situation and a sympathetic stranger.

'They are called Lord and Lady Cumbria. He was at Oxford with Philippe. Philippe told me he was "an awfully nice man" and a great friend, and that he would look after me. But she is horrible.'

Emma felt momentarily sorry for the peer and his wife, whom she knew slightly, saddled with this impulsive girl. Her husband was obviously a lot older than her, if he were a contemporary of Lord Cumbria.

'Philippe is quite old you see. He's forty.'

Leora peeped at Emma to see what effect this declaration was having. Emma at 45 felt slightly miffed.

'That's not very old,' she said.

'But I'm only nineteen,' wailed Leora.

'Now don't wail. You are very young. It's perfectly all right to have an older husband to look after you in these uncertain times.'

'Anyway, when I got here, they were quite nice to me at first. Introduced me to their children's friends and so on and treated me as one of the young. Then I found out I was pregnant. I told Lady Cumbria and she was obviously horrified. In the heat of the moment she said that now was not a good time to be having a baby. She seemed to bite her tongue after that. She told me to go and lie down and she was picking up the telephone as I left the room. I was afraid she was ringing an abortionist to get rid of the baby.' Leora started to sob again.

'She couldn't possibly do that. It's completely illegal in England.'

'When she came upstairs to my room she looked so grim. She said she had arranged for me to see Mr Lawrence, and just told me he was a doctor who would help me. I've been terrified ever since.'

'Clumsy woman,' remarked Emma under her breath. 'How many months pregnant do you think you are now?' she said aloud.

'I'm not at all sure. I just didn't notice anything different to begin with. Then I realised I hadn't had the curse since I came to England.'

Emma smiled. 'I'm sure Mr Lawrence will be able to tell you when the baby is due. I'm hoping he's going to tell me I'm not pregnant at all, but I have a feeling I must be. I had hoped it was the change of life.'

Emma was really talking to herself. When she looked at Leora again she noticed she looked quite embarrassed. To her, Emma looked far too old to have a baby, as old as her own mother.

'Sorry to be so frank, dear. Look, don't worry. Do you have any other friends here?'

'I had a British nanny but she died.'

'Was she Scottish?' Emma asked.

'Yes. She came from Aberdeen. How did you know?'

Emma had identified the combination of accents in Leora's speech. She just said, 'I thought she might be. Go on.'

'There's only the Cumbrias. They are shutting up the Mayfair house now, and Lady Cumbria is spending the war in Gloucestershire. Their house out there is going to be a hospital and Lady Cumbria is going to run it. I don't think she wants the responsibility of me and the baby at all but she doesn't know what to do about it.'

Emma's mind started whirring; she had travelled up from Surrey to see her gynaecologist. She was dreading going back to the cold, empty house, with only Nanny for company. Of her twin sons, Eric was a teaching fellow at Trinity College, Cambridge, excluded from active service because he had had a leg amputated below the knee after a hunting accident as a boy, and George had joined his father's regiment. Her daughter, Marjorie, was using her secretarial skills in the War Office and seldom came home. Emma had another niggling worry that she could not voice. She was hoping Mr Lawrence would put her mind at rest. In the last few years she'd had occasional pains in her chest. She was hoping that it was heartburn but she feared that it might be something more serious. If it was, then she knew this late pregnancy was going to be dangerous. She really could do with some company at home.

She turned to Leora.

'Look,' she said. 'We are complete strangers, but we have something fundamental in common. We are both going to have babies. You have nowhere in England that you feel welcome. I have a large empty house in Surrey. Why don't you come and stay with me? At least until your husband comes over or you can make another arrangement. We had Belgians to stay in the Great War.'

Leora had been staring at her feet. She looked up at Emma, a frown creasing her forehead. 'It's very kind of you but I can't possibly accept. I don't even want to leave London in case Philippe comes to find me. How will he know where I have gone?'

Her voice sounded pitiful.

'You can't stay in London. Women and children are being evacuated as it is. Didn't you say the Cumbrias were shutting up their London house?'

'I thought I could find a hotel.' Leora looked stubborn.

'I don't think that would be suitable. What would your mother say if I let you stay in a hotel? Anyway, when the baby comes they won't let you stay.'

Leora didn't know what to say. She was alarmed by this plump, grey-haired woman who for some unaccountable reason was pregnant and impulsively inviting her to stay.

'I really can't impose on you—'

Emma broke in. 'You wouldn't be imposing, honestly. I could really do with some company. My husband and one of my sons are in the army, my daughter is working in London and my other son is in Cambridge. I'm all alone. The war does change things, you know.'

Leora noticed through her confusion that Emma really wanted her and wasn't just being polite. 'Where do you live?'

'It's actually not very far from London at all. My husband's family house is perched on an almost-mountain called Leith Hill in Surrey. There's a railway halt at Ockley, the village at the bottom. I'm going back after I've seen Mr Lawrence.'

Leora sat quietly thinking about the Cumbrias. Lord Cumbria was distracted by the war. Leora, with whom he had mildly flirted under Lady Cumbria's disapproving nose, was an encumbrance now she was pregnant. Much as he was fond of Philippe, he really did think it was a bit of an imposition to lumber him with his pregnant wife. This was obvious from his manner. Lady Cumbria was very single-minded. She must do her duty during this war, and Leora was in the way. Leora knew that if she went to stay with Emma, who clearly did want her, and left the Cumbrias, who obviously didn't, she would only be doing herself and everyone else good.

'It really is very kind of you. I'd love to come and stay. Thank you.'

The nurse put her head around the door and said, 'Mrs de Rosemann?' with a bright smile.

Emma gave Leora a little push. 'Your turn first,' she said. 'Don't worry. He's very nice. I've been going to him for years.'

'Nothing like this has ever happened to me before,' said Leora.

'I know the feeling. But when we have babies we have to throw ourselves open to the public.'

Leora smiled and went into the surgery.

Emma sat thinking. If the pains in her chest were her heart, then having a baby wasn't going to do her any good at all. She considered very briefly the possibility of abortion. Not only was it illegal, she knew that people died just from the operation. Anyway, if a baby was there it was her child. She remembered with joy the births of her other three children. She couldn't possibly kill it even if it did kill her.

She went over to the table and picked up the old copy of *Modern Woman* from 1937. She flicked through it, wishing she was as she had been in 1937: unworried mother of three with a comfortable marriage, declining into middle age with few fears about anything.

The war and her inconvenient pregnancy had pulled her out of that backwater. She remembered her first pregnancy. That had been in wartime as well. She and Geoffrey had married in the summer of 1914. War was declared in August. Geoffrey had left her pregnant.

The twins were born while Geoffrey was being gassed in the trenches. He was one of the lucky ones, gassed and taken prisoner, unlike her poor brothers, both killed. Ian at Passchendaele, Jack at Gallipoli. When Geoffrey returned to her after the war, they were like strangers. She was so used to living at home with Mummy and the twin boys she had borne in pain and fear. They were big chaps of three when they first met their father. They were so protective of their mother. It was all very difficult and it took a good year to get to know each other again. Not that they had known each other very well before the war.

They went to the seaside at Littlestone in Kent to try to sort things out between them in the summer of 1919. Emma smiled when she remembered removing Eric and George from her bed to let her husband back into her life. They took a sleeping twin each – pink, warm, damp and identical – and put them back in the spare room. She must have conceived Marjorie around about then. A sweet little round pink blonde thing she had been. That birth had been much easier. Emma began to feel hopeful about this one. The imminence of war had for some reason made them behave like honeymooners again. She thought of Geoffrey – spare, slightly stooped and kind. It made her blush to think about it, a spot of private happiness amid the gathering gloom. Whatever happened to them after this, at least they would have that late flowering of love to remember about each other.

She hadn't told anyone about her pregnancy fears yet. She knew Marjorie would be terribly shocked. She was really rather a prude. She loved lacrosse and bicycling. She'd been such a tomboy as a child. Emma and Geoffrey had sent her to Benenden School for Girls instead of having a governess because she'd been so sporty. It had suited her down to the ground. All greasy lacrosse sticks and purple thighs. Emma, who was educated at home, found the whole thing rather bewildering, but Marjorie thrived on it. It made Emma feel rather weak sometimes when Marjorie was being so capable.

Marjorie had enjoyed coming out in 1937, plump in her white silk and Prince of Wales feathers. It was more fun for her than it had been for Emma, who knew no one and had emerged from the schoolroom weeks beforehand. Marjorie had all her school friends and their brothers to romp with. There had been no marriage proposal though. Then she had wanted to learn typing and shorthand. That had come in useful when the war started. She wore a khaki uniform now, and was General Uloth's secretary in the War Office.

Things had changed so breathlessly since Emma was a girl. She'd been chaperoned when visiting her brother Ian at Trinity. She couldn't believe the prudery of it now.

The door to Mr Lawrence's surgery opened and Leora came out looking a bit pink but otherwise happy.

'Mrs Vane, it is true, I am pregnant. The baby is due in March. I feel so much better now. I'm so pleased we are going to be together.'

Emma came back to herself and smiled at the vivid girl in front of her. Mr Lawrence was charming. He'd cheered Leora up enormously. 'I'll just go back to the Cumbrias and pack. Can we meet at the railway station?'

'Yes, of course. I'm catching the half past five train from Victoria to Ockley. I'll meet you at the barrier. By the way, I know Lady Cumbria a little. If you tell her you're coming to stay with Emma Vane, I'm sure she'll let you go. And don't worry about what you said about her before. She's a good woman but a bit of a stickler.'

Leora turned white. Emma went across and squeezed her hand.

'I won't repeat anything you said, don't worry.' She smiled. 'See you there. And don't lift anything heavy. Get the taxi driver to help you and a porter at the station.'

Emma walked past her, leaving her with these last words of motherly advice, and went into Mr Lawrence's mahogany-lined consulting room.

'Hello, Mrs Vane. How are we?'

The obstetrician was a large man with white hair and half-moon glasses. Emma sat down on the other side of his desk.

'I'm afraid I'm pregnant again,' she said in a resigned voice.

'Well, it isn't as if it's your first, is it?' he remarked. 'How old are we now?' He looked at her notes. 'Only 45 is it? There's nothing to worry about. As long as you take it fairly easy. Hop up on the table. Nurse, will you come and assist Mrs Vane please.'

As he examined her he chatted. The nurse held her hand and squeezed it. In spite of her blithe words to Leora she did hate this bit. It had been such a very long time since it had last been her fate to be probed and prodded. Nearly twenty years.

'Everything seems fine. About three months I would say.' Mr Lawrence left her behind the screen to get herself back together, washed his hands and went to his desk.

Emma sat down again. The doctor made a calculation. 'I should say the baby is due around the beginning of June,' he said. 'Lovely time of year to have a baby.'

Then he paused.

'How long have your ankles been swollen?' he inquired. 'It's normal in late pregnancy. But this looks more long-standing.'

'About five years. I do have one major worry, Mr Lawrence. I get pains in my chest. I hoped for ages it was just heartburn but I remember my father's angina, and I have a horrible feeling it's that.'

'That's not my field, as you know. But I had better have a listen.'

He spent a good ten minutes listening to her heart and

lungs. Then he said, 'I think you should see a colleague of mine. I'm afraid it doesn't sound too good. When women of your age go through pregnancy and birth it can impose a severe strain on the heart. I'm not going to conceal from you that it is a worry. But there are things we can do. And you've always been very well, haven't you? I'm sure you'll breeze through this one, just as you did the others.'

Emma felt chilled. She had expected something like this. 'Ah well, babies come when babies come,' she thought. 'We'll cross that bridge when we come to it.'

She stood up and shook Mr Lawrence's outstretched hand. He escorted her to the door.

'I'll book you in to the nursing home from the end of May. I don't think you should have this baby at home. My heart specialist colleague Mr Murphy will write to you.'

'Is it serious, Mr Lawrence?'

'I've known women with slight heart problems who've sailed through the whole child-bearing business with the right help. Try not to worry – that's the main thing.'

'Thank you.'

Emma went out through the waiting room and down the red-carpeted staircase. She wondered briefly why all Harley Street practices went in for red. Was it to hide the blood? 'Better have a bracing cup of tea and then get home,' she thought. Then she remembered the young woman she'd invited to stay. Well, at least she'd be some company for a bit. Stop her brooding. It was always more fun being pregnant with someone else.

Eleven

1940

TIRZAH ONLY HAD ROOM for the contents of one breast. Leora put her baby daughter down with a hasty kiss. The cries of Emma's unnamed, week-old daughter's piercing hunger echoed along the corridor. As Leora opened the door and stepped out, she could hear Nanny shushing the baby, a tone in her voice that sounded as if she was about to cry herself. Leora hesitated. She had been rebuffed before. Nanny Vane held firm views and had a look in her eye that said Leora was a foreign interloper and had no right to impose on her beloved Emma.

But Leora's right breast was hard with milk surplus to Tirzah's requirements. The front of her blouse was wet and warm with the overflow. She began to run along the passage, her arms crossed over her breasts to hold them steady. She paused, waiting for courage outside the door. She took a deep breath, looking down with amazement at her chest. The pain when the milk had come into her usually tiny breasts had been beyond anything, almost worse than the end of her labour. She had imagined the milk swelling the tissues and pulling her skin away from her chest wall. She shivered. The baby came first. She had what the baby needed and she wasn't going to let Nanny frighten her away. She straightened her shoulders and pulled them back, took another deep breath and set her jaw firmly.

She put her hand on the doorknob. Nanny had been vicious last time. Leora dreaded scoldings and crossness. She had been brought up in almost smothering warmth and love as the youngest of a large family. No one she loved had ever scolded her. Her own nanny had been quite elderly and a darling.

She tried hard to make allowances for Nanny Vane on account of the woman's devastating grief. She had loved Emma, to whom she had come as a nursemaid when the twins were born in 1915, and whose age she matched. Perhaps chill mortality blowing down her virgin neck had also sharpened her mood.

Leora turned the large brass doorknob and slowly pushed the door open.

Nanny sat on the low wooden nursing chair, the baby in the crook of her left arm. The baby's face was scarlet, its eyes and nose thin lines of furious indignation. The wound from the clumsily used forceps was fading fast. Her mouth was a terrifying, elemental black hole from which the noise pumped forth. It spoke once more to Leora's breasts, and she felt the warm tingling rush of another let-down. This strengthened her resolve.

When Nanny looked up from her struggle to get the baby to feed from the red rubber teat, Leora could see that her eyes were filled with tears. Her expression hardened when she saw who had come in.

Leora felt like a veteran in the baby-feeding battle now. She remembered her own early struggles with the screaming Tirzah, when putting her nipple in the baby's mouth had been like slashing it with a razor blade, so sharp and piercing had been the pain. She remembered how the complete conviction of a new baby's screams had taken its toll on her nerves, the paralysing exhaustion of those first weeks of no sleep, the torture of being woken just as you drifted off. Nanny wasn't young. She was suffering from the grief and shock of Emma's death and didn't have a young mother's natural defences coursing around her body to keep her going. No wonder she snapped. Leora decided to be very strong for the baby's sake. The attacks weren't personal. She must feel sorry for Nanny if she possibly could.

Tirzah had settled down in her second month. She slept for four-hour stretches in the night, so Leora felt far more able to cope and less likely to burst into tears at the slightest setback. Her nipples were pain-free now, brown as moles, and her breasts produced the most satisfactory amounts of milk. When she looked at her baby daughter, rounded and plump with the good milk that she herself produced, Leora – spoilt youngest child, married to a much older man who adored her – at last felt in control of something. The power of her success as a mother gave her the strength to face Nanny and do something about the screaming scarlet bundle of hunger.

She walked firmly across the floor. Nanny held the baby tightly, defensively. The stretched gape of the baby's mouth encircled the red rubber nipple without engaging with it at all.

Nanny glared at Leora. 'What are you doing in here?

Can't you see I'm feeding the baby? You're disturbing her.
You made her cry. She was fine until you came in. Go away.'

'No, Nanny,' said Leora gently, trying to inject love into
her voice. 'She has been crying for ages. I could hear along
the corridor.'

'So you think you know more than I do, you hussy?'

This was a new approach that Leora wasn't prepared for.
She decided to ignore it.

'Won't you let me have a go?'

'Why should you be any better at it than me?'

They were both shouting over the baby's cries which
made Leora feel more agitated than she wanted to.

'Please, Nanny, I've got plenty of milk. Let me try.'

The baby stopped crying for a moment, probably to
gather strength for the next assault on their eardrums, and
it gave Leora what she thought was a beady look. Her
face looked so pitifully thin compared to Tirzah's rounded
cheeks.

'Is she taking the bottle at all?' Leora inquired, lowering
her voice now she didn't have so much competition.

Nanny's shoulders drooped. Her face collapsed, and all
the indignant colour seemed to drain out of it. She put the
baby down on her knee.

'What would my poor darling Mrs Vane say?' she began
to sob. 'The baby has lost so much weight since birth and I
can hardly get her to take a drop. Glucose water on a tea-
spoon is really all I've got down her – which is barely
keeping her alive. How she finds the strength to scream like
that, I just don't know.'

'Give her to me.'

Nanny sat barely holding the baby, resting her on her
knees. Leora bent over and took hold of her. Nanny's hands

dropped down by her sides and she began to cry openly. Leora was shocked by how light the baby seemed after Tirzah. Like a bundle of feathers, she thought. Holding her close with her left arm, she bent down to the laundry basket by Nanny's side, taking one muslin square for her own use and handing another to Nanny to wipe her eyes.

'I know Mrs Vane would have been so proud of the loving way you have coped with the baby. Such a terrible responsibility. But it was a lot to ask...' Leora had been going to say, 'of a woman your age.' She felt grown-up at 19 but was tired enough herself with a new baby, and 45 seemed infinitely ancient. It was at times like this that Leora longed for her own mother, after whom she had named her baby. She was far away on the other side of the Atlantic.

She dismissed that whole area of worry from her mind and concentrated on Emma's shrieking, living legacy. Nanny seemed stunned, all the fight knocked out of her by a sleepless week. She stayed on the nursing chair. Leora sat down on the bed and undid her blouse. She pulled the cup off her right breast and, holding the baby close with her right arm, attempted to get her large brown nipple into its small red mouth. The baby screamed all the louder. This was an unexpected setback. Leora had been so sure of her skills. She tried and tried but the baby turned her head away, struggling weakly. Leora's back began to hurt as she crouched over, compressing her nipple between thumb and forefinger and trying to shove it between the protesting jaws.

Nanny stood up. She had come to a decision. The baby mattered more than anything or anyone, and if Leora had that within her breasts that would assuage the terrifying hunger of her charge, then she was welcome to all the help that Nanny could give.

'Come and sit on the nursing chair. You'll be far more comfortable.'

Leora was so grateful, the ache in her back was beginning to scream silently itself. She went over to the nursing chair with its low seat and arms and comfortable supportive back and sank down gratefully. Nanny brought her a footstool to rest her right foot on and said, 'I'll go and get you a cup of tea. It's thirsty work and you could probably do without spectators.'

Leora felt intense gratitude. She had some inkling of what it cost Nanny to let Emma's relict out of her sight for one instant. She just hoped Tirzah was sleeping peacefully.

She took another deep, relaxing breath.

'Now, little one,' she said aloud. 'Let's get you fed.'

She squeezed her nipple allowing drops of the sweet blue milk to fall on the baby's tongue. The effect was instant, unexpectedly so. The wide hollow of hunger made contact with the nipple. The whole of the brown areola disappeared inside the tiny mouth. The baby became all suck. Silent, intent, she had found what she had been shouting for. Leora tentatively sat back and let her get on with it. She obviously knew what to do. This was wonderful, because Leora had heard that babies who had been bottle-fed didn't want to make the extra effort with a human nipple.

Her musings were interrupted by a sudden gush of emotion as she looked down at the small needy head. A tiny hand like a pink spider starfished on the blue-streaked skin of her swelling breast. For a moment she forgot her rounded baby along the corridor. The satisfaction of giving this one what she needed took over. She felt enormous pride; tears came into her eyes for the departed Emma. She could almost feel her motherly bulk in the room, approving, Leora was sure. Perhaps the older woman had foreseen all this.

The baby was drowsing now. Her tiny chin wasn't pumping with the same urgency as before. Then she stopped and her eyes, which had been squeezed shut with the effort relaxed. She slept. Leora pushed her little finger between nipple and lip to break the vacuum and lifted the tiny body, wrapped tightly in its cobweb shawl, on to her Harrington-square-protected shoulder. The bubbles rose from distended stomach to rosebud mouth and Leora laughed aloud with the joy of her achievement.

There was a knock on the door.

'Come in,' she called.

Nanny entered, holding a cup of tea.

'Tirzah's fine,' she said. 'I just checked. She's sleeping like a lamb.'

Nanny had been thinking while she was downstairs making the tea. Mrs Vane was dead and gone. Leora represented the best chance for Mrs Vane's baby's survival. Nanny knew the risks of bottle-feeding. The unexplained deaths were so much more common when fashionable women, keen to get their figures back, let nannies rely on bottles. Also, it was a fiddle, and Nanny was feeling her years. Why not let young, fit, healthy Leora take the strain – and the responsibility? At least until Major Vane and Mr George came home from France. She didn't allow herself to imagine what would happen if neither of them did. She had already dismissed Marjorie as a source of help.

Marjorie had come down on the day of her mother's funeral. She'd taken one disgusted look at the baby.

'Well, Nanny,' she'd said. 'Another for your nursery. Give you something to do, eh?'

Marjorie was hiding her confusion and misery under a bluff and breezy manner. She didn't know what to think. She was a clever girl, but disgusted by all manifestations of physicality. Especially the idea of her parents, whom she regarded as elderly, doing what was necessary to make this battered scrap. It was obviously a bad idea: her mother had gone and died of it. Anyway, she had a job of national importance and she wasn't going to come home and play mummy to this child which shouldn't exist.

Her relationship with Nanny was all too recently that of discipline and nursery teas. At Nanny's only very slight indication that it was her duty to look after her baby sister, her bottom lip had shot out.

'Sorry Nanny, no can do. My country needs me. You're frightfully good with babies, aren't you? That girl Mummy picked up can help you.'

The other shock to Marjorie's virgin sensibilities had been Leora, breasts bursting with milk under her chic French clothes, white skin glowing, red lips, black hair. She was beautiful, sexy, married, and a good year younger than Marjorie. Blonde, permed and slightly overweight in her khaki uniform, Marjorie felt like an elephant. She wanted to go into her old room with its battered copies of *Little Women* and *Swallows and Amazons* and howl for her mother, who'd gone and done this stupid thing which killed her. She had no sympathy left over for anyone else.

She hadn't given the baby a second glance as she'd climbed into the Humber Snipe she'd borrowed from the War Office pool, and driven away down the drive.

Nanny hadn't hoped for much. She knew that Marjorie had been avoiding her mother as the pregnancy became more obvious. She had foreseen that the sisters could not be friends. When the Humber had disappeared from view, she had simply sighed and gone back into the house.

Twelve

1958/1941

WHEN THE INVITATIONS CAME for Tirzah and Hilda to 'Mrs Ralph Bullen at Home', the girls had initially been overwhelmed with excitement. Then they realised they had nothing to wear for a smart dance.

'Two bloody Cinderellas,' said Hilly furiously.

She didn't want to bother her father about it. She knew it would distress him that he couldn't afford to buy them dresses.

'We just can't go, can we?' mused Hilda sadly.

'There must be something we can adapt in the house surely?' said Tirzah.

'Why don't we ask Leora?'

'She's hopeless. She doesn't even know which end of a needle to thread.' Tirzah's faith in the practical skills of her chic mother was minimal.

They looked at each other and laughed. Hilly was wearing a pair of Land Army jodhpurs left behind by someone far stouter than her after the war, together with an old shirt of her father's. Tirzah had on a cotton dress that had been part of the local grammar school uniform. Too short and far too tight across the bust. They giggled.

'What do we look like?'

'A couple of swells.'

It was all right in the summer at Leith Hill. Winters were different. The large, tired old house performed a symphony of chilling draughts. All the heating was concentrated in the conservatory, where Geoffrey sat day in and day out. If the girls wanted to be warm, they had to go in there and sit quietly. Too much noise and movement annoyed Geoffrey. If they were reading and giggled at something, he would always ask crossly what they were laughing about. It usually ended in Hilly or Tirzah reading masses of their chosen books out loud to him.

Geoffrey got very bored by his own limitations. First World War gas and Second World War immersion in the Channel during the retreat from Dunkirk had left him with a single dodgy lung. He suffered bouts of depression that made his physical symptoms worse. It had been brought on by surviving one of his sons, George, killed at Dunkirk, and his wife, dying in childbirth around the same time. He still blamed himself for both these deaths that came so quick, one upon the other.

He did his best to pull himself together but he often felt like a useless old wreck, and was bad-tempered as a result. The one person who could tug him out of his black moods was Leora. His helplessness brought out her strong maternal instincts and she adored him. The role of nurse was not the only one she played in his life. Their relationship was rarely sexual due to his ill health, but she did spend nights in his room sometimes. This had led to problems with the family being accepted in the county. Not that Geoffrey was well enough to socialise, but as the girls grew up and reached 18, he did worry about them.

'Emma would have known what to do,' he said to himself. 'She brought Marjorie out all right.'

Hilly was so different to plump blonde Marjorie, with her thick reddish brown hair and pretty face. Geoffrey thought Marjorie had been very like a piglet when she was born. She was safely married now and in America. Every year they received a Christmas card with a picture of Marjorie and her husband John Wiggins, with John Jnr, Betty and Jean, all blonde, with metal plates on their teeth, standing in the California sunshine. Geoffrey would shiver looking at them. Marjorie had never suggested he come and heal his lung with her in the sun. He was too proud to ask. It irritated him that she had presumed to judge his relationship with Leora and blamed him for her mother's death. After the war, while rationing persisted, she had sent parcels and she was still most generous through the post. He supposed she was a nice, straightforward woman, perfect to be fed to the Americans. She looked so right in the Christmas photographs.

There was no money to buy his younger daughter and her foster sister smart clothes, let alone give them a season in London. How were they ever going to meet anyone? When he wasn't sunk into self-pity he did worry about the girls, so pretty and so close in age. He worried about Leora too, stuck with an old, sick man she wasn't even married to. She was young enough to start all over again, marry someone who could give her what she deserved, leaving him all alone among the dilapidated ferns that had been his father's chief passion.

He remembered the first time he had seen her. After Dunkirk, he'd been very ill with pneumonia and the doctors hadn't wanted to tell him that he'd lost Emma. When the fever had died down and he'd pulled through with the aid of the new penicillin drugs, they told him that he was father to a nameless daughter but that it had been too much for Emma's heart.

It had been too early for such shocking revelations, on top of the news of George's death. 'Why didn't she tell me about her heart?' he kept saying to himself. 'I would have been more careful.'

He suffered a relapse and nearly joined his wife and son in the grave. As he fought for breath, he heard the doctors talking outside the oxygen tent. 'He's dying of a broken heart,' one said to the other.

That did it where modern drugs had failed. He was damned if he was going to do anything as feeble as die of a broken heart. Besides, he had a new daughter and couldn't leave her an orphan. With a monumental effort of will he pulled himself round. He was sent to the Isle of Wight to convalesce and didn't meet Hilly until she was nearly three months old, rounded and plump, the forceps scar just a tiny purple line above her eyebrow.

A sergeant in his company had driven him home. The man helped him out and, leaning on his stick, he pushed open the front door and walked slowly into his ancestral home. It felt quiet and dank. He stood in the stone-flagged hall, listening for life while regaining his breath.

The sergeant brought in his leather suitcase and put it down inside the door.

'Will that be all, sir?'

'Thank you, Evans.'

The man saluted and left.

From upstairs came the unmistakable sounds of a hungry

baby, soon joined by another. 'Twins?' he thought incredulously. 'Again? Why didn't anyone tell me?'

As quickly as he could, which wasn't very fast, he ascended the two flights of stairs to the nursery floor. The cries had ceased when he reached the night nursery door. He knocked.

A voice he didn't recognise, certainly not Nanny's familiar and comforting tones, said, 'Come in.'

He pushed open the door slowly.

On the bed, propped up on pillows, her legs stretched out in front of her, was a beautiful, dark girl. The room was warm and she was naked to the waist. He could see the tops of two babies' heads, with their legs tucked under her arms and her hands supporting them. Each was latched on to a round, blue-veined breast.

'Oh,' she exclaimed, dropping a baby and snatching at a shawl.

The unsupported baby fell off the nipple and began to cry. Geoffrey beat a hasty retreat, burning with confusion. He remembered vaguely something in one of Emma's letters about a Jewish refugee she was sheltering and assumed this was her. He had forgotten completely about her until this moment. What was her name? He would have to ask her.

He went slowly back downstairs and found Nanny in the hall, looking at his suitcase in bewilderment.

'Major Vane! Thank God you are here,' she said.

'Hello, Nanny. Yes, I'm back. Would you be kind enough to carry my case? I'm afraid I'm still a bit weak. I need to have a rest after the journey.'

Nanny picked up the suitcase and followed him back up the stairs to his dressing room. He couldn't face the bed he had shared with Emma, where that fatal pregnancy had begun.

'I was so sorry about your wife, sir.'

'I am sure you were, Nanny. Who is that woman upstairs?'

'Mrs de Rosemann, sir. A friend of Mrs Vane's.'

'I presume that one of those babies she's feeding is mine?'

Nanny was embarrassed.

'When I heard two babies crying, I thought we had another lot of twins.' He smiled faintly.

Nanny smiled tentatively back at him. 'Honestly, sir, she's been marvellous. I don't know what I would have done without her. Little one wouldn't take the bottle, and Mrs de Rosemann insisted on wet-nursing her herself.'

'I bet you didn't like that much to begin with, eh Nanny?'

Nanny blushed. 'Well no, I didn't. I thought I could manage. But she wasn't thriving. Mrs de Rosemann's a good woman. Her husband's disappeared in France. She's very worried about him but she never complains.'

'Poor woman. She's French, is she?'

'Yes.'

'Nanny, would you be kind enough to get me a cup of tea? I think I'll lie down for a bit.'

'Right.'

Nanny turned to go. Geoffrey called after her, 'Will she stay, do you think, to help you with the baby?'

'She's got nowhere else to go, so I presume she will. At least until the war is over.'

Nanny left. Geoffrey lay back on his narrow divan. Later he would find the strength to go and look at Emma's things. Now he thought about the young woman on the bed.

'Beautiful sight,' he thought. He had occasionally seen Emma discreetly feeding Marjorie, but the twins had been three years old when he'd got back from being a prisoner of war, well past breast-feeding. He wondered if Emma had fed them like that. He thought about his practical, loving wife and the twin blown apart by a shell on the Dunkirk beach, and turned his face into the cushion as his eyes filled with tears.

Thirteen

1958

LEORA CAME INTO THE GIRLS' room one morning with a heap of dresses over one arm.

'Darlings,' she said. 'I've been thinking about this party. Geoffrey and I were talking about it last night. He disapproves of Ralph Bullen, says he is an arms dealer who made a good thing out of the war. I told him that you girls must get out and meet people. Something must be done. He didn't resist for long. Poor man, he feels terribly guilty about us all, you know, not being able to give you girls a London season.'

Hilly sat up, rubbing her eyes. 'What are you on about, Leora? There's absolutely nothing we can wear. Mrs Collins, the world's most genteel postmistress, whispered to me that the Bullens were 'fraitfully noovo'. As I was wearing my usual elegant two-piece of Dad's shirt and Land Army jodh-purs at the time, I wondered whose side she was on. Anyway, they'll all be wearing Dior. We can't possibly compete.'

Tirzah lay on her back, looking at the ceiling. 'I'd like something in oyster satin, swept back and caught with dia-mond clips,' she sighed.

'I'm sure you would. Meanwhile we've got what I brought over from France with me before the war. There weren't many occasions for wearing the evening clothes, and it was still packed in the trunk that Lady Cumbria sent on to me. It is mostly from my trousseau, all best quality, my mother insisted – some of it haute couture. There might be a dress or two there that you could wear. There isn't really time to get Mrs Jarvis to run something up or alter these.'

The girls exchanged glances. Mrs Jarvis was the local dressmaker. When they did get anything new, such as school uniform, it was stitched on her Singer sewing machine. She was a bit coy about fitting things closely, so everything she made was very baggy with strange lumps on the seams at random intervals. They shuddered at the idea of an evening dress made by Mrs Jarvis being exposed to the titters of the Bullens' smart guests.

'These were my evening dresses,' Leora was saying, laying them out on Tirzah's bed. 'I wore this one at my first dinner party, given for me by my parents after I married.'

The dress was in oyster satin all right but its skirt was slender and gored. The bodice had puffed sleeves and a sweetheart neckline with a little bow and buttons. It looked like a nightdress to Hilly and Tirzah.

The fashions back when Leora was married were radically different to post-war style. The girls might be lacking in ready cash but they couldn't possibly be unfashionable or dowdy. They didn't want to hurt Leora's feelings but could both feel an embarrassing situation coming on.

'Would you like to try it on, Hilly?'

Hilly climbed reluctantly out of bed. She wasn't as tall as Tirzah but she topped Leora by at least two inches. She slipped off her old nightie, and stood naked while Leora dropped the dress over her head.

'There, darling, you look lovely. Just the thing for a girl's first dance.'

Hilly glanced in the dressing-table mirror. For a start, the dress exposed her large bare feet and bony ankles. For another, it pulled over the shoulders. And thirdly, it was totally, totally wrong for 1958. Christian Dior had made sure of that when he'd launched the New Look ten years before.

She swallowed and thought silently what she should say to cause the least hurt.

'Leora, my darling, I think it's a bit small.'

'We could let it out.'

'But that would spoil it and you might want to wear it again one day.'

'Oh, me? Never. It's a young girl's dress. A dress for a debutante. Not for an old woman like me.'

'Still, it really doesn't fit me at all.'

Leora could see. She had been so fired with hope when she'd woken up that morning. She was desperate for the girls to have a bit of fun. She felt guilty that choosing to live with Geoffrey, rather than being a respectable war widow, had cut her and Tirzah off from her family in America. She had a kind of dream that somehow it would all be all right. She knew it wasn't.

'I'll help you off with it. What about this blue crêpe one? Perhaps it might fit Tirzah?'

'For goodness' sake, Mother. I'm twice your size. I would look ridiculous.'

Tirzah never minded being straightforward with her mother. Her relationship was clearer cut.

Leora's shoulders drooped. 'I know.'

She picked up the dresses and started to leave the room. Hilly chased after her and hugged her.

'It was really kind of you. Let's think of something else. Looking at those frocks gave me an idea. I think Tirzah and I will go to the ball. You can wear one of your own dresses and go with Daddy. Men's evening dress never goes out of fashion. Do you think you could persuade him? It would do him good. You could wear the black lace over pink. It's suitably matronly. You would look lovely.'

Leora smiled sadly and stroked the material. 'We haven't been invited.'

'What?' Hilly was incensed. 'Why not?'

'Probably because we are living in sin.'

'I'll see about that.' Hilly was about to set off to upbraid the new neighbours on the spot.

'Come back, Hilda.' Leora sounded stern. 'You can't go and demand an invitation. It would be most embarrassing. Particularly as you've got nothing much on.'

'Oh.' Hilly looked down. She laughed. 'All right, Mother,' she said and turned, appearing meekly obedient, to come back into her room.

Hilly jumped on Tirzah.

'You are horrid to your mother sometimes. She meant really well about those dresses.'

'It's only because she feels guilty. She knows damn well we should both be in America by now, living in the lap of luxury, miles from this bloody house.'

Hilly felt as if Tirzah had hit her. She froze. 'What do you mean?'

'There's no reason why we should stay in England. All her family went to the States in 1938. My father is obviously dead. It's just that my mother is obsessed with your father.'

Hilly climbed slowly off the bed. She was blushing with shame and misery. She got dressed and left the room without saying anything else.

She was making a pot of tea when Tirzah appeared in the kitchen.

'I'm sorry, Hilly.'

'I don't believe you.'

'I am. I am. It's not our business what our parents do. It's just sometimes I'm so sick of not having any money. I want pretty clothes. I want to go to art school so badly it hurts. I know I'm talented. But I have nowhere to put the talent. I feel so frustrated.'

She bashed her fist down on the kitchen table, angry tears in her dark eyes.

Hilly turned to her foster sister. 'Tirzah, it must be hard for you. He's my father after all. You're nearly grown up; you don't have to stay here.'

'Where would I go with no money?'

'Why don't you write to your relations in America and ask for help with art school?'

'They would never help. Mummy is in disgrace. Why should they do anything for me? They probably think I'm Geoffrey's daughter.'

'You can't be. You were a good three months old when he came back from Dunkirk.'

'I can't write to them saying, "I'm not Geoffrey's daughter – can I have some money to go to art school?" now, can I?'

'I don't think you have to mention Geoffrey at all. Why don't you just say that you are Tirzah de Rosemann, daughter of Leora and Philippe, and you wish to go to art school but cannot finance it at the moment – would they help you?'

'It sounds very straightforward doesn't it? Only to me it seems like begging.'

'Don't be so stupidly proud. You could offer to pay them back gradually afterwards. When you get famous. You could think of it like a kind of scholarship.'

Tirzah smiled at this suggestion. 'Well, it's worth a go.'

'I wish I had some kind of talent that would get me away from here. Or some rich relations to appeal to.'

'What about Marjorie?'

'She doesn't even like the fact I exist.'

'Hilly, something will turn up. Perhaps something exciting will happen if we go to this house-warming party.'

Hilly's eyes lit up. 'Yes,' she breathed. 'Maybe I'll meet Prince Charming in a white Lagonda and he will drive off with me into the dawn.'

'Perhaps you will. You're jolly pretty you know, Hilly.'

'I think we'd better cycle to the library and look at *Modern Woman*. We might get some inspiration about how we can adapt something around the house. We could even use the curtains. Think of Scarlett O'Hara. She managed to fool Rhett Butler into thinking she wasn't poor, didn't she? We'll manage. Anyway, we're not really poor. We just don't have any money. But we must get to that party. I think it's vital for our future.'

'I will write that letter, Hilly. It's a good idea. But I won't tell Mummy. She might be hurt. At least I'll wait until I get a reply.'

'OK. I'm sure they will help. They wouldn't like to think of a family member not having any money. They probably think because she's living in a big house that she's fine.'

'They might not like the idea of art school though. It sounds a bit bohemian.'

'Say you want to learn couture pattern-cutting instead, then.'

'You are immoral, Hilly, suggesting I lie to them.'

'It's a means to an end, Tirzah. Go on; get on with it now and I'll go into town by myself.'

She had another mission before she went there. She put on her tidiest cotton frock. Made by the local dressmaker, it was white with an all-over pattern of blue roses. She had taken Mrs Jarvis a picture from *Modern Woman* to copy, but the result wasn't exactly what she had envisaged. The waist was somehow in the wrong place, and the skirt just wasn't fashionably full. But at least it was clean and quite new.

Alarmed by her own audacity, she had decided to pay a morning call on Mrs Bullen. She tucked the skirt into her knickers to keep it out of the chain and climbed on her bike. She whizzed down Leith Hill to the bottom, turned right through the village and pedalled up the drive to the red-brick Tudor house that Ralph Bullen had apparently bought as a country cottage six months before.

Hilly leaned her bicycle against the large, arched brick porch. She pulled a clean cardigan out of her satchel and put her Sunday felt hat on her head. She had shoes and stockings on as well for a change. She knew she didn't look smart, but she regarded herself as good as anyone, and marched confidently up to the front door.

She rang the bell. A butler opened the door. She had never seen one in the flesh before but, like many things in life, she had read about them so she knew what to do.

'Is Mrs Bullen at home this morning?'

'I shall inquire.'

He didn't invite her inside. She felt cross about this, but could understand it.

He came back. 'Mrs Bullen's secretary will see you in the library, miss.'

He showed her into a large, book-lined room, where a woman little older than herself was sitting behind a desk.

'Hello, you are...?' she asked, looking up from her papers.

'I'm Hilda Vane. I live up the hill. I wanted to see Mrs Bullen.'

'Right.' She put on wing-tipped tortoiseshell glasses and consulted a list.

'Miss Hilda Vane. Are you coming to the party?'

'That is what I have called about.'

'I see.' She waited. 'Well, are you coming?'

'Yes, Tirzah and I would love to. But there's a problem.'

'What's the problem? I don't think Mrs Bullen can see you now. You can tell me about it.'

'I'm sorry, but I can't talk about this to anyone other than Mrs Bullen.'

Hilly was determined, even if she could feel her heart thudding with anxiety.

Miss Jones sighed. 'All right then. I don't think she's busy. Wait here.'

She was gone for some time. Hilly wandered around the walls of books. When she tried to take one out to pass the time, she found they were just false backs stuck on. She snorted.

'Can I help you, dear?'

Hilly swung round. There was an ample lady with startling red hair and a full-skirted shirt-waister in bright turquoise. She had a kind, plump, pinkly powdery face. Hilly liked her at once.

'Are you Mrs Bullen?'

'That's right. You are Hilda Vane? You're coming to our party?'

'I do hope so. But there is a problem.' Hilly swallowed, and then rushed at it. 'You see, you haven't invited Leora and Geoffrey.'

'Who are they?'

'Geoffrey, Geoffrey Vane is my father. Leora is my foster mother.'

'Miss Jones?' Mrs Bullen turned to her secretary. 'Why haven't we invited the rest of the family?'

Miss Jones went scarlet. 'Um, er, um. I don't know. It must have been an oversight.'

'I think it's because they're not married but they live in the same house,' Hilly interjected.

'Ah, I see. Yes, I remember now,' said Mrs Bullen.

Mrs Bullen looked slightly wild with her bright colours and her ample bosom. Hilly was attracted to her like a small child to a parrot. Should she explain? Mrs Bullen looked puzzled but friendly.

Hilly rushed on: 'You see, my mother died after I was born. Leora was a refugee and she'd just had Tirzah so she fed me as well.'

Mrs Bullen smiled sweetly, and turned to Miss Jones.

'Miss Jones, dear, will you give Miss Vane an invitation for...What are their names, dear?'

Hilly was glowing with her success. 'My father is Major Vane, and Leora is Madame Philippe de Rosemann.'

'Ah. French?'

'Yes.'

'Take the invitation to your parents. I will look forward to meeting them.'

'Thank you. I know they will be pleased.'

'You're a good girl to come. And brave. I look forward to seeing you at the party. Goodbye.'

She extended a hand, and left the room.

Miss Jones smiled and gave her the invitation. Hilly left the house without further discommoding the butler.

'Who was that?' Peter, the eldest of Ralph Bullen's two sons, walked into the library. He had seen Hilly crossing the hall as he was coming down the stairs.

'She's called Hilda Vane and she lives in that rotting old house up the hill. It's all a bit scandalous and eccentric,' said Miss Jones.

'How fascinating. Is she coming to the party?'

'Yes.'

'Good.' He strolled out.

Hilly found she had enough money in her purse to buy a copy of *Modern Woman*, and she brought it home so she and Tirzah could pore over it for ideas. They looked in dismay at the neat, permed heads of the models, their doe-eyed make-up, the huge skirts and strapless tops.

'I feel bad about showing this to Leora.'

'Well, don't then,' said Tirzah.

'But she loves fashion. She knows very well that things changed completely after the war with Dior's New Look.'

'I've had an idea. Your family has been living here for generations. You know you said that thing about Scarlett O'Hara? These dresses look rather Victorian with their crinoline skirts. Why don't we look in the attic and see if there are any crinolines up there?'

'Tirzah, you are brilliant. There's bound to be something. The attic is full of clutter. Even if we just use the hoops and corsets, and sew fabric on to them, at least we'll have the right silhouette.'

The two girls bolted for the attic, feeling much more hopeful. They were dismayed when they saw the heaps of dusty rubbish that met their eyes, lit only by cracks between the roof tiles. They had to go downstairs again for candles to see what they were doing.

After wading through piles of yellowing newspaper bundles, broken chairs, old suitcases, boxes of letters and a chandelier on its side, its lights scattered across the floor like icicles, they found some promising leather trunks stacked, luckily, under a sound piece of roof.

'I think it would be best if we took a trunk downstairs and looked there,' Hilly said.

But when they tried to move them, the cases were simply too heavy and the ladder too steep to do it safely.

'We can take armfuls of clothes out and throw them down the trapdoor,' Tirzah suggested.

So they did. Soon there was a satisfying pile of bombazine, velvet and silk, with hoops sticking up out of it like a whale's graveyard at the bottom of the ladder.

They climbed down and hauled the clothes into a spare bedroom. There they tried to organise them into single outfits. A strong smell of mothballs rose from the long-packed clothes. Some of them were hopelessly cracked and stained, the silk linings fallen into shreds. Others were in good condition but far too small. Many dated from periods that would never adapt to the fashions of the 1950s.

'Let's start by looking for the right underclothes.' Tirzah pulled out two calico petticoats with layers of whalebone hoops.

When Hilly turned around to show her something, Tirzah had tied an enormous bustle frame on to her bottom, which looked extraordinary with Geoffrey's old khaki army trousers.

Hilly was holding up a black bodice beaded all over with jet. The waist descended in a sharp point and it had long, tightly fitting sleeves and a high round neck.

'What about this for you?' she asked.

'Shouldn't we be showing a bit of flesh for a party?' Tirzah protested.

'Yes, but we could cut this down into a strapless bodice.'

'I see. Is there a skirt to go with it?'

'I think so.' Hilly began tugging at an area of black, and pulled out an immense satin skirt, with jet beading around the hem.

'Put it on. We'll see if it fits.'

They were seized with excitement. There seemed such a wealth of possibilities.

Tirzah slipped out of her clothes. She stood wearing a vest and pants, tying the strings of the crinoline petticoat around her waist. When she slipped into the skirt, it wouldn't do up.

'Oh dear, they all wore corsets in those days, didn't they?' said Hilly, squeezing and hauling her foster sister into the clothes. Tirzah could not get her arms even halfway down the narrow sleeves so Hilly tried just fitting the lower part of the bodice around Tirzah's slender waist. It just fitted if Tirzah breathed every ounce of air out of her lungs, not a situation that could last for more than a few seconds, but Hilly ran off to get scissors from the sewing room to cut off the sleeves.

'Perhaps we should try and find a corset each?' she suggested when she came back.

Leaving Tirzah to be creative with the scissors she went back into the attic to look. She knew she'd be lucky to find anything. Corsets were the kind of everyday thing that got worn to a shred and thrown away. In the bottom of the trunk were a couple of long slender boxes with pictures of impossibly-waisted Edwardian ladies on them. They looked quite untouched. Hilly lifted them out to look. She couldn't believe it. The corsets inside looked unworn. Of a later period than the crinolines, they were frivolous and pretty in comparison to the austere calico petticoats.

'Tirzah,' she called down through the hatch. 'I've found something wonderful. Stop cutting. I think I've got the answer.'

She scrambled down the ladder and ran to the spare room where Tirzah was puzzling over the bodice.

'Look at these. They would be perfectly decent. Aren't they rather like those Balenciaga ball gowns we were looking at earlier?'

She laid the corsets out flat on the bed. They hooked up the front and laced up the back. From the bottom edge dangled enormous suspenders.

'We may be able to afford some decent stockings, at least,' Hilly remarked when she noticed them.

One was black satin, embroidered with pink rosebuds. It was plain and simple, the extraordinary complexity of the boning visible but not intrusive. It was designed to control the body from armpit to just above the knees.

'How on earth does one go to the lavatory wearing that?' Hilly mused. Tirzah, looking at it critically, suggested undoing some of the bottom hooks to give a little flexibility.

'It is rather marvellous. I think it would suit you better than me, you know, Tirzah, with your black hair. I'll try the other one.'

'Do you think Leora will make a fuss if I wear black? She does hold quite strong views on unmarried girls.'

'Yes, I know, but beggars can't be choosers and the rose-buds are pink. They look hand-stitched to me. Goodness, it's beautiful. Can you imagine getting laced into one of those every day of your life?'

The two girls, standing in plain, drooping Chilprufe vests and pants left over from a less shapely phase of their development, felt their long-neglected desire for pretty things satisfied at last. The other corset was flesh pink, with little frills over the bosom to provide a large embonpoint. Hilly worried that it really did look like underwear and that she wouldn't get away with it.

'Never mind,' said Tirzah. 'We can cut off those silly frills, as your bust is quite big enough already, and maybe dye it if you can't stand the colour.'

'I wonder why they were put away like this, unused.'

'Perhaps they were in someone's trousseau and she was jilted. Or perhaps they went out of style before they wore out. Or perhaps whoever they belonged to died in childbirth.'

'You are morbid.'

'People were always dying in childbirth in the old days, weren't they?'

'Yes. Like my mother.'

'Sorry.'

'Don't worry. It's not as if I knew her, after all. Your mother filled the gap really. I do think that things would have been easier for us if she had lived though. We might have met more people for one thing. Marjorie had a completely normal time being a deb and all that. But there was more money in those days, of course.'

'Where did it all go?'

'Well, Daddy did explain a bit. I didn't really understand.

But it was about property from which he received rents being bombed and then losing the compensation in bad investments. There was also lots of taxes and things. There's still a bit left, otherwise we wouldn't survive at all. I know he feels terrible about it. But he has been so delicate since Dunkirk he couldn't possibly have gone out to work.'

'As for Mummy's family's money, she ain't getting any while she lives in sin. But never mind,' said Tirzah. 'We are young and strong. Who cares about money? Let's get ourselves dressed.'

She was slipping into the black corset as she spoke. She hooked up the front and asked Hilly to lace the back. Her white shoulders rose out of the black satin. She lifted her hair off her neck and looked in the mirror, transformed into a sinuous merry widow.

Hilly felt small and plain, but Tirzah seized the scissors and began snipping at the pink corset. Then she made Hilly put it on and searched among the skirts on the bed for something suitable.

With a cry of pleasure she pulled out a cream lace bonnet veil.

'This'll do it,' she said, draping the lace over Hilly's shoulders.

'We can make you a little lace sleeveless blouse out of this to wear over the pink satin. Look.' Tirzah grabbed the magazine and showed Hilly what she meant. Hope stirred and Hilly looked in the mirror with more interest.

'Now for a skirt. Is this all there was up there?'

'I think so. Shall I have another look?'

'Yes, I can't get through the trapdoor in this crinoline.'

Hilly disappeared up the ladder, suspenders trailing down her legs. Soon, more fabric was walloping down through the trapdoor and the air in the passage was chokingly infused with the naphthalene used as moth repellent.

Hilly dug through the pile like a dog scenting a bone and with a cry of triumph unearthed what might have been the skirt of a wedding dress. 'This is much more suitable for a girl's first ball than yours, Tirzah.'

'Never mind. I will look like a mysterious child bride who has just murdered her husband,' Tirzah replied.

Draped in their finery they went to find Leora. They sashayed into the kitchen, making what they imagined was polite Victorian conversation:

'Fie, Mr P., what a tease you are,' Hilly remarked archly to Tirzah, tapping her with an invisible fan.

'Oh,' said Leora, her hands flying up to her face. 'What are you wearing? It looks like you've been in the dressing-up box.'

But this didn't put Tirza and Hilly off, and they spent all the time until the Saturday of the party, stitching and ironing and dabbing peroxide on to the worst of the foxing. Leora went out and bought them new nylons. In the same trunks they found satin dancing slippers, unused and surprisingly big enough for both of them. They couldn't afford to have their hair cut and permed, so Leora would help them put it up on the night.

On the evening of the ball, Geoffrey called Hilly into his dressing room. Leora had concealed from him the fact that Hilly had gone and solicited an invitation for them. She just told him that it arrived late. He had accepted reluctantly but had managed to get himself swept up in the household's excitement. 'Perhaps they are right,' he thought to himself. 'This could unfreeze things a bit. The girls might have some fun and meet some nice men. Leora could do with a party.

She's been shut up here with me for too long, poor darling.'

Hilly, resplendent in lace and satin, came into his dressing room. He was sitting on his bed examining something in his hand. 'I thought you might like this. It was your mother's,' he said. 'I kept this for you in her memory.'

It was a string of pearls with a diamond clasp. Hilly let her father clasp it under the neat chignon that Leora had achieved for her with hairpins and lacquer. She thanked him, hugging him closely to her, and feeling how thin he was.

She felt as if she was glittering. Every part of her shook and trembled with excitement. Waiting for the local taxi to come and take them down the hill to the Bullen's 'country cottage' was torture.

At last the doorbell rang. Hilly jumped and clasped Tirzah's hand. The older girl was slightly calmer. She could see beyond this moment to art college ahead. She didn't have so much invested in the ball. She hoped very much that Hilly would not be disappointed. She glanced at her. There was bright colour in her cheeks, her eyes shone. The dress they had cobbled together faded into insignificance beside her youth and eagerness. Tirzah pressed her hand and kissed her cheek. Then they all squeezed into the ancient taxi.

Down the hill they went. It was still broad daylight at eight o'clock in the evening. It felt odd to the two girls to be so dressed up in what looked like daytime.

Geoffrey and the driver helped the women out. The girls' crinolines had nearly suffocated Leora in the back and she had made mock-cross French noises all the way. Geoffrey asked the driver to come back for him and Leora at midnight: 'I shall be very tired by then. You two can walk home if you want to stay any later. Or someone might give you a lift.'

They shook down their skirts, tweaked up their bodices and milled about like ducklings, before following in Geoffrey's wake.

Hilly recognised the butler, but it was obvious he didn't recognise her as he took her shawl. Huge triangular flower arrangements scented the air. They could see their hosts through an open door; a toastmaster, scarlet of both face and coat, was announcing the people who had arrived just before them.

Hilly felt she might dissolve inside and was grateful for the tight lacing. She held Tirzah's hand tightly.

'Oh goodness, Tirzah,' she whispered. 'What are we doing here?'

Geoffrey and Leora went first, Tirzah and Hilly following behind. Hilly took a deep breath. She was going to do this, be brave not shy, keep her chin up and look this new world right in the eye. She put on a smile and walked forward.

'Major Vane and Madame Philippe de Rosemann,' announced the toastmaster, rolling the R in de Rosemann.

Hilly could see Mrs Bullen's smiling face. Beside her stood a completely square man wearing spotless white tie, with lots of iron-grey hair. Beyond them were two young men in black tie.

'Miss Hilda Vane and Miss Tirzah de Rosemann,' were announced with the same rolled R.

Hilly found herself in front of Mrs Bullen who bent to kiss her and said, 'I'm so glad you have all come. You look lovely.'

Ralph Bullen shook her hand. Everyone was smiling. Hilly felt warmed by their welcome. They passed on into the drawing room. The French windows were open down one side, and an enormous marquee stretched beyond into the garden. As yet there weren't all that many people. Geoffrey liked to be on time, although Hilly knew it was more fashionable to be late. She didn't mind; she had been eager to see and be seen.

'Come on, Tirzah, let's have a look at everything.'

They glanced around at Geoffrey and Leora. Geoffrey was leaning on his stick, looking neutral. Hilly couldn't help noticing that his stiff white front and narrow waistcoat were rather yellow in comparison to Mr Bullen's. He still looked very handsome and distinguished to her loving eyes. Leora was shining with pleasure. She looked absolutely right, as neat and sweet as a nut, hardly coming up to Geoffrey's shoulder. As Hilly turned away, she was accepting champagne from a passing waiter. Hilly felt incredibly pleased that she had braved Mrs Bullen and got them an invitation. They were obviously fine and Hilly could get on with having fun herself.

She and Tirzah roamed the vast, empty marquee with its pink and white striped walls clashing with the red drugget on the floor. There were round tables with snowy linen surrounded by gilded chairs, arrangements of pink and white lilies and a dance floor at one end. The instruments for a band were set up on a platform. Hilly and Tirzah scrutinised the other women's dresses, and compared themselves with what they saw. On the whole, the pastiches they had produced from the attic didn't look too bad. The only difference was that many of the women were wearing three-quarter length skirts and the dresses tended not to have waist seams. Mrs Bullen was wearing pale blue Duchess satin decorated with paisley patterns in darker blue, and silver and pearl beads. Her bright red hair – 'Obviously out of a bottle,'

Tirzah whispered – lay in perfectly sculpted curls on her large cranium.

More and more guests were arriving now. The girls didn't recognise anyone, but the walking about stage of the dance suited them fine. After the first wave of guests had flowed through the doors there was a lull.

Tirzah and Hilly were admiring a particularly pretty girl in perfectly simple white when Peter and David Bullen came up to them.

'Hello,' said Peter to Hilly. 'Didn't you call on my mother last week?'

'Yes, I did,' she said, looking at him gratefully. It felt good to be noticed and remembered.

David led Tirzah away to get another drink.

'I haven't seen you around here before. Have you lived here long?'

Hilly wasn't sure how to answer this.

'I was born just up the hill,' she said. 'But my family has been here for a while.'

'Oh, right.' Peter was silent for a moment. He was acutely aware that his people had appeared comet-like out of nowhere. Although he was certain that Hilly was not trying to make a point in any way, it always made him uncomfortable to think about it. During the London seasons and at Oxford he was used to concealing the newness of his money. Here it was more difficult with his parents on display.

After Hilly's last visit, his mother had remarked that she was a pretty girl, but that she seemed rather oddly dressed. 'Oh Mother,' he had replied. 'The English upper classes often go about in rags. They know who they are and where they fit in; they don't have anything to prove.'

'Ah,' his mother had said. 'I hope she wears something more appropriate to the party.'

Peter had met many a grand horse-faced girl in London wearing appalling dresses run up by the village dressmaker.

'Don't bank on it, Mother,' he told her.

He took a good look at Hilly now, remembering this conversation. She was beautiful, shining with life and happiness, pink of cheek. There was something odd about her. He looked more closely into her face.

'Good God,' he said out loud without being able to stop himself.

Hilly jumped, a hand flew to her cheek.

'What's the matter?' she asked, thinking he must have noticed how strange her clothes were.

'You're not wearing any make-up.'

'Oh dear. Should I be?' She could see quite instinctively that he thought this was no bad thing. 'Tirzah and I haven't got any. We thought we looked quite nice without it. We did look at the pictures in *Modern Woman* and quite liked all that blue stuff and those cat-like black lines, but you can't buy Max Factor in the village.'

'Don't worry. You look lovely. There really is no need for it. Not when you're young, anyway.'

Hilly smiled at him. Her full lips were just lip coloured, her skin thick and creamy, her cheeks pink with exitement. She had dark eyelashes, sherry brown eyes and reddish brown hair. Her waist was very narrow under the lace top of her dress. There was something a little unusual about the dress but it was by no means unattractive.

'Do you come down here often?' she was saying.

On the spur of the moment, he said, 'I'm down here for the whole of August. There's no one left in London.'

He had been invited to go shooting in Scotland by an Oxford friend interested in his father's City activities. He thought he might decline after all and stay near this elemental creature.

'I've never seen a girl wearing black before,' he remarked, waving a hand in the general direction of Tirzah, sitting giggling with David.

'We did wonder whether her mother might object, but in the end black went better with her hair.'

'She looks sensational. David obviously thinks so too. Both of you do. I've never seen girls like you.'

Hilly longed to tell him where the dresses had come from but bit her tongue. 'Be a bit enigmatic,' she told herself.

The other girls looked remarkably uniform with their short, permed and set hair and their hourglass shapes. They all, without exception, wore blue eye shadow, black eyeliner and red lipstick. Many of them, in spite of extreme youth, had thick, pancake make-up on as well, which made their complexions look curiously deathly. Some had done an especially bad job of it, stopping at the chin line, which looked very odd.

Miss Jones, neat in beige chiffon and pearls, appeared at Peter's elbow. She smiled coolly at Hilly.

'I'm sorry to take you away, Peter, but your mother wants you to help with the seating plan.'

'Are you sure, Jill? Can't you help her?'

'No, she wants you.'

Peter sighed, grinned apologetically at Hilly, and went to find his majestic mother. Hilly went and joined Tirzah and David.

David was squarer than Peter in spite of being younger, and looked more like his father. His hair sprung vividly off his brow, and he seemed to take himself a good deal less seriously. Tirzah and he were discussing art avidly and Hilly sat beside them, dreaming and sipping her champagne and watching the world pass by.

When the time came for everyone to sit down for dinner, Tirzah and Hilly were separated; Leora and Geoffrey were on the same table.

Hilly sat between two young men down from London. This was the only part of the evening she didn't enjoy as much. Her charmless companions talked across her about shooting, mutual friends and parties, and made little attempt to engage her in conversation.

The food, however, was more delicious than anything Hilly had eaten before. She decided not to bother with the two aliens from Mars on either side of her but to enjoy what was before her. The first course was smoked salmon mousse with cucumber, followed by chicken in a creamy, faintly spiced sauce with grapes, served with rice and delicious salad. For pudding there were raspberries with thick yellow cream, no doubt from the local Jersey herd. Hilly was very used to enjoying her own company, and the details of everyone's appearance, and even the dull, exclusive conversation held across her, were of interest.

The band came on to the platform as coffee was being served with chocolates. Hilly felt somewhat full inside her tight lacing, and considered for a moment asking one of the young men to loosen her corset. She smiled as she stood up, excusing herself politely, and went to find Tirzah to get her to perform this vital service away from prying eyes.

Tirzah was seated next to David, and they had monopolised each other throughout dinner. All the young men on the table had been vying for her attention. Her black dress and extreme youth were a startling combination at this party, which was otherwise as conventionally smart as Miss Jones could assist Mrs Bullen in making it.

'Tirzah, will you come with me for a minute?'

Tirzah got up immediately. Loud, exaggerated wails came from her assembled swains. She held herself like a queen in response, a haughty smile playing about her lips, and accompanied Hilly to the bathroom. There, there were maids ready with needles and thread, face powder, Floris soap and a bed to lie on if you felt tired. It was lovely and Hilly thought she could happily retreat up here if she went on being ignored. She could always go home with Leora and Geoffrey at midnight.

Tirzah eased her laces a little at the back and asked Hilly to do the same for her.

'Lovely food. Lovely champagne. Honestly, it was such a treat, I didn't mind that the men sitting beside me ignored me.'

'Did they? That's very rude. David was sweet, and the other men on the table followed his lead. It was all very flirty and fun. There were some nice girls as well. I told them all about where our dresses came from, and they were intrigued.'

'I saw Geoffrey looking very happy at their table as well.'

'Oh good. He does like a party, I know. But being so ill he hasn't had much opportunity.'

'And Leora has positively blossomed.'

Hilly felt as if she was the only one who wasn't having very much fun. She felt a bit dashed, because she had been so excited beforehand. Still, there was lots more evening to go, and Tirzah seemed to have gathered far more young men than she could handle. Perhaps some of them would dance with her.

They looked at their faces in the mirror. Hilly carefully avoided taking advantage of the powder provided, remembering Peter's words. Tirzah dashed the swansdown puff across her fine nose smiling at herself in the mirror.

They went downstairs to see what else they could see. Peter was standing in the hall, looking up.

'There you are,' he said to Hilly. 'Mother stuck me on a table of insufferable debs. What was your table like?'

Hilly thought once more that she had better not tell the whole truth.

'Lovely,' she said, smiling and referring to the dinner.

'Would you like to dance?'

The band had started playing in the marquee and Peter led Hilly on to the dancefloor. She felt a bit uncertain about her dancing, although Leora had taught her and Tirzah to foxtrot and waltz to the ancient wind-up gramophone. The odd thing was, she seemed to anticipate Peter's every move. It felt strange and magical. She knew she was dancing very well and so was he.

She noticed him looking down at her with a puzzled expression. It reflected a feeling she had inside herself as well. They seemed to fit together like two halves of a nut inside a shell. The dancing couples around them retreated. Perfection. This was perfection, she thought.

She had never been so happy in all her short life. Peter stayed with her for the whole evening, dancing, talking, drinking champagne, walking in the moonlit rose garden and finally kissing her in the black shadow of a huge yew hedge. Things became a little unreal after a while. She tried to stop drinking the lovely cool fizzy champagne, as she knew that she wasn't quite as sober as a well-brought-up girl should be. Peter was practically carrying her everywhere anyway, so she never disgraced herself by falling flat on her face.

She forgot about everyone else. Leora came to say she was taking Geoffrey home, that he was tired but they had both had a lovely time talking to old friends and making new ones. Ralph Bullen had been particularly kind.

The party went on and on. Then it thinned out. The sky began to flush pink on the horizon. Peter led Hilly once more into the garden, and birds were singing. She felt exhausted. She had never been up so late before.

They sat on a stone bench and she went to sleep on his shoulder.

'I think I had better take you home, little one,' he said.

'Yes please, only not now. I'm happy here,' she murmured.

'You can't stay asleep here,' he said. He helped her to her feet and took her around to the garages to collect his car. It was slightly chilly in the dawn. He wrapped her in an old fur coat and put her in the front seat of the open-topped MG. She snuggled down and fell more deeply asleep.

Fourteen

1959

HILLY'S MIND STOPPED its panicky whirling. Peter had told her to follow him to London, but she was fairly certain that he hadn't meant like this. With a humble view of her talents, she had looked in *The Lady* magazine for a job with children. Now she was working as a mother's help for the Strickland family, a young couple with two small boys living in Chelsea. They had grander ideas than Mr Strickland's job as a car salesman should allow.

She quickly realised that the Stricklands couldn't afford a proper nanny and were a bit confused about how to treat her. They wanted her single-handedly to fill a servants' hall that existed only in their collective imagination. At the same time, Mrs Strickland wanted to be friends with her. It wasn't too bad so far. She had arrived the week before, and settled in before trying to work out how to see Peter without him thinking she was chasing him.

She lay on the old army camp bed in the box room they had partially cleared for her and slowed right down into her somnolent body. London was hot with Indian summer – even though it was October – a sharp exciting chill infused the air as the sun went down. Hilly's skin felt warm and dry as if taken over by some benevolent fever. Sweat broke out on her scalp and she lay very still purposely unmoving – wanting what? She knew exactly what. What had passed for love between her and Peter.

She remembered Peter's hands, which she had felt duty bound to brush off like dirt, but which unlike dirt she had been desperate to welcome on to her body. She had struggled under the unendurable tension between what she wanted and what he wanted, and what her upbringing told her she could not let him have. She pressed the base of her spine into the lumpy mattress. So odd, she thought, that you had to be shown by someone you didn't know very well the way around your own body.

She couldn't lie to herself – it was Peter who had revealed just what blissful sensations were possible. She'd had a vague idea from reading trashy novels that making love was meant to be delicious and exciting, but biology diagrams at school had made the whole thing simply embarrassing. Until, in that punt tied up beneath the willows on the lake, quite screened from the house in a green leafy tent, their kissing had aroused her so much that she couldn't help opening her legs and letting him touch her. He smiled when she cried out, her eyes opened wide by the extraordinary sensation, like being run away with by a horse. When she had been in the middle of it she hadn't known how it was going to end or even if it was ever going to end without her dying. She had been frightened. When it died away and a languorous relaxation had replaced it, she lay in his arms in the greenish dappled light. He had the tact to stop kissing her then and just held her against his chest, surprised by her surprise.

When she had recovered herself a bit she looked up at him. He propped himself up on one elbow. She glanced down and couldn't help noticing the bulge in his cream-coloured flannels. He turned to look at her.

'It's your turn now, darling.'

'What do I do?'

He looked at her amused. 'Don't you know?'

'No, actually, I don't.' She felt slightly indignant. She was gradually coming down to earth from a planet she'd never visited before and Peter sounded so matter-of-fact.

'You mean you've never done anything like this?'

She knelt up on the cushions of the punt.

'If you must know, until last week, I'd never even kissed anyone I wasn't closely related to.'

'My goodness me. I'm glad I came down here.' He pulled her down on top of him, his hands on her bottom under her thin, short dress. 'Look, I'm not going to risk getting you pregnant. It really is your turn to do something for me.'

He took her hand. She could feel the unexpected hot hardness like a sand-filled sock under his fly-buttons.

'Undo it.'

She unhooked the waistband and began to unbutton him, slipping her hand in with infinite daring. Peter groaned, so she assumed she was doing the right thing. The skin around the top was loose so she pulled gently downwards fearful of hurting him. It seemed caught at the back by a thread of skin.

Peter lowered himself from his elbows with a sigh. 'It can take quite a lot, you know,' he murmured.

She pushed the skin back over the rosebud end and then pulled it down again.

'Do it a bit faster,' he said.

She did; grasping the stem firmly in one hand, she moved her hand up and down. Peter was frowning and she stopped for a minute and bent over him.

'Am I hurting you?'

'No, no, go on, for goodness' sake. You can go a bit faster.'

She did. It gave her cramp in the muscles on the inside of her hand. He began to curl up and shudder. She recognised the nervous electrical activity from the new sensations her own body had produced.

He seemed to convulse. She felt frightened and wanted to let go, but he clasped her hand more firmly around himself and with his other hand covered the end with his handkerchief. She felt something warm, wet and viscous. He fell back on the cushions. She washed her fingers in the lake, thinking about biology class and all those tiny half-beings like tadpoles in the cool water.

She wanted to ask Peter if what she had just done for him – and he for her – was an adequate substitute for the marriage bed. She felt a little embarrassed as he lay back with his eyes closed, quite withdrawn from her. She looked down at his face. His skin was lightly tanned, his nose finely modelled with sharply defined nostrils and his hair sprang back from a high, rounded forehead, straight, thick and dark brown.

She felt anguish in her stomach looking at him. He had been hers for a minute, in the palm of her hand. Now he looked so remote. She shivered with remembered sensation and felt herself dissolving with emotion. Was being in love like this, then? A roller coaster that varied in speed between giddy plunges into physical pleasure and slow hesitating climbs to abstract affection?

She lay down on her back beside him feeling awkward. He rolled his head towards her and kissed her cheek.

'Thanks, darling,' he muttered.

She felt better immediately and asked what she wanted to know.

'Is sexual intercourse like that?'

His face was very close to hers. A lazy smile lit up his warm mouth.

'It is a bit. Sex is more mutual. You aim to come at the same time ideally. It can also be not nearly as nice as this. Not nearly so warm and comfortable.'

The wine, the sun, the delicious sensations, had robbed her of shyness.

'Tell me about it,' she said.

'I'll only get excited again. Really, you have a lovely body.' His hands were unbuttoning the front of her dress. She wasn't wearing anything underneath and he slipped his hand inside over one breast.

'Hilly by name, hilly by nature,' he muttered into her neck. Then he pulled his hand out again and did her up. 'Naughty, naughty. I think we'd better be getting back.'

Hilly felt disappointed. She was beginning to love the feel of his warm dry hands on her skin. Her nipples had particularly enjoyed the attention.

'Honestly, Hilly, I've obviously got to protect you from yourself. I've never thought about being a chaperone before. I think I'd be quite good at it – much better than some dried-up old spin who never knew what powerful forces she was protecting her charges from. You're damned responsive, you know. Some women don't seem to feel a thing.'

Hilly felt that this was a flattering comment. She finished buttoning herself up, smoothed down her hair, put her shoes back on and took a deep breath to steady herself and move into a different plane where bodies weren't so clamorous for attention. She focused on the willow branches dabbling in the lake, and thought how dull the green of their leaves looked in August, compared to the electric fireworks of spring.

Peter looked at her breasts, somewhat squashed by the outgrown dress.

'You would look wonderful in the right clothes,' he said. 'Do you own a bra?'

'Yes, but it doesn't fit me very well and it's uncomfortable.'

'I know, I'll take you shopping in London. Would you like that?'

Wouldn't she just? Something started to niggle at the back of her mind. She drew imperceptibly away from him.

'I'm sorry, I couldn't.'

'Why not? We could go up for the day, have lunch, look at the shops. Get you kitted out with something that at least fits. It would be my pleasure.'

'I'm sorry, I couldn't possibly do that.' Hilly felt like crying. All that lovely mutuality. Then this. She felt grubby.

Peter was looking into her face. 'What's the matter?'

'Please just take my word for it. I can't possibly go up to London with you.'

'I'll square it with your father. I'm sure he won't mind. He seems to like me. And I am being very responsible. I would let you go with me to London.'

'It's not that.' Hilly was acutely uncomfortable.

'What is it, then?' Peter sounded impatient. His mind had run ahead, had begun to anticipate a touch of the old Pygmalions and didn't like to be thwarted. He flattered himself on his taste in women's clothes. Hilly had a lovely waist, good breasts and ankles. She'd just suit a full-skirted, tight-waisted dress. He thought of Mrs Hornby, whom he visited sometimes in St John's Wood, teasing but professional, her voluptuous flesh bulging out of the top of her merry widow waspie. He had already begun to visualise Hilly's firm youth confined in just such a delightfully constricting garment.

'I promise you, we'll have such fun. Please, Hilly. It would give me pleasure, it really would.'

'I've just given you pleasure and now I need to be paid for it – is that right?'

'What are you talking about?' He couldn't understand the chill that had entered her voice. 'Of course I'm not going to pay you.' A thought struck him. 'You might just as well pay me. You seemed to be enjoying yourself enough.'

Hilly unbent. She giggled. She put her hand in her pocket and found a threepenny bit. She pulled it out and gave it to Peter.

'What's this?'

'Payment for my pleasure. I'm sure it's not enough but it's all I've got at the moment. Which is also why I can't come with you to London. Because I can't afford it.'

'I can though. You haven't come over all scrupulous have you?'

Hilly had a lot of pride. She knew who she was and where she fitted in. She was all for love and sex and passion. She didn't want anyone ever to feel they had to pay her for what she would freely give. She could not go to London with Peter and be treated to a day unlike her normal days, just after sharing her body with him.

'Peter, no. And that's the last thing I am going to say about it.'

He looked dejected, and she felt sorry that she had built what was no doubt a completely innocent proposal of fun into the dirt of a tart's transaction.

'Oh, well. I'm sure you know what you are doing. Mum and Dad are packing up the day after tomorrow anyway, as Mum wants to catch the autumn season in London. We won't be back down here until Christmas. I don't suppose you could come up to London and stay with friends?'

He sort of knew this wasn't possible. He was just trying to make the situation seem normal. This really beautiful girl was from a very good family but one so fallen on hard times as to be poorer than he could understand. His father had made his million when Peter had been too young to remember what things had been like before. Money had never been an issue for him, and he didn't know what its presence or absence could mean.

'Look, Hilly, I think you're a very special girl. You don't seem to be full of all the nonsense that the debs are. They're obsessed with marriage and babies and money and going to the right parties. I'm bored stiff with them. But you are something else. What we just shared seemed so natural and right. You weren't all coy about it. So many other girls would take, but then refuse to give in return, come over all modest and pretend that they didn't know what I meant. I loved the frank way you just got on with it. I loved your serious expression as you tried to get it right. But I'm worried about you. What are you going to do stuck down here meeting no one?'

'Oh, I don't know. Help Leora look after Daddy. And read. I love reading.'

'Don't you want to go to university or something?'

'I'd love to. But look, Peter, you have to understand. There isn't any money at all. I'm stuck until some nice curate asks Daddy for my hand in marriage.'

'That's not right. This isn't a Jane Austen novel. You could do anything you liked. You could come up to London and get a job.' He felt frustrated. She had begun to look dull around the eyes and her mouth drooped.

'You can't just stay around here in a kind of dream. You're eighteen for God's sake, not twelve.'

'You don't understand, Peter. There's nothing for me. Daddy is really very sick now and needs lots of looking after. It's not fair to leave Leora alone with him, particularly as Tirzah's family in America has sent her money to go to art school as her father was killed in the war. Marjorie is in America, Eric is in India, so there's only me. I'm lucky to have Leora to help me.'

'Why does Leora stick around if she's got family in America?'

'I think she loves Daddy. He definitely loves her. When I was sixteen, he explained things to me. He is very honest.'

'What do you mean?' Peter asked gently.

'Well, she's his mistress I suppose.'

'Oh, I see.'

'They're just like an old married couple now. When Geoffrey came back from Dunkirk after Mummy died, he found Leora looking after me and Tirzah. She actually wet-nursed me and probably saved my life. He fell in love with her and she with him. It seems strange as she didn't know where her husband was, but she'd only been married a couple of months before they were parted by the war – perhaps she didn't know him very well.'

'War does funny things to people,' said Peter. 'Death and all that. Makes people feel sexy.'

Hilly tried not to look shocked. She paused. Then she said:

'I think I knew about them before he told me. He also explained carefully that she wouldn't marry him because she didn't know whether her husband was dead or not.'

'I see.' Peter unbuttoned her dress again and buried his face in her breasts.

After a while he said: 'Hilly. I do adore you. Can we wait until Christmas and then think about what to do next? I'll be down sometimes for shooting and so on. I can see you then. But really I think we'll have to be patient and wait. I haven't sorted my own life out yet. My father might be rolling but he hasn't given me a bean. He always made it clear to me that after Oxford I was on my own.'

He absent-mindedly played with her nipples, his voice slightly muffled by the proximity of his face to her chest.

Hilly felt warm and light. Every time she'd been with Peter, part of the tension had come from not knowing whether any of this was real. She'd had so little physical affection in her life that his attentions came to her with extra loading. Without a mother, hugging at home was rare. The warm lengthy cradling in his arms and his sudden kisses were all so new to her unaccustomed skin. What he was saying now told her that his emotions might be engaged as well. She had been making heroic efforts not to cling to him at the end of each of their meetings, so distant did the prospect of more of the same seem to her. Her dignity was very important to her. She'd read enough to know that clinging, along with weeping and moaning and wanting more than a man was prepared to give, were all likely to induce revulsion.

Fifteen

IN THE QUIET HOT CAPSULE of August in the country, nothing of the outside world intruded. Peter could revert to his sensual, physical, uncomplicated self. His social insecurity about the newness of his money couldn't prick the bubble of his brief affair with Hilly. But seeing her in Fortnum & Mason's Fountain Restaurant in Piccadilly, he felt dangerously out of control and exposed. For one thing, she didn't fit in; she was out of context. No make-up and cheap-looking clothes. She was sitting waiting for him when he arrived, and if she hadn't spotted him hovering in the doorway, he would have scarpered and dealt with the consequences later.

Her face was blurred with insecurity. Her eyebrows gathered in an anxious frown. Her lips twitched as she tried to smile at him. He came round to her side of the table and bent down to kiss her cheek. For a faint second the firmness of her skin and its complete lack of powdery scent drew him back into her bubble. He took a seat opposite her and grasped her hand under the small table.

'Darling,' he said softly.

Her lips, narrow with anxiety, blossomed into the kissable width and fullness that he had adored. He warmed himself with the thought that he was doing the right thing by her. He wished they were back in the punt and his hand was inside that absurd, straining bodice once more. On the other side of the table, dressed in a thin tweed suit with ghastly buttons, and a garish green felt hat, her charm was almost non-existent.

Sitting there in silence, he became aware of familiar voices behind him:

'Isn't that the man you were dancing with so much last night?'

'Oh God, yes.'

'Who's he with? Can you see?'

'Never seen her before.'

'She's rather pretty. Doesn't look like "One of us, dear" though.'

'I think she looks frightful. What on earth has she got on her head?'

'Funny of him to bring her here. I wonder why. Lyons Corner House would be more her style.'

'Perhaps he's giving her a lovely treat up West.'

Peter prayed with all his might that Hilly wouldn't realise what they were talking about. He recognised the girl's voice. It was the Hon. Violet Steen. He had danced with her a lot at the Motcombs' dance the night before. Very pretty she was too. She had been wearing a Dior knock-off in pink and black striped Duchess satin. It was strapless – what his father called a 'gownless evening strap'. She had been the only girl he had met so far who pulled her bodice down, rather than tweaked it up all the time. He'd found her very alluring. Violet had pressed against him most encouragingly in the conservatory, although hoops, tulle and the stiffening of her petticoats had allowed very little contact below the waist, and the stiff boning above had meant that touching her breasts was a very academic exercise.

He could see Hilly looking at him questioningly and felt irritated. This was his world, his life – what was she doing in it? She belonged in some sex-drenched rural idyll. She was the shepherdess with tumbled petticoats behind a haystack. She was for pastoral lovemaking with no strings. She was Chloe or Phyllis to his lovelorn but irresponsible shepherd. What was she doing buttoned into cheap tweed in the most sophisticated and urban of environments? He was angry and embarrassed by the voices behind him, but he couldn't help being influenced by them into seeing her as they did: cheap, gauche, unsophisticated, very, very young and inexperienced. He hardly knew her; why was he taking such a risk with his reputation by appearing with her in public? Really, they were right. Lyons Corner House would have been far more suitable.

'I haven't got much time,' she was saying, her physical agitation very apparent. 'I've got to baby sit this evening.'

'What exactly are you doing in London?' he asked.

'Well…' She was blushing slightly. The urban air had done no good to her complexion at all and it seemed dulled. Peter remembered its almost crystalline, pearly texture, all over her body – the bits she'd allowed him to examine. He stirred physically at the thought, but the sensation died down when he looked at her again. It simply wasn't the same girl. She looked like a housemaid on her day off.

'I'm working for a family in Chelsea, looking after their children. Collecting them from school and helping with homework – not that I am much good at that.' She tried to laugh, but it came out as a choking cough. The city dirt in the air was getting to her lungs.

'Why on earth are you doing that?'

'Well, you did suggest I come to London and get a job. I'm not qualified for anything else.'

'For God's sake, that's not a job for someone like you.'

She was quite still, her face looked set. 'What do you mean, "someone like me"?'

Peter had the grace to feel embarrassed, which made him angry once again. 'You know very well what I mean. Do they know who your father is?'

'No. And they don't care. And nor do I.'

'But surely your father minds you being a servant?'

'Goodness, I hadn't thought of it like that. I'm officially a mother's help. It's nice being in Chelsea, near Tirzah. Although she's too busy studying to see much of me. Also, when she came to tea, and Mrs Strickland came home in the middle of it, she wasn't very welcoming to poor Tirzah. She kept making bright remarks about how wonderful it was that there were so many girl art students these days. And how liberating trousers were. And how washing must be difficult in digs. Until poor Tirzah felt she must leave. I could see how she was feeling, but I couldn't do anything about it. You see, I wanted to keep the job…' Hilly paused, then she muttered: 'To be near you.'

'Oh God,' thought Peter. 'I am so stupid, why did I say anything to encourage her to come to London? She doesn't fit in. I can't possibly be seen going around with a nanny. They'd all laugh at me.' Back into his consciousness came the voices of Violet and her man friend sitting at the bar. They were talking about a dance that night to which Peter hadn't been invited. Hilly was talking in a soft voice, but he didn't want to hear what she was saying.

'They're bringing out the younger girl this year. You know, Penelope. Antonia is engaged already, I hear.'

Violet said, 'Oh really. Who to?'

Her voice sounded sharp. The query, which she had tried to keep casual, was of excruciating, all-consuming importance to her. An engagement ring was the desired end product of all the teas, lunches, cocktail parties, race-meetings, dances, hair appointments, make-up and dancing lessons – as a brass ring was on the merry-go-round. They were very similar in lots of ways – lights, colours, music and a ring at the end of it. If you managed it first time round the circuit, you won. If your second season didn't produce a proposal, you were pretty well on the shelf.

One part of Peter's mind was aware how stupid and shallow all the social jockeying was. But its grip on him when he was in its physical area was difficult to unstick.

'Old Jerry Stanford-Cooper.'

Peter, tuned into Violet more than he was to poor Hilly sitting opposite, heard the relief in Violet's voice.

'Oh God, he's been hanging around on the deb scene for simply years. He must be at least thirty-five. He's asked everyone to marry him. Antonia must have been pretty desperate.'

This was fairly inaccurate, Peter knew. But if a man got engaged, particularly to a long-term player, he couldn't be seen to be merely fussy about marrying the right person. He had to be a hopeless, unattractive failure.

'He's awfully short isn't he,' Violet drawled on. 'I've only danced with him once and couldn't help noticing that he had hairs growing out of his nose.'

The man roared with laughter. 'He's rich though. Family's sitting on coal.'

Peter felt gratified that Violet had danced with him more than once. He unconsciously touched his own nose.

Hilly picked up her knitted woollen gloves off the table. She'd sipped her tea, but the sandwiches were untouched. The cress lay sadly around them. Then she dropped one of her gloves on the floor and, bending to pick it up, hit her head on the table knocking her hat off. 'What are you doing down there?' Peter's voice sounded impatient.

'I'm just picking up a glove and my napkin.'

He bent down to look, catching her kneeling on the floor surreptitiously dabbing her eyes with the stiff linen.

'Do get up.'

She rose to her feet. He could see perfectly well that she was crying. The tip of her nose had gone pink in contrast to the strained, bleached look of the rest of her face.

'Oh God, is she blubbing now?'

Peter seemed acutely tuned in to Violet's carrying tones.

'Looks like a housemaid in trouble. What has naughty Peter been up to?'

He turned around now, certain Violet meant him to hear and torn between his two selves: the kind, clever man who'd rocked Hilly's delicious body against his chest under a willow tree in August, and a socially insecure creature scrabbling to fit in with the in-crowd. The kind boy would have cuffed Violet's pancaked face with the back of his fingers and called out the supercilious man with her. The London Peter smiled, embarrassed, and hoped against hope that tea with Hilly wouldn't be held against him.

Violet smiled warmly back at him. 'Peter, darling, how are you?'

He found himself saying, 'All the better after last night, Violet.'

'Will you be at the Bateman dance this evening?'

Peter felt the blind panic of the uninvited.

'Well, no actually. I have to have dinner with my parents.'

'Couldn't you come on afterwards?'

He knew she knew that he hadn't been invited and was playing with him. He felt the sharp cruelty. But it was part of the game. He couldn't just pick the bits of the game that abraded his soul the least; he had to play it all.

'Actually, I haven't been invited.'

Violet had scored for embarrassing him. He now scored for being what he thought of as coolly honest.

'By the way, this is John Highmore. Darling, this is Peter Bullen. From Surrey.' She giggled.

Peter remembered Hilly and his manners. He didn't want to, but he had to introduce her. He also knew that when they heard her voice they would immediately identify her, however odd her clothes were, as one of them.

The thought made him turn around, a relieved smile on his face. But Hilly had vanished. Stricken with guilt he ran over to push through the revolving door. Looking both ways, he thought he could just see the back of her ghastly suit disappearing around the corner into Piccadilly. It was getting on for six o'clock. His chin drooped on to his chest as he turned and went inside to have a cocktail with Violet and John.

Sixteen

SHRILL UNBROKEN VOICES came up to Hilly through the still air. It was a sullen, grey, late autumn afternoon and she was off duty until teatime. She lay in her chilly attic room on a narrow cast-iron bedstead too crooked and chipped for the dormitories downstairs. The boys seemed far away, with their skinny knees, emphatic remarks and sudden, extreme violence. Images rose in her mind of cuffings and raggings. They weren't adverse to more girly methods of inflicting pain either, like hair pulling and pinching. Their ears were always dirty.

Hilly sometimes attempted to do something about the younger ones' ears with a grey flannel moulded over one finger. The orange wax and black dirt were immovable. She wondered what their mothers did about it at home. Not very much. The deposits seemed archaeological. Her mind strayed from ears, noses and knees to her own position.

When she had had to leave the Stricklands, Hilly went home to see Leora and Geoffrey. At least Peter had jolted her out of penniless apathy in her tatty old family home. She now felt the independence of earning, even a pittance, and knew that work was the key to her future. It was no good relying on men to rescue you: you had to rescue yourself. But she didn't want to try being a nanny again. It was too difficult dealing with other people's social unease and trying to live 'as a family' – let alone being exposed to predatory frustrated husbands.

She had found the post of under-matron at Lodswell Preparatory School for Boys advertised in *The Times*. She'd applied, been interviewed and given the job within days. It was hard work. Instead of two little boys she had to deal with 150. But there was no one to object if she scolded them for being rude, and she could even report them to the headmaster if they were really awful. Some of the older ones were quite nice and friendly, some of the little ones endearing. The masters ranged from strange old bachelors to slightly less strange younger bachelors. The headmaster's wife was kind, and Hilly had been granted compassionate leave very easily on the occasions when her father's lung had started to give severe cause for concern. She was pleased with her new job.

She'd managed to push Peter to the back of her mind and settle into the school routine, getting to know the staff and establishing a place for herself. One of the masters in particular interested her. He was one of the younger ones – in his late thirties, she judged. He was a form master but he also taught art. She had been shocked when she had noticed his hands, knotted and bent with scar tissue. Sister had told her the scars were caused by war wounds, but she didn't know any details.

'Mr Jerusalem's dreadfully sensitive about it,' she'd said. 'Whatever happened, he got a medal for it. The boys all adore him and wouldn't dream of being cheeky about it.

They know it would upset him. He was an artist before the war apparently. His hands ache unbearably if he does more than the odd quick sketch. I gave him some pomade divine to rub into them. I hope it helped.'

Hilly had seen some of his pencil sketches: a boy's head bent over a book, figures running on the playing fields, Sister disappearing down a corridor. The headmaster had had them framed and hung around the school.

They began talking at lunch when they were seated on the same table. Mr Jerusalem had a very light touch with the boys and Hilly learned a lot about how to relate to them from him. A few weeks into the autumn term, he sent a note to her via one of the boys, inviting her to have a drink with him in the local pub.

She sent a note back accepting, immediately. She needed for her own peace of mind to forget about Peter. She couldn't love someone as shallow as him, one minute overwhelming her with affection, the next embarrassed to be seen with her in public. Stephen Jerusalem might have been older, but he was gentle and kind and his face was pleasing. He had thick black hair and an interesting oriental look around his eyes. When he wasn't smiling and laughing with the boys, his expression was still and withdrawn.

He intrigued her. Besides, she was healthy and young and knew a bit about sex now, and he was the only remotely attractive man for miles. She laughed at herself when she realised this.

When she came off duty after lights out, she went up to her room to change out of her uniform. She felt a vague excitement at having a date at all. Her life had been very dull. She put on a clean blouse, nylon stockings and the tweed suit and green hat that she had worn to meet Peter.

It wouldn't look out of place in a country pub.

She laced up her brogues, set off down all the flights of stairs to the bottom and left by the back door. It was dark, so she took a torch. He had asked her to meet him in the village as he had come off duty a lot earlier. She felt free as she strode down the yellowish drive and out through the gates. She turned left and walked along the right-hand side of the road the half-mile into the village. There were two pubs, the Bull, which was rather a low dive, much favoured by the local agricultural workers, and the Swan, which had pretensions to be a road house and was built in the mock-Tudor style of the 1930s. She went into the saloon bar and saw Stephen sitting on a stool talking to the landlord. He looked around as she came through the door and a smile lit up his face. She warmed herself on his happiness at seeing her.

He slid off his stool and led her to a table. Then he asked her what she would like to drink. She had no idea, so she chose pink gin because she thought it sounded sophisticated, and he brought it back to her, faintly roseate, bitter and strong. Then he went back to the bar and picked up his pint.

'Right,' he said, as he settled himself beside her on the plush banquette. 'Tell me all about yourself.'

He smiled and looked so genuinely interested that she started telling him all about home and who lived there. She didn't, of course, tell him about Leora and her father. He was very interested in Tirzah and told her he had been at the Slade School of Art before the war.

He asked questions that prompted her to tell him more. Talking to him made her home seem exotic and interesting instead of just ordinary. He bought them more drinks and carried on prompting her. She noticed that she had heard precisely nothing about him, so she tried to tease out what she could. The atmosphere changed immediately.

'I'm just a dull old schoolmaster and have been since I was invalided out of the Navy,' he replied.

She wasn't going to be thwarted, however, and cleverly hit upon the subject he was really interested in: the boys, and their various talents as artists.

'I'm so lucky with the headmaster. He is unusual in that he is really interested in art instead of just Latin. Lots of the boys from Lodswell go on to develop fine abilities at public school and at least as many go to art school as to Oxbridge.'

It was obvious to Hilly that Stephen was an excellent teacher. She wanted him to teach her; she felt so ignorant and under-educated in his company. He was flattered by her attention. The all-male atmosphere of a boys' prep school wasn't conducive to courtship and he had never been drawn to the other permed, prim and proper under-matrons, who left with monotonous regularity when they found that the masters were mostly not the marrying kind. Sister was a dear, but gruff and at least 60. There was something unusual about Hilly; he couldn't put his finger on it. She seemed hungry for life and free of pretensions.

They went out often after that. The headmaster's wife was a bit frosty about their relationship at first, but noting that everything was conducted in public, relaxed her vigilance. In her view, Hilly was a little too free in her manner – it was a good thing she wasn't working in a public school. At Lodswell even the oldest boys were more interested in cricket and rugby than the undoubtedly pretty Hilly.

Seventeen

'WOMEN AREN'T ALLOWED to go to Jewish funerals. I've never been to one before.' Leora let go of Hilly's hand and walked away through grass still crisp with frost.

Watching Geoffrey's narrow coffin descend into the earth was an end and a beginning for her. She had to get on with her life. She wasn't even 40 yet. The last 18 years had been a matter of bringing up Tirzah as best she could. She felt a lingering guilt sometimes about her daughter. In all honesty she should have followed her family to America as soon as the war was over. But she had married Philippe de Rosemann, an older man she hardly knew, in order to grow up and get away from the smothering love and spoiling of home. She'd tasted independence and, anyway, by the end of the war she had been in love with Geoffrey. She hadn't known how long he would live. She couldn't have left him. There was also Hilly, her foster daughter. Having probably saved her life, she had wanted very much to see her safely through to adulthood.

On their last night she had lain down fully clothed on the

bed beside her lover. Geoffrey sat propped up on pillows to assist his breathing; the nurse was downstairs making tea.

He awoke. Looking straight ahead at the wardrobe, he said, 'Emma? George?' in a pleased and questioning tone of voice.

Leora was ashamed of the jealousy that had jolted her. She remembered Emma with gratitude and love. She had never known George.

She put her hand on his thin arm. 'Geoffrey, darling, do you need anything?'

He turned his head very slowly and looked straight at her. In the same tone, he said, 'Leora?' He seemed to smile. Then his breathing came with more difficulty than before. She was just climbing off the bed to fetch the nurse when the look in his eyes stopped her. She stood beside him, bending to put her arms around him, to hold him tight and keep him with her. She felt his hand touch her waist. Her cheek was near his mouth, and he seemed to be trying to say something. His lips fluttered against her skin.

'Leora ... love.' His breath rattled in his throat, and she tried once more to pull away and get the nurse. He shook his head mutely.

She felt as if she herself were unable to breathe and clung to him, her cheek pressed to his. The struggle was brief and Geoffrey was quiet. She knew the desperate attempts to suck air into that damaged single lung were over. All was very still. She held him for what seemed like ages. Then, from being there even after he was still, he just wasn't. Geoffrey had gone. With him went any ties to the great rotting house on the hill.

For years, her responsibilities at Leith Hill had seemed so much more real to her than her life with her family before the war. She'd been afraid that she might never be allowed to grow up to make a decision for herself; that after the war, if she took Tirzah to America, her daughter might be swept up into the same kind of claustrophobic ease. Then again, Tirzah would have had the benefits of money and an expensive education. Leora didn't think her daughter was any the worse for the austerity of her upbringing. She had an extraordinary artistic talent and the art master at the grammar school had fostered it perfectly adequately. Tirzah was happy and as independent as she wanted her to be.

Leora gazed at the gravestones all around her with unseeing eyes. It would be best if she left for Paris as soon as possible. She needed for her own sake as well as Tirzah's to try to find out what happened to Philippe. He had no other relations left in Paris.

She had already written to her family to tell them what she was going to do and that she would come to America afterwards. Tirzah had been accepted at Chelsea School of Art; Hilly had a job she seemed to enjoy. If either of them needed to, they could join her across the Atlantic as well. In a curious way it was a relief that Geoffrey had died. Hoping that he would somehow get better had exhausted her. The certainty of losing him was easier to bear. She began to look forward. She would never forget Geoffrey, or Philippe for that matter.

Hovering near the grave as the sexton arrived with his spade, the two girls watched Leora's slender back from across the cold graveyard. Tirzah kissed Hilly's cold cheek. 'I'll just go and see if Mother's all right. She hasn't cried yet, you know. I think she's very shocked.'

'OK.' Hilly tried to smile at Tirzah, but her mouth trembled uncomfortably, so she bit her lip instead.

'Don't stand here watching them fill the grave.'

'I won't.'

Tirzah went and Hilly turned towards the lychgate.

'Hilly.'

She'd been ignoring him but she couldn't forget that he was there. She continued on her way, physically aware of his presence. It felt wrong to be so alive that her skin wanted to jump off her bones, in spite of her grief for her father.

'Hilly, for goodness' sake, stop.'

She realised she was practically running in her attempts to get away from him and her own desire. He broke into a run himself, caught up with her and grabbed her arm. She stopped and stared at the ground.

'Please let go of me, Peter. Someone might see. One of your smart friends maybe. Don't want to be seen consorting with a servant, do we?'

She couldn't bear to look at him. An image of her languid self in the punt flashed upon her inward eye. He held her arm tightly. She could feel his sudden anger transmit itself through his fingers.

'Hilly. Look at me. I'm sorry, OK?'

'You're sorry, are you? That's nice. Perhaps I'll let you mess about with my body a bit more if you say sorry.'

'Hilly, I know I behaved badly and I probably deserve that kind of beastliness.'

'I'm upset, right? My father died. I loved him. He was the only parent I knew. I've got an excuse to behave badly. I don't think you did though.'

'Hilly, I'm so sorry. I came down from London when I heard. My parents are away but I thought I must come to Geoffrey's funeral to represent them.'

'So correct, aren't you.' She sneered while her guts turned to water at his touch.

'I wanted to see you to say sorry for that awful business in the Fountain. I really didn't mean it to happen; it was a mistake.'

She nerved herself to look up at him at last.

'Peter, I don't care about that and I don't care about you any more. So you don't have to feel responsible, OK?'

'I don't. I just want to know what you're doing now.'

'Something suitable for my qualifications. I'm an under-matron in a boy's prep school.'

'I've got my car outside; can I give you a lift home?'

Hilly looked around for Tirzah and Leora but they must have left in the hired car after seeing her with Peter and assuming that he would look after her. Hilly had kept very quiet about meeting Peter in London.

'All right.' She let herself be pulled. The skin on the inside of her arm was humming with his hand's contact, and transmitting waves of nervous energy across her breasts.

Peter had a battered pre-war Jaguar – Ralph certainly didn't spoil his boys with extravagant allowances. He shrewdly wanted them to make their own way in the world, as he had. Peter opened the passenger door for Hilly and then climbed in himself. He sat staring straight ahead through the windscreen. 'I don't want to take you home. I want to take you off somewhere by ourselves.'

Hilly sat silent. He was honest, anyway. No hypocrisy about inappropriate behaviour at funerals. Last summer he had introduced her to her body. It craved him now. She was finding it hard to see beyond that, but dusk was falling and Leora and Tirzah had arranged a small tea party for the funeral guests.

'I really must go back and have a cup of tea and be polite. It would look very odd if I didn't turn up.'

Peter had been gripping the steering wheel. He relaxed slightly.

'I'll take you there, then.'

Hilly turned to him on the squashy leather seat. She put her hand on his forearm. 'Afterwards, perhaps?'

He turned and smiled at her. Then he bent forwards and kissed her.

'I haven't forgotten anything, you know,' he said. 'I really am sorry. You must believe me. What happened last summer between us was far more important than what happened in London; I want you to remember that.'

He started the car and drove back to the house where Hilly and Tirzah had been born. When they arrived, Hilly jumped out and told Peter to park in the old stable yard. That way they wouldn't be blocked in and could get away quickly.

'What are you planning?' she asked herself as she entered the house. She took off her coat, hung it in the glass porch and then went through into the drawing room.

Leora, who loved parties, had bought a case of sherry. She understood from an ancient book of etiquette she'd found in the library that this was what the British drank at funerals. Mrs Dawson, who cleaned for her, had gathered the village ladies and made a good tea: 'To keep the chill out, dear. Hanging about in graveyards is very unhealthy.' They'd hired a shiny silver urn and were dispensing the tea and brown sherry.

Hilly felt thirsty and hungry. She took a huge, scalding cup of tea and swallowed it in big, thirst-quenching gulps. Then she accepted a glass of sherry and downed it, holding out her glass for another. Taking a ham sandwich, she went over to speak to the vicar.

'So sorry about your father, Hilda. Such a brave man. Very quick at the end though, wasn't it. I am very sorry that you are orphaned at such a young age. Have you thought what you will do?'

'The house will be sold now, and I've got a job. Tirzah is at art school in Chelsea. Leora is going back to Paris. Marjorie is in the States and Eric is in India running his school. They couldn't get over for the funeral.'

'I don't think I've met Marjorie?'

'She's my sister. I've hardly met her either. She married during the war – a Lieutenant Colonel Wiggins. She's got three beautiful children and lives in California. She's much older than me.'

'Ah, I see. Oh, look, Leora has emerged. I must go and have a word with her. Many condolences once again. But I am sure your dear father has gone to a better place. He was good man.' The vicar said this with complete sincerity, holding Hilly's hands in his and looking into her face. Then he went.

Hilly poured herself some more sherry. The reckless feeling that had come over her in the churchyard returned. She looked around for Peter. He was on the other side of the room with Tirzah. As she walked across, village ladies, the odd regimental friend and neighbours murmured their condolences. There was a good turnout in spite of Geoffrey's unconventional relationship with Leora.

'Hello, Tirzah. Good turnout isn't it?'

'Yes, it really is. I think a lot of people were very fond of Geoffrey. I know I was.'

Peter said, 'Are you staying here tonight, Hilly?'

'Yes, I am.'

'Would you like to come for a drive?'

'Oh yes, Hilly, do go. It would do you good to get away from all this for a bit,' said Tirzah, then turning to Peter. 'She's been in the house for weeks, nursing her father. She needs a change.'

'Yes,' said Hilly coolly. 'A drive would be nice. I'm just going to get myself another drink.'

She felt excitement rising under her ribs. The pain of her father's loss was pushed into the background. She turned her back to the room and swallowed another glass of the dark amontillado sherry. Then she went back to Peter carrying a full one.

'I'll just have this one and then I'll come.'

Peter looked at her. She was wearing a black suit with a black turtle-neck underneath. Her skin was very pale with red circles on her cheeks. Her eyes glittered. She had succumbed to having her lovely bright brown hair cut and it was in a short curly perm. She finished her drink and put the glass down.

'Shouldn't I stay and help clear up?' She knew what Tirzah would say. 'No, don't worry. I'm going to put Mummy to bed and the village ladies have offered to do everything. I've got to get up to London for class early tomorrow.'

Peter began to play Hilly's waiting game.

'I could give you a lift to the station now?' he asked, his eyebrows slightly raised.

'No, I'll stay here with Mummy. I think she's exhausted. Thanks a lot, but I want to look after her a bit.'

'Fine. Coming then, Hilly?'

He took her arm and drew her away. The guests had

thinned out, and she shook a few hands and thanked people for coming as she led Peter out through the kitchens and the back door to where the Jaguar was waiting in the stable yard. It was dark by now; Peter held the door open for Hilly before getting in himself.

In the leathery gloom he seized her and began kissing her frantically. She pushed him away.

'For goodness' sake, someone might come out. This is very shocking behaviour at a funeral. Don't you realise I'm recently bereaved?'

'Sorry. God, I always seem to be saying sorry to you. I'm not sorry about kissing you. Let's go.'

He put the car into gear and they moved off, headlights lighting up the tatty stable yard as they swung out into the drive.

'What's going to happen to the old place?'

'Daddy left it to Marjorie, Leora and me in equal parts. But Leora has renounced her share because her family in America will welcome her back now. Eric had some separate settlement when he was twenty-one. We'll have to sell it.'

'Not much of a market for these big old places that need a lot spending on them. Unless a school wants it or something.'

'I know. I don't expect very much once death duties have been paid and Marjorie has had her share.'

'What's Marjorie like? I've never met her.'

'I've only met her once. She was so desperate to get away from home after my mother died that she married the first man who asked her and ran away to the States.'

'Why was she in such a hurry?'

'Daddy said she was a bit of a prude and was terribly shocked when my mother was pregnant. Then, when Leora stayed on after Daddy came home, that was too much for her and she fled.'

'Leora was more of a nurse than anything else, wasn't she?'

'Except that she truly loved my father and stuck with him through thick and thin for eighteen years. Disapproval, social ostracism, his poor health. I don't know why she did really, except that after the war there was nothing for her to go home to in Paris. Her family stayed in the States, and any cousins had been shipped out to concentration camps. I don't think she could face the French after that.'

'I don't blame her.'

They drove on for a bit in silence.

'Do you want to come back to the parents' house? They're away. It would be just us.'

'What are you suggesting, Mr Bullen? And me so young and innocent.'

'Don't start that again, please, Hilly. I promise you that nothing will happen that you don't want.'

'That's just what I'm afraid of.'

'You are a little tease. Do you know that?'

They were driving along in a deeply sunken lane, the headlights illuminating roots of trees that veined the sides. Peter espied a track and swung the car into the turning, driving away from the road and around a corner so that passing motorists could not see them.

Then he stopped the engine and turned on the inside light.

'Do you want a cigarette?'

'OK. It'll go nicely with the sherry.' Hilly drew a half-full bottle out of her handbag, took the lid off and had a long swig.

'How much of that have you had?'

'I don't really know and I really don't care.'

She rested her head on his shoulder. It was warm in the car and quiet. The front seat was a soft, leathery bench. Peter began to undo the buttons of her jacket. His hand found its way through her waistband and under her jersey.

'You've got such incredibly smooth skin,' he mumbled into her neck.

She stubbed out her cigarette, which she wasn't enjoying, in the ashtray and took another swig of sherry before putting the cork back in her bottle. Then she gently pushed Peter away, took off her jacket and pulled her jersey over her head.

'I see you've invested in a bra,' Peter said. He was leaning against the window watching her slip the straps off her shoulders, and take it off.

She lifted her bottom off the seat and pulled her skirt down over her hips. Then she pulled off her knickers and threw them into the back seat. Peter leaned over and put the blow heater on. 'Are you drunk, darling?'

'No,' said Hilly inaccurately. 'I'm in love. With you.'

'Good, because I'm in love with you too and I think you look wonderful like that.'

Hilly had failed to remove her stockings and the dark-coloured tops made her look like a legless Greek marble statue in the faint light.

After a bit, Hilly said rather quietly, 'That hurts.'

Peter groaned.

'Shall I stop?'

'I think so.'

'I'm sorry. This was a mistake. I'll get out of the car. You can put your things back on.'

The atmosphere of reckless abandon had left them. Hilly, back to herself, couldn't imagine what she was doing naked in a car in the woods. Peter walked away, smoking and trying not to mind. Hilly dressed. When he turned back, she was sitting demurely in the front seat.

'I feel rather sick,' she said.

Peter leaned across her and opened the car door. She put her head out just in time.

'I don't know what I'm doing,' she said, when she had recovered a bit. 'I think you'd better take me home.'

Eighteen

PETER STARTED THE ENGINE and drove them both back to the house. They said good night to each other in constrained voices. He kissed her cheek.

'Look, I'm sorry about everything. It all seems so complicated. Will you be all right?'

'Oh, yes, I'll be fine. I've got to go back to work tomorrow. I had a few weeks leave to look after Daddy, but now it's all over I must go back.'

'Why did you leave those people in Chelsea?'

'It was OK for a month or so but then Mr Strickland wouldn't leave me alone.'

'What did he do to you?' he asked.

'He used to stay late at work and Mrs Strickland was always out at cocktail parties – I believe she was an ornament of the young married set. Anyway, he'd come back from work. To begin with it was quite nice, a bit of company...'

Hilly shivered as she remembered. Strickland had offered her sherry. She'd accepted like a fool and he'd insisted she sit beside him on the kitchen sofa while he made jocular remarks about slumming it with the help. His face was red and his breath smelt of alcohol. She felt uneasy. Eventually she said, 'Mr Strickland, I must just go and check the children.' She tried to stand up but he grabbed her arm, pulling her down and spilling the remains of her sherry.

Before she knew what was happening, he was on top of her, wrenching up her skirt and scrabbling at her pants, his fat lips squashed on to her face, his awful slobbery tongue pushing into her mouth. Her head was wedged into the corner of the sofa and she felt as if she was suffocating. He raised his body slightly to undo his belt and she saw her chance, bringing a knee up sharply between his legs. He cried out, leaping backwards off her, clutching himself in agony.

She had seized the opportunity, slithering off the sofa and running as if her life depended on it up the stairs to her room. There was a key in the lock; she turned it. About ten minutes later he followed her and tried to get in, swearing and hissing through the door. 'Come out of there, you little bitch...'

She was terrified he would wake the children. Then she heard the doorbell. Mrs Strickland was always forgetting her keys. He stopped abruptly and lumbered down the stairs to let his wife in. Hilly heard them both start up a few minutes later. The sounds ceased when their bedroom door banged shut.

She'd unlocked her door and crept out and across the top of the stairs to the children's room. They slept soundly. Perhaps they were used to it. Hilly hadn't known very much about children at that point. They looked quite sweet when they were asleep. Awake they were bad-mannered little boys of six and seven, whose mother did nothing to correct them when they were rude to Hilly. She felt helpless and didn't know how to respond, although her instinct was to give their bare legs beneath the little grey school shorts a sharp slap.

She'd gone back into her room to pack her few things into her canvas bag. Down the stairs she crept as quietly as she could, her coat over her arm. The front door was double locked. Her heart in her mouth, she cast around for the mortise key and found it on the hall table. Out she went, closing the door quietly, double locking it again from the outside and posting the key back in through the letterbox.

She had left the Strickland family forever without her last month's pay. A week later an envelope with quite a lot more cash in it than she was owed arrived at Leith Hill, postmarked Chelsea but without a note. It looked like Mr Strickland's secretary had typed the address.

Then she'd walked straight to Tirzah's digs, where Tirzah and her friends were all still wide awake, sitting up drinking coffee, smoking and talking. Tirzah took one look at Hilly's white shocked face and sent the others back to their rooms.

Hilly told her foster sister all that had happened and they shared the narrow divan. They couldn't sleep as it was too uncomfortable so they talked all night. Tirzah did most of the chatting; she wanted to tell Hilly about Dougal, the Scotsman who had just arrived at Chelsea. Hilly was quiet. This growing up business seemed to her very hard. She wished she had a real talent like Tirzah, which would drive her to do interesting things. She couldn't bring herself to tell even her beloved foster sister about her humiliation in Fortnum's.

When she'd finished telling Peter why she'd left Chelsea, he said, 'Bastard! Well done for cracking him in the nuts. Still you can't blame him – I can't resist you. Look, Hilly, darling. I just think it's the wrong time for us.' He lit a cigarette.

'I suppose so.'

'You're nineteen and I'm twenty-one and we've both got a lot of growing up to do.'

'Mmmm.'

'Father said that I must see the world a bit. He's worried that I'm being idle in London. I didn't tell you this earlier, but he's suggested I go to Hong Kong to help expand his business there.'

'Mmmm.'

'What do you say I go for a couple of years and you do your job and then I could come back and we can see where we are. You'll be twenty-one by then and grown up.'

'A couple of years,' Hilly repeated. 'Right. You go off to Hong Kong and I stay here being an under-matron, and then what?'

'Well, I would be making a living and I could support you properly.'

It seemed infinitely remote as a possibility to Hilly. Two years – anything could happen in two years. She had heard about the fishing fleet of girls who, having failed to find husbands in England, went to the colonies to try their luck. It seemed unlikely that Peter would come back for her. She didn't want to say so; she was too dazed with love, grief, shock and alcohol. She had a thumping headache from the sherry and felt quite unreal.

'Darling, I must go now. You will wait for me, won't you?'

'Did you come down for Daddy's funeral or to tell me you were going to Hong Kong?'

'Both really. I wanted to tell you that we couldn't be together yet. But if you could wait I will come back for you.'

'You didn't make up your mind to go to Hong Kong because of what happened in the woods?'

Hilly had to know the answer.

'No, darling, of course not. I had already decided and we aren't engaged or anything, after all.'

He paused and smoked for a bit.

'Are you all right? I didn't hurt you too much, did I?'

'No, I'm fine.' There was a dull soreness between Hilly's legs but she didn't want to tell him about it.

'I wanted to be with you again like we were in the summer. But it wasn't like that, was it?'

Peter was silent.

'Will you hug me?' she asked in a small voice.

He ground out his cigarette in the car's ashtray and put his arms around her. Her thick auburn hair smelt like rain and earth. In the dim light her skin shone again with the crystalline clarity that it had lost in London. He kissed her gently, and she kissed him back. There was no one around; all the lights in the house were off apart from one in the hall. He slipped his hand under her skirt and found bare skin.

'I lost my knickers somewhere in the car,' Hilly whispered in his ear.

'We'll find them in a minute.'

It was too much for Peter this time. She murmured softly but consented. He tried hard not to get carried away, but found to his joy that she had no objection this time. Somewhere in the back of his mind, a warning sounded. He exercised an almost impossible forbearance.

Afterwards they lay across the front seat of the big car utterly relaxed. Hilly pulled herself together quite fast.

'Peter darling, you're squashing me rather.'

'Oh, Hilly. I do love you. What a lot of time we've wasted. I wish I didn't have to go to Hong Kong. Father has put a lot of pressure on me.'

'Don't worry, you'll come back.'

'Yes, I will, and then I promise we'll get be together and do that properly all the time.'

'Wasn't that properly?'

'Not quite. I withdrew so you won't get pregnant.'

'I thought that's what you were doing. Do you know something, Peter? It was better like that. It felt better.'

'Good.'

'I'm exhausted. I must go to bed. Don't fall for any of those fishers of men I hear about.'

'What?'

'You know, the fishing fleet.'

'Oh no, they won't be interested in me. They are all much older anyway, looking for rich old men. I'll have the memory of you as a benchmark.'

Hilly laughed contentedly. It occurred to her that they got on better after making love than before.

She got out of the car. Peter found her knickers and asked if he could keep them. She was rather shocked and took them away from him. They kissed for the last time.

'Goodbye, Peter. 'Til we meet again. I will miss you.'

'Goodbye, Hilly. I'm flying to Hong Kong the day after tomorrow. I promise to send you a telegram as soon as I arrive. Don't forget to write back. And thanks, my darling.'

'Not at all,' she said, disappearing into the house.

Nineteen

1997

A TRACE OF SOFTNESS in the dead London air lifted Dora's spirits when she went to pick up the paper. On Mondays she bought the *Guardian* for the Media section, on other days *The Times*. When she felt like being amused, it had to be the *Telegraph*. Nowhere else did you find stories about dangerous toxic waste turning out to be pickled cauliflower.

She had found the tiny dusty newsagent around the corner from her new flat. It belonged to two kind and ancient Englishmen who gave her credit until the next day if she didn't have enough cash on her. Its chief advantage was that she could examine the whole magazine rack without embarrassment. The top shelf, while occasionally displaying a semi-nude supermodel, was devoted to the glossies: *Tatler*, *Modern Woman*, *Vogue* and *Harpers & Queen*. And it wasn't very high up, as both proprietors were tiny.

There were no shiny buttocks subdivided by lacy G-strings (which looked so uncomfortable, she thought), no wet-lipped mouths hanging open in simulated ecstasy to embarrass and irritate her, no bloated silicon valleys straining for freedom.

She remembered Guy's strange collection of 1950s' magazines, which she'd found in his flat. Black-and-white picture after picture of busty, fully-clothed women tying themselves and each other into intricate almost yogic postures. He'd come in while she'd been giving herself cramp kneeling on the floor looking at them. She'd gone red.

'Oh, that's the way into your knickers, is it?' he'd inquired languidly. 'How exhausting.'

He'd taken them away from her and put them up on a high shelf in a cupboard. 'You don't need to look at those, darling, really.'

He'd pulled her to her feet and kissed her and then gone to make her a cup of tea. When she remembered how funny and original he was, how completely charming, it was very hard to do without him – even after all these years.

He was so completely shameless and so beautiful with his large, dark-lash-fringed grey eyes and wide soft mouth. Sometimes she forgot the thoughtlessness, the idle words that cut right through her composure. She only remembered him looking at her sadly near the end and saying, 'You're a good person, you know, Dora.' She understood now that her stupid virginity simultaneously repelled and attracted him.

In spite of romantic disappointment, she couldn't deny that there was something utterly delicious about living alone at last. After her father had died, there had been just enough cash for her to put down a deposit and get a mortgage. She'd bought an empty attic space high up in an Edwardian mansion block in Bayswater. She had toyed briefly with the idea of buying a two-bedroom flat and renting out the other room, but felt a bit old for communal living – kitties, squabbles about the heating bill, alien tooth marks in the cheese. So she shed her flat-sharing persona and became an eccentric spinster in Moscow Road, living among the Greek widows and itinerant Australian bankers.

She'd trekked around what felt like dozens of overpriced cupboards until she found her home. It turned out to be on the eighth floor of Smith Court; a single room about twenty feet square, with a tiny hall and pegs behind the front door, and two small cubbyholes built into the walls; rudimentary. It wasn't a flat at all when she'd first seen it; just a space, probably originally a maids' dormitory. A window had been wedged open by damp and had let in generations of birds.

The feel and smell of it had reminded her of the attic in the house where she'd been born: dusty floorboards, a sad little grate full of hay and grey pigeon feathers; a slight whiff of long-dead bird, sepia flowery wallpaper stained with brown patches of damp and peeling off in strips under the window.

Moving in immediately hadn't been an option, but the square room fed something deep within her and she'd found the confidence to beat down the price. It had been sold on behalf of an anonymous company which had bought it speculatively (probably sight unseen) and then gone bust.

With the young estate agent, she'd gone up and up in the old-fashioned lift on a hot June evening. It was stuffy under the eaves and Dora went over and pushed one of the windows open. The evening air was sweet, blowing from the park with no scent of the traffic fumes that stayed at ground level. She'd looked out over the roofs of Bayswater towards the gleaming dome of Whiteleys and felt content.

Standing in his white shirt sleeves, jacket flung over one shoulder, the seemingly 15-year-old estate agent ('Call me Dave') had implied that the whole world was panting with desire for Flat 84F.

Dora had looked him straight in the eye. She knew he didn't see her as female and desirable. She had been wearing a sensible navy dress with gold buttons, and patent leather court shoes, because of lunch with one of her favourite commissioning editors – the ancient doyen of very grand interior design who'd produced *Englishman's Castle* magazine every month for the last 40 years. Something fanciable to Dave would almost be another species.

She had wanted the attic very much. She didn't show Dave how much. No one else wanted it at all as it turned out – and an affordable price was agreed. Because it was above the top floor, the service charge was manageable as well.

She had asked a trusted colleague to recommend a builder. He also fed her an architect, Graham English, who had a habit of standing too close when talking to her. Every time she retreated, he would follow, until she had made a complete reverse circuit of her new home. She felt she had been given a good practical demonstration of the dimensions. Perhaps he'd learnt this original approach to improving clients' spatial awareness at the Architectural Association.

She forgave him when he came up with some good ideas for maximising the space, and put it down to short sight rather than lechery. One cubbyhole became her bedroom. Graham had thought her eccentric for wanting a single bed but had then become excited about the possibilities. The bed was raised and built in just under the window, so that she could see out over London while lying down.

He'd insisted on double-glazing to prevent drafts at the bottom, but she could open the window at the top and let in a breeze that stirred the cotton muslin with which she'd draped the bedposts. There was a little ladder that took her up to the platform on which she put her well-sprung mattress, and lots of drawers underneath.

The largest space became an open-plan kitchen and living room so she could cook comfortably for her friends and have them near her with glasses, chatting and not shouting pitifully for attention through the kitchen door. In the other cubbyhole, Graham created a pocket bathroom with a combined hip-bath and shower.

She had insisted on a ceiling fan for stuffy summer evenings, even though a breeze blew in from Kensington Gardens through the windows at both ends. She had the chimney cleaned and lined so she could have an illicit wood fire in the winter – so high up that no one would detect its delicious scent and ban it.

It had all been ready within three months. She had given a noisy party packed with fellow journalists, which nearly destroyed her relationship with her neighbours on the floor below before it had formed. On her first night, she had felt like Frances Hodgson Burnett's little princess – after Ram Dass had crawled across the roof and left all the magical treats in her attic. The little princess had a mutually supportive relationship with a rat. Dora felt that her rat had rather let her down.

On the Tube to work, Dora looked at her *Telegraph*. She still read the court page and looked at who was getting married to whom. After a positive flood five years ago, it had settled down a bit and she didn't see anyone she knew nearly so often – or go to nearly so many weddings.

She had managed to get a seat, and her eye travelled up the column from bottom to top looking at the Misses and Esqs in bold for any familiar surname.

'Ah,' she thought. 'Some grand relation of Guy's is getting married. Who's the Hon C. D. G. Boleyn, I wonder?'

She froze. She thought her heart would stop beating. Her breath came in gasps. The woman sitting beside her looked around curiously. Dora was shaking.

The engagement has been announced between Guy, only son of Lord Northiam of Colchester and Mrs Janet Moore, and Lady Amabel St Clair, younger daughter of the Earl and Countess of Cumbria.

'But he can't,' she said out loud. 'He's married to me.'

The woman stood up and moved away, to be rapidly replaced by a young man deep in the *Financial Times*. Dora got a grip on herself.

It all came rushing back: the cooling coffee, her acute embarrassment. How long ago was it? Years and years and years. The ugly ring still hung around her neck on a chain, but she'd hardly seen her husband since and then usually only in print. It was a strange way to conduct a marriage, but it had happened, hadn't it? They had never consummated it though, so perhaps it had worn off.

If you disappear, you are legally dead after seven years, aren't you? In the middle of that thought she was astonished to feel a ripping pang of jealousy right across the liver. She realised she must never have stopped hoping.

Having said she would give him time, she'd quickly got into the habit of denying any involvement with him. Yes, she'd known Guy Boleyn, but wasn't he in New York selling Pre-Raphaelites now? She'd heard he was rather successful. He became part of the Studio 54 crowd, English ex-pats bent on having mindless fun. He'd also been welcome in grand drawing rooms of New York's leading social X-rays.

'I bet they all think he's just darling,' thought Dora sourly.

There had been times when she thought she would die of loneliness and misery. She couldn't tell anyone. She had promised not to and she was horribly set on keeping her promises. The reality of her marriage shrivelled more rapidly to her, as she could never expose it to another's scrutiny.

She had gone out into the fields one night near her parents' house and shouted her misery at the moon. The moon had just stayed where it was, not caring whether she was married or dead. Just once she had seen Guy in the flesh. She had been at a restaurant opening with some friends. It was a typical 1980s party – loud, brash and expensive. Champagne had flowed; the restaurant was over several floors of a Soho warehouse, with a different theme to each floor.

'Didn't you used to know Guy Boleyn, when he lived in England?' someone had asked her.

'A bit. Why?'

'Well, he's here.'

She thought she would choke on her amusing miniature fish and chips wrapped up in a pink triangle of the *Financial Times.*

'Where?'

'Over there. He's completely pissed and looks terrible. He used to be so pretty.'

Dora had looked where he was pointing. She'd hoped that she didn't love him any more. That he had become ugly, bald, fat and debauched.

But he hadn't. Drunk, yes; glazed, yes. Heartbreaking, yes. He had seemed to look right through her and out the other side.

Dora had left abruptly.

Now this. He was engaged to Amabel St Clair, who sounded like a drag queen or a stripper, but was genuinely grand. Amabel was a well-known model who'd been around for years – a true English rose, serene and beautiful with long, straight, lion-coloured hair. As different from dark and faintly oriental Dora as diamonds are from coal.

Twenty

WHERE WAS SHE? It was very dark and Dora always slept with her curtains open. It must be the middle of the night. London basked in an orange glow, so she wasn't there. Her skin felt crawly with an ancient fear. Alone. In the dark. It pressed in upon her. The silence lent the darkness a velvety texture. Had she gone blind? Perhaps she was in a sensory-deprivation cell. Why? She curled into a foetal position, still as she could manage in the silent black room. She had to be dreaming. She'd wake up in a minute.

Then she remembered. The appalling knowledge of what she was planning to do crashed into her consciousness. She was in a bed and breakfast in Gloucestershire, where Guy was to wed the tall and willowy Amabel.

Guy hadn't invited her to 'the wedding of the year', as *Hello!* had described it. There was bound to be tight security. But Dora had a secret weapon. After all, no one could be more fittingly present at Guy's wedding than his lawful wedded wife. She'd checked. Marriage didn't just wear off after seven years if you didn't consummate it. Nor could

Guy divorce her without her noticing. She hadn't signed or seen anything. Perhaps he was just hoping she'd keep quiet. Or perhaps he believed it wouldn't mean anything if he hadn't screwed her. She did feel sorry for him – and for poor Amabel, whose wedding day she was possibly going to ruin. She hadn't made up her mind yet, though. She might just witness it and keep quiet.

For a while after she'd discovered what Guy was planning, she'd just accepted it. He must know best, she'd thought. He always had before. Surely he would get in touch, arrange for the marriage to be annulled, ask her to sign something, if that brief miserable ceremonial had meant anything significant at all?

But she hadn't heard from him, not since that last kiss on the top of her embarrassed head fifteen years ago. Dora hugged herself. She could choose to have everyone staring at her. Brides must feel like this on their wedding morning, she thought. Maybe Amabel was feeling the same thing right now.

As a MAW – model, actress... whatever – as they were rudely known, she wasn't bad. At least she did something for a living and wasn't just a Notting Hill trustafarian like so many of her contemporaries. She was with the Cornice model agency, which specialised in girls who either were, or looked as if they were, out of the top bracket. Ralph Lauren was always scooping them up to model his pseudo-English clothes. She'd recently had a minor part in an Edith Wharton adaptation on the television. Dora hadn't been able to help herself. She had taped the programme and played Amabel's bit over and over again, analysing what Amabel had that she hadn't.

Dora had honestly believed she was over Guy. For years she hadn't thought about him much. Since the end of the

1980s she had managed to be merely interested and not winded when anyone talked about him. Damping all that emotion down had a paradoxical effect. The announcement in the *Telegraph* was like a drill hitting crude. Thwarted love, desire, hate and passion had erupted.

She had considered telephoning him but something had held her back. She had called the Citizens Advice Bureau instead to find out exactly where she stood, giving a false name and explaining the situation. The advisor had been very sympathetic. Dora misrepresented the circumstances a little to cover her tracks. But the essence was true. She had married a man in the 1980s but he had deserted her. Funny to use that word – deserted. It made her feel helpless, which is not what she had been at all. The marriage had never been consummated and might just as well never have happened. Did it still count?

The woman on the other end of the telephone had been very definite. As far as she was concerned it counted just as much as any other marriage in law, unless a divorce had taken place subsequently. She checked with her solicitor colleague and called Dora back to confirm it. If the man in question got married again without getting a divorce then it would be bigamy, fair and square. Although very few people were prosecuted for bigamy these days, it was still an offence and Dora had every right to consider herself married to Guy.

Dora didn't know what to feel. It was like a dream or a joke. She felt she had no right to marriage. Somehow she'd put herself aside from the mainstream of her friends by her rash last-ditch attempt to hold on to an impossible man. Guy must have regretted it almost immediately. He had run as fast as he could from the mess he had made.

Dora had simply shut down. They had never slept

together – it seemed perverse to her. He'd gone on at her so. Saying 'no' had become such a fixed habit that it seemed obvious to her to continue with it. What had she been waiting for? Something utterly unreal called 'true love'. She had been so uncertain of Guy that she'd felt he must prove himself by marrying her.

She never thought he would go through with it, that sleeping with her would be such a draw that he would risk his freedom at such an early age. And his freedom was greater than most. With a trust maturing when he was 25 he could go anywhere, do anything. Dora, older than him and trust-free, had not yet realised how dreadfully bad for people inherited money could be.

He'd chosen to marry her and he hadn't even bothered to claim the prize. It was humiliating. She had occupied a unique place in his life after all – married but not mated to him.

She'd never been a traditional bride: the centre of attention, packaged in gruesome white, swathed in acres of netting and with a ridiculous family tiara on top. She'd worn that horrible silk dress that had gone to Oxfam six months later, a mascara stain on the sleeve where she had inadvertently wiped her streaming eyes, haunted with Dora-shaped misery.

But now, finally, she had the opportunity to star at a wedding. Swinging into action, she had thought about who would have been invited. She chose the most shambolic of possible targets – Richard Tate – and invited herself around for a drink on the pretext that she was researching a piece on people who lived in Streatham, and would he be interested in giving her some tips.

'God, Dora, haven't seen you for years. Read your stuff

sometimes. Jolly good. You always make things sound funny. You're not going to laugh at me though, are you?'

'Would I do that to you? After all we've been through together?' Dora could feel herself pitching camp.

'Do come and get drunk with Donald and me. We'd love to see you.'

'Thanks, I will.'

She had found Richard and his boyfriend Donald sharing a little early 19th-century flat-fronted house in what estate agents would call 'a pretty, tree-lined street' – basically a street with a few poisoned urban trees in dog-shit-strewn gaps in the paving slabs.

Dora glittered, and the boys rose to her bait like fish to a silvery lure. She subtly pumped them about Guy's wedding, pretending she thought it was so funny that he should have found what he always dreamed of – a wife who could keep him in luxury. Richard and Donald surpassed themselves in bitchiness. Amabel's hair came in for particular amusement. Donald was a successful hairdresser, and Amabel went to a hugely over-hyped competitor of his off Grosvenor Square. Dora learned that this reviled practitioner was going to be flying by helicopter (his own, not Lord Cumbria's) in and out to do Amabel's hair for the ceremony.

Richard, who was an antique dealer and a very old friend of Guy's from his Portobello days, got left behind and bumbled fatly off to make some supper. Donald and Dora soared away on an arc of detail: the dress, Versace probably (would there be any fabric involved or just this year's trademark chromed chains? – which would be very virginal, Donald thought); the flowers – Paula Pryke, who else? The caterer? Lorna Wing – an advocate of the new simplicity, doing nothing but Whitstable native oysters and caviar apparently. The

Rolling Stones would be there, and Billy Kidd, but whether they would be playing or just standing about was not known. There was to be a dance afterwards in a special kind of floating marquee erected in the abbey ruins adjoining the Cumbria country seat.

Dora casually made her way over to the mantelpiece to look at the invitation. When Donald went to see if Richard needed any help in the kitchen, she quickly scribbled down the RSVP name and address planning to answer the invitation, and hoping that the organisation had a breach she could slip through. She knew Guy's divorced parents would each provide a list of their guests, and she was sure that Guy's list would be completely hopeless, probably separate torn bits of paper with unreadable names scribbled on them – he had dreadful handwriting. Amabel's mother, glossy and beautifully organised, would have a fixed future-mother-in-law smile by now.

She had heard of people answering invitations they hadn't received. It was the kind of thing she wrote about for *Tatler*. Sometimes it worked, and you were just included on the security list. Sometimes it didn't, and you received a rude letter telling you not to show your face. After spending a happy evening with Richard and Donald she had gone home to bed to continue plotting her way into Guy's second wedding.

The next day she went to Smythson in Bond Street and bought their most expensive thick cream laid writing paper and envelopes. She also purchased some dense black ink that was almost matte on the page and got out her twenty-first birthday present fountain pen with the gold nib. She practised a bit before writing her reply in loopy, sloping, old-fashioned-looking, slightly shaky writing. On the off chance that they would recognise her by-line, she used her late grandmother's name.

> *Miss Emma Vane thanks Lord and Lady Cumbria*
> *very much for their kind invitation to Guy and*
> *Amabel's wedding on 3 June 1997 at 3 o'clock,*
> *and is sadly forced to decline due to a previous*
> *engagement.*

She added a PS:

> *Would you please let me know where Guy and*
> *Amabel have their wedding list so that I can send*
> *them a present.*

'That should get the ball rolling,' she thought.

Sure enough, a stock-typed reply signed by Lady Cumbria arrived a couple of days later. It read:

> *So sorry we shall not have the opportunity to meet*
> *you at Amabel and Guy's wedding. Their wedding*
> *lists are at the General Trading Company, The*
> *Conran Shop and Thomas Goode.*
> >   *Yrs Eileen Cumbria.*

Dora had reviewed her financial situation. Her savings were now dedicated to getting herself to the wedding, beautifully dressed and as bona fide as she could manage. Rather like a real bride, she couldn't think beyond the point of the wedding. She chose the most expensive and traditional of the three wedding list choices, Thomas Goode, and she went early one Saturday morning. It took a long time to choose a present to strike precisely the right note with Lady Cumbria and the unknown Amabel. The Cumbrias had obviously chosen Thomas Goode to service the requirements of exceedingly rich elderly relations. The General Trading Company was for more conventional contemporaries and slightly less rich relations, and the Conran Shop for the couple's fashionable friends. She knew that Lady Cumbria would stick rigidly to these social assumptions about where each gift had come from. Of course really grand relations would give family silver or jewellery and not go near anything as vulgar as a shop.

Dora hoped that the expensive paper, use of the title 'Miss' as opposed to 'Ms', the old-fashioned ink, deliberately copper-plate writing and choice of present, would lead Lady Cumbria to believe that she was an elderly, rich spinster relation of Guy's, possibly from whom he had expectations, and to whom he had posted an invitation without reporting back to base. It probably wouldn't surprise Eileen Cumbria in the least.

The wedding present Dora chose in the end cost the earth and was as far away as the moon from anything she would normally have bought. She regarded it as an investment. If all went according to plan she would get it back. She had checked with the shop that a cash refund would be in order, 'If that is what the happy couple would prefer'. It was a set of six cut-crystal sherry glasses that were not on the list.

She told the shop that she was Miss Vane's social secretary – if anyone should ever ask – and paid with cash, explaining that Miss Vane was a bit eccentric and didn't believe in credit cards. She asked that the gift should be addressed to Lady Cumbria, and made out one of Thomas Goode's cards: with loving best wishes to bride and groom from Emma Vane. This part of the plan depended on Guy taking no interest in the wedding presents, at least those from Thomas Goode. Paintings and pots by friends would, of course, be a different matter.

The next step was her wedding outfit. She went to Harvey Nichols and spent the rest of the day trying on beautiful clothes and hats with the help of a kindly shop assistant, who evidently believed she was going to spend a lot of money. The hat was an ethereal meringue of black tulle, chosen to top off a Tomasz Starzewski suit in black silk herringbone tweed, edged with matching satin ribbon and tied with discreet bows down the front instead of buttons. The jacket was cut low and curved over her breasts with a fitted waist and bracelet-length sleeves. The assistant had kindly run off to Lingerie to fetch a Wonderbra to give her a cleavage.

The skirt was fashionably knee length. The black hat extended down over her face in a sculpted veil and was lit up at the front by an enormous, blood-red silk poppy. She also bought very high-heeled black Manolo Blahnik sling-backs, black silk stockings, a French Lycra girdle suspender belt and the Wonderbra. The assistant stood back and looked at her wearing the whole lot. Dora had already explained it was for a wedding.

'Whose wedding, Miss? Because I wouldn't like to be the bride.'

Dora knew all about retail flattery and the emetic effect it had on customers' credit cards. The woman sounded almost frightened. When Dora looked at her own eyes in the mirror, gleaming through the diaphanous veil, something stared back at her that was unfamiliar and alien.

Everything was folded with tissue and packed into bags.

The hat had its own box to protect it. Dora went downstairs to the perfumery, still in the grip of her private nuptial ritual, and bought from the Guerlain counter completely new make-up in strong colours she no longer used. Blood red lipstick, gleaming black mascara and instant eyeliner (she hoped her hand wouldn't be shaking too much when she put it on), and porcelain foundation, slightly pearlised. Then she went home, hung the clothes in her cupboard, and sat down to write the next letter in her correspondence with Lady Cumbria.

> *Dear Lady Cumbria,*
>
> *I do hope you don't mind, but the previous engagement, which would have prevented me from attending Guy and Amabel's wedding, has been cancelled due to the death of an old friend.* [She felt the detail, and the sense of a life drawing to its close, would carry the day]. *I wonder if I could now be included in the list for acceptances? If this is inconvenient, please let me know.*
> *Thank you so much.*
> *I look forward to meeting you on the day.*

She received a charming note back, this time handwritten, saying of course Miss Vane must come – so sorry about her friend's death – and delighted good wishes. In the same post came a friendly letter from Amabel, thanking dear Miss Vane so much for the lovely sherry glasses – she could visualise herself and Guy, as the sun was setting, sitting on their terrace sipping sherry etc, etc. Dora laughed at this. Guy never in his life, as far as she knew, voluntarily drank sherry, unless there was absolutely nothing else – not even neat Pimms. It was clear that Lady Cumbria had fallen for her elderly rich cousin act and passed it on to Amabel. No one was ever so rich that a fat legacy didn't come in handy, and it didn't do to dismiss relations who replied to invitations on Smythson's most extravagantly thick paper.

So Dora was all set up for Guy's wedding. Only one thing was missing. What scent should she wear? When she had known Guy, he'd always worn L'Heure Bleu. He probably smelt of something far more masculine now. She went and bought a bottle of that to complete her preparations for her private destructive rite.

Twenty-one

THE DARKNESS HAD FLED but the sun was still low in the sky when Dora woke up again. She got up and went to look out of the window. Light flooded at a shallow angle across the wet lawn. She could hear a blackbird. There was a faint mist wreathing about the feet of the undulating hills. The bed and breakfast she had chosen sat halfway up a Gloucestershire hillside and the view was lovely.

Mrs Lewis had explained the night before that she ran the bed and breakfast so that she would have money to spend on the garden. The grey stone cottage was a second home; they had a house off the King's Road. Mrs Lewis told Dora she liked to be in the country as much as possible, particularly in the summer. She felt stifled in London and the garden there was tiny. The children had left home now so their two rooms were free. The temporarily absent Mr Lewis (away on business) would pay for everything else but couldn't see the point of spending money on plants – they just grew, didn't they? Would Dora like breakfast on the terrace? The forecast was very hopeful. Happy the bride the sun shone on, eh?

The room Dora was staying in had the pleasing clean shabbiness of a certain kind of solid English family house. The chintz curtains had naturalistic red roses on a cream background, except on the edge nearest to the window, where they had faded to the palest possible pink. The window was wide and low. Dora curled up inside her tatty Victorian nightie and sat on the wide window sill with her arms around her knees, dreaming and looking out at the gradually lightening garden.

The wedding ceremony itself was to be held in the next village's church at three o'clock, followed by a reception at Cumbria Hall – on the lawn if the weather was fine. Then everyone was expected to go back to their house parties for a rest and to change into black tie and party dresses. But Dora's imaginings stopped at the ceremony. Dora was relying upon some sign when the moment arrived that would tell her how to act. What that sign would be she had no idea. She was living moment to moment with no real plan any more. Even if she did nothing, she didn't think she'd have the nerve for the reception – let alone the receiving line.

The dewy morning made her feel sentimental. She wondered how Amabel was feeling a few miles away. Was she awake too, contemplating her future, excited, happy, wondering what was going to become of her? Dora suddenly felt loving and generous towards her. When they came back from their honeymoon, perhaps Dora would remind Guy and they would make some quiet and private arrangement to annul their own marriage. It seemed terribly cruel to disrupt the path of true love. It wasn't Amabel's fault, after all.

Guy wasn't hers to interfere with; he never had been. What did she think she was doing? She considered the money she had spent ruefully. Oh well. She'd just have to work extra subbing shifts to make up for it or get more US commissions that paid better. The suit was really beautiful; it would do for all grand occasions from now until she was 90 if she didn't put on weight. She hoped Amabel and Guy would have the sense to change those dull sherry glasses for something more exciting.

Dora felt the guilt and misery that had lain in wait behind the jealous energy drain away. Perhaps she could free herself finally from the grip Guy had maintained on her life and find someone else. It wasn't too late. This was what the wedding ceremony today would mean to her: an end to her subconscious hopes and a new start for her as a free woman.

It might not be legal, but privately she would allow today's ceremony to cancel out the dismal, perfunctory business that had taken place in Chelsea years before. She felt so good and generous that she considered going to the reception as well. She would know plenty of people. It would probably be fun. Guy wouldn't challenge her; he'd crashed enough parties in his time.

She went into what must have been the old nursery bathroom across the passage. A faded frieze of ducks traipsed around the walls. She ran a deep hot bath in the enormous, cast-iron tub, with its straight, no-nonsense feet, and dripped in some of Mrs Lewis's Floris Rose Geranium bath essence, very relaxing to the nerves, she understood from a piece she had written about aromatherapy – just what was called for in her tangled circumstances. She pulled her nightie off over her head, put her beautifully blow-dried hair in a bath-cap and slid into the water.

She plastered blue Clinique Beauty Emergency Mask over her face and lay back, breathing in the intoxicating fumes of rose geranium and mint and distracting herself with an ancient book of Giles cartoons. When she began to feel too soggy, she got out, wrapped herself in a towel and went back to her room. It was still only nine o'clock. She had booked herself in for two nights as she didn't want to arouse her hostess's suspicion by only booking one. Mrs Lewis knew all about the Cumbria wedding, and was aware of the dance in the evening. Dora planned to come back to the house after the ceremony, pack, pay for two nights, and drive back to London unscathed, free, a new woman.

She was so relieved that she had decided not to make a scene. Scenes weren't really her thing, and all the plotting and planning had disrupted her life too much over the last six months, as well as proving very expensive. Now she could go back to her quiet life in her nest, writing pieces and going out subbing, reading and visiting friends. She had rather given up on the man front. The last man to take her out to dinner seemed to assume she was desperate for sex. He'd pounced, been rejected and then come over all huffy. Dora could see that he was thinking that she should be grateful at her age. It turned out he had a long-term girl-friend who was waiting at home. They had an 'open' relationship apparently. Dora couldn't think whom that might benefit. Shags were easy to find – but she wanted a husband. She'd recently interviewed the celebrated society matchmaker Heather Heber-Percy for a piece on marriage brokers in the modern world. Perhaps she could provide a gentleman farmer. It would be practical, like an arranged marriage. After what she had been through marriage-wise, practicality would be a relief.

She dried herself in the sunlit bedroom, standing on the faded and worn pink carpet. She let the sun touch her naked body and shivered as she caught a glimpse of herself in the mirror.

Her dark, straight hair was newly cut into a most precise long bob that emphasised the slightly exotic look around her eyes. On the whole, she wasn't displeased with her looks. She wasn't willowy, sinuous Amabel, with her long, straight, honey hair, large brown eyes and pouting mouth. She began to feel very generous again. What right had she to interfere between two people who were enough in love to get married on this glorious June day? Her business with Guy's affections was deep in the past. She must forget it now. It was over.

It was turning into such a beautiful day. Lucky them. Did she feel any kind of a grudge? She stood stark naked and examined every corner of her mind. Her own wedding day had been one of those grey and chilly spring days which are all the more depressing because April has already delivered some sunny promises of the coming summer.

She went over to the bedside table and picked up her watch. It was the time she had agreed to have her breakfast. She threw on a bra and knickers and a cotton dress and raced down the stairs and out on to the terrace. Mrs Lewis had laid the table and put out half a grapefruit in a bowl. There was a copy of Saturday's *Telegraph* by her place, an insulated cafetière, its plunger still sticking up, and a thermos of hot milk beside it.

'I've fallen on my feet here,' she thought to herself. In her happiness and relief she was able to feel truly hungry for the first time in months. Misery always made her thinner.

When she found that the grapefruit had even been cut the way she liked it, the way Hilly had always cut it for her, each segment separated from its pith, she felt completely happy. She poured herself a large cup of delicious coffee as Mrs

Lewis appeared with a full English breakfast in one hand and a rack of toast in the other.

'That was lovely, Mrs Lewis, thank you so much. No one has cut a grapefruit for me like that in years.'

'That's all right, dear.' She smiled.

She put the hot plate and the toast down in fr⟨...⟩ra.

'Would you like me to put up the sunshade? It really is very bright.'

'That would be lovely, thanks.' Dora looked with pleasure at her fried egg, tomato, bacon and sausage. She couldn't remember the last time she had eaten such a breakfast or indeed any breakfast. She wondered what Amabel was eating or whether she was too nervous to eat.

She devoured it all and then hoped she would still fit into the amazing tight-waisted suit. She worried that she would be too hot but remembered the fine but robust silk herringbone tweed and the real silk lining. She read the whole newspaper from beginning to end and even noted a shopping piece she had written a couple of months before had made an appearance. That seemed to her to be a good omen. She idled away the rest of the morning, playing with her face and seeing how the hat looked best.

Then it was two o'clock. She'd refused lunch. Breakfast had been enough to fill her up for a week, she said – although in fact the effect had been the opposite. She always found eating a big breakfast made her very hungry for lunch but she didn't want Mrs Lewis to go to any more effort for her. She felt light and strong in the shining day. Her skin, which she had luxuriantly massaged with cocoa butter, smelt faintly of chocolate, and gleamed with health. It was very white. She seldom sunbathed.

It was time to begin to dress. Her mind came back from

its wanderings and began to dart about. Her stomach fluttered. She slipped into the old-fashioned-looking shiny Lycra girdle with its dangling suspenders and pulled up the thin, sheer, silk stockings, careful not to snag them on her nails. She bent forward to fit her breasts into the Wonderbra, marvelling at the effect it had on her cleavage, and put her silk-clad feet into the low-cut, high-heeled satin sling-backs. Then she looked at herself in the mirror again. She looked like nothing so much as those bondage ladies in one of Guy's 1950s magazines and was taken straight back to his stuffy little basement flat, full of curiosities, pots, pictures stacked against the walls, his own easel and paints. The bare, grey floorboards. The smells of coffee, joss-sticks and slight staleness that at 23 and in love she'd been happy to overlook.

The feeling of elation evaporated. It was no good pretending: she was still in love with Guy. She felt silly and artificial. What was she doing getting all dressed up to watch him marry someone else? She must be mad.

She sat down on the edge of the bed, deep in thought, her knees pressed together and her high-heeled shoes splayed apart.

'I'll just go to the church. Then I'll drive straight back to London. I won't come back here. I'll pack and pay now before I go.'

That decided she stood up. She took the little curved knee-length skirt down from its hanger and stepped into it. It was slightly looser than it had been when she had bought it a month before but it was so well cut that it still fitted.

'Anyway,' she thought, 'the loose waist won't show under the jacket.'

She put on a low-cut shell of oyster satin with spaghetti straps that had come with the suit. That was the lovely thing about very expensive clothes – they came with extras. She slipped on the jacket. It had large concealed poppers to fasten it down the front. The bows were merely for show. She tried on the hat to check the whole effect. The veil, which could be folded back, covered her eyes and nose – but they could still be seen dimly beneath. When hats like this had been shown on the catwalks, there had been a great fuss about faceless women. It served her purposes admirably. Last of all, she outlined her mouth with the deep, matte lipstick, which matched the blood-red poppy on the hat. Really the whole effect was very striking, she had to admit.

It undoubtedly suited her exaggerated desire for ceremonial. After all, this was as much a turning point in her life as it was in the bridal couples'. Why shouldn't she look dramatic?

She was sure the other wedding guests would surpass themselves in the hopes of a picture in *Tatler*, *Modern Woman* or *Harpers & Queen*. It would probably make Dempster as well. The artier minor royals were expected. Some of them were very dressy indeed and one of them in particular had exquisite taste in clothes.

In accordance with her new plan, she packed. Then she picked up her bag and hatbox, once more containing the spectacular hat, looked around the room for anything she had forgotten and went downstairs.

She was loading the car when Mrs Lewis came rushing out.

'Are you off to the wedding then?'

'Yes, Mrs Lewis. I've decided not to stay tonight. I don't feel too well so I think I'll go back to London straight after the reception. I would like to pay for two nights though, because of the shortness of notice.'

'Are you all right? You look very pale.'

Dora quickly improvised.

'I get these migraines. They come on very quickly. But I've got some drugs which hold them at bay.'

Mrs Lewis frowned.

'Look, don't worry about paying for the second night.'

While Dora wrote out the cheque, Mrs Lewis said quietly: 'Was he your boyfriend?'

Dora stopped writing for a moment and shut her eyes.

'Oh dear, I am sorry.' She squeezed Dora's arm. Dora managed a shaky smile but couldn't say anything except goodbye and thank you.

The front of Mrs Lewis's cottage faced on to a lane where Dora had parked her car. She waved, speechless with suppressed tears, and drove away. It was Mrs Lewis's sympathetic tone that had pierced her shell. She'd never dared tell her own mother about Guy. It had all happened so quickly, and her mother in some subtle way disapproved of boyfriends. By the time they were married and Guy had gone to New York, there was nothing really to tell. So Dora hadn't. No one else had known the full extent of her misery; she'd hidden it well. Mrs Lewis's kind blundering intrusion had touched an unused nerve.

'Don't cry,' Dora told herself. 'Your mascara will run.'

She stopped the car a few hundred yards down the road and looked in the mirror. Her face looked surprisingly cool, pale and composed.

'That's what expensive make-up can do for you I suppose,' she thought ruefully.

Approaching the church, she swung back into plotting mode. She might have decided not to disrupt events but she wanted to stick to the rest of her plan up until the very last minute. She parked some way away from the other guests' cars, on the other side of the church. This was to minimise the risk of bumping into anyone she knew.

She was going to arrive as late as she could and slip in at the back just before the bride. The only risk was that Guy would be following the latest fashion for bridegrooms and greeting his guests at the door. If she timed it just right he would have gone up to the front pew to join his best man before she walked in. In her experience, grooms stared grimly ahead of them from that point on, until the bride arrived, heralded by the music they had chosen lovingly together.

It was no good; she did feel angry and hurt – and excluded, left out. Shreds and patches of that old feeling when one hasn't been invited to a party were there – along with jealousy, thwarted love, weary waiting and a sense of drama. All very complicated and really rather mad. She sat in her car, opened the hatbox and took out the incredible hat. Looking in the driving mirror she fitted it on to her head, pulling down the veil to hide her face. Then she looked in her handbag. Yes, it was there – a copy of her marriage certificate, for which she had gone to Somerset House, after she had spoken to the Citizens Advice Bureau. Just in case, she told herself. He'd rushed off with the original, no doubt thinking this would give him control over what he had just done.

She got out of the car, her little bag with its precious cargo clutched in her hand. She felt shaky and chilled. She very deliberately shut and locked her car door, balancing on the verge on her vertiginous heels.

Then she began to walk slowly towards the church.

Watching in the driver's mirror, she had noted that the stream of guests had slowed to a trickle of rushing, raffish Notting Hill types. It was five minutes after kick-off. Dora counted on Amabel being a fashionable 15 minutes late. She didn't want to have to push past her in the porch, tripping over adorable attendants as she went. There seemed to be dozens of bridesmaids in late-eighteenth-century-style white muslin dresses, with pink satin sashes, pink buckled shoes and little bonnets trimmed with flowers and feathers. They carried beribboned baskets of apples between two of them, so took up quite a lot of room.

She looked at her watch and began to hurry in classic wedding guest manner, teetering slightly and holding her hat with one hand. There was only the faintest breeze but the hat was such a puff of a thing that it might just take off. She could see the enormous old black Rolls coming the other way. It wouldn't be hired; the Cumbrias probably had garages stuffed with grand motor cars.

'Oh heck,' thought Dora. 'I'm not going to make it.'

Then she noticed Guy standing by the door. He was looking the other way, towards the bride's Rolls, and hadn't seen her. She slowed down and looked at her feet, taking deep breaths to steady her nerves. She heard a man's voice say, 'For God's sake, Guy, come into the church or you'll still be down there when Amabel arrives. She won't be pleased.'

To Dora's relief Guy vanished.

The Rolls was just drawing up by the lychgate as she entered the church. Luckily, as the congregation was huge. Dora knew that lots of friends, particularly of Guy's, had been assigned to reception-only status. Most of them, being among the more ungodly, hadn't minded. She walked in. A smooth young usher whispered urgently, 'Bride or groom?'

She whispered back, 'Groom.'

He was looking at a list. 'Are you family?'

Dora toyed momentarily with the idea of telling the truth.

'No,' she said. 'Can I just slip in at the back? I'm sorry I'm late. The bride is just arriving.'

This distracted him from his list and Dora took the opportunity to slip into a pew on the right-hand side at the very back. The other people, all middle-aged strangers, shuffled up a bit, smiling. She had been right: spectacular hats sprouted all over the church. Hers seemed quite understated in comparison.

She began to look at her service sheet. All the old favourites were there: Lord of All Hopefulness, Corinthians etc. The church bit obviously wasn't the point of this wedding. It was knees down and then knees up as quickly as possible afterwards. She peeped through her veil at Guy's back. She had never seen his best man before. Then she realised he must be Amabel's brother – he looked rather like her. Guy had a great talent for friendship, only he chose rather eccentric people, none of whom would have been deemed suitable best men by Amabel. Dora's heart sank. Was Amabel taming Guy?

Guy turned around and looked down the aisle. Dora froze. She was pretty invisible but she was sitting at the end of the pew. She lowered her eyes and glanced up through her veil. Would he sense that she was there? 'Why should he?' she scolded herself. 'He hasn't thought about you for years.'

Even though their relationship had lasted no real time at all, the subterranean pull between them had been very strong. When she was feeling optimistic about herself, she thought it must have been this mysterious force that drew her into the secret marriage; when pessimistic, she knew it for weakness and over-romanticism.

The organ began to play the wedding march from Lohengrin – 'a surprisingly conventional choice,' thought Dora. 'Perhaps it's postmodern.' There was a rustling beside the door. Everyone stood up. Waiting at the altar end of the church were three bishops of various heights and a cathedral-sized boys' choir.

Dora looked over her shoulder to see the bride arrive. There she was, her back to the bright day, leaning on her father's arm. Her dress couldn't have been more of a contrast to the attendants' rococo prettiness. As Amabel strode past, Dora could see it was made of very fine cream suede, skimming and moulding her perfect body without visible seams. The neckline was modest, the sleeves came right down to her fingers – but she was completely on display.

Her braless breasts were unnaturally buoyant, the nipples visible through the second skin. The dress fitted to the knee and then flared out into a short train, artfully tattered all around the bottom. Her completely flat stomach, the slender waist and curved front of her thighs, even her kneecaps and tummy button, could all be seen. She had to be naked underneath; there was no visible panty line.

On her head was a diaphanous cream chiffon square, held in place by an art deco diamond tiara. Her hair was pulled back into a tight chignon, exposing her glorious golden cheekbones. She looked remote rather than ecstatic.

Dora switched her attention to Guy. He had turned to watch his fate coming towards him. Dora braced for the happy, uncertain, pink face of even the coolest bridegroom, but found herself suppressing a gasp. Guy looked dreadful. He'd always been slender but even in the *Hello!* spread he'd looked quite normal. Now he looked gaunt, grey. Dora's heart sank. What on earth had happened to him? Dora thought she caught a strong whiff of desperation before he turned back to the business in hand.

Her heart started thumping. What should she do? People were always nervous at their weddings, but not like that. She had never seen such a haunted bridegroom. Perhaps she was imagining it. Could she be superimposing her own feelings on to her lost love? She had been so sure that she would be able to control herself, that she wouldn't need to carry out her plan and disrupt this 'joyful occasion', as the chief bishop was calling it.

During their short association Dora had noticed a strange thing about Guy. He might take every drug offered to him, drink everyone else under the table, sleep with anything that moved and have friends from a wide variety of exotic backgrounds, but underneath he had a streak of deep-dyed conventionality. Was that why he had actually nerved himself up to marry Dora?

Perhaps he was remembering that he was already married and was afraid of being done for bigamy? No, Dora felt that wasn't it. His misery seemed focused on the present, not the past. For a brief instant he had looked so strangely at the undressed beauty walking demurely up the aisle on her father's arm. The paparazzi outside the church must have had a field day: no wonder she had been delayed. No one had been that undressed in public since Elizabeth Hurley, even if Amabel was revealing only her finger tips and face.

What on earth was Amabel up to? Displaying herself like meat on a slab at her own wedding. Dora's good intentions flew out of the Victorian stained-glass windows.

Guy was hers by right. She had the evidence in her bag.

She was going to rescue him from whatever demon was haunting him at this bigamous wedding. She was going to save him from himself.

The largest of the three bishops was intoning, 'If any of you know cause or just impediment why these two people should not be joined together in holy matrimony ye are to declare it...'

Help, she'd nearly missed it. She stood up. At first no one noticed. Then one of the flanking bishops did, and nudged the officiating one, who'd already gone on to the bit about the dreadful day of judgement. He stopped and glared at her, hoping she would sit down and let him get on with it. But Dora had fire in her belly and no time to think; she couldn't back down now.

She took a deep breath and stepped out into the aisle. At the click of her heels on the terracotta tiles, silence fell. She couldn't believe how brave she was being. All the doubts and scruples had fallen away. Amabel was no blushing bride who would strive towards mutual support and love for the rest of her married life. This looked to Dora like a publicity stunt designed to boost a flagging career. She remembered reading somewhere that she was being considered for the next James Bond film.

'Excuse me,' she said. She cleared her throat.

She had everyone's attention now. The bishops stared. Nothing like this had happened to any of them before.

Dora took off her hat. She noticed Guy turned to look at her dully, as if he wasn't in the least surprised. Amabel just stood there still facing the altar. Dora addressed herself to her.

'Look, I'm terribly sorry about this. I know my timing is dreadful.'

'Yes, yes,' said the bishop testily.

'But Guy is already married to me.'

There was a gasp. Amabel, so cool she hardly flickered, said, 'Oh shit.' She turned and almost ran down the aisle. Pushing past Dora, she threw her single arum lily on the ground and disappeared through the sunlit door.

The best man turned to Guy and said, 'You bastard.' He hurried out after his sister. Her parents, looking daggers at Dora, followed him.

Dora felt small and foolish and bad. The congregation sat down, unsure what to do with itself. 'Why, Dora?' said Guy wearily. 'Why now? Why didn't you call me and we could have sorted it out beforehand? You're a little drama queen, you know that?'

Dora noticed some colour had come back into his cheeks. She thought he looked better than when she had first seen him in the church. Perhaps it was just anger. She hurried towards him.

The bishop leaned over and said, 'Let's not do this in public. I suggest you both come into the vestry.' He straightened up and announced to the congregation, 'We'll just get this sorted out. If you would remain in your places.'

Dora could hear suppressed snorts of laughter coming from the back of the church.

The bishop turned around in a lordly manner and proceeded up into the vestry that was to one side of the altar. Guy, manners unimpaired by events, allowed Dora to go first in the ecclesiastical wake. He followed, grimly silent. The congregation began to murmur. They were annoyed that the main drama would be taking place behind closed doors. The organist, with great presence of mind began to play soft funereal music.

Dora felt she was caught in a bubble with Guy and the bishop. It all seemed like a parody of the wedding she had never had: retreating into the vestry for the formalities, the removal of the veil – with Amabel playing an unduly sexy Odette to her modest Odile. When she looked around, she saw Guy's parents had caught up. His mother looked grim. His father was saying in hushed but angry tones, 'How could you be so irresponsible! You're thirty-six for goodness' sake. I was just beginning to think that you were settling down at last. When did this happen anyway? I knew nothing about it. Who is this?'

Dora caught Guy's father's eye. He stared at her rudely. They were at last in the peace and privacy of the vestry.

'Well?' demanded Guy's father. 'Are you just a jealous little troublemaker or is there something behind this?'

'Look,' said Guy. 'I'm sorry. I'm afraid she's right. It's true. At least I think it is. This is Dora Jerusalem. I married her in the 1980s in Chelsea Registry Office – mainly because she refused to sleep with me and I wanted to teach her a lesson.'

'What?' His mother looked astonished.

'I know. It sounds stupid. When I met Amabel again and she made it so clear that she wanted to marry me, I didn't bother to think about the implications. I haven't really seen Dora since, except in the distance.'

'Huh. So much for sexual liberation,' put in his father. He turned to Dora and said, 'Look here, why didn't you say something before? You must have known Guy and Amabel were engaged.'

'I - I don't know. I felt a bit mad about the whole thing. Guy was playing with me then; I thought I would return the favour.'

'Can't blame you, I suppose.' Guy's mother spoke for the first time. 'How long ago was this?'

'Oh, years…'

'And you never married anyone else?'

'Of course she didn't, Mother. She's married to me. However badly I behaved she seems to have taken it all far too seriously.'

'Guy, you'd better go and find Amabel and see if you can make it up with her,' his father suggested. 'Although she looked like nothing on earth, I must say. Did you have any idea she was going to wear the Emperor's new clothes?'

Guy didn't answer. He didn't look at Dora again. He walked out of the vestry and down the aisle, followed by curious stares. From the back of the church came whistles, catcalls and cries of, 'Way to go, Guy.'

Guy's mother turned to Dora and said, 'I'm Janet Moore, Guy's mother. We have never met, I think?'

Dora nodded, her eyes fixed on the floor.

'Well, this is Guy's father, Lord Northiam. We're divorced and have been for years. Which is what Guy should have done before marrying Amabel. Silly boy.'

'Do you have any evidence?' Lord Northiam asked.

Dora brought out the photocopy of the wedding certificate. He took it from her.

'I still don't understand why you had to do it so publicly. I do think it was thoughtless. Did you not consider anybody else's feelings?'

'I am sorry. I suppose I didn't. It was all so awful. It took me years to get over it. I don't suppose I have got over it really, if I can behave like this. This isn't the real me, you know.'

'Leave her alone, Northiam. Guy's wasted years of her life, don't you understand? Not just a bit of disappointment for a spoilt little rich girl like Amabel.'

Dora caught what she thought was an approving glance from Janet and gave her a small sad smile. 'I think I'd better go now,' she said.

Janet was scribbling on a small piece of paper.

'Come and see me in London when all the brouhaha has died down.'

The parish priest, who had replaced the bishops by this time, offered to show Dora out of the back of the church, 'as there are a lot of photographers out the front.'

He was very kind, taking her arm and patting it. Dora began to cry.

'It's not as if I didn't mean to cause trouble because I did,' she wailed as he led her away. She glanced back at Lord Northiam; she thought he looked defeated. She pulled away from the priest and went back to him.

'I am really sorry,' she said to his averted face. 'But I truly loved your son and if I could have been his wife properly I would have done my very best to be a good one. I'm not just some flake.' Then she left him, following the priest out of the vestry door.

'My car is parked on the other side from everyone else's,' she explained.

'So you planned all this did you?' The vicar looked amused.

'To be honest with you, I had decided not to do it – to sort something out afterwards.'

'What made you change your mind?' he inquired gently, as they picked their way between the overgrown grave-stones.

'His face,' she said simply.

'What about his face?'

'He looked desperate, as if he needed rescuing. It made me realise how much I loved him and that I was willing to risk everything to get him back.'

'Do you think this is the best way to get a man back? To make a public fool of him?' He was still speaking gently.

'Probably not. I don't know.'

Twenty-two

HAVING UNDONE THE PADLOCK with difficulty, Dora pushed open the sagging door. The room was dim and dusty. Distemper flaked and powdered off the bulging walls. 'It must be an old dak bungalow,' she thought. There were two charpoys pushed together in the middle of the brick floor, their mosquito nets looped up on hooks above them. Their feet stood in little unglazed pottery cups to keep goodness-knows-what creepy crawlies out of the mattress.

She had chosen the cheapest hotel in the backpackers' bible and hoped she wasn't going to regret it. In India you got used to very primitive conditions. She had shared shower cubicles with enormous cockroaches contemplatively munching hair in the drain. In an old hippie hostel dormitory, she had woken inches away from one of the bearded blond gods of Valhalla breathing softly deep in his dreams. You had to accept strange experiences in India. Dora flexed her shoulders; all the London knots and tensions had untied themselves on the road from the airport.

It didn't smell bad – only of dust. She shrugged her rucksack on to the nearest charpoy and went through to look at the 'bathroom'. It was a tiny, dark, brick-floored cupboard with tap, bucket and squatter loo – very much what she had come to expect.

She had been on the bus all day and felt grubby in every cranny, so she shot the bolt on the bedroom door and stripped off her clothes. Fetching the sandalwood soap in its little aluminium box and a sponge, she went into the faintly foetid bathroom. The air was warm so she filled the bucket with cold water and began to sluice and scrub herself down. Feeling much better, she padded on wet feet back into the bedroom to fetch a towel.

As she wrapped herself up, she was glad to note that her breasts hadn't lost their shape – even though she'd lost quite a lot of weight. The all-pervading smell of piss in the air and anxiety about Guy had removed her appetite. She dried herself, folded her lunghi around her waist and tucked it in, and put on a long T-shirt. She was very thirsty and longed for a cup of tea. It was a bad idea to be out on your own after sunset. She wanted to be safely locked into her room by the time the sun dipped below the sea. Money belt strapped on under the T-shirt, she picked up pen and notebook and went to find a café on the beach.

On the way she performed her usual ritual, asking to see the visitors' book and scanning it for Guy's name. It wasn't there. Tomorrow she would set off around all the cheap hotels doing the same thing. Tonight she would rest and enjoy herself.

When she had visited Guy's mother a week after the aborted wedding, Janet had told her that Guy had tele-phoned just once to say that it was no good with Amabel and that he was going to India 'to think things through a bit'. Janet wanted him to come and see her, but he said he had too much to do before he went. He had already rented his flat to a friend – 'for tuppence a week', as his mother had put it. He had been going to move into Amabel's flat after the wedding.

She also told Dora that he'd tried to go around to Amabel's place to retrieve his clothes. She hadn't answered the bell and he luckily investigated a pile of bin bags on the pavement – he knew it wasn't dustbin day. The Notting Hill inhabitants hadn't followed their usual pattern and helped themselves as, sure enough, his entire wardrobe was there. Guy had obtained his visa in 24 hours, bought a bucket shop ticket to Delhi and left.

Janet knew why Amabel hadn't answered the door, because Lady Cumbria had told her. Amabel was on her honeymoon in Phuket in Thailand, and not alone either. She couldn't help feeling happy that Amabel had found consolation so fast. It helped Dora to justify her behaviour to herself.

Her hotel was very near the beach, and Dora had noticed an open-sided café a couple of hundred yards away as she had walked from the bus. She went back there, ordered tea, which came in a glass, and ladoos, the only Indian sweetmeat she could tolerate – sweet crunchy balls of fried vermicelli. She had a look at her Lonely Planet guide with its long list of hotels she'd crossed out.

When the vicar had helped her into her car, she'd thought she'd better drive away just in case the press found out where she was. They probably weren't interested in her but it didn't do to hang around. She had kicked off her high heels and driven about five miles before turning off down a track into a small wood. She got out of the car and took off her jacket, slipping a cotton dress over her head and removing the skirt underneath. She put the suit back on the padded hanger.

She had rolled off the stockings and suspender belt and put on some cotton knickers before getting back into the car and driving on barefoot. While she had been changing she had decided to go and see Hilly. She didn't stop to telephone her; she just drove on to the motorway, down to the M25 and round to the Kent turn-off, arriving at home just as the day was dying. It was a beautiful evening to finish off a heavenly day. She stopped the engine, took off her safety belt and just sat for a moment. Hilly appeared around the side of the cottage in her gardening hat, wearing a faded sundress, rubber gloves and cut-down Wellingtons.

'My goodness, Dora, what are you doing here?' she said as she went over to shut the gate.

Dora got out of the car and went to her mother. She tried to put her arms around her, but Hilly went stiff and pulled away uncomfortably, apologising under her breath. Dora's heart sank.

'Mum, I've done something rather dreadful.'

'Well, you'd better come inside.'

'Mum, did you hear me? I've done something dreadful today.'

'I've just got to get out of these sweaty clothes and have a shower. I've finished for the day luckily. Then we can talk.'

'Please listen to me. I feel terrible. I don't know what to do.' Dora started crying. She always hoped her mother would be able to comfort her, as she had years ago, before prep school. But from that point on, Hilly had grown more and more distant. Dora had found refuge from her mother's eternal busyness in her father's study. She had long since learned not to confide in her. Hilly always seemed so disapproving of everything. It had been particularly bad when Dora's father had died. She didn't see her mother cry once. Dora wondered what on earth she was thinking and couldn't imagine. When Dora had wept bitterly, missing her father's voice on the telephone, his interest in her and often-expressed love, Hilly had simply left the room.

Now she turned to her only child. 'What on earth are you crying about? Come into the house.'

Dora did as she was told. She left the beautiful suit and hat in the car and brought in her overnight bag. She padded softly across the gravel, mortifying her bare feet on the sharp stones. The back door opened directly into the kitchen, which was warm from the Aga. 'English summers are never warm enough to justify turning it off,' Hilly would say. 'As soon as you do, it's one of those dismal rainy days again and you wish you hadn't.'

'I'll just take my bag upstairs.'

'Your bed isn't made up. You'd better get some sheets out of the airing cupboard.'

Dora went, muttering to herself, 'She's not in the least bit interested in me. Why the hell did I come back here? If Daddy were here, it'd be different. We'd be in his study with the door shut, giggling over it, and he would tell me exactly what to do next. Mum is worse than useless.'

Dora's father had died three years beforehand. It was cancer of the liver and he had declined very quickly. She remembered how brave and glorious he had been, even when he was quite yellow with jaundice. He'd had the grace to laugh about that. 'Marvellous suntan,' he'd said. That was after the local vicar had given him the last rights. He had been so desperately thin and tired. Of course, he was much older than Hilly, 20 years, but still much too young to die. A painful frown creased Dora's forehead every time she thought about him as she tried to suppress her tears.

She fetched sheets from the cupboard in the bathroom and made up her little bed. Her room was very much as it always had been: plenty of china animals, shelves of books – Beatrix Potter, *Improving Your Pony*, *Angélique and the King*, *Complete Chaucer*, *Our Mutual Friend* – reflecting different phases of her life. In the capsule of her room echoed the intense happiness she'd felt every time she'd come home from boarding school.

Her mind shied away from the events of the day. She hoped very much that the dance was going ahead anyway, that Amabel had the spirit not to waste a party. She felt almost guiltier about the flowers and the caterers and what it had all cost than she did about the emotional impact. She was convinced that Amabel didn't really love Guy, that the whole thing was a well-staged publicity stunt to boost Amabel's acting career now she was getting too old to model. 'I'd better be right,' Dora told herself.

She found an old cardigan and a pair of tennis shoes and put them on. There was a slight sharpness in the air. She went down to the kitchen.

Her mother was stirring something on the Aga. 'I'm making some supper, do you want some?' 'Oh Mother, of course I do.'

'All right, all right.'

'Wrong foot, right from the start, as usual,' thought Dora, and then she said. 'I've just got to make a phone call – would that be OK?'

'I suppose so.'

Dora went into her father's study. It looked much the same as it had when he was alive, only much tidier. She sat at his desk and rang directory inquiries, asking for the Cumbria's number.

'I have three listings here,' said the operator.

'Estate office, gardener or house?'

'House, please,' said Dora, hoping it wasn't ex-directory. Surprisingly, it wasn't.

She dialled the number, unsure of what she was going to say until someone answered the telephone.

'Cumbria Hall?' said a female voice. It didn't sound as she imagined Lady Cumbria would speak.

'Hello,' said Dora. 'I was at Guy and Amabel's wedding this afternoon and I'm still in the area. I was wondering if the dance is still happening?'

'To whom am I speaking?' said the voice, sounding bewildered. 'There was an announcement in church about that.'

'Ah,' said Dora, thinking fast. 'I slipped out when the disturbance happened and didn't hear it.'

'Oh, I see,' said the voice. 'Well, Lady Cumbria asked me to tell everyone that, in spite of the distressing incident, the party would go ahead as planned. After all, everyone is in house parties. It was all so beautifully organised it seemed such a pity to cancel it.'

'That's marvellous. Well done, Lady Cumbria,' said Dora, feeling immensely relieved.

'Are you not staying in a house party?'

'Er, no . . .'

'Who is this?' the voice sharpened suspiciously.

'Goodbye. Thanks for letting me know.' Dora put the telephone down and sat back in her father's chair. She had wanted to ask how Amabel was, but hadn't dared. She could find out next week.

She went back into the kitchen.

'You haven't changed, have you?' Her mother was standing with her back to the Aga, arms crossed. Dora stared at her bewildered. 'I haven't seen you for months and you breeze in here and go straight into your father's study.'

'But, Mum, I just went to use the...'

'He's not there any more, is he?'

'Mum...' She could see her mother's eyes glittering with unshed tears. Dora went towards her impulsively seeking to take her in her arms. Hilly seemed to tense up. Ugly sobs jerked from her mouth.

'Mum, what is it?'

Dora held her mother's rigid upper arms and tried to draw her towards her.

'I'm sorry I haven't been here much but I've been so busy with the flat and everything...'

Hilly was weeping openly now. Through her sobs Dora could hear her saying that Dora was heartless. That she never came near her old mother now her father was gone. That she was cold.

Dora protested, all the time trying to pull her mother into her arms.

'Leave me alone.' She struggled wildly, pushing Dora away with her elbows. Dora was crying by this time as well.

'What do you mean, Mum? You never needed me. You were always so busy yourself. I thought you didn't mind whether I came or not.'

Hilly pulled copious sheets of kitchen roll down and wiped her face. She silently handed a piece to Dora to do the same. They were still standing far apart from one another.

'Of course I minded. You're my daughter, aren't you? As you got older you would always go straight to your father as soon as you came home and shut the study door. I used to stand outside listening sometimes to the sound of your voices and laughter. I felt so left out.'

'Mum, I didn't know. I didn't think you were particularly happily married. I always thought you didn't like me much. You were always so sharp with me. Dad was such fun.' All the certainties of home took on new shades of meaning. She realised that she had been avoiding home now her father wasn't there, without thinking about her mother much at all.

Hilly changed the subject abruptly, 'Would you like a drink? I put a bottle of wine in the fridge.'

'That would be lovely.'

Dora reeled while her mother poured wine into glasses. A curtain seemed torn away. The thoughtless patterns that had developed seemed so normal. Her father had had time for her. Her mother was always busy with her committees, her administrative job in the local boys' prep school, her friends, the house, the garden, the freezer. Her father wrote art history textbooks, rather slowly dictating his copy into a tape recorder for the local typist to transcribe. He always had time to talk to her when he wasn't abroad looking at pictures.

They sat one on either side of the kitchen table. Dora looked into her mother's face with interest. She was only 57. Although her skin looked blotchy with tears, Dora could see how pretty she still was. She had a deep and ample cleavage in the neckline of the sundress and a neat waist. Looking at her objectively, Dora realised she wouldn't be surprised if Hilly found another man.

'Mum, I really had no idea you minded. You never seemed to have the time to just stop and talk. When I first went to boarding school, I came back in the holidays longing for you. I remember once you said you would come up and wash my hair. I sat in the bath for hours, waiting for you, while the water got colder and colder. You never came. I eventually did it myself. You had forgotten me.'

Hilly took a sip of her drink.

'I'm sorry. I thought it would be easier for you to be away from me so much if I didn't coddle you in the holidays. I just didn't know much about how mothers ought to be; as you know, I didn't really have one.'

Dora digested this.

'Why did you send me to boarding school so young? Lots of the other girls' parents lived abroad, but you didn't.'

'Your father insisted.'

Dora blinked. Then she felt angry. 'I suppose you can say that now he's dead. So he can't deny it. That's really weak of you. I know he really loved me.'

Hilly looked at her wearily. 'He did love you. Only he couldn't get on with his work with you around, being noisy in the house. So it was easier to send you away. Believe me, Dora, I didn't want to lose my little girl. I had to work to keep us all going, and getting that job as head matron at Kenton just about kept us afloat. It meant I could work in term time and be around in the holidays to look after you.'

'Daddy worked. He was always working, wasn't he?'

'Yes, he used to write his books. They didn't make a lot of money. Luckily he inherited this house from his uncle. But we both needed to earn to keep things going. We had to pay your school fees.'

She suddenly felt sympathy for her mother.

'He stopped teaching at the local college when you were quite young, you see,' Hilly went on. 'He had to leave his original job when we got married.'

Dora absorbed this, but didn't feel like probing further.

'You said you did something dreadful today?' Hilly asked, changing the subject.

'I disrupted a wedding.'

'You did what?'

'I never told you, but I got married when I was twenty-three.'

'You did what?' Hilly stood up. 'Why did you never tell me?'

'Frankly? You didn't seem any too interested in my life. And I didn't tell Daddy because I was embarrassed and ashamed. You see, Guy told me to keep it a secret until he inherited his trust fund. He was afraid his parents might not approve.'

'Oh dear. I haven't been a very good mother, have I? I was so determined not to interfere, you see. I wanted you to feel free to do whatever you liked. The idea in those days was to let the children make their own mistakes, and keep your mouth shut. I didn't want you to get trapped into marriage too young, as I was.'

'It just made me feel you didn't care what I did. So I went and did something silly.'

'Well, there were much sillier and more dangerous things you could have done, I suppose. When did you get divorced? I always wondered why you didn't have boyfriends or get married. The boys you brought home all seemed to be gay, although I never wanted to say anything in case I hurt your feelings.'

'That's just it, Mum. I didn't get divorced.'

'You mean your husband tried to marry someone else and you stood up and stopped the wedding?'

'Well, yes. Yes, I suppose that's exactly what I did.'

'Who were you calling just now?'

'I was just calling the bride's home to make sure they didn't cancel the party. You see, it was going to be the ball of the year and if that had gone up the spout as well I would have felt terrible.'

Hilly snorted. Then she began to laugh.

'Not many people get the opportunity to stand up and stop a wedding, do they? There must be something odd about you.'

'For goodness' sake. He was legally married to me. He couldn't then go and have a lovely society wedding with somebody else, could he?'

'I suppose you didn't hear until it was too late to do something about it beforehand?'

Dora looked guilty.

'Well, yes, actually. I did know beforehand.'

'You must be an exhibitionist, then.'

'I suppose I am. But I really wanted to see them together before I could make up my mind what to do about it. And I couldn't think of any other way to see them together without arousing suspicion, except at their wedding.'

'How odd of him to invite you.'

'He didn't. I crashed it.'

'Right, I see. Do you want another drink?' Hilly went to the fridge to fetch the bottle. 'By the way, are you all right?' she inquired with her back to her daughter.

'Yes, Mum, I think I am. I think it's a relief to have done it. Now I must take the consequences and I'm quite happy to do that.'

'Do you still love – what's his name? Guy, was it?'

'I think that is what all this is about. I never stopped loving him. If he walked in now I would go off with him without a backward glance.'

'Oh. Just when you and I seemed to be getting a bit closer for a change.'

Dora swirled the dregs around in her glass. Then she said, 'Mum, you know I believe that the relationship between parent and child is really up to the parent.'

'Oh, so you think our relationship is my fault?' Hilly voice didn't sound angry, merely interested.

'No, it's not exactly your fault.' Dora squirmed inwardly. There were so many no-go areas with her mother. Her face could shut like a trap and Dora wouldn't normally dare to venture further for fear of being snapped at. Today she felt brave, though, and carried on.

'I know so little about you. You never talk about your childhood or your youth. I am sure you have your reasons.'

'Please, Dora, I don't want your amateur psychology. Look at what you've just confessed to doing. Who is this man you married anyway? You can't have lived with him – I think I would have noticed that at least. When I telephoned you were always at that house you shared in Fulham with those flatmates.'

'You're doing it again, turning the conversation away from you to me. What is it? Please, Mum. Now Daddy's gone, I've only got you.'

'I see. I'm a substitute for your father now, am I?'

'OK. I'm clumsy.'

'Do you remember who was doing the cooking, cleaning the house, growing vegetables, looking after the garden? And when you went back to school I had to go out to work as well. At least your father had organised decent life insurance for himself so I could retire early.'

Dora felt ashamed. She realised how many of the comforts of home she had taken for granted. She looked at her mother. 'I'm sorry. I didn't realise. I was here so little I wanted to cram as much of Dad in as possible. You must also acknowledge that it was your choice to do all the work. I am sure he would have helped if you'd asked him.'

'Men of his generation just didn't. Remember he was twenty years older than me. He fought in the war, for goodness' sake. I was born in 1940. I don't know if he ever talked to you about the war.'

'No, he didn't. That seemed to be his no-go area. I was rather grateful that he chose to live in the present.'

'Well, he was in the Navy, as you know. He was invalided out.'

'Yes, I knew that.'

'Did you know why?'

'I thought those scars on his hands might be something to do with it. I didn't like to ask.'

'Well, he suffered from shell shock. Bombers attacked his ship most unusually. They dropped something called fragmentation bombs designed to explode above ground to cause maximum casualties with flying shrapnel.'

'How horrible.'

'While the others all went below, your father ran in the opposite direction to help a young sailor who'd fallen. Just as he seized him around the chest to drag him to safety, another shell exploded. The sailor's body shielded your father from the worst of the shrapnel, although he got it in his hands and arms. He was a promising young artist before the war, but the torn tendons made his hands too stiff. '

'Did the sailor he tried to save die?'

'Yes, instantly. Absolutely peppered. Your father didn't realise he was dead for a bit and sat on the deck holding him in his arms. I believe he was very beautiful and your father was rather in love with him.'

Dora gaped. The skeletons were positively tumbling out now. 'Was my father gay?'

'Not really,' said Hilly. 'But he helped out when they were busy.'

Dora found herself laughing. Then tears began to pour down her face again. She went and knelt beside her mother's chair, putting her arms around her waist and resting her head on her knee. Hilly put a hand on her shoulder.

'I do love you, darling Dora. Always have.'

Dora cried all the harder. She was surprised she had any tears left. She shivered and ached with tiredness.

'The pregnancy was a bit alarming, though,' Hilly went on.

'Because your mother had died in childbirth?'

'No, not that. She was forty-five and had a bad heart. She should never have had another baby. I was only nineteen and fit as a fiddle.'

'Why, then?'

'Because at the time I wasn't absolutely sure who your father was.'

Dora leapt to her feet.

'What on earth do you mean?'

'I'm sure now that you are Stephen's child. You look awfully like photographs of him as a boy. Those exotic eyes are very distinctive.'

Dora, already disturbed enough by the events of the day, felt frantic as her world slipped out of control.

'You hypocrite! You always made out what a bad idea it was to sleep with people before marriage. You were always so discouraging about boyfriends. All the time you were cutting around – conceiving me. You bitch. I think I'd better get back to London. No wonder I'm so fucked up about sex.'

Dora made for the door.

'Wait, Dora, please. There was only ever one other man. And I only slept with him once. Actually, we didn't even sleep. It was rather more perfunctory than that. I really loved him too and desperately wanted to be with him, but he went abroad and got engaged to someone else. So, I married your father soon afterwards. Then I had to work and run a home, and having no parents and nowhere to go, I missed out on the sixties completely. I suppose I may have been a bit jealous of your freedom. But if what you mean about being "fucked up" about sex is that you never joined in with the promiscuous seventies, then you must be glad now, aren't you? What with AIDS and herpes and all the horrors I read about in the papers?'

Dora was staring at her mother. She'd never heard her speak like this before. 'If you must know,' she said. 'I never lost my virginity. Came pretty close to it a few times. But I went and married Guy so young, and stayed faithful to him. Besides which, men more or less stopped offering when I passed thirty.'

'You never slept with him?'

'No. He went off to New York straight after our pathetic excuse for a wedding. I never saw him again to speak to until today.'

Hilly got up to open another bottle of wine. They'd finished the last one.

Twenty-three

'Darling, I've just been talking to your mother.' There was something in Tirzah's voice on the telephone that made Dora feel anxious and guilty.

'How can I express to you how sorry I am.'

Dora was bewildered.

'What about?'

'I had no idea that you had actually gone and married him. Why didn't you tell me?'

'I don't know. I was embarrassed, I suppose, that it hadn't ended in everlasting love – like you and Dougal, or Selwyn for that matter.'

'What a waste of all those years.'

This made Dora angry.

'Why does everybody keep saying I have wasted my time? For goodness' sake, I've had a really interesting life, thank you. Why should having a man be the only justification for my existence? You of all people, Tirzah, should know that there's a lot more to life than marriage.'

'Darling, I'm sorry. I didn't mean to offend you. But this

so-called marriage does seem to have prevented you from finding anyone else.'

'Who cares? I don't.'

'But you might have wanted children. I know your mother was longing for grandchildren.'

'I'm not some kind of baby-making machine to gratify her frustrated maternity. Why can't anyone be pleased with the things I have created? Thousands and thousands of published words on hundreds of subjects. I am independent; I earn a good living, doing something that interests me. Why does everyone think it's such a tragedy?'

'If you feel like that about it, why are you going to look for him?'

The fury drained out of Dora, like air from a balloon. 'I'm sorry I shouted at you.'

'That's OK, darling. Any time. You still love him, right?'

'I suppose I do. But I don't know him any more. I feel love beaming out of me but I am perfectly aware that he isn't receiving it, like NASA trying to contact other planets.'

'Oh, I don't think love is ever futile. Look at Our Lord's love for us. So many of us aren't tuned in to that.'

'Yes, Tirzah.'

Dora didn't take too much notice of this. Loving and marrying Selwyn had converted Tirzah to Christianity and she would bring it up sometimes. Dora respected Tirzah's commitment and admired the beautiful sculptures that had come out of it, particular the Mothers. They combined the Sorrows with the Babies, and were based on concentration camp photographs of dignified but naked Jewish women with children in their arms and calm expressions.

And the scultpures reflected another change in Tirzah's

life. Nine months after marrying Selwyn, at the age of 43, in the crypt of Canterbury cathedral, she had had the first of two children. She had always assumed while married to Dougal that she was barren. When she found herself to be pregnant, to her complete amazement, she talked to the doctor who had treated Dougal for the testicular cancer that had killed him. He told her that Dougal had probably always been infertile.

Tirzah hadn't been sure what to feel about this. Her new Christian faith helped. Mary came first, followed by Peter 14 months later. For a good three years, Tirzah existed in an ecstatic milky melee. When this subsided, she began to sculpt her Mothers. Dora judged Tirzah to be a very fulfilled woman.

Tirzah continued, 'Dora, I do feel guilty about it, though. I feel I might have given you the idea that marrying him might solve all the problems in the relationship. It was still so close to Dougal's death and I knew I was falling in love with Selwyn. I was confused and I'm afraid I said things to you that I shouldn't have. Do you remember, you came and spent a night after a party?'

Dora remembered vividly; that was where the idea of marrying Guy and sorting out the details afterwards had crystallised in her mind. She sighed. She had always been so willing to give Guy time and space, but possibly not quite so much as he had taken.

'It wasn't your fault, honestly, Tirzah. I was young and foolish and desperately in love. I had this absurd idea that my virginity was something significant. I wish I had just lost it quickly at Cambridge, like all my friends. I would have been so much less naive all this time.'

'Right. Well, you have my blessing in whatever you

choose to do. Please don't expect him to be pleased to see you, that's all.'

'I'm not expecting a miracle,' said Dora, inaccurately. 'I just want to sort it out once and for all and get on with my life. I did hope that witnessing him marry someone else might do that. He looked so desperate and miserable though. It didn't look right.'

'Have you considered that you might be wrong about that? That he was just nervous of the commitment? That they did love each other very much?'

'I don't know about that. Guy's mother told me that Amabel went on the honeymoon with another man – a film producer who had been at the wedding and sat with Lord and Lady Cumbria in the front pew.'

'Oh, I see.'

'She was beastly to Guy when he went to apologise. She wouldn't even see him.'

'You can't blame her for being angry.'

'No. But I don't think she loved Guy. I don't think she would have made him happy. Her stuffy-looking brother was his best man. He had lots and lots of good friends who would have been happy to do that for him. I felt she was trying to sanitise him, to change him into what she wanted, instead of accepting him as he was.'

'You can't know that, Dora. This could all be self-justification.'

'I know, Tirzah. I'm going to India for other reasons than to find Guy. That's just what has set me off. I've never travelled anywhere much for very long. I missed out on backpacking when I was younger. I just want to say sorry, if I bump into him, and sort out the details. I have already talked to a solicitor about arranging a divorce for when I get back.'

'That sounds very sensible.'

'I'm looking forward to a bit of independent travelling. I've sold the idea of the mature gap-year trip to several of my commissioning editors. I might even do a book. Please, Tirzah, I'm not wasting my time just chasing a man across the globe.'

'I know. Do come and see us when you get back. Your goddaughter will want to hear all about it. Before I know it she'll want to run off to India herself.'

'Give them all my love.'

'I will.'

'Love you.'

Dora rang off. She had long since learned to edit the truth about her dreams. She moved through her life in a state of hope. It was one of the things that Guy had found so attractive about her.

Twenty-four

Dr Simon Monroe barked 'Enter!' and a woman pushed open the creosote-painted door and crossed the beaten earth floor to his desk. He glanced up, before returning to the haemoglobin graph he was calculating. For a moment he thought she was a local, with her dark hair, tanned cheekbones and oriental eyes. But local women wore gonchas – wrap-over robes – and were often adorned with hanks of grubby freshwater pearl, turquoise and coral jewellery. This woman was wearing Helly Hansen climbing dungarees and a thick jersey.

'Are you Dr Simon Monroe?' Dora began. As soon as he heard her voice, he became irritated.
'Yes. What is it?'

He was used to home-counties girls, travelling on their own, barging into his office armed with some flimsy introduction. Simon was in India to get away from precisely the life they represented.

'Excuse me, I was wondering…'
'Yes, what?'

'Do you know a man called Guy Boleyn?' Dora asked.

At last he looked up properly and snapped, 'Why?'

'Well, I heard he might be in Ladakh.'

'Who told you that?'

'The manager at the Benaulim Beach Resort in Goa. They said you brought him up here after he had been ill.'

'You one of the girls who are always chasing him?'

Dora didn't answer, but looked down at her sensible khaki canvas Indian Army boots. He added a couple more figures to the graph paper, before asking: 'How well did you know him?'

'Quite well.'

'When did you last see him?'

'Earlier in the summer.'

No one else had come looking for Guy yet. Light dawned:

'You're not the woman who screwed up his wedding, are you?' She wasn't what he had imagined. In his mind's eye, the woman to blame for Guy's most recent problems had been a slutty little troublemaker.

'Yes, I'm afraid I am.'

'Right.' He didn't say anything more. 'Vengeful cow,' he thought to himself. 'Just when Guy had found some kind of stability, she goes and screws it up.'

Guy hadn't told him much, just that he had tried to get married in June and a blast from the past had turned up and put a stop to it. 'Not that I blamed her,' he had remarked. 'We were legally married.' The whole business had set him off again on a downward spiral of depression.

Simon had been taking a break from Ladakh, combining a beach holiday with volunteering at Panaji hospital, when he was asked to examine a European case. The emaciated man had no papers on him, and couldn't – or wouldn't – answer questions. He had bad amoebic dysentery and the hospital staff had stabilised him, but didn't know which consul to contact.

As soon as the man opened his eyes, Simon recognised his boyhood friend Guy Boleyn. After that the doctor had nursed him back to health. It turned out Guy had collapsed with dehydration and been robbed on a remote stretch of Benaulim beach. He hadn't been taking the kind of care of himself necessary to stay healthy in India.

'You were Guy's first wife then? What's your name?'

'Dora Jerusalem. In a way I suppose I am. Do you know where he is?'

Simon sighed. He'd been putting Guy's whereabouts to the back of his mind for the last week and didn't really want to face up the problem now.

'I think you should sit down,' he said.

Dora did not sit down. 'Please, tell me where he is?'

'Well, I'm afraid I am not quite sure. He left a week ago, but the jeep he was driving was found in the Indus river. It seems it had gone off the road.'

'And Guy?'

'We just don't know. He may just have parked it and not put the handbrake on before setting off. He was on a walking mission to take haemoglobin samples in a series of villages off the road. Something we do regularly, to keep track of the nutrition programme. There's no way of contacting him.

'His rucksack and equipment were not inside the jeep, so we thought he probably just went off. Even so, I took the precaution of alerting the police and the army and they've checked all the usual places that heavy objects are washed up.'

He glanced up and saw the woman looked horrified, but he couldn't stop: 'The good news is they haven't found a body or his luggage. The bad news is that the Indus is a powerful river, given terrible force by the narrow gorge it flows through in the Himalayas.'

Dora finally sat down. Simon could see she was trembling.

'Have you been searching yourself?' she asked.

'I couldn't. I have had to run the project here single-handed. I did a lot for Guy after I found him in that Goa hospital. I'm sorry, but I have to admit I got a bit tired of it.'

'That's completely irresponsible. Have you told his parents?'

'Well, no, I haven't. He's always survived these scrapes before. I'm simply waiting for him to walk through that door.'

Simon suppressed feelings of irritation and felt defensive. This was his world. He made the decisions. She had no right to question him. He noted the haunted look in her eyes. 'He can be very self-destructive, you know,' he said, more gently.

'I remember him getting depressed, but I didn't realise it went as far as suicide.'

'I don't believe he would ever actually commit suicide on purpose, but he had a habit of doing little or nothing to prevent trouble. He got into a mood occasionally even at prep school. It was amazing he survived his childhood.'

'Aren't all little boys reckless?'

'Yes, but this was different. He would get a set expression on his face that always made my heart sink. I would feel cowardly about turning back. I was always large; he was small and skinny. I suppose that's why he survived the thinnest branches and thinner ice.

'After he got to Dartington it was worse because he had access to all kinds of drugs. His parents' break-up didn't help. It wasn't just drugs either; it was motorbikes, and he would go swimming in the river at any time of year when he was in a particular mood. If the result was no future, he didn't really seem to care.'

'I only ever saw him depressed once,' said Dora. 'I just thought he had been bingeing – you know, coke and booze. Although I didn't do drugs myself, it wasn't such a big deal in the eighties, was it?'

Simon leaned across his desk and noticed her rucksack.

'Do you have anywhere to stay?'

'No, I came here straight from the bus station.'

'Look, you had better come home with me now. I've finished here. I'll tell you a bit more about what is being done.'

'Right.' She stood up. 'Thanks very much, but I think I should go and look for him myself.'

'What makes you think you will be more successful than the police or the army?' he said, incredulously.

'I've been looking for him all over India. I've traced him as far as here, and I'm not going to give up now.'

'Look, Debbie...'

'I'm called Dora.'

'Sorry – look, Dora, what do you know about Ladakh? You'll only get lost and then be more of a problem than that silly self-destructive idiot. I don't know why I took responsibility for him. It always led to trouble, even at school. Bugger it.'

Simon had another look at Dora. He had been feeling bad about not going out searching for Guy himself – relying on the local authorities. She did look strong and sensible. She was wearing the right clothes and no lipstick or anything silly.

He prided himself on being an excellent judge of character, and he quickly made a decision. 'Are you fit?'

'Yes, I am reasonably.'

'Right, I'll tell you what you can do. I will lend you Dorje. He's from a Tibetan exile family and he's a professional climber and guide loosely attached to the Food and Nutrition Fund. You'll have to pay him, as he isn't on the roll, but you can go with him, just to check out a couple of the villages that Guy was meant to be visiting. We haven't seen anybody from either recently. They're bringing in the barley harvest, which tends to keep them busy and out of Leh. Maybe Guy's holed up and embarrassed to tell me about the jeep. He always did break my toys.'

'Having said that, he's probably on his way back into Leh by now. The trouble is that there's no way of getting in touch with the outlying villages.

Guy's tour was meant to go on for days, and that was what Simon was going to allow him. He wasn't meant to be alone, but he had done the first round with Dorje, had a good map and compass and knew the way. The villagers would accompany him between villages.

But then again, perhaps Guy was dead. Simon knew he was going to have to face up to it and tell Lord Northiam and Mrs Moore at some point. He had kept putting it off, knowing that each day he did so was making more trouble for himself. People were always going off on long walking tours, but if he had been in the jeep when it plunged 20 feet into the Indus, then he was very unlikely to be alive.

He could see that Dora was shocked and needed to do something. He knew the therapeutic effect of action as opposed to inaction. She had come this far; she might as well go further. He also didn't particularly want Dora hanging around in Leh, pestering him for news. That might go on for the whole winter. She might run out of money or move in with him. He shivered with disgust. He didn't much like women.

'You're dressed for it anyway,' he told her.

'I met some Australians in Goa who were going home and sold me their clothes and equipment.'

'Good. I'll give you a list of supplies you will need. You can leave any excess baggage in my house. Dorje is completely reliable. He won't molest you.'

'Really? Does he speak English?'

'Yes. Very well. He was brought up in Delhi. But don't expect conversation. There isn't much oxygen as you go higher, so save your breath for walking. Look, are you sure you want to do this? It's pretty primitive out there. No lavatories, and no bushes to squat behind either.'

'I'll be fine. I can look after myself.'

'You can stay the night in my house. I've got a spare charpoy. I'll tell Dorje what's expected of him and how much you'll be paying. Tomorrow, I'll drive you up to where the road ends.'

Twenty-five

'THIS IS IT, THEN – the end of the road.' Simon pulled the jeep round in a tight circle so that they were facing back the way they had come. He got out and pointed over the edge to where the Indus boiled in its gorge.

'The other jeep was found a bit further back, where the gorge is shallower. It's quite possible that he just failed to put the handbrake on or leave it in gear. That would be just like him.'

Simon had lain awake for a long time the night before, while Dora slept on a charpoy in the sitting room. He asked himself why he was so reluctant to drop everything and go in search of Guy. At prep school they had been such friends. In spite of his greater bulk, Simon had always followed Guy's lead – usually deep into trouble. Guy had been asked to leave a year early for repeatedly going out of bounds and hadn't been able to take his Common Entrance – another reason why he had gone to Dartington. Simon had invested a lot in his early friendship with Guy. He was helpless before him and easily bent to the smaller boy's will.

No body had been found. It was typical of Guy to give him an almighty fright. There was the time when he had fallen out of an apple tree in Simon's parents' garden and lain white and still on the ground. In an agony of terror Simon had run screaming into the house for his mother. When they rushed out, Mrs Monroe as white as Guy had been, he was laughing at them from the top of another apple tree. He hadn't been invited to stay again. Simon's father, also a doctor, had thought that Guy was an appalling influence and that his relationship with Simon was unwholesome. Their friendship was confined to school after that, and then to the occasional meeting in the holidays in London.

Simon hadn't seen Guy for ten years when he first recognised him in the hospital bed in Panaji. He realised that there wasn't a great deal wrong with Guy that the right antibiotics, rest, electrolytes to restore the balance of his blood, and decent food wouldn't repair. He was worried only by his stubborn silence and his black depression.

Simon had nursed him back to bodily health in the two remaining weeks of his holiday. When Guy was well enough to leave hospital he had installed him on the other charpoy in his beachfront hotel at Benaulim. Guy hadn't seemed very grateful, although he had gone along with Simon's suggestion that he stay off cannabis. Simon had been very relieved when he had examined him not to find needle tracks on his arms.

When it was time for Simon to go up to Delhi in order to fly back to Ladakh, he had suggested that Guy accompany him. 'The nutrition project could be the perfect distraction,' he'd thought. 'Stop him feeling so sorry for himself all the time to help people who have nothing – not even sufficient iron in their blood to live long lives.'

Guy had accepted apathetically, but he quickly became interested in the scheme to improve the lives of the malnourished women and children whose haemoglobin he was learning to test. The poverty and deprivation suffered by the average rural Ladakhi, and their constant cheerfulness in spite of it, seemed to be hoisting him out of his self-pity. The exercise and plain but good food, a lot of it grown in Simon's little garden, were also improving his appearance and mood. But then the jeep had been spotted in the Indus.

Did he love Guy? He felt more comfortable with loving the human race in general and no one in particular. Apart from some abortive attempts at nurses and fellow medical students when he was studying at Barts, Simon had steered clear of the whole business of love and sex. He poured his energies into alleviating suffering if he could. The NHS was no place for him: too few opportunities to fly by the seat of his pants, too many people telling him what to do. He wondered whether Guy's potent early charm and lack of interest in rules might have influenced his unstructured and adventurous approach to his medical career. Simon's background was far more likely to have slotted him into home-counties general practice, plus wife and kids, like his father.

Simon had been hoping to send Guy back, fired with knowledge and enthusiasm, to raise funds among his rich friends. But now he imagined him washed up on a grey, deserted little Indus beach. He might never be found, alive or dead. There were plenty of anonymous bleached bones in the Himalayas, some human, some animal. Simon felt peculiar about the way he was thinking. He had had such hopeful plans about Guy finally doing what he, Simon, wanted him to do, instead of the other way round. But he had slipped once more from Simon's grasp and vanished.

Dora climbed out of the jeep and settled her rucksack and sleeping bag on her shoulders with Dorje's help. It was quite late in the afternoon – they needed to climb up and over a steep and craggy outcrop before finding the first dwelling and somewhere to sleep. Simon had been delayed by a dispute with the local health workers. Dora, fearing that she would have to climb in the dark, asked if Dorje might drive them so they could get to the end of the road before the light failed; but Simon couldn't spare the jeep.

So by the time Simon had swung himself slowly into the driving seat, Dora was in nail-biting agony. She wondered if he might be doing it on purpose. She had formed the impression that he thought she was silly to be going, and was merely humouring her with a light walking tour. She didn't know the confusion in Simon's heart.

At last they were climbing. She turned round on the narrow, steep track and looked down at Simon. Already he was far below, looking up. She waved. She couldn't see the expression on his face but his hands stayed in his pockets. He turned and climbed back into the jeep as Dora set herself at the slope and walked on upwards. Night began to fall. She could still see Dorje's pale blue jacket in the gloom in front of her, but she had to keep her eyes on the path to prevent herself from tripping. She began to toil and then to slog. She didn't dare look up, because when she did, the top seemed far away and she wasn't sure if she was going to make it. She tried taking deep breaths of the oxygen-starved air. She scrambled on hands and knees in more than one place and began to pant. It was very steep. Dorje's voice came down to her out of the gloom.

'Don't worry, it isn't so steep after this. Just get to the top. It's easy on the other side.'

He didn't even sound puffed. Dora didn't trust herself to answer. Her body inside the Helly Hansens was bathed in cold sweat. Her lungs were screaming for oxygen. She felt shaky and bedraggled. She thought she might be going to cry with relief when she risked a look up and saw Dorje silhouetted against the sky. This gave her heart, and she scrambled the last few yards to join him.

'Very good,' he said, hauling her on to the ridge. She bent down and held her knees, gasping for breath. In the dim twilight, she couldn't see anything beyond that would indicate human habitation and her heart began to sink again. She thought she had better put her trust in Dorje though, and get on with it.

He let go of her arm and jumped. She was startled but realised that he was several yards below her, sliding on the loose stones of the scree. He looked back up at her.

'Jump, and dig in your heels. It's perfectly safe – the scree will catch you.'

She felt she didn't have a lot to lose. She was desperate for something to drink and to get out of the gathering gloom, and this seemed like the quickest way down. She jumped, keeping her weight on her heels, digging them in as she descended. She slid towards Dorje and he held out a hand. She caught it and he jumped again. She went too. Wild exhilaration seized her as they plunged down the hillside surrounded by clouds of dust, stones rattling with them, to the bottom.

She didn't even notice the effort it had been such fun.

'That was good,' said Dorje. He let go of her hand and set off along a narrow path.

They had to walk for another two hours to get to the small farm where they were to spend the night. Dorje would not let her drink water, which made her uncomfortable. But she had put herself in his hands in the strange parched moonscape, so she did what she was told. There wasn't a single blade of grass. She could feel her lips drying to a crisp as she walked, and blessed her Australian beach acquaintances who had given her some squalid-looking lip-salves. She had been going to throw them away. One of the girls had told her, 'I know they look revolting and second-hand. It's not just vanity though. You will bless us when you get there.' She did now as she kept one in her pocket and smeared it regularly on to her mouth.

Dorje called back to her, 'The farm is just ahead.'

Dora could see nothing. She was walking in his wake quite blindly. They descended into a small valley where there were some stunted trees, and she could just see a building with no lights showing.

Dorje went up and knocked on the door, pushing it open at the same time. A small amount of firelight spilt out and Dora's heart lifted. The farmer had long black hair, shaved as far back as the midpoint of his cranium in a straight line. He was wearing an indescribably dirty goncha in natural-coloured wool. Dorje and he were negotiating. It seemed that they could not come inside.

'He has girlfriend with him,' Dorje explained, shrugging as he came back to her. 'We can use the animal enclosure.'

Dora just went along with whatever was suggested. She was delighted that it was so dark, because there was no kind of lavatory and the trees were slender and wouldn't provide cover. She didn't dare think what she would do in the morning. She slipped away and disentangled herself from her Helly Hansens. The night air was cool on her bare skin. After she had peed she lifted up her jumper and let the breeze dry her off.

Dorje had lit a fire when she got back and was boiling water from the stream. He made sweet tea and then threw Maggi instant noodles into the remaining water for their supper. Dora sank down beside the fire and sighed with pleasure, enjoying the moment, trying not to worry too much about past and future. By the time they had eaten and drunk their tea, it was quite late. Dora took her boots off and crept into her grubby but superior sleeping bag. She rolled up her jacket to pillow her head and looked up into infinite space. The sky was deep blue, the stars clear clean pinpricks of white light. She had decided not to think about Guy until there was the least possibility of finding him. She fell asleep feeling minuscule but content under the turning sky.

She slept well on the hard ground, but when she stood up, last night's climb told on her muscles and she groaned. Dorje was already boiling a pot of water. She looked round for somewhere to have a discreet pee and saw a reasonable-sized rock a little further down the valley by the stream. She took her toothbrush and a flannel and managed a kind of wash.

There were cold chapattis and jam for breakfast, with the usual sweet tea. Then the companions got themselves together and set off again.

'It will take us until this evening to get to the next village. When we have asked about Guy there, we will go back to the Indus, cross it and go to a village on the other side.'

'Right,' said Dora. 'How do we cross the Indus?'

'Don't worry. There's a rope bridge.'

Dora thought she would face up to that charming prospect when she got to it. They walked through a blasted landscape, pale beige and scattered with scree, indented with small valleys and softened only by the occasional stand of birch trees and rushing streams. She longed to drink from the crystal clear, cool water. Dorje would never let her. He explained that, if there was a village further up, she would be bound to get ill. And drinking cold water when she was hot in mid-walk was a bad idea as far as he was concerned.

In spite of this, Dora found the walking enormously restful – on and on, swinging one army boot in front of the other. There was the odd scramble up a steep bit and often a scree-jumping session on the other side, but nothing as severe as the first outcrop. Dorje told her that he had once seen a man carry a donkey over one steep place. Prayer flags, ragged bits of coloured muslin with lettering on them, flew from the tops of sacred piles of stones called stupas.

They walked along the sides of valleys, often climbing at a very shallow angle. Dora picked up a staff and used that to haul herself along. Dorje kept up quite a pace, which suited Dora because her natural impatience drove her on.

The air was so clean and empty. It was late in the year, but there was still power in the sun. She smeared the lip-salve all over her face as it contained a sunblock. As the sun dipped in the sky, she began to hear clonking bells.

'What's that sound?'

'It's the harvest,' was all Dorje would say.

They rounded the end of a valley and were confronted with the village where they were to spend the second night. It was an Old Testament setting. The low houses were exactly the same light sandy beige colour as the landscape from which they were formed. The dark squares and oblongs of windows and door were all that punctuated the washed-out scene. A little outcrop of humanity in a desert. She walked past a small, walled enclosure containing extraordinary wooden carved figures.

'Very old,' commented Dorje.

Directly in front of Dora was a man winnowing with the help of a team of horses. The barley lay in a great primrose disc on the ground. A row of four horses were harnessed at their backs to a single spoke, stuck out from a turning hub in the centre. A man led the outside horse round and round; their trampling loosened the grains from the ears of barley. It was the bells around their necks that Dora had heard clonking.

Dorje led her into one of the houses. It took a moment to get used to the dim light. She saw she was in a kitchen. It had wooden roof beams, and a woman was stirring a cauldron over an open fire to one side. She wore a dark red goncha, rather like a woollen dressing gown, bound around the middle with a wide sash. Her hair was black and plaited. She had filthy knots of semi-precious stones in her ears. On her back was a baby. Dora tried to have a look but the woman courteously hid it from her.

'The baby is too young to be seen by strangers,' commented Dorje.

'Tell her I am sorry.'

He said something. The woman smiled, showing gaps between her teeth, and went on rolling brownish sausages out of dough and dropping them into a broth which smelt like nothing on earth. Very sweaty old feet was the closest description Dora could come up with.

'What is she cooking?' Dora asked.

'Dried meat soup.'

'Ah.' Dora was terrified that she would be offered some and wasn't sure how she was going to swallow it.

Dorje, seeing her face, said, 'Sheep died of foot and mouth last winter. I'll tell her it's against your religion to eat meat.'

Dora was relieved.

'You must remember various things here,' he instructed her. 'Avoid showing the soles of your boots at all times and if you are offered chang, you must accept.'

'What is chang?'

'It's the local beer.'

'Is it strong?'

'It can be.'

Dora took a deep breath and resigned herself to an interesting evening.

'Do they have a lavatory here?' she asked.

Dorje asked the woman of the house. Then he turned, beckoning Dora to follow, and took her down ladders, across tiny courtyards, through dark gaps between buildings until they came to a yak's stable. They climbed another ladder, and Dorje pushed aside a piece of sacking that hung over the entrance.

'In here,' he said. 'I'll wait.'

Dora thanked him. She stepped into the roofless enclosure on top of the stable. There were two holes side by side in the mud floor.

'Sociable,' she thought.

She squatted over one, looking down at the stable floor a few feet below, hoping not to pee on a yak. Afterwards, Dorje led her back to the kitchen. Dora dreaded the idea of getting drunk and having to have a pee in the dark. She would have to avoid this chang after the first polite gesture.

Dorje lit a little fire on the other side of the kitchen, where there was another rudimentary hearth. The smoke escaped through a hole in the black, faintly gleaming ceiling.

The men of the family started to come in. There was a child of about seven, with bright red cheeks, wearing a felt slipper on one foot and a broken Wellington boot on the other.

Dora sat down, carefully concealing the soles of her army boots, smiling at everyone who caught her eye. One of the men handed her a Duralex glass, exactly like the ones she had drunk out of at prep school, full of cloudy pale yellow liquid like lemonade. As he gave it to her, he squidged a tiny piece of yellow butter on to the brim.

'Dorje, what's this?' she called, smiling maniacally at the assembled company all the time.

'That is chang.'

'Why is there a piece of butter on it?'

'That is yak butter. They are honouring you.'

She noticed that the woman served the men but didn't sit with them, and she assumed she was an honorary man for the evening.

There wasn't much she could do to communicate. Dorje came back to her and handed her a bowl of noodles, which she ate. He had some chang. She drank hers slowly. It tasted faintly sour, perfectly pleasant and not particularly alcoholic.

'Do you want to try salt butter tea?' Dorje asked her.

'I might as well,' she replied.

The woman had been brewing it since she'd finished making the dinner, and brought it to her now with many smiles. Dora took it and sipped. The greasy hot salty layer on the top was balm to her lips, sore in spite of the lip-salve. The tea underneath was unexpectedly refreshing.

'It's obviously the perfect drink for up here,' she remarked to Dorje, who just smiled. He was pouring toasted barley flour and sugar into his second cup to make tsampa, a kind of porridge. Dora decided to decline this. It was a relief to give up on the chang.

Dorje asked after Guy, but no one here had seen him and they were too busy with the harvest, they said, to bother about what went on in the next village.

When it was time to sleep, Dorje led Dora outside on to the roof and they lay down. Dora was asleep before she could even begin to feel strange in relation to the sky.

The next day they swung back towards the Indus; walking in single file, in silence, stopping only for lunch and a drink of tea. It was mid-afternoon before they saw the river again.

They were nearer to the source. The river flowed swiftly through a deeper, narrower gorge, about twenty feet in all from side to side. There was a rope bridge, with two canvas seats hanging from it, one each side of the gorge. Dora was terrified. The rope looked horribly weak and feeble and she was sure it wouldn't bear her weight.

Dorje turned to her. 'I'll go first and show you what to do.'

'Are you sure it's OK?'

'Yes, it's easy. I'll come back and help you into it.'

'How do I get out of it the other side?'

'You can practise getting in and out this side with my help.'

Dora was not reassured. She watched Dorje wriggle and slither into the harness, drop over the edge, catch hold of the rope and begin to pull himself across, wavering and swaying with each tug. She felt sick with fear. Then she remembered why she was there. 'Guy could be immobilised on the other side. That might be why the people on this side don't know where he is,' she thought. She swallowed.

She watched Dorje scrabble on to the top of the facing

cliff – which overhung slightly – still wearing his harness, then slip it off and stand up to wave. The other harness was now just below her.

'For goodness' sake, Jerusalem, don't be such a weed,' she scolded herself. She gestured to Dorje that he was to stay there and she would come over on her own. She felt he might be more help getting her out on the other side.

She swung the canvas seat up on to the ridge. There wasn't much leeway. Sitting down, she pulled the harness up over her hips, her legs dangling in space. Tentatively, she did as she had seen Dorje do, and slithered over the edge with her eyes shut. She prayed as she felt herself momentarily in space before the rope took up the slack, and she opened her eyes to see she was dangling over white rushing water thirty feet below. Then she grasped the rope, looked where she was going and pulled. The wooden pulley creaked rhythmically. It seemed to take ages, but finally she was on the other side, dangling under the cliff, wondering how to get up and over. Then she noticed some little hand and foot holds cut into the rock.

Dorje was peering over the edge. 'I'll pull a bit but you must climb. Don't worry, the seat is quite strong enough to catch you if you fall.'

'I'm not going to fall,' thought Dora. She remembered Simon had told her that Dorje had climbed Everest. She was determined not to appear wet before him. She clung to the rockface and began to climb.

For one sickening moment, the weight of her rucksack seemed to pull her backwards. Dorje gave an almighty tug and she landed on her face on the gravelly cliff top.

'Good. Good,' he said, helping her off with the harness.

She stepped out of it gratefully and tossed it over the edge. They set off again in search of Guy.

'This village is not like the last,' said Dorje. 'Dr Monroe helps them with projects but they don't finish them in time.'

'Why?'

'They drink too much chang.'

'Oh.' Dora was thoughtful. 'Dorje, does that mean I have to get drunk too?'

He gazed at her incredulously and began to laugh. 'Oh no. They aren't so worried about what you do here.'

'Sounds like just the right place for Guy,' she thought to herself.

Over the top of a small rise, coming the other way, they saw a Ladakhi man. Dorje hailed him and asked the usual questions.

The man started talking volubly. Dorje turned from him to Dora for a moment and said, 'I think he's there.'

Dora's stomach did a flip-flop. 'Typical,' she thought. 'Find the only nest of soaks in the whole of the Himalayas and hole up giving everyone a nervous breakdown.'

Dorje conversed with the man some more before filling Dora in with the details.

'This man says there is an American in the village with a bad leg. His brother was walking home from Leh, taking the path on the opposite side of the Indus to the road, when he saw a jeep go over the edge and into the river. It's very narrow and powerful there. The American climbed out through the jeep window and tried to get to the bank, but he was swept away downstream. This man's brother ran along the path beside him, thinking he would drown.'

Dora had an absurd vision of a rowing coach cycling along the banks of the Cam, bawling the stroke through a megaphone. She had once seen a coach ride straight into the river. She giggled. Dorje looked faintly surprised. She shook herself to concentrate. This must be Guy they were talking about. Wasn't she meant to care more about him than anyone in the world? Hadn't she come four thousand miles to find him?

Dorje was still translating what the man had told him. 'So this man's brother went on until he could find a place to climb down. When he got to the bank, the American was nowhere to be seen. He looked upstream and saw him caught by a rock. His head was in the water and he wasn't moving. This man's brother managed to get back to him and pull him out.'

'Why didn't he then go on down to Leh to get help?' Dorje questioned the man.

'It takes too long to walk down to Leh. And the American didn't want to go; he wanted to carry on with the project. He managed to get to the village although he seemed to be in pain.'

'How is he now? It must be more than a week?'

'Apparently he can't walk at all now. He wanted to wait for his leg to get better so he can get back to the road, but Mingmar here decided that he had better get help. He didn't tell the American because he didn't think he wanted him to. They don't want the responsibility up there any more though.'

'At least he's alive,' said Dora with relief. 'But he must be badly injured.'

'I doubt there is a skilled healer in this particular village.'

Dorje seemed to be waiting for her to say something, so Dora made a decision.

'Dorje, I will go with this man to find Guy and do what I can for him. Can you get back to Leh in the dark to get help?'

'All right – it will be quicker going down as I will walk

direct to the river. I've got some first-aid things in my ruck-sack, which I will leave with you. There's morphine if he is in a lot of pain.'

Dora thought to herself that she wouldn't let him have that. He could stick to paracetamol until he was under medical supervision. She wasn't sure what he had been up to since she had last seen him and she didn't want to take any risks.

'Thank you, Dorje. You've been great. I am sure we've found him.'

Dorje was slightly worried about letting her go off on her own to the notoriously drunken village, then he remembered that the last village had assumed she was some kind of man. She was thin enough. Dorje explained to the villager what they were planning to do. Dora shook his hand, having packed away the little red box of drugs, and they parted on the narrow path.

Now Dora knew where Guy was, she wasn't in the least worried about him. All she worried about was where she was going to find enough privacy to have a pee when she got there. She figured Guy might be able to help her and she strode on behind the dark maroon back of her new guide. He didn't seem to be drunk, she thought with relief.

It was getting quite dark by the time they got to the village, but Dora could see that the place had a shambolic feel. The last village hadn't been neat, but this one resembled a medieval village in a Monty Python film. Mingmar led her into one of the larger houses. Once more she found herself in the kitchen. She peered around in the gloom.

'Where is the American?' she asked, her heart beginning to thump in her chest. He led her through a low doorway, pushing aside a woollen hanging as he went, and waved a hand.

The room was startling after the monochrome gloom of the Ladakhi houses she had visited. It had no windows and was lined with brightly coloured fabrics, with a raised bench built out from the walls around the sides. There were Tibetan rugs on the floor and a long low painted table down the middle. It was surprisingly beautiful after the squalid appearance of the village outside. A small oil lamp burned on one of the tables.

Dora peered around. Leaning on one elbow, propped up by pillows and reading a book in the faint light of the lamp, was a European. She called softly, 'Guy?'

He started and dropped the book. 'Who's there?'

She didn't know how to play it. In the end it had all seemed to happen very fast. She tried the cool approach.

'Hello, Guy. It's me, Dora.'

There was silence for a moment, then he said wearily: 'I travel thousands of miles. I drive a jeep into the Indus. I do everything I can to get away from—'

'From what, Guy?'

'Bloody women,' he said. His voice sounded cold. 'Can't you fucking well leave me alone for five minutes?'

'I left you alone for years,' she said quietly. 'I'm sorry I'm disturbing you. I'll go now.'

She turned, shock and desolation seizing her, pushed the woollen hanging aside and left him to it. She would go and sleep on the roof, then she would somehow get Mingmar to help her return to the road. The authorities could take over now.

'I hope he gets gangrene,' she thought fiercely. 'Bastard.' Then she realised something. 'He didn't ask me to come and find him. In fact he ran a long way away to escape from the whole mess. Why was I so stupid as to think he would be pleased to see me? He wasn't last time. What a waste of time and money.'

She'd been carrying her little load of love around, longing to bestow it upon someone. She had found Guy when she was very young. She had tried to give it to him. He had been reluctant to receive it. Now she was trying to force it on him, miles from anywhere, where he couldn't escape. Wrong, wrong, wrong, she thought sadly.

She walked out through the main kitchen doorway and climbed up the outside staircase on to the roof. Sitting on her rucksack, she watched the peerless blue of the sky darkening into night.

'This is it,' she said to herself. 'I must give it up. It's over.' She felt a sob rising from her stomach. Her eyes filled with tears of self-pity.

She heard the clonking of a bell below, and looked down over the parapet. A man was leading a yak up from the harvested patches of field. Her bladder felt very full. She watched where he went and climbed down to follow, hoping to have a quiet pee in the warm breathing company of the big black beast.

When she came out of the stable, intending to go back up on to her roof and eat chocolate for supper, there was a child waiting for her.

It took her hand in its grubby one and began to pull her back to the house from which she had come.

'What are you doing?' she asked.

The child didn't understand. He just grinned up at her and continued tugging. She went back in through the kitchen doorway past a smiling woman, wearing a winged hat covered in cowrie shells like a kind of mermaid nun.

She blinked as she entered the room where Guy lay.

There was a gas lantern burning brightly now, and the detail of the painting and hangings leapt out at her in all their oriental glory – scarlet, malachite green, lapis blue. Guy was at the other end of the room, propped up on his cushions, his legs covered by a blanket.

He wasn't smiling, just looking neutrally at her. She remembered that he could have very good manners and was probably employing these inbred reflexes now, however little he wanted to see her.

'Come and sit down, Dora. Would you like a cup of tea?'

'Thank you, Guy.'

She was transported straight back to his Chelsea basement. She had never known a man so keen on tea as Guy.

She sat down, hiding the soles of her boots. The woman of the house came in with the paraphernalia for salt butter tea on a little tray. Guy said something to her. She smiled.

'Have you learned the language?' Dora asked.

'I had lessons in Leh and the children have been teaching me here. I had nothing else to do while I waited for my leg to get better.'

'I sent Dorje back to Leh to get help.'

'Well, there's no other way to get out of here without walking.'

'I imagine they could send a helicopter.'

'Yes, I imagine they could too. But I don't see Simon doing anything so generous after what I did to his jeep.'

'He was pretty pissed off.'

'He always had a sense of humour failure if anyone broke one of his toys.'

Dora was proud of herself. There she was, cool as a cucumber, making polite conversation in the middle of nowhere over yak butter tea. Pretty British behaviour, she thought to herself. 'How is your leg?'

'Hurts like hell. That's why I snapped at you before. I jumped and the pain shot through me. I almost blacked out after you stalked off.'

'I didn't stalk off. I thought I made a dignified exit.'

'If I were you, and I had come all this way to find someone and they had been that rude, I would have stalked off. I bet you resolved just to leave me to stew in my own juice, didn't you?'

Dora smiled reluctantly. 'Yes, I did. I thought I would leave Simon to look after you and go home to get on with my life. You have completely screwed up this year for me, Guy Boleyn. I haven't earned a penny and I've been spending money like water on pursuing you.'

'Well, the more fool you.'

'I suppose I am a fool, really.'

'You are. I'm not worth it, you know.'

'Aren't you? Are you sure about that?'

'I don't know. But I do know that I haven't been so happy for years as I have been since I came to Ladakh. Not since the early part of our time together in eighties.'

The bright room, Guy, everything felt so surreal. As if in a dream, she came straight to the point:

'Why did you leave me after we got married?'

'I was a coward. I couldn't face explaining. I just didn't think I was ready for you. I wanted to make an independent life for myself. To grow up a bit. I figured if I married you, you would have to wait for me. You did, didn't you? It was quite obvious from your exhibition performance at my near-miss wedding.'

'I did. Idiotically – year after stupid year. Now I know

where I stand I will be able to give up this silly obsession and get on with my life.'

'Who are you calling a silly obsession?'

'You. Or at least the you I fell in love with, who probably didn't exist.'

'Do you still love me, Dora?'

She didn't say anything. She looked into her cooling cup of salt butter tea and swirled the melted yellow fat around and around.

'Well, do you?'

'Why the hell do you think I am here?' she muttered angrily. 'I thought you might be dead when I heard the jeep was in the Indus. Simon seemed so calm, so unwilling to do anything about finding you, that I was comforted. Then I thought that, since I was here, I would have a bash at finding you.'

She turned to him. He was looking incredulous, as if he had just realised that she hadn't been on a chance holiday, but had quite deliberately set out to find him in the vast expanses of the sub-continent.

'How did you know to look for me up here?'

'Your mother thought you had gone to Goa – so I went there first and visited all the hotels hoping to find your name. Finally I did, at Benaulim Beach Resort, and I was told a Dr Simon Monroe of the Food and Nutrition Fund in Ladakh had brought you there from the hospital.'

'Of course it was difficult to get up here because of the war in Kashmir, but I managed. My Uncle Eric in Delhi, whom I've never met, pulled some strings. Lots of his old pupils from when he ran Abu College are in government. Anyway, I got a permit and up I came. Then I met Simon and the rest you know.'

'Christ. You are persistent.' He said, in a kinder tone. 'I don't know how I feel about anything at the moment, Dora. You will have to give me some time.'

'OK. You've had quite a bit of my time already. I am sure you can have some more.'

The woman of the house came in with two steaming bowls of soup. It smelt slightly better than at the last house. The dried meat element seemed to be missing. She put the soup down in front of Guy, who thanked her. Then she said something to him and he smiled and replied.

He turned to Dora. 'Go with her. She asked me if you were my wife and I said you were, which is perfectly true. She thinks you look dreadful and wants to do something about it.'

Dora stood up, feeling dazed. The woman laughed and took her hand, leading her into the room next door. She carefully pinned the hanging over the doorway and began to help Dora take her clothes off. Dora hung on to her thermal vest and long johns. Then her hostess opened a big chest and drew out a black velvet goncha with bright pink binding on the edge and a bright pink silk waistcoat. She helped Dora into the coat-like goncha and pulled the sash very tight around her slim waist. Then she stood back, laughing again.

Dora looked down. The dress reached her feet and crossed over her bosom, coming up high under her chin. The romantic costume intensified her sense that she was dreaming. She thanked the woman. It was undoubtedly an improvement on Helly Hansens. She picked up her clothes and went back to the coloured chamber.

Guy smiled properly at last: 'You know, you look rather local dressed like that with your eyes and your tan. You are even nearly dirty enough.'

'Well, I haven't washed for a few days,' said Dora. 'Will you thank her for me? It is nice to wear a dress again.'

'Eat your soup,' was Guy's reply.

She did. It didn't taste of much, but she was hungry. Then Guy had some of the tsampa and Dora suggested she should have a look at his leg. She went to get her rucksack down off the roof, expecting a bit of a sprain as he was making so little fuss. He had been so lucky to survive his ducking.

'You can look at my head as well,' he remarked as she returned.

She gently turned his head to look, and had to suppress a gasp. The long, blond hair – bleached by the Indian sun since the wedding – was matted with dried blood at the back. She touched it gently. He winced. She decided to leave well alone and let the doctors deal with that. Then she carefully took the blanket off his leg.

His trouser leg was cut away and she could see the flesh underneath was badly swollen and bruised below the knee. She thought for a minute that it might be infected, but the skin wasn't broken which she took as a good sign. She retained a calm manner as she bent over and sniffed. It didn't smell worrying. Then she touched it. It felt hard and hot.

After a moment, she said, 'Did you really think that this would get better by itself so you could walk home?'

'To tell you the truth, I didn't much care. I was perfectly happy to hang out here until something or other happened.'

She bit her tongue to stop herself scolding him.

'Right,' she said. 'All I've got is paracetamol. Would you like some?'

'Might as well.'

She thought he was being exceedingly brave, if somewhat foolhardy. That night she hardly slept. His temperature went up as the evening drew on and his restless muttering kept her awake.

She lay on her back, her arms under her head, thinking to herself, 'This is the first time we have ever slept together. Some wedding night.' She didn't share this thought with Guy. She dozed eventually, dreaming of helicopters and woke to find Simon in the act of kneeling down beside Guy to examine his leg.

'Good morning, Dora,' he said when he saw she was awake and watching him. Guy didn't seem to have woken up properly and was still muttering restlessly.

'This doesn't look very nice but it's just a simple closed fracture I think. I am going to give him a shot of antibiotics as a precaution, and a sedative for the journey. There's a helicopter parked down on the fields. They're coming up with a stretcher for him. You can come too if you like.'

He seemed very calm. He was a doctor, after all.

'Simon,' she said, considering him. 'Why didn't you come looking for him? Or send Dorje?'

Simon looked into her eyes. For the first time she noticed he looked sad. He spoke rapidly under his breath. 'This can't go beyond this room, but I was certain he was dead and that his body would be found at any moment. I didn't want to be the one to find it. So I left it to the army.'

Dora stared at him. 'So all that reassuring stuff about handbrakes being off and the luggage missing from the jeep was lies?'

'Most of it, yes.'

Dora stared at him in astonishment. She thought she had better not pursue it. Guy was alive and seemed to have got away with few injuries. There was no point in going backwards.

She pushed the blankets aside, reassured about Guy's health, hoping that Simon would not look too intently at her grey thermal underwear. She pulled on her outer clothing and folded the beautiful goncha over her arm to give back to the woman of the house. Two Indian paramedics arrived and lifted him gently on to the stretcher, carrying him out and down to the helicopter, Dora following behind. Simon stayed to talk to the headman and pay for Guy's accommodation.

When Dorje had come walking into his office to tell him that Dora had gone on with a villager who claimed to have pulled an American with a bad leg out of the Indus, Simon had felt appalling guilt that it hadn't been him.

He hadn't told Guy's mother, at Guy's firm insistence, when he had first discovered him in the charity hospital in Goa, surrounded by derelict, elderly Italian junkies whose government couldn't be bothered to fly them home. But he had extracted her telephone number from Guy on the pre-text of filling in an official form to allow him to work for the agency. As soon as Dorje had arrived with the news, he had gone to the telephone exchange to book a call to London.

Guy's mother had sounded concerned, but not unduly surprised, when Simon told her that Guy had had an accident, and Simon was able to ask her for his insurance details.

'The medical insurance is with American Express,' she had told him. 'I thought that would be the easiest. I suggest you get in touch with them. If you hang on, I'll give you the claim and reference numbers. Is Dora there by any chance?'

'Yes, she's with Guy.'

'She wasn't in the jeep?'

'No. It happened before she got here. She went to find him when she heard.'

'I'd better call her mother with the news. She must be worried about her. Do you know her mother's number?'

'No I don't.'

'OK, I'll find out. She has such an extraordinary name, it shouldn't be difficult to trace. Thank you, Simon, for telephoning. How are your parents?'

'Fine, thank you, Mrs Moore.'

'Oh, and thank you for looking after Guy. You always did, as far as I can remember.'

She had rung off having given him the Amex insurance information. Simon felt confused but thankful that he could get Guy decent treatment. There was an excellent American hospital in Delhi; he would book him in there.

The helicopter took them back down to Leh, where Guy was X-rayed in the little hospital. There it was found that there was an uncomplicated break just below the knee joint of his left leg and that his skull was intact. How he had managed to walk so far on it was anybody's guess. Splints were applied to steady the leg and Simon arranged for Guy and Dora to get on the next plane to New Delhi, where it could be properly set and put in plaster.

Twenty-six

IT WAS A CHILLY dull October day. Dora had no idea that India could be cold. She was glad that the only clothes she had were the fleecy Helly Hansens and thermals so essential in Ladakh.

She rang her Uncle Eric from the hospital after Guy had been wheeled into surgery. This close relation was an unknown quantity to her. She knew only that he was 25 years older than her mother Hilly was, and that he'd been conceived, together with his twin George, in the first careless rapture of her grandparent's marriage.

Dora walked out of the white, hygienic hospital into the New Delhi street to hail a three-wheeler. She bent to speak to the driver.

'Residency Apartments, please, Mayo Street.'

'I am sorry?' he said.

She repeated the address. He looked mystified and called over a passer-by. 'What is she saying?' he asked.

The other man turned to Dora and said, 'What is it that you want, please?'

'I want to go to the Residency Apartments in Mayo Street, please,' she said.

He turned to the driver. 'She wants to go to the Residency Apartments in Mayo Street.'

Light dawned on the driver's face, 'Ah,' he exclaimed. 'Tell her to get in.'

The other man turned again to Dora and, with great courtesy, invited her to enter the vehicle. She thanked him. She had become used to India over the last months. The entire conversation had been conducted in English.

The little vehicle rumbled and squeaked over the potholed roads, avoiding cows, families of four on scooters, children selling newspapers and holy men sitting in the road. They arrived at the huge Lutyens apartment building originally built to house officials of the Raj and now sheltering everyone from Uncle Eric – a 'stayer on' – to the minister for food.

Rain began to fall from the grey sky as Dora scrambled out, dragging her rucksack, and paid the driver. Then she rang the bell on the huge, solid gate, big enough for an elephant to gain access. The porter came and peered suspiciously through a peephole.

Dora said in her most imperious manner, hoping he wouldn't notice how grubby she was, 'I am the niece of Mr Eric Vane. Please would you let me in. He is expecting me.'

The peephole snapped shut. There was a delay, then another, person-sized gate opened to let her in. The red-turbaned porter led the way through the courtyard to an arch with a pink stone staircase leading upwards.

'Mr Vane's apartment is on the first floor,' he said.

'Thank you.'

Dora shouldered her rucksack and climbed the wide shallow stairs. Two doors led off the landing, each with a little brass holder and a card. She peered at the one on the left. 'Ranjit Singh' it said in perfect copperplate engraving. The one opposite said, Eric Vane, BA Hons (Cantab), MA, FTC. She rang the bell.

A middle-aged man in a white high-buttoned coat and red turban opened the door.

She repeated, 'I am Mr Vane's niece, Dora Jerusalem. He's expecting me.'

A smile lit up the man's face. But he didn't say anything or introduce himself. He just relieved her of her rucksack and led the way through the hall.

The proportions of the apartment were like those of an Edwardian mansion flat, but it was lighter and airier. It was immaculately clean, but everything was old and faded.

Dora followed the man into a room opening off the end of the hall. Her uncle was sitting in a winged armchair. There was a small fire in the grate.

'Ah, Dora,' he said as if he had seen her the previous afternoon. 'Forgive me if I don't get up. I find this cold, damp weather makes my joints rather sore.'

Dora saw a slender old man with a sweet smile.

'How is my sister?'

'She's very well, thank you, Uncle Eric.'

'And, more to the point, how is your husband?'

'He was unconscious when I left him. Because the leg hadn't been set after it broke, it was healing up badly – they're going to have to re-break it.'

'Poor man. That is very painful. I broke my leg very badly as a boy out hunting. It never healed properly. It had to be amputated in the end. I suppose these days they would have been able to mend it.'

'I don't think it was a bad break in the first place, thank goodness.'

'The American hospital is marvellous, I believe. As good as anything in the West. I understand your husband didn't want to be flown back to England?'

'No, he wants to stay out here as long as he can.'

'I'm very glad. Living here as I have for so many years, I haven't seen anything of my family. I was so looking forward to getting to know you a bit. And your husband.'

Dora found it extraordinary to hear Guy referred to in this way. She supposed she should just let it ride. It was too complicated to explain the strange nature of her marriage.

'Now, I imagine you would like to wash. Then we can have some tea. Salim, will you show Mrs Boleyn to her room?'

Salim turned and went out of the room. Dora, with a smile at her uncle, followed him.

What she really wanted was a long hot soak in the huge tub she found in the bathroom off her bedroom, but she knew it wouldn't be polite to keep Uncle Eric waiting. She stripped completely and washed herself as quickly as she could at the basin. Then she put on clean underwear. She had a few flimsy cotton dresses left over from Goa but it was really chilly. She decided to put her Helly Hansens back on but replaced the army boots with camel-skin slippers with pointed toes. Then she brushed her hair and returned to her uncle.

He was sitting where she had left him, reading *The Times of India*. Salim came in with a tray of tea. Uncle Eric asked her to pour.

There was a lifetime of catching up to do and yet Dora didn't know how to open the conversation. When they were both supplied with thin slices of bread and butter and cups of tea, Uncle Eric said, 'Your mother wrote to me once, asking for a job as matron at Abu College, the school I ran in Gujarat. But she was only nineteen. I felt it might be a bit much for the boys. I had to turn her down.'

'She never told me that. She made a career in boy's prep schools in England. She started in Lodswell, then moved to Kenton where she ended up as bursar running the school's finances.'

'Well done her. Do you work?'

'Yes, I'm a freelance features writer for newspapers and magazines.'

'Ah, how interesting. Were you in India to do some research?'

'Yes, I was.' Dora felt she couldn't explain the real reason. They talked about the various stories she was going to write.

'My mother used to write,' he told her. 'She was a very clever woman, though woefully under-educated. But she read all the time to make up for it. I loved her company. It was such a shock when she died.'

'Your sister Marjorie seems always to have blamed my mother for that.'

'That was sad too. They could have been good friends. I think it was very hard for your mother growing up in that irregular situation. Not that I wasn't grateful to Leora for looking after my father all those years.'

'I've only met Leora once. I thought she was a darling.'

'She was a very spirited and brave young woman. I still miss my mother sometimes, and George of course.'

'Were you identical twins?'

'We were, and very close.'

He looked into the fire. Dora remained quiet.

After a bit, Uncle Eric took his stick and began to stand up. Dora moved across to help him.

'Thank you, my dear.'

'Now, I must have a rest. I do hope you will join me for dinner.'

'I need to go out and do a bit of shopping, if you don't mind.'

'No. Not at all. Salim will tell you the best places.'

Twenty-seven

'WHEN YOU WERE BEING TAKEN to be X-rayed, the doctor told me you should stay in hospital for a bit after you had the leg set and plastered. How do you feel?'

'Really not too bad. I'm lying down, aren't I? That's all I would do in hospital. I would be bored rigid. I thought it would be more fun to come and be with you,' Guy said lightly.

'Well, I hope you don't have a fit or something,' Dora retorted.

'Honestly, Dora, the X-ray showed a simple break, so I didn't need surgery. They just put me into something the anaesthetist called a "twilight sleep" to set the bone. Intravenous Valium apparently – rather fun.'

The male nurses had pushed their arms under Guy's body and legs and lifted him on to the trolley. In the fracture clinic, the anaesthetist had introduced himself as Dr Bhabani and inserted a line.

As he had drifted off, Guy had begun to dream he was back in his Chelsea basement, sitting on the sofa, joint in one hand, cold beer in the other, Hellman's mayonnaise with a knife stuck in it, open on the table before him. In spite of the familiarity, he'd felt uncomfortable. Glancing up he'd seen that the room was packed with women and girls. Not a party either, because they were all facing him and silent, pressing much too close.

In his dream he could neither move nor speak. Gradually, he recognised a face here and there. Thelma, but as he had first known her – slender, naked for some reason, her fair crimped hair covering her breasts like a Cranach Venus. Evangeline, dressed as a pirate. Lesley, in nipple-revealing corset. Those twins in black wigs from LA that a friend had had purchased for his thirtieth birthday. Imogen. Geraldine. Poppy. And a very dead-looking Alba. Pressing closer, they had all begun to decay like the dancers in the *Thriller* video.

Guy had tried to scream as they seemed to cover his face with something and push him back. He choked, gasping for air. Taking a desperate breath, he felt the blessed relief of oxygen sinking to the bottom of his lungs.

Then he had found himself back at home in the woods, lying on moss. Not alone, but no longer oppressed. Whoever it was beside him filled him with pure joy, as the sun, falling in warm droplets through bright young beech leaves, warmed his skin. A cool hand had touched his wrist. He heard laughter and smelt flowers. Arms wrapped around him, breasts pressed against him: 'Dora,' he sighed.

'No, not Dora, just Dr Bhabani.' Then Guy was awake, but the fear and joy of his dream stayed with him as he was wheeled into the plaster room. After that, all he'd wanted to do was to get back to Dora and test whether the dream had had any meaning.

'How did you get here anyway?' Dora was asking him.

'They left some crutches in my room. You gave me your uncle's address. I waited until the plaster felt good and dry, and then just hobbled out when the place was a bit dozy in the afternoon to get a taxi.'

'Did it hurt?'

'Well, I did feel a bit queasy, but they'd given me plenty of pain killers and I reckoned I'd be fine once I got back here.

'Your uncle's a nice old boy. When his bearer had made me comfortable, as he put it, he came to talk for a bit. He said your mother had rung before I arrived.'

'Right. I'll have to speak to her at some point. Maybe tomorrow.'

They were silent for a moment. Dora was sitting on a chair by the bed and Guy reached out to take her hand. She smiled at him and squeezed his fingers gently. Guy remembered how much her happiness had always warmed him long ago. Something of his dream came back to him then – the incredible joy and he said suddenly:

'It wasn't just my fault, Dora, you were older than me. Better educated. You seemed independent, earning your own living and so forth. I thought you must know what you were doing.'

'I did try to tell you how I felt.'

She leaned on the padded headboard. The room was very quiet. He pulled her gently towards him, and put his right arm around her neck, drawing her face to his to kiss her lips.

He was pleased when she joined in, opening her mouth slightly. Her arms moved to embrace him and, just as in his dream, he felt her breasts pressing against his chest. With his left hand, he discovered the zip on her Helly Hansens and pulled it down. There were several layers of clothing under that.

'Wait...' She said, pulling away from him. 'What are we doing?'

'Kissing,' said Guy. 'I remember doing an awful lot of that the last time round.'

'No, what is going on? I don't know what is going on.' She looked as if she was going to cry.

'Do stop talking, Dora. Don't you see? It doesn't need to be complicated any more? It can just be simple now.'

'Can it?'

'Yes,' he said firmly. 'I want to see what happens if I kiss you. If I like it and you like it we can see what happens next. After all, if we both like it, we might also like being together properly. What do you think?'

'OK.' He was wearing far less than her, just a loose cotton shirt and trousers. She took her mouth away from his and stood up.

'Hang on.' She went over to the door and shot the bolt across.

'Oh, Dora, what are you doing?'

She turned, looking embarrassed. 'You don't want my uncle's bearer to come in, do you?'

'God, no.'

Guy watched Dora take off her clothes. 'I don't suppose anyone has ever before performed a striptease while wearing mountain-walking gear. Really, I'm not sure Helly Hansens suit you. You look much better without them.'

'I don't think they're meant to be pretty,' Dora remarked, looking down at the fluffy, blue, cold-proof garments lying at her feet. She was naked now, sans thermal vest, jersey, long johns and all. The skin on her arms, face, feet and neck was brown. She hadn't had time to sunbathe. She'd spent so many days questioning backpackers in cafés and walking around all the hotels. The rest of her was shining white in the gloomy room, her breasts full and round.

Guy started to swing his heavy leg off the bed.

'No, stay there.'

He sat obediently on the edge.

'Look at me. Am I mad?' she asked.

'I don't know yet,' he said, considering. 'But I'm very keen to get to grips with you right now, even though you do look like a gypsy horse or something – white in the middle and brown at the edges.'

'You are all right, aren't you?'

'Apart from a broken leg and a bang on the head, yes, I'm fine. Why?'

Then he saw what she meant. 'Oh that. Well, I had every test you can think of just before I didn't get married, if you see what I mean. Amabel's parents insisted. They'd had me checked out by a private detective before they called the caterers. He didn't detect that I was already married though, did he?' Guy was grinning now. 'And, before you ask, I haven't slept with anyone since Amabel. And not often with her, I can tell you.'

'Why did you ask her to marry you?'

'I didn't. She asked me. I had a certain amount of spurious fame of my own after I found a lost Pre-Raphaelite, at least in New York, where she was modelling. She's my age, you know, old for a model. Anyway, she hoped to get into films. The easiest way to lots of exposure was to get married and sell the story to *Hello!*'

'Why did you say yes?'

'She's very pretty and charming when she wants to be. I was quite flattered she chose me. I'm not adverse to publicity myself. At least, I wasn't then – anything to sell a few more pictures. I wanted to move back to England. I was fed up with New York. Everyone works too hard and I was exhausted. My friends kept dying of AIDS. It got pretty grim.'

'I can imagine. I lost friends too.'

'Look. Don't let's get distracted. I do want to explain why I tried to commit bigamy. Stupidly, I got swept along by the wedding plans. Lord and Lady Cumbria went into overdrive – glad to marry her off to an Englishman I suppose. I felt I couldn't back out, even after there was gossip in Dempster about her "close friendship" with an American film producer called Ned Colpus. When I confronted her with it, she denied it.'

'Was that the big bloke in the front pew?'

'Yes. When I got up to stand at the front of the church and saw him there, I was furious. Sheer hurt pride.'

'If she wanted a wedding, why didn't she marry him?'

'He wouldn't. He was paying alimony to four ex-wives already.'

Dora hesitated, then said, 'I think she went off on the honeymoon with him.'

'I'm not surprised,' he muttered. 'I wouldn't be surprised if she'd planned to do that all along.'

'So you were forced into marriage twice. Goodness, Guy, you must feel quite persecuted.'

'Dora, you are getting off the point. I can't rush over and grab you. So please will you rush over and grab me as you're the one who is naked.'

'We are married, after all,' she stated slowly, as if trying to convince herself. She walked over and sat on the edge of the bed beside him, hugging her knees to her chest.

'Do you think we could consummate our marriage, Dora? When was it?'

'April 1982.'

'Please forgive me for not remembering, but I've been training myself all these years to pretend it didn't happen at all. Half the time I was so wasted I could believe it was just a dream.'

'A bad dream?'

'No, just a dream. Unreal.'

He put an arm around her. She rested her head on his shoulder.

'I've so much to say to you and I want to hear you speak too. I used to dream about you all the time to begin with. Dreadful, guilty dreams, where you were dead, or married to someone else or horrible to me in various ways. I dreamt about you again in hospital today.'

'I'm glad I lived on in your imagination.'

'When I was very drunk, I think I used to tell people that I had only ever loved you.'

'I know. Some of them told me. I used those kind of conversations as small occasional coals to heap on the fire I kept burning.'

'Why did you keep it burning, do you think?'

'I just never met anyone else half as funny, as nice, as beautiful as you.'

'You're making me blush. Look, I love talking, but don't you think we should get into bed?'

'Now?'

He pulled off his shirt and swung slowly back onto the pillows. Dora climbed under the covers beside him and lay down.

'I have to be honest, Dora, my leg does ache a bit – I'm not sure I'm good for much. By the way, are you still a virgin? I'm sorry to ask, but it puts a different complexion on things if you are.'

'Guy, I've never slept with anyone. Before I married you I didn't because I was too much of a coward, and since then, because I was married to you and believe very strongly in marital fidelity. And because I am a crazy fool who doesn't know what's good for her.'

'And you had nothing to be faithful to and God knows I never gave fidelity a moment's thought.'

They turned towards each other, reclining on their elbows, face to face.

Guy considered what to do next. 'I think I could manage to get on top if you didn't mind the plaster.'

'I do think it would be easier this first time, if you could.'

She lay back and Guy rolled over on top of her, his plaster cast awkwardly dragging over her left leg. She suppressed any reaction to the discomfort this caused her. Guy slowly manoeuvred himself with her help. She couldn't help yelping when he actually penetrated her.

'Sorry, darling. Does it hurt?' He looked down at her. 'I've never had a virgin before. This is the kind of wedding night our ancestors would have had.'

'Only without the plaster cast.'

'Yes, but you being a virgin and us not using any contraception, it's all very traditional.'

Having pushed his way in as gently as he could, he just lay there on top of her.

'I'm not sure I can do much now I'm here. Are you all right? I'm not squashing you?'

It was uncomfortable for Dora but she smiled up at him. It was over – the moment that had loomed so large in her life. She felt enormous relief and sighed deeply.

'I think we'd better call a halt there, for both our sakes.'

She kissed him and he withdrew and rolled carefully off. He groaned.

'It bloody well hurts still,' he said.

'That's what comes of walking about on a broken leg. You were incredibly lucky. If that Ladakhi hadn't seen you and pulled you out in time you would have drowned.'

'I wonder what I have been spared for. Sorry, Dora, did that hurt a lot? What did it feel like?'

'Like something inside me being broken.'

Guy pulled aside the covers and looked down at the sheet. 'You are bleeding so I suppose I have to believe you.'

'Do you think we should hang the sheet out of the window?'

'No, but I do think I should get you a proper wedding ring. This hideous thing was the one I bought on the day, wasn't it?' It still hung around her neck on a chain. 'I just grabbed the first one I saw. I am sorry.'

His voice was fading. She kissed his lips. He smiled. She got out of the bed.

'Where are you going?' he mumbled.

'Just to have a bath. It's been a long journey. I feel dusty.'

'Mmm.'

Dora wrapped herself in a kimono that was hanging on the door and padded into the huge and elaborate bathroom. The Edwardian building had every comfort and convenience available in 1909. She hadn't had a hot bath since she had left England four months before. She shook a handful of Mysore sandalwood bath salts into the steaming water and climbed in.

'Even if nothing happens after this, I am happy,' she thought. She felt a lump rise in her throat.

One of the great pains of her strange, fruitless, faithful

marriage was that she could never have children. It came to her as she lay in the sweet-smelling steam that the end of her virginity meant the possibility of motherhood. What did they say rather soppily about children? That they dwell in the house of tomorrow? Well, she'd spent the last 15 years dwelling in the house of yesterday.

'I must have been mad,' she thought. Then she considered that she wouldn't be where she was now if she'd been sensible and got a divorce and not been such a hopeless romantic.

When she was quite wrinkly and had scrubbed every inch, she went back into the bedroom and lay beside her sleeping husband. Propping herself on one elbow, she looked down at his face.

There were purple half-moons under his eyes and his dark lashes lay over the thin, transparent skin. His nose was dusted with freckles and the sun-bleached hair was beginning to recede slightly on either side of his widow's peak; but his lips were as soft and tender as they had ever been. She kissed them and lay back, sighing with happiness.

Twenty-eight

'Hello. Is that Mrs Jerusalem?'

'Yes.'

'This is Janet Moore. I'm Guy's mother.'

'Ah,' said a cool voice on the other end of the line. 'What can I do for you?'

'I just wanted to tell you that I've had news of your daughter from India today. She's fine apparently, and she's found Guy.'

'I didn't know he was lost.'

'Well, it seems he drove a jeep into the Indus - which is quite typical of him – and then disappeared into deepest Ladakh. Dora went and found him. He broke his leg.'

'I'm sorry to hear that. Thanks for letting me know. By the way, I thought Dora said he was called Guy Boleyn?'

'Yes, it is. I divorced his father Peter and married again.'

'I see. Peter Boleyn?'

'He's Lord Northiam now. One of Mrs Thatcher's life peerages for services to the Conservative Party. Actually, that's unfair – he donates lots of money to far worthier causes.'

'I used to know someone called Peter Bullen.'

'Probably the same person. His father upgraded the spelling of his name, and quite a lot of other things about himself in the sixties.'

'I see…'

'Look, Mrs Jerusalem. Shouldn't we meet? Say lunch in London? I think we've got quite a lot to discuss.'

'How old is Guy?'

'He's thirty-five.'

'Where did you get married?'

'In Hong Kong. Why? It was a whirlwind romance, a terrible mistake. It only lasted as long as it did because of Guy. When did you meet Peter?'

'A very long time ago.'

'Well. Shall we meet?'

'I think we should wait until Dora and Guy get back from India.'

'If they decide to make a go of the marriage we can have a party for them,' suggested Janet. 'Do pass on my best wishes to your husband.'

'He died a couple of years ago.'

'Oh, I am sorry.'

'Did Peter ever marry again?'

'No. There's no Lady Northiam.'

'OK. Well, thanks very much for letting me know about Dora. I'm sure she'll telephone when she gets near a phone.'

'Guy was admitted to the American hospital. That's what his friend Simon Monroe said.'

'I see. Thanks. Goodbye, Mrs Moore.'

'Goodbye, Mrs Jerusalem.' Hilly put the phone down, her heart pounding.

She had to face up to it. There was a very slim chance

that Dora and Guy were half-brother and sister. She knew that up until now they hadn't slept together. She prayed the broken leg would act as a chaperone until she could warn Dora. It had been a chance in a million that they should meet, let alone fall in love and get married.

She had never been entirely sure whose child Dora was but didn't like to think about it. Except when jealousy gripped her heart, when she stood outside Stephen's study and listened to her child and her husband laughing inside.

She was transported straight back to what it felt like to be 19; terrified and abandoned in stuffy 1950s England. Hong Kong had seemed so far away. Her hands shook as she made herself a cup of tea. Why hadn't she realised that Boleyn and Bullen were the same name? But Dora had never told her about Guy when she had been going out with him – or not going out with him, or whatever she was doing prior to her wedding.

'You are a jealous old woman, Hilda Jerusalem,' she told herself. 'No, you are a wicked old woman. You have probably ruined your daughter's life.'

She sipped her tea and planned what she would do next. Before her father's funeral she'd shared the odd kiss with Stephen on the way back from the pub, but nothing more. After the funeral, she had cooled off for a bit. Stephen had looked hurt, but he accepted it graciously, aware of the age difference and shy about his hands.

Then Peter's promised telegram hadn't arrived. Ten days went by and she'd heard nothing. Surely it didn't take that long to fly to Hong Kong? She began to be frightened that she was pregnant. The tenuous connection between them seemed irrevocably severed. Panic had driven her back into Stephen's arms; for comfort, but also for cover.

Stephen had been touchingly pleased when she said she would go out with him again. They walked back from the pub in the chilly moonlight over the playing fields.

She hadn't planned it. She really hadn't, had she? But she'd allowed herself to be drawn into the shelter of the cricket pavilion and they had kissed. She couldn't help responding to the warmth of his mouth.

He'd pushed the door open and they'd gone inside to stand close together in the darkness. It felt so good to be held tightly and desired by someone who adored her. Stephen had told her then that he wanted to marry her. She hadn't replied, but they had lain down on a pile of cricket pads and coconut matting. Something had dug into her back making it difficult to concentrate. She hadn't enjoyed the love-making that time. To him, her silent consent had been her acceptance of his proposal and he was glowing with pride and joy the next day, when he announced his engagement to the headmaster.

The headmaster had been annoyed. He didn't want married masters. They made demands. He had to pay them more. They weren't so controllable. The school was his livelihood and he had made a nice pile to retire upon. He told Stephen he would have to leave.

Stephen made certain arrangements before presenting Hilly later that day with a fait accompli. She was dazed, and allowed herself to be swept along on the tide of his passion. Stephen was kind, mature, loving and interesting. Why not just go along with what he wanted? Peter, an unreliable snob, had seduced her in a car and then disappeared to the other side of the world. If she was pregnant, he'd hardly throw up his career and come back for her. To her mind, there was no contest.

With no reason to wait, they had a very quiet wedding by special licence in the local church a week later. Hilly wore a new mauve wool suit with a velvet collar, and a blue felt hat. They went up to London after the ceremony and moved into rooms that Stephen had rented.

She had led such a sheltered life that just being in the capital was exciting and distracting. She spent time with Tirzah, and Stephen slipped seamlessly back into the art world, getting a job in an old friend's gallery very quickly.

It had been easy to forget about Peter. Stephen went out of his way to keep her amused. Her body responded to his, and she began to enjoy her new grown-up freedom as a wife. And then, nine months later, a mother.

Her life had been unlit by any great passion, but it hadn't been dull either. She believed earthshaking love probably existed only in fiction. When Dora started school, she went back to work as a school matron, studying accountancy and bookkeeping in the evenings. By the time she had retired, she had become bursar of Kenton Prep. She would have liked more children, but they never came.

The only major problem was her sense of exclusion from Dora and Stephen's relationship. Sometimes she'd wanted to burst in, shouting, 'She's not yours, she's mine.' She knew she couldn't give way to that ignoble urge. Stephen adored Dora. It would have shattered the frail structure of her marriage. It probably wasn't true, anyway.

She missed Stephen. Not all the time, but she was surprised at how much. She missed him coming out of his study every evening like a trapdoor spider sniffing its dinner. She thought how dreadful it was that there was so little time to sit and contemplate the luck that brought you together with someone you could love. Or at least tolerate. It was only after a person was dead that their finer qualities could be mulled over.

She shook herself. None of this had ever mattered until now, but she couldn't just hope for the best. What if Guy and Dora had a baby with genetic problems? Even a very slim chance that they might be too closely related had to be faced.

She telephoned Eric in Delhi. He talked to her as if they met every day, which was a relief. He must be over 80, she thought. He told her that Dora had arrived and seemed very well and happy. She had gone out shopping.

Hilly wanted to tell him not to let Dora and Guy sleep together but didn't know how to without shocking her monk-like older brother. 'Do you know how Guy is?' she asked.

'He had a broken leg and a bruised head, I believe. They're keeping him in for observation. These days they don't amputate, you know. Not like when I broke my leg.'

'I see.' Thank goodness Guy was incapacitated.

'I believe Guy and Dora have been married for some years,' said the gentle old voice on the end of the line.

'Yes, but they were parted for a long time.'

'Ah. I have offered them the use of my little house on Mount Abu.'

'That was kind.'

'Please come and see me,' he said. She could hear from his voice that he meant it.

'Yes, Eric, I will.'

Hilly put the phone down. It was all so unreal. She had an irrational memory of a book she had read called *Fear of Flying*, which advocated completely responsibility-free sex. How could there be any such thing? What had she started in the front seat of the old Jaguar, drunk on sherry and grief, all those years ago? The consequences might ruin her daughter's life. How sensible Dora seemed to her distraught mother, hanging neurotically on to her virginity.

She rested her head on her arms and howled. She didn't know what to do. She was glad Stephen was dead, so he didn't have to learn about the muddle and mess of her late teens. Some of her tears were for him.

Should she ask Eric to get Dora to ring her and explain her fears over the telephone? Or should she tell Dora to come straight home? She knew how stubborn Dora could be, particularly now happiness was within her grasp. There would have to be a very good explanation. Only a blood test would put her mind at rest. Then she had an idea.

The American hospital in Delhi was bound to be state of the art. Perhaps they had these new DNA-testing facilities and could help. She needed to talk to them and find out. Then she should really fly out to Delhi and explain the whole thing to her daughter and son-in-law face to face.

She went to fetch her American Express card and telephoned international directory inquiries.

Twenty-nine

THERE WAS A WAY to find out for sure, but it was going to be complicated. Hilly sat down at the table, rubbed her face with her hands and tried to calm down. What the hell was she going to do now? Her relationship – if you could call it that – with Peter had been a brief fling between two passionate young people, nothing more. After the invention of the pill it became commonplace.

But in the late 1950s, nice girls who would were rare. It wasn't surprising that Peter had come back for her willing body. All that talk of marriage was just a way of getting inside her pants. Peter could have had anyone he wanted. He obviously forgot her as soon as he arrived in Hong Kong. She'd certainly never heard from him again.

Stephen had been so different. He had never failed to exhibit his feeling that it was almost miraculous for him to have gained a wife and child. He was a man whose huge talent had been thwarted at an early age by physical injury. Although he had written many books, his primary creative urge to draw had been frustrated. Dora, in some ways, had

replaced drawing in his life. That was one reason why he
adored her so much.

He always loved Hilly as well. She winced when she
thought how brisk and impatient she could be with him sometimes. How he just took it quietly and never complained.

Somewhere deeply buried she missed Peter too. She felt it
was perfectly possible to love two men at the same time.
Hang on, what was she thinking?

She had never loved Peter, surely? Wasn't it just a summer
interlude, an infatuation?

She couldn't help remembering the crazy excitement...
Sharing a bicycle – Hilly riding side-saddle on the crossbar –
careering down a dusty track and falling off into the ditch at
the bottom, she scraping her knees, Peter bashing his head.
Lying entwined on the grassy verge, tangled in the bicycle.
She hadn't thought of that for years.

It came to her that she was bored. Early retirement had
seemed like such an idyll to begin with. Stephen's carefully
nurtured life insurance – a gift from the dead – had washed
her out of the world of work. He had been well aware that he
would leave a youngish widow and had expressed his love
for her unselfishly. But she had worked all her adult life. She
was used to the pressure of cramming everything around a
working day. Used to the rhythm of school term and holidays. She felt restless and rather lonely. It had been so lovely
to have Dora with her, to feel their relationship begin to
unfold. All this might destroy that tender plant. She needed
more in her life than the house and garden, always had. She
was still quite young. Not your usual retired person. Now
there was this extraordinary, fateful conjunction between her
child and Peter's. The undeniable excuse to get back in touch.

Before calling the American hospital, she had spoken to

the blood transfusion service of the local hospital and found out the procedure for establishing whether Guy and Dora were related. Somehow, she needed to drain a bit of blood from those arms that had rocked her so many years ago. If she could send some of Peter's blood to India, there was a chance that the doctors out there could do an ALA test and discover quite quickly if Peter was or was not Dora's father. DNA was more difficult and would take longer.

Wild ideas about creeping up behind Peter with a syringe and extracting a little blood by stealth from a Savile-Row-upholstered buttock popped into her head. That would be a fitting punishment for her humiliation in the Fortnum & Mason's Fountain. No, she had to bite the bullet, or she might be done for assault, which would be a terrible waste of time. She must call him – there wasn't time to write and get him to consent.

Hilly went to fetch a copy of *Debrett's* from Stephen's study. There he was: Lord Northiam of Colchester, created in 1980. Married Janet Davies, daughter of Sir Humphrey Davies Bt, 1959. Marriage dissolved. His hobbies included birdwatching. There was an address and he had the humility to publish a telephone number. No anonymous 'House of Lords, SW1,' for him. Hilly began to like him. She wondered why he had never married again.

·She dialled the number. A young woman answered.

'Lord Northiam's office. Can I help?'

Straight through. Hilly paused.

'Who is calling, please?'

'Oh, yes, hello. Could I speak to Lord Northiam, please?'

Hilly felt sorry for Peter. After all these years, what a shock it would be. But there wasn't time to regard his sensibilities with a slow lead-up to the facts.

'Who shall I say is calling?'

Wonderful, Hilly expected to be told he was in a meeting in the usual 1990s way. 'Could you tell him it's Hilda Vane?'

At least he would be slightly off guard. He would be bound to remember the extraordinary name of Jerusalem and associate it with the last shock he had received. Hilly couldn't help but relish the drama that awaited her on the telephone. She realised just what a buzz her daughter must have got from disrupting a smart wedding. 'You frivolous woman,' she told herself, breathing deeply to keep calm while she waited for Peter to come on to the line.

'Hello, this is Peter Northiam. Can I help you?'

He didn't remember. It can't have meant anything to him. She felt irrational disappointment.

'Hello, you probably won't remember me, but...'

'Oh, but I do remember you. Very clearly.' Gracious, after more than thirty years. Hilly couldn't help being flattered. 'Didn't you get married? Don't you use your married name?'

'I do. Only I thought you would be even less likely to know who I was.'

'How could I forget?'

Hilly remembered that it was mid-afternoon. She wondered whether he had had a good lunch and was inclined to flirt while the 1939 Armagnac swirled about in his blood. She hoped it would also anaesthetise him a bit against the shock.

'Peter, there is something I need to discuss with you.'

'Goodness, what on earth can that be?'

Hilly paused. How could she put it? 'I don't know if you remember my father's funeral, but...'

'Vividly, I'm afraid. I asked you to wait for me when I went to Hong Kong. I'd been there for no time at all, when I heard you'd married someone else. My mother saw it in *The Times*. I was having fun in Hong Kong, but I was quite determined to come back for you. Your bumpkin charm was very potent. The girls I met in Hong Kong – what did you call them? – were all like the ones in London but older and more desperate.'

'The fishing fleet.'

'No, you had another expression, which resonated in my mind when I got there. Ah, I remember: fishers of men. Very irreverent. But you were, weren't you? I liked that.'

Hilly digested this in silence.

'Why, Hilly? I really meant it.'

Hilly felt disinclined to discuss obstetrics with someone she hadn't seen for more than 30 years, but she had made up her mind to be blunt. Time was short. How short she didn't know.

'I thought I might be pregnant so I married the first man who would have me.'

'Ye gods. You can't have been. I was so careful. Anyway, why didn't you tell me? I would have married you.'

'But you got married as well, didn't you? Very quickly.'

'I heard you were married. Janet was slightly more fun than the other women. It didn't last. I think I wanted to pay you back for being so faithless. I felt you had kicked me very hard in the balls and I couldn't understand why.'

'Peter, I'm sorry, but I didn't really ring up to reminisce. I have to ask you a favour.'

'Is that why you rang? What do you want from me?'

Hilly could detect in his voice the suspicion of a rich man much leeched upon.

'Some of your blood,' she said bluntly.

'Heavens, Hilly, you were always a bit surprising, but my blood? Why?'

'It might help to explain things if I tell you that my married name is Jerusalem.'

There was a silence.

'Are you still there, Peter?'

'Yes.'

'Dora is my daughter. I never had any other children.'

'Right.'

'As you probably know, she is with Guy in Delhi. It looks like they might be getting on rather too well, and I just don't know what to do.'

'You think Dora might be mine?'

Thank goodness for Peter's quick mind.

'Not really – she looks very like Stephen when he was young. But you were dark as well and I really do just have to make sure. My local blood transfusion service said that to do an ALA test, which is fairly conclusive, they would need your blood. I hoped I wouldn't have to involve you. I thought this new DNA-fingerprinting business was totally straightforward and they would do it over the phone.'

'Right.'

Hilly hoped that Peter had grasped what she was talking about and would take charge. But the silence went on and on.

Finally he spoke.

'Hilly, Dora burst into my life a few months ago, disrupting my son's wedding and landing me with a huge bill for the whole thing, which Lord Cumbria felt I should pay as it was all Guy's fault. There were nine hundred guests all together. They drank as if their lives depended on it. I have certain negative feelings towards your daughter as a result. Why she couldn't have sorted it out before the ceremony I just don't know. Perhaps you, as her mother, can tell me.'

'I had no idea she had ever married anyone. I didn't know

anything about it until she came down here after your son's wedding. She was in a terrible state. So upset. But also I think very relieved that she had done it. I have to tell you that I haven't had the best and most confiding relationship with my daughter. It would have been so much better if I had. I might have been able to help. She was very close to her father though.'

'Didn't she tell him?'

'No. At least, I'm not sure.'

'Have you asked him?'

'He's dead.'

There was another pause.

'I'm sorry.'

'So am I, but there we are. He was much older than me and had been badly injured in the war. I couldn't expect him to live for ever. I have a bit of money. Can I help out with the wedding expenses?'

'That is very sweet of you, but no. From something Guy's mother said I am fairly sure it wasn't a love match and Amabel was after a bit of publicity. She went off on her honeymoon with some film producer whose mistress she was before, during and after apparently. Anyway, I offered to pay for a proportion, and he was satisfied with that. Poor Cumbrias. I don't think they know what hit them with that daughter of theirs. Solid county people really, plenty of money though – managed to avoid Lloyds. The world of showbiz might just as well be another planet as far as they are concerned.'

'Peter, sorry to bring you back to the point, but Guy and Dora are legally married, and we must find out if they are more closely related than they should be before they consummate the marriage.'

'Oh, yes. I must say, from the moment your daughter walked up the aisle looking like a modern version of the Merry Widow, life has been much more exciting. I really was very careful, you know. I don't believe she is mine.'

'Well, let's hope not.'

'She's got balls, I must say. She came back to me and told me that she truly loved Guy and would have been a good wife to him if she'd been allowed to be.'

'I'm sure she would have. She is thoroughly competent and independent and also very loving. He'd be lucky to get her.'

'I'm afraid I was rather unfriendly. The shock you know, meeting one's daughter-in- law like that – at one's son's wedding to someone else.'

Hilly interrupted him. 'Unfortunately, we need to tidy up this detail before anything else can happen.'

'All right. I suppose we had better get the blood to India as soon as possible.'

'Yes, we must.'

'I'll sort it out if you would just give me the hospital details.'

'OK.'

Hilly dictated the address and telephone number of both the hospital and her brother, and left it to Peter to get a sample of his blood flown out.

She put the phone down feeling bitterly sorry for her daughter, and dreading the impossible conversation.

Thirty

Uncle Eric was having breakfast when Dora came into the dining room. Guy was uncomfortable and stiff when he woke up. The painkillers had worn off and she was quite frightened by his pallor. His freckles looked darker than usual as the tan seemed to have drained out of his face. She'd helped him hobble to the bathroom. He had looked a bit exasperated.

Dora knew she must ring the hospital and either get a doctor out to examine him, or get him readmitted for some less-clumsy nursing.

'How's your husband?' asked Uncle Eric.

'He's not too good. I don't think he should have left the hospital quite so soon. Can I telephone?'

'Yes, do. The phone's in my study.'

Dora hurried through. As she put out her hand to dial the number the phone rang. She picked it up. It was her mother.

'Dora, is that you?'

'Hello, Mummy. How are you?'

Dora felt warmer towards her mother. She realised that the wariness was receding. Their relationship had improved in the days she'd spent in Kent after the wedding.

'I'm fine.' Hilly sounded flurried and Dora became anxious. 'What's wrong?' she asked.

'There's something I need to talk to you about. Where is Guy?'

'What? Oh, he's here.'

'What's he doing there? I thought he was in the American hospital. His mother called me.'

'He was bored in hospital. Once they'd set the leg and put it in plaster, he escaped and came to Uncle Eric's flat. He's not so good today though. I was just about to call the doctor, as he should probably go back in.'

Hilly took a deep breath.

'Did you sleep with him?'

'What? What business is that of yours?'

'Dora, darling, I'm sorry. It has all been my fault. I'm really sorry.'

'How can it possibly be your fault if I sleep with my husband?'

'Are you sitting down?'

'Of course not. What are you talking about? You're frightening me. Aren't you happy that I am happy at last? That I found him? That he loves me?' As Dora said this she hoped so much it was true. The anguish made her sharp. 'Are you still jealous of me? That I am happy?'

'No, no. It's not that. Please, Dora, listen to me. Darling, I love you so much. But I might have done something to cause you pain.'

'What?'

'Please sit down, and listen.'

Dora pulled Eric's desk chair over, took a deep breath and did as she was told.

'Are you sitting down? Darling, please...'

'Yes, I am sitting down. What? You can't disapprove of me sleeping with Guy. After all, we are married. I love him. I did sleep with him, in fact. I'm not a virgin any more. Right?'

'Oh dear. I had hoped the broken leg might stop him.'

Dora gasped. 'For God's sake, Mummy. What do you mean?' She didn't want to explain the exact details of last night with her mother but she seemed to expect it. What century were they living in?

'Did you use contraception?'

'As a matter of fact, no. But it wasn't a very complete act if you know what I mean.'

'Oh.'

'Mother, what is the matter?'

'I don't know how to tell you this.'

'What?' Dora's voice cracked. 'You think he might have AIDS, that's it, isn't it? Well, he definitely doesn't. He had every test you can think of before his wedding. That ghastly woman insisted.' She could hear her voice getting more hysterical as she went on: 'He's clean as a whistle. Hasn't slept with anyone since, or injected drugs or anything. Don't worry, I knew he had been pretty louche. But I didn't let him touch me until I was sure.'

'No, it isn't that either. Do you remember me saying that I was only ninety-nine per cent certain that you were Stephen's child?'

'Yes, I remember something, but there was so much else going on I just thought you were being a bit over-dramatic. I look so like Stephen. I loved him. He was my father. I'm glad you didn't tell me any of this before he died.'

'The point is...'

'What's the point?' Dora snapped.

'I really didn't want to tell you over the phone. I was hoping to fly out and talk to you. I even tried to get the American hospital in Delhi to do tests without informing you. But they refused. Not surprisingly, I suppose.'

'Mother, I can't stand this. Get to the bloody point. Why should we have blood tests? Do I have some kind of genetic problem? Don't worry, I won't have conceived. It's inconceivable.' Dora was coming down off screaming pitch.

'No, no. You are perfect. But the other man I slept with was Guy's father.'

Dora dropped the phone. Silvery swirls of light passed across her vision; she felt hot and sick and slid off the chair.

She opened her eyes to find Salim waving an ancient green bottle of smelling salts under her nose. Eric hovered behind him.

'Are you ill too, Dora?' he asked. 'You can pick up some nasty fevers out here.'

Dora sat up. He head hurt. She put her hand up to it and found a bump where she had caught her forehead on the sharp edge of the desk.

'Salim heard a noise and came in to find you on the floor. Your mother was still on the telephone. He told her you would ring back.'

She groped around in her foggy mind. Then she stood up slowly and looked in the mirror. The eyes that looked back at her were Stephen's. Her hair was very dark – like Stephen's. Guy was dirty blond going slightly white at the temples. His father, whom she had met so briefly, had grey hair, thinning on top. Mrs Moore had white hair and blue eyes. If you tossed all those genes up in the air, what did you get when they landed?

She hated her mother at that moment with a bitter, acid loathing. She thought of the times she'd tried to confide in her – but she'd turned away or changed the subject. She'd shown no interest in her pain, tiredness, disappointment and stress. How she had longed to lean on someone. And her amusing, clever, damaged father? He'd loved her, but he wasn't going to engage with her either. Wrong generation. Stiff upper lip. Didn't know the meaning of the word stress.

Dora's thoughts were disordered by shock. Now her mother had stepped between her and the only man she'd ever wanted.

It was probably a pack of lies. Some kind of horrible trick. Why was her mother trying to spoil her happiness? Then sense prevailed: her mother might have faults, but she wasn't a fantasist or a liar.

Uncle Eric stood beside her, leaning on his stick.

'What is it? What's upset you? Was it something your mother said?'

Dora didn't know where to start. 'I'm sorry, I can't talk about it. It's too complicated. Is it OK if I ring her back?'

Eric nodded, too polite to press this unexpected niece. He had his own secrets. 'Of course, I'll leave you in peace.'

He left the room and Salim followed him.

Dora was already dialling the number, wild with impatience and fear. 'Mother?'

'Darling, are you all right?' Her mother sounded worried. 'Look, I'm so, so sorry. You've waited so long. I know I haven't been the best mother… I will make it up to you, I promise.'

'Bit bloody late,' said Dora. 'So what do we do now?'

'I am pretty certain you're Stephen's child, but I have contacted Peter Northiam and he's spoken to the American hospital. His blood is being couriered out overnight. They might be able to do a test called ALA that detects some kind of chemicals in the blood and is quicker than DNA testing. I knew you would want to know as soon as possible, so I called him.'

Dora was reeling with shock. She remembered the father at the wedding, staring after his son. He'd looked so sad.

'What did he say when you asked for his blood?'

'He was really very nice about it. He doesn't think he is your father.'

'Look, Mum, I don't blame you. I know you were left alone at a young age and just had to get on with it. I know the fifties were not like the nineties for single mothers. You must have been scared. But please let's not talk any more now. I've got to go and tell Guy. For goodness' sake, don't tell a soul.'

'I love you so dearly, my precious daughter. Really, after this I will try to make things right.'

'Hmm,' grunted Dora, and felt a huge lump rising in her throat. 'We'll see how this turns out. I might never want to speak to you again.'

'Please...'

'Joke, Mum. Don't worry. Call you later.'

She went to find Eric to try to explain.

'I have to talk to Guy,' she told him. 'We both need to go to the hospital. They might be able to help with something.'

'Are you ill?'

Dora tried to smile.

'No, Uncle Eric. I'm fine. I think.'

'Oh, good.' He looked puzzled. 'I'll let you go now. When we get to know each other a bit better, I will no doubt understand.'

'Yes, I'm looking forward to that too.' She wanted to say: 'She's your bloody sister, why couldn't you keep her under control?' But she knew that Eric hardly knew Hilda. She kissed his papery cheek. 'See you later.'

She telephoned the hospital, asking for an ambulance. Apparently the orthopaedic surgeon had hoped Mr Boleyn would turn up again at some point. He was probably in considerable pain and in need of drugs.

It was time to break the news to Guy. How was she going to tell him? Should she wait until he was recovered? The ugly word 'incest' began to whisper its nasty sibilance in her mind.

They had slept together. It had been a most significant act. It had been meant to symbolise a new beginning, a consummation after such a long wait. But it might just have been a squalid incident. The sort of thing that the Sunday tabloids picked up and crowed over, muckraking. She shivered. Pregnancy was very unlikely.

Then she shook herself. She was Stephen's daughter until proved otherwise. Guy must go back into hospital and have his clothes taken away so he couldn't get to her again until all this was sorted out. His poor condition was a good enough excuse for avoiding sex.

Guy was watching her as she came through the door. He seemed a bit warm but quite cheerful. Perhaps a little too cheerful, feverish – chatting happily about their trip to Mount Abu. She put on the act of her life. She couldn't bring herself to kiss his lips. So she sat down on the bed beside him, put her arms around him and pressed her lips to his hair, which smelt faintly of disinfectant.

'Guy, you have to go back to hospital. I can't look after you properly here.'

'I need painkillers. It is really nasty inside this plaster, a sort of combination of itchy and agony.' He rested his head on her bosom. 'I do love you, Dora. I think I started loving you when we got the giggles together at that party. Do you remember?'

Dora just murmured into his hair. She wanted to cry. Last night she had reached out and grasped what was now so freely offered. Now she might not be able to have him. Just when he wanted her. The promise of happiness seemed to blow away from her like a leaf to be caught for a wish. She had to tell him. He wasn't a child to be protected from uncomfortable truths. It was his business as well as hers. The doorbell rang just as she was finding the right words.

'Guy,' it rushed out.

'What?' He seemed lost in a feverish dream. 'Guy.' She pulled away from him. He flopped back on the pillows looking bewildered. 'I don't know how to tell you this less brutally...'

'Tell me what?'

'I've just been speaking to my mother. She says she slept with your father. Guy, she thinks there's a remote possibility that I am your sister.' She knew she was handling it badly.

'Oh, for God's sake, Dora. What are you talking about? Sounds like a fifth-rate soap plot. Is this one of your jokes? Now, when you know you've finally got me?' He smiled. 'A bit sick. Spirited though. Very funny actually. Well done, Dora.'

Dora could hear the feet of the paramedics in the passage outside the room. 'No, no, it isn't a joke, Guy. She really did.'

His eyes dulled. 'I can't imagine why you are saying this. When did you find out?'

'Just now. I was so shocked I fainted. I banged my head.'

He shut his eyes. She wanted sympathy but he wasn't remotely ready to deliver. There was a knock on the door.

'Hang on a minute,' she called, then turned back to Guy. 'Look, I don't look anything like you. I look like Stephen. I don't think we have any genes in common at all.'

Now she was babbling.

'Right, I'm fed up with this, and with you, and my leg hurts like buggery. Just let those guys take me back to the hospital. And stop talking.'

'I'm coming with you, as they need to take a sample of my blood. My mother spoke to your father and got him to send some of his blood there. They can do a blood chemicals test called ALA that they use in paternity cases.'

'Just shut up, Dora.'

The paramedics came in with a wheelchair. One of them injected a mild sedative to make the journey easier for him. Dora felt him slipping away from her. He wouldn't meet her eye and allowed them to help him into the chair. They left the room, and she trailed along behind them.

'Don't let her in the ambulance. I want to be on my own,' he said.

It was understandable, she supposed. He wasn't well. She could feel her own heart thumping painfully in her chest. What if she was Peter's child? Her imagination raced ahead to a quiet annulment. Guy lost to her for ever. She couldn't see happy family reunions after this. Glowing faces around the Christmas tree were completely out.

Under these thoughts was a sick feeling. How could he trust her after this embarrassing incident? Even if she was Stephen's how could they be together after this gross suspicion? She had known it was too good to be true.

Guy was gone. Why had she been so honest? Why had

she chosen to tell him now, instead of after the result? The front door closed.

Uncle Eric appeared.

'Dora? Don't you want to go with him?'

'He's in too much pain. I'll get a cab.'

'No, Salim can take you.'

'Thanks,' she said dully.

So the happiness of her whole life was to last a couple of days at most. She must live and live and live and never be loved and happy again. Her forehead ached with unshed tears. Salim appeared and she followed him down and climbed into Eric's ancient Ambassador motorcar. The ambulance was just turning out and they followed it.

Her mind raced ahead to prepare for the worst. She would never see Guy again. Never have that sense of warmth and completion she had had in his arms. He would recover and be flown home. What would she do?

As in the furthest corner of Pandora's box, there was a tiny hope. She couldn't help it. That was how she was made. A person without that kind of hopefulness would have been much more practical about getting the marriage and babies that she wanted.

The Ambassador delivered her to the hospital entrance. Guy had gone in through the A&E entrance around the side. She couldn't imagine how she would explain what she was doing there to reception. Which department could she possibly ask for?

She went up to reception and stood lost for words.

The nurse said to her, 'What can I do for you?'

'Oh, right. I have come for a blood test. ALA. For paternity. Where should I go?'

The nurse looked unfazed. 'Your good name?'

'Dora Jerusalem.'

She consulted the ledger. 'Yes, I see. Phlebotomy is expecting you. Take the passage to the left. There's a white swing door with a round window. You can't miss it.'

Dora didn't dare ask what phlebotomy was. She thought it might be a kind of radical brain surgery for the very depressed. Oh dear. There was the door. She stopped for a minute to collect herself, took a deep breath and pushed through into a large light room divided like a ward into curtained-off areas. The reception desk was just in front of her.

The nurse looked up and smiled. 'Dora Jerusalem? Please sit down. We'll be with you in a moment.'

A curtain was drawn back and Dora invited behind it. The nurse bared her arm and tapped the vein to bring it up a bit before inserting a needle (Dora looked away) and drawing out a small syringeful of dark blood.

'That's all now. I'll just put a little plaster over the puncture. The other bloods have arrived and are being processed as we speak. We will have the result for you tomorrow.'

'Oh, I thought today.'

'No, it has to be done overnight. We realise it is urgent and are doing our best.'

Dora longed to find Guy but she was pretty sure he didn't want to see her. She knew how volatile he was – how quickly his mood could change. He was so easily plunged into despair. Perhaps this was all for the best, she told herself. 'Could I stay married to his risk-taking behaviour and extravagant gestures?' she wondered. Behind her attempts to persuade herself that losing him was a good thing was her lifelong belief in the redeeming powers of love.

She went back through the main entrance to find Salim

waiting for her with the Ambassador. He held open the door and she climbed in, stunned.

The next day she went back into the hospital as early as she felt was decent or reasonable. Guy hadn't rung or been in touch at all. She'd called to find out how he was, to be told he was sleeping under sedation, as they had had to cut off the plaster. There was a worry about infection underneath and it had needed a special dressing. Poor Guy, she thought.

Salim dropped her off. She told him to go home but he said Eric had asked him to wait. It was a different nurse in reception and she gave her name.

'Can you please wait? The doctor will come to fetch you,' she said.

Dora sat down and waited. About 20 minutes later, after Dora had found she couldn't sit down but needed to do some pacing, the doctor came and took her into an empty side ward.

'I am going to tell you immediately that all is well. You are not blood relations. I am ninety-nine per cent certain. The ALA test is pretty accurate, but we will be doing DNA just to make sure. Lord Northiam has paid for the full battery of tests.'

Dora burst into tears.

'Does my husband know?'

'No, he is still sleeping. Do you want to tell him?'

'I'd rather not.'

'It is up to you, but I think it would be better that he gets the good news from you.'

Dora wasn't so sure. Guy had rejected her rapidly and completely the day before when doubts first arose. It was as if he was longing for an excuse to do so, that he couldn't keep up the effort of love and happiness for very long. Now she wished she hadn't told him at all. Maybe they could have retained the illusion for a little longer, at least until he was mobile enough not to be dependent on her.

He might never have known. Had she completely blown it?

The doctor showed her to his room.

She pushed open the door and went in. Guy was lying on his back, his head slightly turned to one side, his eyes closed. He was breathing easily and looked cool. She touched his face to make sure and his grey eyes opened.

'Hello, Dora. What are you doing here?'

'We've got the results.'

'Oh, right.' He turned his head away. 'Well?'

Nerves always brought out Dora's worst jokes. 'We're cleared for folk dancing.'

'But not for incest?' he asked, still not looking at her.

'No, no, that's not what I meant at all. I'm Stephen's.'

'OK. That's good, I suppose. Won't have to share Peter's inheritance with you.'

She laughed, but then noticed he wasn't even smiling. 'What do you mean, Guy?'

'I really won't, Dora.'

The last little hope hiding in the corner of Dora's carefully cherished box flew up and dispersed in the bright Indian air.

Thirty-one

2009

IT WAS SEVEN O'CLOCK AND DORA snapped awake in her cabin bed floating high above Bayswater. It was going to be such a busy day that she didn't mind not getting a precious extra hour of sleep.

She jumped down and went through into her kitchen to make a cup of tea. While the kettle was boiling she had a shower and washed her hair.

What should she wear? She thought black and white and deep red lipstick. She needed to look confident, as the day started with a script conference – posh term for a meeting – bang on ten in Soho Square with the scriptwriter who might, just might, get her first novel filmed. She'd sold the option but wasn't naïve enough to think that meant there would be a movie at the end of it.

After that, lunch with her agent to hand over the new synopsis. Then the best bit: her first book-signing in Hatchards in Piccadilly. She thought of the hours she had spent browsing the shelves, longing and longing to be part of the bookshop world. And now she was. Or might be, if anyone turned up.

The paper thumped through her letterbox. How the crumbling old mansion block had changed since she'd bought the tiny flat all those years ago. It now had a lift that worked all the time, instead of just when it felt like it, so you didn't risk a coronary just going home up the stairs – and people would deliver.

She drank her tea and scanned the *Telegraph*. Arriving at the court page she smiled, remembering the shock of seeing Guy's engagement to Amabel and the ghastly mess she had made of things afterwards.

It had been the making of Amabel. She wasn't a talented actress, but the combination of family tiara, aristocratic blonde good looks and virtual nudity had done for her what safety pins and a Madame X bust had done for Liz Hurley.

Guy been a media darling back then, having discovered a valuable Pre-Raphaelite painting hidden under a huge 1960s abstract slashed white canvas. He'd noticed very subtle textures in the white paint resembling Pre-Raphaelite waving hair and had taken an experimental knife to one corner. Underneath lay Millais' lost masterpiece, *Sir Galahad and the Loathly Lady*, and the rest was history. It had been cleaned, mended and snapped up at auction by one of the country's most famous theatrical knights for a record-breaking £5.6 million.

It hadn't belonged to Guy, so he didn't make his fortune. But he did make the front pages of the newspapers and a fat commission. Then he dropped out of sight after his non-wedding and the momentum of fame had ground to a halt.

Amabel had married at least three times since then and fitted in a love child by a mystery politician as well. Her parents were sometimes photographed smiling in a slightly strained manner in the background of a *Hello!* spread to mark the christening or yet another wedding. 'This time, it's the real thing,' Amabel was always quoted as saying. Quite without irony.

Poor Guy, he might have been a kept man by now if it weren't for me,' Dora thought. Sitting in the clear June morning light, she looked into the silver hand mirror left to her by Leora and painted out the shadows under her eyes.

It was getting late. She checked her bag and fled with her mobile in her hand. The lift came in seconds and down she went. Hurrying towards the Central Line, she searched for H on the keypad while trying not to bump into people and lamp posts, and dialled.

She thought she might just catch Guy.

'Darling. Is everything OK?'

'Hello.' He sounded a bit strained.

She pictured the titanic struggle to get two clever, wilful, stubborn children with alternative ideas to dress, eat and go to school. It told on both of them.

'Yes, Esme says she feels sick, but it is Monday, and Torin is sulking because I won't let him watch a cartoon. So all is much as usual.'

'I miss you.'

'And I you. Wish I was with you.'

'What if nobody comes?'

'They will, don't worry.'

'They might not.'

'If they don't, get an earlier train. We can have a drink in the garden and watch the sun go down.'

Guy was very good at priorities these days. His default mode now was a sunny garden, a cup of tea or a cold glass of something delicious and the sight and sound of his wife and children.

With her overactive imagination, she could visualise herself sitting alone and ignored behind a pile of books. She decided to give it ten minutes and then she would bolt home. She couldn't bear the humiliation of the shop assistants pretend queuing to encourage the non-existent punters.

'Tirzah rang,' Guy went on. 'It was mostly about the exhibition, but she sent her love. She'll be staying the weekend before the opening in September.'

'Oh, lovely, lovely. We should get Mum and Peter too, and make a bit of a party of it all.'

'Excellent idea. Must take the kids to school. Bye, darling. And good luck.'

It was the ordinariness of it all that gave her constant joy. Their squabbles about who did what as they calibrated their relationship into a pattern for life.

During her long wait for Guy, in her low moments, she had found it difficult to understand the point of Dora. When she'd heard her friends wail about being tied down by a baby, she'd wanted to scream, 'I want those ropes, those leaden weights. I want to touch the ground.'

Like a hot-air balloon that has lost its moorings she'd felt adrift, floating through life, semi-transparent. A cloud. Smoke.

Then solid happiness had taken the shape of Guy's return, the children and their house near Bath. But it was no fairytale, and real life inevitably intervened. The worst bit had been their money worries. Guy had taken such a huge risk investing both in his Bath art gallery, and in an internet site to try and capture an international market.

Dora had worked as a copywriter in a local advertising

office to keep things going while the art business built up – bored to tears writing about feed and combine harvesters, and being preyed upon by the married managing director. She never saw enough of her children, but was so exhausted by the end of the working day that she snapped at everyone when she got home.

Guy invested in more and more art, thinking that the internet would bring him the customers he needed. But the dot-com bubble burst at the end of the 1990s and Guy's trust fund had vanished, to be replaced with huge and terrifying debts. They had remortgaged the house, which meant that Dora had to work harder than ever to help keep up the payments. Guy had descended into a black gloom and began drinking too much and staying up most of the night.

They all but stopped talking and only kept up a front for the children's sake. Dora's hard-won happiness began to peel away, which she enjoyed in a perverse way, like peeling off a scab. She almost desired to be let down so she could say to herself, 'Serves you right. You never deserved a reward for all that soppy waiting.' Only the thought of her children had kept her moored to the shifting ground.

Then, just at their lowest point, Tirzah had doubts about her long-standing dealer. Large sums of money seemed to be missing and she was hardly known in the UK despite acclaim at the Venice Biennale. She had come to Guy for advice because she liked and respected him, not for any other reason. As their romance had been so – well – romantic, Dora had never been able to admit to those who loved them that it had all gone wrong.

Selwyn had driven Tirzah up from Kent, where he was now Canon Theologian at Canterbury Cathedral. They'd all had a lunch pregnant with expectation – and then Guy had taken Tirzah into his office for an hour's chat over coffee.

The sun had long since sunk when they emerged looking for cold white wine, Guy happy and energised because his ideas – which he'd been formulating while watching helplessly as her old dealer frittered away her potential – had poured on to fertile ground.

An atavistic curved female figure, the face just sketched, a crescent moon on the forehead – a memorial to the Princess of Wales for one of the London parks – had made Tirzah a celebrity. Other high-profile commissions had followed due to Guy's relentless efforts on her behalf. As the internet finally took off, his online gallery had displayed her work to a truly international audience. The Boleyn Gallery in Bath was as well attended on opening nights as anything in Cork Street.

Guy's success had meant that Dora could stop wittering on about pony nuts and herbicides. They had a hut built in the garden with an electricity supply, so that she could write in comparative peace. She didn't know how she managed to hold a sentence in her mind while rushing out to deal with shrieks – but only if they hit that particular note that meant pain rather than fury.

She had even landed an agent with her first full-length manuscript, and had been so excited, but as the relentless tide of rejection letters flowed from publishers, she'd given up. It was so frustrating; but Dora had never stopped secretly hoping. She went back to freelance journalism, and would spend a couple of days in London every week working in contract publishing to help pay for their life and to support herself.

The rest of the time she looked after the children, with the growing feeling that she might never make it as a novelist and would have to accept her fate.

She was endlessly grateful to Tirzah for giving Guy a chance and the confidence he needed to succeed again. But Tirzah had shut her up, saying: 'Nonsense, darling. He's the best there is for artists like me. He did me the favour.' Now figurative sculptors beat a path to his door. Their marriage was repaired, and she no longer turned away from Guy at night.

It was at that point that she'd tried fiction again. A short story made it on to Radio 4. She won a magazine competition with another one. It was included in an anthology that did well. Dora was published at last.

How different it could have been without Guy. If she had evaporated one day, she believed that no one would have wondered where she had gone.

Thirty-two

1997

A SCRAPING NOISE WOKE DORA. It was pitch-black outside. She reached to turn on her bedside light. Click and then nothing. Power cut. The darkness was so thick she could sink her teeth into it. Gripped by fear, she groped for a candle and matches on the bedside table. The tiny yellow flame flung massive shadows around the room.

Kamal was at least a hundred yards away, asleep on his charpoy in his small home. Uncle Eric's summer home was so isolated she'd lain rigid with fright the first time she'd heard a sambar bark in the forest.

Kamal had lived there for ever; first with his wife and children and now with one remaining son who wasn't quite right. He was caretaker and cooked for Eric when he was there. Salim got summers off to go to his family in the Punjab.

Dora hadn't been sleeping well and woke up most nights. She was prone to fits of weeping that came over her like summer storms. She supposed she was mourning for hopes that were now, finally, dead and buried.

Uncle Eric had accompanied her up from Delhi and introduced her to Kamal. He'd shown her how to get around, dug out his old typewriter for her and generally settled her in. Then he'd gone back to Delhi, where he did educational consultation with a range of Indian schools in spite of his age.

The solitude had suited her to begin with – by daylight. The daily visits from Eric's old friend and deputy head Bani Singh were soothing and gave her something else to think about. They would sit and talk and sip nimbu pani – cold water with lemon juice squeezed into it and a pinch of salt. She had had to get used to Kamal waiting on her, and accept it without jumping up and trying to help.

Seven sisters – dusty brown birds that always travelled in groups of seven – would peck around in the dust at their feet. Bani Singh told Dora about the horrors of Partition, the rapid withdrawal of the British, the Ghandi family and the rest of Indian history after Independence. She learned a lot.

The rest of the time she had spent reading Eric's collection of Indian anthropology and archaeology books. She tried not to think about Guy. When she let down her mental shield, intense feelings flooded in – confused reactions to coming to India, finding him and rekindling her dormant love. Sometimes she would walk to the edge of the plateau and look down. The plains were so far below her that she felt like the children in Narnia, blown by Aslan's breath off the cliff edge.

Yet when she ate egg curry and chapattis on the tiny verandah and watched the sun do its precipitous dive, she couldn't regret anything. The evenings were chilly and Kamal would light a fire for her. Small inklings of happiness crept over her as she watched the flames.

She'd planned to spend a month in Mount Abu and had a

week to go to 'recover her poise', as Uncle Eric had put it. Then she was off to Calcutta to do six months with Mother Theresa. The idea had come when she'd met an American on a train who'd been there already. They'd talked through the night, as neither of them had booked berths, and she had been very interested in his motives and views. She thought she would interview all the Westerners she met and write a book about the kind of people who are drawn to help the destitute and dying – like Simon Monroe. If that didn't put her minor romantic misadventures in perspective, nothing would.

There it was again. She was sure there was something or someone outside on the verandah. She contemplated slipping out of the back window and going to wake Kamal but was frozen to the spot. Perhaps it was an animal. The house was locked.

Then she heard the door handle turning and felt sick with fear.

'Dora?' She thought she heard her own name, called softly. Then again, 'Dora? Are you there?'

The breath went out of her in a long sigh. If whoever it was knew her name they were unlikely to be goondas intent on rape, murder and robbery.

'Who is it?' she ventured, sliding her legs over the side of the bed and picking up her candle. 'Kamal?'

'Dora, it's me, Guy. Oh shit...'

Dora hurried to the door, fumbling for the key.

'What's happened?'

'I've just banged my leg on something. It's so dark.'

Dora opened the door and insect screen cautiously, shivering in the night air. Guy was standing on the verandah. He had a small rucksack on his back, a crutch under one arm, and a rather dim torch in the other hand. He was wearing what looked and smelt like an old Afghan coat. Glancing down, she could see his leg was still in plaster – his trouser leg flapped where it was cut away. There was a walking iron on the bottom to stop the plaster crumbling away.

'Can I come in?'

'Yes, of course.'

Dora went ahead, making sure he could see by the light of the candle. She squatted down in front of the fireplace and began to scrumple pieces of *The Times of India* to get the fire going again. She heard him drop his crutch and rucksack and lower himself into a chair behind her. When the fire had flared up she steeled herself to look at him properly. The light was dim but she thought he looked cheerful.

'How did you get here?'

'I took the late bus and got into town about nine. Thought it was too late to come out here and booked myself into a hostel. Then I woke up and decided I couldn't wait any longer. I bribed the sweeper to wake a cab for me. Eric had given me directions. Getting from the gate to the verandah was the worst. I caught the cast on something. It's throbbing a bit.'

'Would you like a cup of tea?' she asked, putting off the moment. What had he come to say? She knew he was basically a decent and honourable person. Perhaps he couldn't leave her in suspense any longer before dumping her. Although it seemed a long way to come with your leg in plaster in order to dump someone. A little curling flame began to flicker in Dora's heart.

'Yes, thanks.' He smiled at her.

Dora padded into the dark kitchenette and lit the gas under the kettle. Arranging the tray carefully, she felt her heart lift at the thought of the two of them being in the same place once more. But it was so quiet in the other room. Was this just another dream?

Shaking her head, she pinched her forearm, half expecting to wake up, but found herself standing up in her camel-skin slippers. Perhaps she was sleepwalking? Bewildered, she carried the tray back to the fireplace and almost jumped to find Guy gazing into the flames.

She began to shake as she put the tray down. He glanced up at her and smiled again. The scent of poorly cured goatskin filled her nostrils, and she knew for certain she wasn't dreaming this time.